**"I'm wondering why you duck every
personal question I ask you—"**

Holden couldn't take it anymore. He claimed her lips. Just when he was sure she'd push him away, she sighed, softened, and opened her mouth to let her tongue tangle with his.

And she gave. He'd known she would; she was so generous, so caring. She had a heart as big as the world, and though she tried to guard it, her heart was wide open.

So, he told himself as he slipped his hands into the glory of her hair, he'd just have to guard it for her, be careful not to offer more than he wanted, or let her give more than was good for her.

Still, he took the kiss deeper, tasted the sweetness of her, swallowed the sexy little moan she made and felt his control begin to crumble.

He wanted more, needed her like his next breath.

ACCLAIM FOR

TEMPTATION BAY

"Sullivan's contemporary debut deftly combines intrigue, romance, and witty banter...The sizzling passion between Dex and Maggie propels this page-turner forward to its explosive conclusion."

—*Publishers Weekly*

"4 stars! Sullivan brings a sensational sense of place to her first Windfall Island novel, immersing readers in the Maine island and its fascinating population—most notably her heroine, whose fortitude and no-nonsense exterior cover a heart of gold. Sullivan builds the tension between her lead characters and crafts a relationship so compassionate and reciprocal it is simply irresistible."

—*RT Book Reviews*

"Intriguing, sassy, and entertaining...It will keep you anxiously awaiting the next novel."

—*HarlequinJunkie.com*

Hideaway Cove

ALSO BY ANNA SULLIVAN

Temptation Bay

Hideaway Cove

ANNA SULLIVAN

FOREVER

NEW YORK   BOSTON

Copyright © 2014 by Penny McCusker
Excerpt from *Secret Harbor* copyright © 2014 by Penny McCusker

Forever
Hachette Book Group
237 Park Avenue
New York, NY 10017

www.HachetteBookGroup.com

Printed in the United States of America

First Edition: July 2014
10 9 8 7 6 5 4 3 2 1

OPM

Forever is an imprint of Grand Central Publishing.
The Forever name and logo are trademarks of Hachette Book Group, Inc.

The Hachette Speakers Bureau provides a wide range of authors for speaking events. To find out more, go to www.hachettespeakersbureau.com or call (866) 376-6591.

The publisher is not responsible for websites (or their content) that are not owned by the publisher.

To Michael, the best things in life are worth waiting for—and you deserve the best.

Hideaway Cove

Prologue

Helluva night," Jamie Finley said as he and his crew loaded the last of the crates on the horse-drawn wagon that would carry the illegal booze to their stash in Hideaway Cove.

Like the others, including his son, Emmett, Jamie's eyes strayed out to sea, where a pair of ships rode at anchor twelve miles from shore, at what those who flouted the U.S. government's Prohibition law had come to call the Rum Line.

Two hours before there'd been three ships lit up like Christmas and raging with the wild party that hopped nightly, just out of reach of the Coast Guard, from one deck to the next. Then one of those ships, the *Perdition*, exploded and sank beneath the restless and hungry waves of the Atlantic Ocean.

Like the group on the beach, the other two ships had gone respectfully quiet and dark. Every ship's captain feared fire at sea, but when a ship was loaded to the hatches with alcohol-based cargo, even the smallest spark took on a whole new threat.

"Da," Emmett Finley said softly, and when his father turned to him, he opened the flap of his coat to show the face of the baby he held against his chest. The baby they'd found on their little boat when they returned from the *Perdition* with their load of bootlegged booze.

She slept fitfully, her tiny body warm against Emmett's. Perhaps too warm.

"You're right, son. We ought to get the babe in out of the weather."

"What're you going to do with it?" Floyd Meeker asked.

Jamie bumped up a shoulder. "Laura will know best."

"You're going to let a woman decide?" Meeker huffed, disgust digging the normal sour and disapproving lines on his face even deeper.

"My wife is as good as anyone else. Better than most, when it comes down to it."

"Not on Windfall. It has to go to those who make the decisions for the island."

"No." With a speaking look to his son, Jamie Finley stepped over to Meeker, drew the rest of the men away from Emmett and lowered his voice. "The babe can't be given over to the coppers without putting everyone at risk."

Meeker jerked his head to where Emmett waited. "That's a fine blanket wrapped around the child."

Not to mention the jewel Jamie had seen around the baby's neck before his son had shown the presence of mind to cover it up. "Her people will be looking," he said. "She didn't come from that ship, not to begin with." Of that he was certain.

"If she's found here," Meeker said, "We'll go into the deepest, darkest hole them Fed bastards can find, and then they'll use the excuse to tear this island apart."

"We're agreed, then. We keep our business this night a secret. All our business." Jamie made eye contact with each of his compatriots, saw them nod—all except Meeker, who stepped forward.

"I'll take her, then," he said. "You have enough on your plate, Finley."

One of their crew laughed uproariously, incredulously. The other rocked back on his heels, quietly amused.

Jamie just shook his head. "No."

"But—"

"You haven't got a nurturing bone in your body, Meeker."

"I only want—" Meeker began, swallowing back the rest of his objection as the other men turned on him, their intent obvious in their set expressions and fisted hands.

Windfall Island had no sheriff, no law enforcement personnel of any kind. Windfallers dealt with their own, under a code of justice that went back to the island's first settlers. That justice was swift and unforgiving.

Jamie rested a hand on his son's shoulder and turned him toward home, leaving the others to ensure Meeker's silence.

And silence, of a different kind, was what he shared with his son on the long, cold walk. The stars shone bright, sharp points of light in a sky that had gone from cloud-covered to clear in the hours since they'd first set out for the *Perdition*.

They scented the village first, the rich aroma of wood smoke seeming to warm air frosted with winter and ripe with the tang of the ocean. As they rounded a curve of shore, lights shone from windows, comforting as they made their way along the crooked streets to their own little house. And the sound of weeping that sliced through the walls.

"Stay by the door," he told Emmett when they walked inside. The only light came from the banked fireplace across the room, and although his wife's tears were stifled now, sorrow seemed to weight the air.

Laura Finley had strength to spare, as much strength as God had ever given a woman. That didn't mean she'd never shed a tear, and under other circumstances Jamie would have left her to it, as he never knew how to handle such emotions. This time, though his eyes were dry, what moved her to tears broke his heart as well.

"Maddie is bad off," she said when he joined her by the fire, where she leaned over the crib he'd made with his own hands before Emmett's birth. Their infant daughter, not yet a year old, lay so still and silent within, her skin pale and translucent as moonbeams.

"She's a Finley," Jamie insisted. "She'll fight it off."

"Sometimes I have to lean close to make sure she still draws breath."

"Laura." Jamie lay a hand over hers, waited until she straightened, then tipped his head to where their son waited.

Emmett opened his jacket, let his mother see the child sleeping in his arms.

"Jamie," Laura breathed, then her voice sharpened to a knife's edge. "Take that child out of here."

"Shhhh, Laura, listen to me," and he told her what they'd witnessed on the beach.

"I heard it," she said dully, "I felt it." Then she bent back to Maddie, and he understood that it had made no impact on her, not with their daughter fighting for her life against an enemy they had no way to defeat.

A measles epidemic had run rampant through the island. The very young and the very old had proven especially susceptible. The rest of them could do little but stand by and watch their loved ones fade.

"Take the babe away before she sickens. Please, Jamie. I couldn't bear to see another child take ill. Wait," Laura said as he turned to go. "Can...Can I see her again?"

Emmett came a step or two closer, turning to put the baby's face into the light from the fire.

"Look how rosy her cheeks are."

"She's awful warm, Ma," Emmett said.

"No wonder, out in all that damp and cold with naught more than a blanket to keep her warm. God willing, she's only taken a bit of a chill."

Like his wife, Jamie turned back to their daughter. The difference between the two infants, so close in age, but miles apart in health, drove like a knife into the heart.

Still, many a frail child had come back from death's door, while a healthy, well-fed one succumbed.

"Go on now; take the child over to the Duncans'. Claire will know what to do."

"But they've sickness there, too."

Laura lifted her gaze to her husband's. "It's over for them."

"What happened, Da?"

Jamie reached into the child's blanket and removed the jeweled necklace, depositing it in his pocket. "We'll find out soon enough, boy." And out they went, though he hated leaving his wife and child again.

Seeing as the Duncans lived just across the way, it took mercifully few moments in the breath-stealing cold to reach their home. Joe Duncan opened the door at Jamie's knock, stepping back to invite him and Emmett in. Once a man of high energy and infectious good humor, now sorrow carved deep lines on Joe's face and stooped his shoulders.

Their daughter Elizabeth had sickened with the measles at the same time as Maddie, but although Jamie searched Joe's face, he couldn't read the outcome. When Claire Duncan came out of the back room, though, Jamie knew immediately.

"Maddie?" Claire asked.

"We'll know soon." Jamie had to stop, swallow against the band of fear and sadness tightening his throat. "Laura said your wait is over."

Claire's eyes filled, and when she reached out, Jamie caught her hand in his own, then clasped Joe's shoulder.

"Emmett." Claire dashed her hands across her damp cheeks, then stopped when she realized the boy had his arms full. And what he held.

As Jamie related the bare bones of the story, she flew across the room and gathered the baby up, already clucking about the child being damp and feverish.

"A soaked nappy doesn't help," she finished, stripping off the beautiful pink blanket with no more than a quick, envious sigh for its fineness.

"Laura was right to send you," Joe said, watching his wife hurry out to fetch a dry diaper and some of their own daughter's clothes. "Claire boiled everything in sight, even swabbed the floors and walls with lye soap. Would've boiled me if she could've wrestled me into the pot." He looked down, his jaw working for a second before he managed words again. "I'd've jumped in if it woulda meant..." he broke off when his wife came back in, the two of them sharing a long look.

"You tell Laura we're praying for Maddie," Claire said. "For all of you."

"She'd say to tell you she's returning the favor."

"No need now." Claire stared off toward the bedroom before meeting Jamie's eyes again, working up a little smile for him. "You'll let me know. About Maddie."

"I will." Jamie turned to collect Emmett, and found him asleep on the bench by the fireplace.

"Boy is done in," Joe said. "Why don't you leave him here? It might be best, considering..."

Jamie nodded once, pulled his watch cap back on, and slipped out the door to go keep vigil with his wife.

It would be over, one way or another, by dawn.

Chapter One

Present Day. Windfall Island, Maine.

Jessica Randal, Jessi to her friends and family, had been born and raised on Windfall Island, Maine. At the tender age of seventeen, her high school diploma so fresh in her hand that the ink was still wet, she'd found herself pregnant and engaged. Nine short months later, the boy she'd thought her soul mate had left her high and dry and she'd given birth to the real love of her life.

Benjamin David Randal arrived with little fuss or fanfare—a contented, happy baby who'd refused to cry even when the doctor slapped him sharply on the bottom. Seeing as he possessed the dreaded Y chromosome, Jessi knew for certain he'd give her trouble. She vowed he'd be the only man who would—as he'd be the only man in her life.

Most of eight years had passed since that life-altering day, and she'd made a good life for herself and her son. She didn't have a college degree, but she took enough online courses so that when her best friend, Maggie Solomon, started her charter business with nothing more than a used airplane and a drive to succeed, Jessi had climbed on board and never looked back.

Maggie owned two planes—or had before she'd lost one to the icy grip of the Atlantic—and a helicopter now, along with a pair of ferry boats. She spent as much time as she could in the air. Jessi made that possible.

As ten percent owner and one hundred percent business manager of Solomon Charters, Jessi handled the scheduling, drummed up business, kept the place stocked in everything from toilet paper to aircraft fuel, and juggled the bills to keep the wolves from the door—for the business, and for herself and her son.

All in all, she was pretty proud of herself, satisfied in her work, and fairly content with her personal life.

"Mom?"

She turned toward the sound of that voice and thought, *make that deliriously happy*. Looking into the face of her son, how could she not be?

"What's up, Benj?"

He paused in the act of loading his backpack. "Where are we going on vacation next summer?"

"I'm not sure." She gestured to his pack. "Work while you talk or we'll be late. How about Boston, or maybe Gettysburg?" she tossed out, because summer was a long way off and she hadn't given vacationing even a passing thought. "What do you think: Freedom Road or battlefield ghosts?"

Benji stuffed some papers in his backpack, flopped in a book, and heaved a sigh. "History stuff again?"

"I thought you liked history stuff."

"It's okay." He sent her a sidelong glance. "They have history in other places."

"Oh? What other places?"

He shrugged. "Everywhere, even Disney World."

Jessi bit back a smile. "I don't know, Benj. Disney World?"

"It's not just rides and cartoon stuff, Mom. I looked it up in school." His little voice rose with excitement as he made his pitch. "They have animals, like in a zoo but they get to wander all over and you have to look at them from a train kind of thing. And there's stuff about countries and presidents and science."

"And this idea just came to you out of the blue?"

He hunched his shoulders. "Danny Mason is going with his family."

And Danny was bragging on it to all the other kids in school. Not that Jessi could blame him; Disney World was the Paris of the pre-teen set.

"Auntie Maggie could fly us there," Benji said, "and some of the hotels are pretty cheap— I mean," he screwed up his face, "affordable. Some of the places are afford-able, Mom, like for families, you know? So we could still stay in the park."

But there was airline fuel, airport fees, a rental car, admission tickets, and meals for a kid who ate like he had two hollow legs, and souvenirs, because why go all that way and bring back only memories? And she kept those details to herself. Bad enough that Benji had gone to the trouble of researching hotel prices; she wouldn't have him worrying about money, not at his age.

"You've never said anything about Disney World before. Do you want to go just because the Masons are going?"

He thought about it for a second, which made her smile—and tear up just a little. How many seven-year-olds took the time to think through an answer—an answer about a proposal he'd clearly already put considerable thought and study into?

"I don't know. I want to be a pilot, like Auntie Maggie. I guess that means I kinda want to go everywhere."

"London? Moscow? Budapest?"

"I'm just a kid," he said, and though his back was turned she could tell an eye roll went along with the comment. Then he zipped his backpack and turned, giving her a sunny smile. "I'll hit those other places when I grow up. *We'll* hit them, Mom."

And the tears filled Jessi's throat so she could only smile and ruffle his hair as she nudged him toward the door. The way he assumed they'd always be a unit warmed her heart, and broke it a little, because she knew he'd leave her one day. She intended to do everything in her power to make sure he could and would. Children were meant to grow up and lead their own lives, and it was the task—and burden—of their parents to make sure they were prepared. When the time came, she'd swallow back tears again as she saw him off.

But that day was a long time coming, she reminded herself. For now, for all the days until then, he still belonged to her. Only her. "I've always wanted to go to Budapest."

"Really?" He looked up at her, brown eyes alight with curiosity. "Where is that, 'xactly?"

Jessi sighed loudly and for effect. "It's a good thing you're going to school for a few more years if you don't even know where Budapest is."

"I can look it up only . . . How do you spell it?"

Laughing, Jessi gave him the letters after they'd climbed into the car. Benji copied them down on a scrap of paper, barely finishing before they pulled up in front of Windfall Island's little school.

He stuffed the paper in his pocket and opened the car door, but instead of getting out, he turned to her. "We could get a dog," he said. "Instead of going to Disney World, I mean."

Jessi shook her head, amused. "Consolation prize?" He'd asked her for a dog at least a thousand times, but somehow he always managed to find a new angle. "Only you, Benj."

He gave her a bright, mischievous smile. "I'll talk you into it," he said, tossed in a "'Bye, Mom," and jumped out of the car, too old to kiss her in front of his friends anymore.

She'd gotten used to that, even if she waited until he'd gone inside before she turned the car—and her thoughts—toward work. Best to concentrate on what she could have, what she could do. To remember that while it would be amazing to give her son a once-in-a-lifetime dream, by getting through every day, every week, every year, by sending him to college, she'd be giving him the tools to realize all his dreams.

Windfall Island perched just off the coast of Maine, a long, narrow, unforgiving spit of land edged with rocks too damn hard for even the relentlessly pounding surf of the Atlantic Ocean to wear down. Her people were just as hard, just as unforgiving, and just as moody as the Atlantic—not to mention they ran the gamut from mildly eccentric to downright off-kilter.

Holden Abbot had come to Windfall Island to do a genealogy of the residents. All the residents. According to his research, the island had been settled by those on the fringes of society, sailors who'd jumped ship, men who'd broken laws, and runaway slaves. Fugitives from justice all. They'd left a legacy of insularity, paranoia, and a severe dislike for any form of law enforcement—maybe because, over the centuries, breaking the law had often meant the difference between survival and starvation for the people of Windfall.

Laws weren't broken on a regular basis anymore, at least not the big ones. Nowadays tourism provided. The season, however, had ended with the falling leaves and dropping temperature. The last tourist had vacated the island long before the wind became cutting and the surf turned deadly.

Hold wasn't a tourist, but he was an outsider—which had proven even less tolerable to the citizens of the island. At least the male citizens. The women tended to be a lot more welcoming. Rabidly so.

Except for the one he wanted to get to know.

Jessi Randal seemed mostly oblivious to him— friendly, helpful, and sort of vaguely flirtatious without putting any real intent behind it. Without ever saying no, she kept him at arm's length. Then again, he'd never outright asked her for a date because hearing her say no— well now, that would be a true rejection.

She walked in, petite, pretty, and looking so fresh and so sunny it seemed she brought spring in with her. And there, Hold thought, his blood sizzled, his nerve endings tingled, and a weight seemed to settle on his chest, making it just a little hard to breathe.

"What's new, Mississippi?" She peeled a puffy coat the color of fresh lemons off her curvy little body, and when she turned and leveled her bright smile and dancing green eyes at him, he couldn't have kept a thought in his head with duct tape and wire mesh.

"I know you Southern boys like to go slow, but it can't possibly take this long for you to come up with an answer. You only need one word, like *fine* or *good*."

Being from the South, Hold generally took his time over, well, everything. Jessi made him feel a powerful impatience; he just didn't want her to see it. So he sat back, folded his arms and played it cool.

"Unless you're up to something nefarious and you don't want to tell me about it."

"Not me." Unless, Hold thought, she considered it nefarious to picture her naked. Which she probably did.

"Okaaay, so let me try this again. What's new?"

"Not a blessed thing, sugar."

"Well then." She sat at her desk, and although the phone began to ring, she only looked over at the old-fashioned wall clock, which stood at one minute to eight.

She waited, watched the second hand sweep its measured way around the dial to dead on the hour, then plucked the receiver off the ancient black desk phone and said brightly, "Good Morning, Solomon Charters. Hold Abbot?" She looked over at him, grinning hugely. "Let me see if he's around."

Hold slashed a hand across his throat, shook his head, even got to his feet, prepared to beat a hasty retreat before he had to talk to the Windfaller on the other end of that call—probably female and ready with a proposition he'd have to find a non-insulting way to fend off. He'd just about run out of charm, and for a man who hailed from a part of the country where charm was as much a part of the culture as pralines, that was saying something.

Jessi rolled her eyes, but said into the phone, "He's not here, Mrs. Hadley." After a "Yes," a couple of "Mm-hmmms," and some scribbling, she said good-bye and hung up the phone, holding out a pink message slip. "How about dinner?"

Hold crossed the room to brace his backside against her desk, just near her right elbow. "Sign me up, sugar."

"Boy, you're good at that," Jessi said. "The little lean, the eye contact, and the way you call me 'sugar' in that slow, easy Southern drawl. Smooth as Bourbon. Laureen Hadley is a goner."

"Who? What?"

"Laureen Hadley. You're having dinner with her tonight." Jessi handed him the pink message slip. "Eight sharp, which is quite the sacrifice for Mr. Hadley since, according to Mrs. Hadley, eating that late will wreak havoc on his digestion. Mr. Hadley is always one taco away from complete intestinal meltdown, so that's really no big surprise."

Hold stared at the slip a minute, then wadded it up and tossed it in the trash. "I'm not having dinner with the Hadleys. I'm busy tonight."

"Of course you are," Jessi said in a way that told him she thought she knew exactly what he'd be busy doing. Or rather whom.

She reached into the top drawer of her desk and pulled out a stack of pink message notes and handed them over. "Take your pick."

Hold dropped them in the trash. "I'm busy then, too."

"Why do you encourage them if you're not interested?"

"I don't encourage them."

She twisted around in her chair, rolling it back a couple
feet so she could stare at him, brows arched. "What do
you call flirting?"

"Harmless fun. A way to pass the time, make a woman
feel good about herself."

"Harmless for you, maybe. Around here it's like making yourself the only bone in a roomful of starving dogs.
Once they get done swiping at one another, the last one
standing is only going to..."

"Gnaw on me a little while?"

She gave him a slight smile. "For starters."

"You made your point, Jessica. From now on I'll only
flirt with you."

"At least I know you don't mean it." She rolled back to
her desk, pulled a stack of paperwork over in front of her.

"What makes you think I don't mean it?"

"I don't know. Maybe the fact that you flirt with, oh,
every woman between legal and the grave? What would
make me any different?"

"I don't know," he parroted. "Maybe the fact that I'm
attracted to you?"

She rolled her eyes.

"It's true, Jessica. I'm saving myself for you. Ask any
woman between legal and the grave. They'll tell you I'm
all talk and no action."

"I have no interest in your love life."

Not for long, Hold thought as he pushed off her desk.
And he was running out of patience. Sure, he'd only been
there a couple of weeks, and while he'd wanted Jessi from

the moment he saw her, he'd decided to give her time to get used to the idea. She was, however, being purposely, *stubbornly*, obtuse.

Or maybe there was something more at work this morning.

Hold slid the stack of papers out from under her unseeing eyes. "Want to share your problem with Uncle Hold?"

"You're not my uncle."

He grinned, settled beside her again. "Glad you noticed."

She shot him a look. "It's not that big a deal, just something Benji sprang on me this morning that I'd like to make happen."

"Maybe I can help."

"It's something I have to do myself."

"Why?"

"Because Benji is my responsibility."

"I get that, but why do you have to do it alone? Maggie would do anything for you, no questions asked—Maggie and Dex," he said, referring to her best friend and majority owner of Solomon airlines, and her fiancé. "So would I."

"Then it would be Maggie and Dex doing it. And there's no way I'm asking you for help."

"Why?"

"Because I hardly know you."

"And you don't want to admit you're attracted to me?"

"Back off, Abbot." She shot to her feet, did the backing off herself. "Benji is my son, and if he wants to go—whatever he wants, I'll damn well make it happen without going begging to my friends. Or complete strangers with egos the size of"—she tossed her hands in the air—

"something really big," she finished, clearly at a loss, but so damn gorgeous he wanted to scoop her up and kiss her until all that glorious temper turned to a different kind of heat.

"What are you grinning at?"

"You," he said, holding himself back with what could only be called an Herculean effort. "You're beautiful when you're mad."

Her mouth dropped open. "You...I...Stop saying things like that."

"I'd rather show you anyway, sugar."

She lifted her hands to her cheeks, not just pink now but hot red. "Hold—"

"Why don't you tell me what Benji wants?" he said because he'd pushed her too far, and he didn't want to hear her give him a single reason why they couldn't be together.

"It's just so"—she dropped her hands, laughing a little—"ridiculous."

But it had upset her, and it didn't take much for him to reason out why. "It can't be easy to raise a kid by yourself, no child support."

Jessi sat back down, crossed her arms. "Really? Do tell."

Hold smiled indulgently. "I know you own ten percent of Solomon Charters, but you're putting most of the profits back into the business if you want to grow it at all, and especially right now, when you've just lost the Piper..." He trailed off at the look on her face—a look that had nothing to do with being reminded of Maggie's near-death just a few days before, resulting in the loss of her first airplane. And when the tone of her voice matched the look, he knew. He'd just made an ass of himself—a supercilious, condescending ass.

"Oh, don't stop now," Jessi said. "I find it truly fascinating how you can tell me all about my life without ever asking a single question."

"Uh..."

"Let me guess. You've been asking questions, just not to me."

"How do I respond to that observation without putting your back up any more than I've already done?"

"Apologizing would be a good start," she said with a perfect mix of disappointment and reproach.

Hold suppressed the urge to hang his head, dig his toe into the carpet, stuff his hands in his pockets, or otherwise give physical presence to the guilt he felt. "I wouldn't have to apologize if you'd talk to me once in a while."

"I talk to you all the time."

"Not about anything personal."

"That's because my personal life is none of your business. Which I keep telling you, and you keep ignoring."

"Doesn't that tell you how serious I am about getting to know you?"

Jessi just shook her head, turned back to her desk. Dismissed him again, like she always did. "You want to get to know me? Start with my genealogy, Hold." She shot him a glance, eyes sparkling, a hint of laughter in her voice. "Maybe I'll turn out to be the long lost Stanhope heir, and all my troubles will be over."

Money, Hold thought sourly.

He could have told her it didn't solve every problem, but that would raise questions he wasn't ready to answer. Jessi believed him to be a simple researcher; he hadn't told her, or anyone, that he came from one of the wealthiest families in the country.

Because he'd yet to meet anyone it didn't matter to on some level.

He could honestly say the women he dated didn't always go into the relationship because of his money, but once they found out, they changed. Every last one of them.

What he felt for Jessi...He didn't know what he felt for Jessi, or what she felt for him. But he wanted a chance to find out before his money complicated everything.

Jessi sighed. "It's a nice dream, inheriting a fortune. Not having to live from paycheck to paycheck would certainly make life easier."

"Money isn't everything," Hold murmured, although he couldn't brush off the ease it put into his life—the freedom, for instance, to be here on Windfall Island for who knew how long, working a job that didn't even net him a paycheck.

But he understood there were people who would do anything, say anything, be anything, to get it. He had first-hand experience.

Chapter Two

The day passed in a blur; Jessi made sure it did despite the fact that Solomon Charters had hit its slow season.

There were no daily ferry trips back and forth to the mainland, with their inevitable emergencies, large and small, to be dealt with. There were no tourist flights, in and out, to be scheduled around the commercial airliners, so Solomon Charters could maximize flights to the mainland.

There were, however, private charters, taking Maggie farther afield now that the company's good reputation had begun to spread. Maggie still picked up the mail a couple times a week; she still flew goods in and out and, in her flight suit, battered leather bomber, and aviators, she put an irresistibly dashing face on the business.

Someone had to keep the lights burning, though. Someone had to pay the phone bill and juggle the budget so they got past the lean winter months without burning through all the money they'd put aside during the summer glut.

"Jessica," Hold called out in his honey-dripping southern drawl.

And someone, she added to her thoughts, had to pump the island's residents for information useful in solving Eugenia's mystery. She glanced over her shoulder, to the small back office where Hold worked—even if that meant she had to work alongside a man who sent her senses haywire just by breathing.

She walked into the little back office. Hold smiled, and it wasn't just her senses—everything inside her yearned. The need had been growing for weeks, and now it all but overwhelmed her. The idea of giving in to it was so damn tempting—he was so damn tempting.

It had been nearly eight years since she'd vowed Benji would be the only man in her life. She liked to think she'd held steady because she was strong. Truth to be told, she'd yet to meet a man who made her regret that vow.

Hold looked up again from the scatter of books and papers in front of him, smiled again, and for the life of her she couldn't do anything but smile back.

And what harm could there be in looking, she asked herself? Holden Abbot was a prime specimen of the troublesome male species, and she had eyes, didn't she? And needs. Even if she'd gotten used to ignoring those needs, it didn't mean she'd forgotten how it felt to have a man's hands on her. Hold had such incredible hands, wide palms and long fingers she imagined would be just a little rough at the tips, a little calloused on the palms.

She could still remember the glory of a man's body against hers, and Hold's body, well, she liked the planes and angles of him, liked the easy, graceful way he carried himself, and she could imagine—had imagined—

"Jessica," he said again.

Her gaze snapped to his face, heart-stoppingly handsome even when it wore a lazy, self-satisfied smirk she knew came at her expense. He hadn't missed the way she'd been ogling him, and he tipped his head, gave her a come-along look. He'd made it clear he'd be only too happy to have her do more than look.

She wouldn't, and not just because of a promise she'd made herself eight years before.

Because along with everything else, she could still remember how it felt to have her heart broken. And hers wasn't the only heart she had to protect now.

She squared her shoulders, gave her nerve endings a stern talking to, and promptly put her foot in her mouth. "Was there something you wanted?"

His smirk widened into a full-on grin.

She turned on her heel.

Hold followed her. Of course. And settled his very nice backside on her desk, just by her elbow.

"Does the phrase *personal space* mean anything to you?"

"If I had my way there'd be a whole lot more personal between us, sugar, and a lot less space."

She didn't look up at him, just pointed, stiff-armed, to the little office.

"Before you send me back to my cell, I wanted to ask you about the Butler family," he said, the name coming out as *Butlah* in his drawl, bringing to mind that scene of Rhett carrying Scarlett up a wide sweep of stairs in *Gone with the Wind*.

Hold certainly had the muscles for it, she thought, and her house had stairs. Narrow, pokey stairs with a turn in the middle. If he tried to carry her up, she'd hit her head and wind up with a concussion. Which was just what she'd deserve.

"It's a pretty common name," Hold said when she failed to respond. "Any idea how we can narrow down the search?"

"My mother told me Mrs. Butler died in the seventies, and Mr. Butler just picked up and moved the family. Here one day, gone the next. They had a son, but word came back that Mr. Butler remarried and had a couple more kids." And she was babbling, damn it, because as long as she was thinking about the Butlers, she could keep herself from jumping Hold Abbot. "I'll ask around, see if anyone knows where they landed."

"We could ask around together," Hold said.

He set a neat stack of papers down in front of her, and now she noticed how he smelled, too. She closed her eyes, just for a second, and drew him in: soap, man…

"Right here," he said, pointing to an entry in what turned out to be one of the island journals Maggie and Dex had borrowed from Josiah Meeker's private collection.

Jessi concentrated almost desperately on the entry, not only old and written in spidery handwriting, but badly smudged as well.

"Can you make it out?"

She glanced up without thinking, and found herself caught in the depths of melted-chocolate eyes. Hold had a way of looking at her that made her feel as if she were the only woman in the world.

And he knew it, damn him.

She picked up the papers, shoved them at him. "Go away."

"What's got you all het up?"

"You. And before you smirk at me again, it's not a good thing."

"How is it I always manage to put your back up?"

"It's not—" She huffed out a breath. "It's the condescending way you talk to me—to women," she amended hastily. "Might as well just pat me on the head."

"It's not your head I want my hands on."

"All of me is off-limits."

Hold shoved off her desk and paced away, whipping around to scowl at her. "I just want to get to know you, Jessica. What's wrong with that?"

Nothing. But all she said was, "You know as much about me as you need to."

"And you think you know as much as you need to about me."

She shrugged.

"Then where's the harm in having a little supper together?"

"On this island? Are you serious?"

"So folks'll talk. Flapping jaws're about as dangerous as a bag full of butterflies, my granddaddy always said."

"No offense to your granddaddy, but words can hurt as much as sticks and stones."

"Not if you let them fly right by you. C'mon, darlin'. It's two people sharing a meal and a conversation. I promise I won't push you for more than that."

Jessi looked up, met those warm brown eyes, and accepted that she wanted to believe him.

But she'd been taken in before by a pair of guileless eyes, fooled by a beautiful trust-me smile. She saw those same eyes, that same smile, on her son, every day. Benji didn't have a dishonest bone in his little body, but it reminded her, every day, of the mistake she'd made—not in having him. No, she'd made her mistake long before Benji had ever been conceived.

Hold Abbot might look like the most honest, most sincere, most straightforward man in the entire world, but how could she trust him when she couldn't trust her own judgment?

"You've been hurt, sugar— Don't poker up on me," Hold added when she did just that. "I didn't ask."

"But you got the story anyway." When you lived in gossip central, it was impossible to keep anything private. It didn't make the sting any less for knowing he'd seen her skeletons. "Gives you kind of an unfair advantage. You knowing about my past while I don't know the first thing about you."

He leaned a hip on the corner of her desk. "By all means, let's even the playing field."

She didn't think the playing field would ever be even, not when he looked at her like that.

He gave her one of his disarming smiles, and, God help her, she couldn't bring herself to open that door.

She just didn't want to know anything that would lower her opinion of him. Or worse, raise it. He was nearly irresistible as it was; if he got any better she'd be toast.

"It doesn't matter," she said. "Unless you're willing to move to Windfall, settle down, and help me raise someone else's son."

"Getting a little ahead of yourself, aren't you?"

"No. I have a child, Hold. I don't have the luxury of casual relationships. It's not fair to Benji to let him get attached to someone, only to lose that person when the relationship ends."

"So you won't let anything happen between us unless it could lead somewhere permanent?"

"Yes."

"Is that supposed to scare me off?"

"Frankly, yes."

He simply stared at her, his expression slightly... bemused, was the best way she could put it.

"It's always worked before," she muttered self-consciously.

Hold narrowed his eyes. "Benji is how old?"

"Seven."

"And his father left?"

"Before he was born," she said crankily.

He grinned from ear to ear. "Interesting."

Jessi felt the blood rise to her cheeks, felt the heat spread until it seemed as if her whole face was flaming.

But when his grin softened, when he brushed his fingers over her cheek, the heat turned to need, the soft kind of need that moved through her and left her empty and aching. She fought back, eased away before she could turn her face into his hand, just so she could feel the warmth of his skin on hers.

When she finally met Hold's gaze again, she was absolutely steady, absolutely sure the need couldn't leak through. "I won't get involved with anyone unless there's a chance for a real relationship, Hold."

"We could take it a day at a time, and see what happens."

For a second, just a second, she wanted it so badly she felt almost desperate to take what he offered. The reality of spending her life alone far outstripped the theory of it.

She had friends she could turn to, but having a partner, a husband, to build a life with, to make memories with: to be a family...She shook her head and stopped torturing herself with what ifs. "This is a ridiculous conversation when we both know you aren't the marrying kind."

He straightened away from her, and she could all but feel the anger rising off him. "You don't know anything about me, but you'll make me the villain so it's easier for you—"

"You're right." And it shamed her. "I'll apologize for saying that, Hold."

"But not for seeing me as a man who can't commit."

"It's not..." she spread her hands, at a loss to make him accept what he simply didn't want to believe. "I'm sorry."

"You should be, Jessica, for thinking so little of me after such a short time. And for selling yourself short."

"I'm not selling myself short."

"Just one more thing I'll have to change your mind about," he said with the kind of steel she'd never heard in his voice.

"I'm not in the habit of changing my mind."

"Women do, with troubling regularity."

"Not the ones I know."

Maggie Solomon breezed in, fresh off a charter to Portland, tall and beautiful, cloaked in the kind of confidence that couldn't be taught, and that drew people to her like moths to a flame.

It was a testament to her own level of upheaval, Jessi thought, that she hadn't even heard Maggie's helicopter set down on the tarmac, let alone noticed the outer door opening.

Hold grinned. "Here's living proof."

"No you don't," Maggie said, dumping her clipboard on Jessi's desk. "However I got involved in this discussion, you can take me right back out of it."

"I was just telling Jessica, here, how much I admire a woman who can admit the error of her ways."

"Maggie never admits to being wrong."

"Damn straight. Admit you're wrong, and a man will never let you forget it."

"Referring to any man in particular?"

They all turned toward the door, but not before Jessi saw Maggie's face light. And why not? Jessi asked herself, stifling a sigh as Dex Keegan walked in—tall, ruggedly handsome, and a bona fide hero—and planted a kiss square on Maggie's mouth. And Maggie, who'd always refused to risk her heart, rested her hand on Dex's chest—her engagement ring-adorned hand—and leaned into his kiss.

Dexter Keegan, private investigator, had started the search for Eugenia Stanhope, and along the way he'd fallen in love with Maggie. It had taken Maggie longer to let Dex into her life. But she'd finally done it, finally admitted she loved him.

"That could be you," Hold said in Jessi's ear.

"I have no intention of kissing Dex," she said, brushing him away with the back of her hand, "And if I did, Maggie would probably drop me out of a plane at ten thousand feet."

"I was talking about me."

"You want to kiss Dex?"

"Ha, funny. Let me know when I've won our little bet."

"We don't have a bet, and if we did you'd be the last person I'd surrender to." Just to make her point, she met his eyes. And she was caught. The air between them seemed to ignite—

"So," Maggie asked, "anything exciting happen today?"

Jessi tore her eyes off Hold, but when she opened her mouth, she couldn't force words from her dry throat.

"Nothing interesting has happened since Mort tried to kill you," Hold said glumly.

Just a week ago, Maggie had been identified as a possible descendant of Eugenia's, and an attempt had been made on her life. Her jack-of-all-trades handyman, Mort Simpkins, had been the actual perpetrator, but they all assumed one of the Stanhopes had pulled the strings.

Since Dex was the PI, he'd be investigating—quietly—the family, with a view to figuring out which one of the Stanhopes didn't want to share the family fortune. Then he'd be coming back to Windfall, to Maggie, to start their life together.

It made Jessi deliriously happy for Maggie, and unbelievably sad for herself.

"Seriously, Jess, are you okay?"

Jessi blinked, looking over at Maggie. "Where'd everyone go?"

"Hold and Dex are back there." Maggie jerked a thumb toward the little office she'd once used as her own space, but had given over to Hold so they could keep the genealogy locked away from prying eyes.

"Giving us a girl moment?"

"Yeah, probably."

Jessi smiled. Maggie might be in love, but emotion, any kind of emotion, still made her twitchy enough to set her to pacing.

Being the good friend she was, Maggie didn't let a little personal discomfort hold her back. "You haven't answered my question."

"There's nothing wrong with me."

"Just the same old stuff?" Maggie smiled faintly. "Want some advice?"

"From you? On my love life?"

"Who said anything about love? Remember, you told me not so long ago, just to take Dex out for a spin, not to get emotionally involved."

"And you told me to go to hell."

"Not quite those words."

Jessi sighed, wishing it could be so easy. "It's different for you, Mags."

"Because you have a child to worry about? I'm not suggesting you make Hold a part of the family, Jess."

"What? Just have meaningless sex? Like you used to before Dex?"

"Well, gee, wasn't I a slut," Maggie said dryly.

"No, Mags, I mean, it's not like you were jumping from bed to bed or anything. Just once in a blue moon. But...I don't know. It's been so long."

"It's like riding a bike, Jess."

"I'm pretty sure if I tried to ride a bike after all this time, I'd fall off."

"Yeah, well, maybe a little pain is worth it."

Spoken, Jessi thought, like a woman who had no idea how it felt to be deserted by the man she loved.

* * *

The main building at the airport consisted of a wide, usually empty lobby, done in seventies black and white tile with seventies chrome and black Naugahyde furniture. Past the lobby was Jessi's work space, as crowded and full of life as the lobby was empty and soulless. Just off Jessi's domain was another room, smaller yet, that had once served as Maggie's office.

Maggie's desk had been cleaned off, and the walls that had been covered by maps of the world crisscrossed with the most common flight routes instead held long sheets of white paper. Hold had marked the sheets with solid or dotted lines and the names, when known, that it took to create a genealogy for the people of Windfall Island.

Jessi saw wide and notable gaps, one of which included—or rather failed to include—the Randal family.

Windfall Island Airport represented Maggie Solomon's life's work. Since Jessi owned a percentage, it was her work as well. But not her life.

Her life was her seven-year-old son. She would cheat, steal, or murder to keep Benji safe. She would lie, too, or at least turn her back on the truth.

Still, none of the three other people currently crammed into that closet of a room pushed Jessi to fill in her part of the genealogy—Jessi or anyone else on the island with children. The enemy had already proved ruthless enough to murder on the mere suspicion of a Stanhope connection; he wouldn't scruple over the life of a child.

"I've been working on ruling out—or in—the families who have moved away from Windfall Island," Hold said. He moved over to indicate the section of the chart he'd been researching. "So far they're out. I've gone back a hundred years, just to be sure, and I haven't found anyone among the families that have left the island who fits the requirements for possible relationship to the Stanhope family."

"Fast work," Dex put in. "Tracking down almost nine decades of people moving in and out of the community."

"It was fairly easy, actually. It's a small community, which keeps it manageable. Eugenia went missing in thirty-one, so I took the census from the year before and compared it with each one after, then searched for the missing families. I'm still tugging on a few strings, tying up a loose end or two."

"But you don't believe they're going to lead any-where meaningful," Jessi said. She knew this, as she'd been helping him play out those strings in the hopes that one of them would help unravel the mystery of Euge-nia's fate.

"No," Hold agreed, "but we have to follow them until we know for sure they don't take us anywhere."

"So at this point we're pretty much left with the fami-lies still in residence," Maggie observed when none of the rest of them chose to voice the obvious. Her vivid blue eyes shifted, met Jessi's worried green ones.

"Me, you mean," Jessi said. "I'm the same age as you, Maggie, the same generation. It makes me a possibility. And Benji—"

"No one is taking a shot at Benji, Jess. As long as Dex and I are around—"

"And me," Hold put in.

"The point is, you and Benji are safe as long as the rest of us are breathing. But we can't protect everyone, which means we can't put anyone else in danger, either."

"We won't have to if we can find out which one of the

Stanhopes is homicidal about keeping the family fortune intact."

"That's where I come in," Dex said, his gaze going to Maggie. They'd both known his investigation into the Stanhope family members would take him away for a time.

And although Jessi knew her best friend well enough to see the unhappiness in her eyes, Maggie's lips curved into her trademark smart-ass grin. "At long last, peace."

Dex stepped up to her, ran his hands from her shoulders down her arms, linking his fingers with hers. "You'll miss me."

"Not until tomorrow, right?"

"Yeah." He blew out a breath. "The sooner I go, the sooner I'll get back."

"Then I say we stop wasting time." Maggie headed for the door, tugging him along behind her. Not that Dex objected, or that either of them had eyes for anyone but each other.

Jessi watched them until they disappeared through the door to the lobby. When she looked around, her face heated because she knew Hold had heard the sigh she hadn't tried to stifle, and saw the longing she couldn't hide.

He stepped over to her but she jerked away before he could brush the fingers he'd lifted over her face.

Hold didn't push it. Or rather, he came at her from a different direction. "My invitation for tonight is still good."

"What about Laureen?"

"Doomed to disappointment." He exhaled heavily. "As am I, it appears."

"I'll be having dinner with Benji, like I do every night."

"I didn't take you for a coward."

"Then you didn't look close enough."

He lost his irreverent grin. "I only said that to get a rise out of you."

"But?"

"How long are you going to hide behind your son?"

"Oh, at least the next ten years, give or take," she said breezily. But she wasn't hiding behind Benji; she was standing in front of him, where she belonged.

"Does it ever occur to you that you can protect him too much?"

"He's seven. There's no such thing as protecting him too much."

"Jessi, I don't want to hurt him. Or you."

But he could, so easily, and wasn't that what really frightened her? "What exactly do you want, Hold?"

"A chance to get to know you, and for you to get to know me."

"It's not that simple." She allowed herself to move away from him. Okay, that coward comment had stung, and she'd stayed put if only to show him he hadn't gotten to her. But he had.

That long, strong body, the smile that seemed to light up the room, the way his eyes met hers and made her want to just let go and believe.

She'd been there before, she reminded herself.

She'd been taken in by a sunny smile and the attention of a handsome man—or boy, as the case had been. She'd believed Lance Proctor when he'd said he loved her, when he'd said he'd marry her. When he'd promised they'd be a family, the two of them and the life they'd created between them.

She'd been devastated after he ran off, those first days when she'd held her pregnancy a secret. When she'd believed he'd come back. He hadn't; she'd had to stop believing, and eventually she'd gone to her mother.

Doris Randal had cried. And although the memory of it still broke her heart, Jessi had to content herself with the knowledge it had been the only time she'd caused her mother that kind of pain. The tears at Benji's birth, and all the ones after, had been happy ones.

Her mother had been gone almost two years, and not a day went by that Jessi didn't miss her in a dozen ways, large and small. Not a day went by that she didn't remember the example her mother had set, that she didn't struggle to find that kind of strength within herself. Her mother had become her rock, Jessi remembered—hers and Benji's.

Now Jessi had to be the rock.

"Jessi?"

She looked over at Hold and thought, *the bigger the temptation*.

"Benji doesn't ask about his father much," she said, working her way carefully through her explanation as she gave it. "He used to ask, once he started spending time with the other school-age kids and realized they all had one and he didn't. I tried to explain to him, you know, that his dad being gone had nothing to do with him."

"But he doesn't believe you."

"He thinks I'm sparing his feelings."

"And you don't want to bring another man into his life

who'll leave again. I wish I could tell you I'll stay, Jessi, but we've known each other barely two weeks."

"I'm not asking for assurances, Hold. I don't expect you to make lifelong plans that include a ready-made family. But I don't do anything until I consider how it might affect Benji."

"I think he's a stronger kid than you're giving him credit for. He must be with you for a mother."

"That's flattering—"

"And you think I'm just blowing smoke up your skirt."

"You don't know me, Hold. Not really." That was part of what troubled her. She was going on instinct, and she couldn't trust hers. "Why are you pushing so hard?"

"There's something about you, Jessi." And now she could tell he was being careful with what he said. "The minute I saw you, there was something. You felt it, too. Are you going to deny yourself a chance to get to know me, and vice versa, because you don't know how to explain it to your son?"

"Today? Yes."

Hold shot her that lightning-quick, sun-bright grin. "That means there's hope for tomorrow."

"It'll still be no tomorrow."

"Then I'll just have to keep asking."

Chapter Three

Friday morning dawned fresh and bright, the early October sky a crisp, clear blue. Jessi greeted the day still wearing her favorite and most tattered sleep shirt, and a robe that had seen better days.

Benji had gone off to school already, ecstatic to be allowed to walk with Bobby Cassidy from next door, ten years old and everything Benji aspired to be, with his skateboard skills and a cute little air of worldliness. Braving thirty-degree weather didn't seem like such a treat to her, but it was only a few blocks, and really, what could happen on an island where the children were well-known and every adult watched out for them?

It gave her the peace of mind to lounge at her little table, eating a breakfast she'd actually cooked rather than scarfing down a bagel on the way to the airport. A whole weekday off to spend as she liked, she thought blissfully as she sipped her second cup of coffee. Eight glorious hours to herself after a long, stressful week in the company of a man who couldn't seem to take no for an answer. And that, she allowed, wasn't really the problem.

No kept getting harder to say. *That* was the problem.

Worse, she'd actually begun to miss Hold's harassment when he wasn't around, to feel as though her world spun with a little bit of a wobble. As if, she thought, the Earth was a carnival ride with one of the stabilizers missing.

Life was certainly that, she decided: a carnival ride. Needing Holden Abbot around to keep her on track? That would be true craziness—

Her front door flew open and Hold burst in.

Jessi jumped out of her chair, dripping coffee cup and all, and scooted around behind the table before he could grab her up. "What? What's wrong?"

"You didn't show up for work this morning."

Jessi could only stare, trying to reconcile the simplicity of his words with the panicked race of her heart.

"What are you talking about?"

"You. Not showing up this morning. You're always there at precisely seven fifty-seven."

Jessi plunked her cup down, plucked a napkin from the table holder and wiped her hands. "There's nothing precise about it." Actually there was, since she dropped Benji off at school at pretty much the same time each morning, then drove to the other end of the island. But she wasn't giving him that.

"Are you sick?"

He reached out, and she couldn't evade the hand he laid on her forehead. Stupid, small table.

She brushed him off. "Jeez, can't a girl take a day off once in a blue moon?"

"Of course, sugar, I just wish you'd told me."

"It's—"

"None of my business. See, I have been listening."

"Sure. Now you're just ignoring."

"I'm only concerned about your welfare, Jessica."

"Whether or not I want you to be. Some people would call that stalking."

"What would you call it?"

"Arrogant, high-handed. And annoying, because you're mostly harmless."

"Am I?" Hold said softly, and the way he looked at her made her pulse jump.

She gathered the edges of her robe together with one hand. "I said mostly," she managed, the words weak and thready, not just because the breath had stalled in her lungs, but because her thoughts had scattered, incinerated in the heat flashing through her.

Hold leaned forward to peek over the table. "Nice legs."

The hand clutching her lapels trembled on the verge of letting go. Giving in. Hold's knowing grin stopped her. "They're the same legs I had yesterday."

"But you always have them covered."

She edged behind a chair, and when his gaze lifted, pushed at her hair. It had to look like a rat's nest, she thought, scowling at him because he was enjoying her discomfort. "You can go now."

"I could use a cup of coffee."

"They have coffee at the Horizon."

"Yours is better."

"Don't let AJ hear you say that," she said, ignoring the little pop of foolish pleasure. "Or Helen."

AJ and Helen Appelman owned and operated the Horizon Inn. Once a tavern dating back to the island's beginnings, it was a hotel now, and did a heck of a tourist business in the summer. In the winter it was mostly empty. Hold was likely the only guest right now. He was renting one of the efficiencies.

"You have your own kitchen, as I recall."

"Hot plate, sink, mini fridge." He wrinkled his nose. "I'm a lousy cook. I usually eat in the dining room."

And not alone, from what she'd heard.

"Why don't you get dressed, and we'll go out to breakfast?"

"I've already had breakfast."

He lifted his nose and sniffed the air like a hound, lifting the newspaper she'd dropped over her plate.

"Omelet."

Hold put a hand on his stomach. "Any chance I could convince you to make me one?"

"No." But she wanted to. Not to show off her cooking skills, but because it seemed such a—a couple sort of thing to do. Lazy morning, breakfast together, hands brushing as they traded sections of the paper, which would lead to their gazes meeting. And when her eyes met his, as they did now, she felt it all the way to her toes.

And she wanted.

It was all just a little too tempting, seeing as she'd spun the fantasy in her own mind. Not only tempting, but dangerous, she decided, bracing a hand on the chair in front of her, if only to remind herself she stood in her own home. Where she lived with Benji. Alone, just the two of them.

"Good-bye, Hold," she said.

"What are you up to today?" he asked, then immediately held up a hand. "I know, none of my business."

Hold stopped at the end of Jessi's front walk, looked back as the front door closed smartly behind him, and grinned. Couldn't help himself. Jessi had asked him to leave, politely at first. Then she'd pulled out her stern voice, and when that didn't work, she'd planted both her little hands on his back and physically shoved him through the door.

On the one hand, he mused as he put his feet in motion again, she'd kicked him out. On the other, now, he'd gotten her hands on him. Not the way he'd intended but that time would come, he told himself, still grinning as his thoughts ambled with the same Southern leisure as his feet. He could move fast when he wanted. Mostly, though, he took his own sweet time. The getting there, to his mind, was as interesting and entertaining as any destination. Why rush it?

Jessi Randal was turning out to be one of the rare exceptions. If he knew her—and he was beginning to know her—she wouldn't spend the day shut up indoors. She'd be out and about, her smile as sunny as her coat, brightening up the town and everyone in it. The woman moved like lightning, he mused, plowing through her work with the kind of alacrity that made a Southern boy's head spin. She talked fast, she walked fast, she moved almost constantly and at a pace that exhausted him just to see it. Except where he was concerned. She had only one speed there, and it was full stop.

Still, there were moments—or more like split seconds in her case—when he could see he was getting to her. A considering glance his way, a flush in her cheeks, and a woman didn't get irritated by a man—not the way she did anyway—unless she was fighting her own attraction. Hell, she'd as much as admitted it to him, hadn't she?

The trick was getting her to act on it, turning those seconds into moments. And he was just the man for it, for wearing away at her resistance like water carved a landscape. Inexorable, unstoppable, irresistible, he added with another grin that had the woman across the street staring. He nodded politely, as if he hadn't just seen her walk into a light pole.

As she hurried away, head down, cheeks red, his cell phone buzzed against his hip. He pulled it out, read the display. He was already smiling when he accepted the call, even before the voice on the other end said gruffly, "Where the hell are you?"

Hold looked around and realized he'd wandered into the main part of the village, more familiar now, but still foreign to someone who'd grown up in the warm, fragrant heart of Dixie. "You'd never believe me if I told you," he said to his brother, James Abbot.

"You've been gone a fair while, bro. Don't you think it's time you got back to your real life?"

"I'm busy."

"Doing what?"

"Stalking a woman."

"Well, that's a switch." Hold could hear the laughter in his brother's voice. "Usually you're the fox and some woman is trying to hound-dog you into a corner, hell bent on marriage."

"Haven't been caught yet, have I?" And he had no intention of being caught. He liked to keep his relationships short and light.

"Not since your close call."

Too close, Hold recalled. It had been just days before his wedding when he'd discovered his fiancée was after his money, his family name, and the ease she could buy with both.

"Look, bro, I can only imagine what you went through."

Not even close. Maybe it had been two years, but he'd had his heart fucking shattered, Hold thought savagely. He'd been made to question everything about himself, most especially how he could be so blind, such a terrible judge of character. How could a man like his brother, with a wife who looked at him like the sun rose and set at his instruction, understand how it felt to have your world so completely overturned?

"Point is," James continued, "Miriam Burton was one of a kind—the worst kind. There's got to be a woman out there who might have bad enough taste to love you in spite of your unfortunate looks and ridiculous personality."

"Only one?"

"It only takes one. 'Sides, I don't want to scare you when you're making such good progress. I mean, look at you, venturing away from Abbot House all by yourself."

His brother's sarcasm, more than all the motherly hugs and fatherly pep talks, helped remind Hold that the past was the past as long as he had the strength to leave it there.

"Let me know when Alicia comes to her senses and dumps you," he said to James, "because she realizes it's me she's wanted all these years."

"Sure, that'll happen right after a mutant virus turns us all into zombies, and she sees you as her next meal."

"So this is why you called? To insult me?"

"Kids want to know when Uncle Hold is coming back," James said with a shrug in his voice.

"Wow, and they're not even zombies yet?"

"No, but they're young, they have no taste."

"Maybe you're the one with no taste."

"Jimmy," he said, referring to his son, "eats crayons. Suzy," his daughter, "drinks air and pretends it's tea."

"Maybe you should feed them once in a while."

"Funny. Mom told me to remind you about the charity ball in Boston."

"I'm on top of that," Hold said.

"Your assistant is on top of it, you mean."

"That's what assistants are for, son. You ought to trust yours enough to take a day off once in a while."

"Can't. The world will grind to a screeching halt."

"Your ego is a thing of monumental proportions."

"You only say that because Mom loves me best."

Hold caught a bright flash of color out of the corner of his eye, and said, "Gotta go," even before he turned to see Jessi appear out of the cross street leading to her house.

"But—"

"Love to Mom and Dad," he said, and disconnected.

At the end of the island closest to the mainland, sheltered from the worst blasts of Lady Atlantic's changeable temper, lay Windfall Village, a conglomeration of buildings cobbled together over the better part of three centuries from whatever building materials came to hand. As some of those building materials were a direct benefit of the ships that had run afoul of the Lady in the midst of a tantrum, the result was an interesting mix of stone and wood, metal and glass, in an architectural style that could best be described as Repurposed Quirk.

In the beginning, the basic mindset had been about making the structures serviceable. Nobody cared what a building looked like as long as the roof kept out the weather. With tourism now the main source of Windfall Island's income, paint colors ran the gamut from sun- and sea-faded to bright as a button, and in the summer there'd be colorful awnings and umbrella tables. But just now, with the trees bare, the late autumn sky the color of pewter, and no tourists thronging the narrow streets, the village looked forlorn, a little down in the mouth and somewhat shabby at the edges, like a grizzled old uncle who'd seen better days but was nevertheless dear to the heart.

Jessi couldn't imagine living anywhere else. She'd forwarded Solomon Charters' phones to her cell, but as it was quiet this time of year, with few visitors to be flown in or out, she felt light and happy. Free.

And then she spotted Hold across the street, shoulders propped against the wall of the apothecary, hands in his pockets, one ankle crossed indolently over the other. He looked like an ad for...It didn't matter, not with his tall lean body set off by slacks the color of deep, dark chocolate topped by a beautifully worn leather jacket. His burnished hair was uncovered and ruffled slightly in the wind, and even when he straightened, he wore an expression that could best be described as "bring it on."

Barely an hour had passed since she'd found the strength to kick him out of her house, and there he was, lurking on the edge of her peaceful day, tempting her.

Jessi lifted her chin, focused her eyes ahead, and sailed

right by. When he fell into step with her, she said, "Uh-uh, stalkers are supposed to skulk half a block behind so they can hide in doorways and pretend to be innocent."

"Where's the fun in being innocent..." Hold trailed off when she glanced at the sign on the door where they'd stopped. "The Clipper Snip."

"The Clipper Snip," Jessi repeated with a lot of satisfaction and a little edge of snark. "What better way to spend a morning than being pampered?" Not to mention it was an estrogen-fueled gossip fest Hold wouldn't want to enter without body armor and a Taser. "Coming?" she said sweetly.

Hold's eyes wheeled from her to the door Jessi was slowly inching open. "I, um..."

"I'm sure the girls will be ecstatic to know you're going to hang out with us for a couple of hours. You can entertain them with all the fun stories of how you lost your innocence."

"You're enjoying this."

"Oh, yeah." She tugged the door open, letting out a puff of warm air laden with the unique stew of chemicals and perfumes common to such establishments the world over.

But when Hold called her bluff by taking her elbow, she balked. No way was she walking into Gossip Central on his arm. Even worse would have been walking away, especially when he moved his hand to the small of her back and gave her no choice.

But two could play that game. "Hello, ladies," she said brightly, "Look who the wind blew in."

Every eye in the place turned in their direction.

Hold took an immediate step back, helped along, no

doubt, by the combined weight of all those avaricious stares battering him simultaneously.

And when he backpedaled some more and it appeared he was leaving, the place broke into pandemonium. Jessi was elbowed out of way as the Clipper Snip's patrons surrounded Hold—which was fine with her since a safe distance only made the picture that much more entertaining.

"You need a cut?" Sandy asked him, her fingers already sifting through Hold's hair, judging the weight and texture of it.

"Uh, no." Hold said, sidling back as far as he could manage without trampling anyone. "I'll just, um...Jessi, can I have a word?"

She would've held back, made Hold sweat it out another minute, but Sandy shoved her forward. Hold took her arm and drew her back to the door. He didn't speak.

"You wanted a word," she reminded him, but his eyes shifted over her shoulder, and when she glanced behind her she understood why.

Women studied displays, perused magazines plucked at random from the tables by the lobby chairs, studied their manicures, all within easy earshot of the front door.

"Strange," Hold said, "but I seem to be fresh out of words at the moment."

"Well, here are four for you. Get lost and stay lost."

"That's five...Okay, four. If I cooperate with the first part of that statement, will you have supper with me?"

"Benji," she said simply. But there was such sad resignation on his face, Jessi couldn't help but soften. "It's how it has to be, Hold."

"No, it really doesn't. But I know you believe that,

so . . ." He pulled open the door, and although she knew he was baiting her, the question just popped out.

"So?"

He looked back at her, and this time his grinning face was bright with the fun of the contest. And edged with so much conviction that, for the first time, she felt a thin sliver of doubt. "Wait and see."

"Don't fall asleep on me," Sandy Rogers, owner and operator of the Clipper Snip, warned Jessi. "You're the only level-headed person in the place at the moment. 'Sides me, of course."

As Sandy had her hands buried in Jessi's conditioner-drenched hair, busily massaging Jessi's scalp, Jessi responded with a sound that fell somewhere between a moan and a purr. But when Sandy tweaked her hair, she made the effort to form actual words. "Not sleeping. Not talking, either."

"Because?"

"People talk back."

"Ask questions, you mean. And who can blame them when Maggie snapped up that handsome lawyer?"

As a cover story, Dex had told everyone he practiced law when he arrived on Windfall Island, so everyone still believed him to be a lawyer. Only she, Maggie, Hold, and George Boatwright, the sheriff, knew the truth.

"And Holden Abbot," Sandy continued, "is still available. And close, since he spends all his days out at the airport."

"But he spends his nights at the Horizon," Shelley Meeker sniped. "For the life of me I can't imagine what could possibly be the attraction all the way out there."

"First guess?" Maisie Cutshaw chirped in from under a head full of foil squares. "It's about as far away as he can get from anyone named Meeker."

Shelley stuck her nose in the air and simply ignored Maisie. Jessi couldn't have agreed more. Shelley's father, Josiah, owned and operated the island's antique store, collected island documents, and considered his family in a class by themselves. The other Windfallers agreed wholeheartedly. Anything that separated Meeker from the rest of them was okay in their book.

Shelley had inherited her mother's porcelain beauty, and her father's better-than-thou attitude. She was spoiled, superior, and absolutely vicious when she didn't get her way. She'd wanted Lance Proctor, back when they'd been in high school; she'd never forgiven Jessi for having him. "Why's he sticking around this boring little speck of an island anyway?" Shelley wanted to know.

"I imagine you'd have to ask Holden Abbot that question," Jessi said. She got back silence. It didn't take her long to interpret it. "Oh, you already have. And what did he say?"

Shelley sighed. "He looked right into my eyes, and I couldn't have cared less what came out of his mouth."

"I know just what you mean," Maisie said. "That Dex Keegan is one prime piece of male real estate. But Holden Abbot..." She shook her fingers as if she'd burned them. "Only thing could make him better is if he were rich. Right, Jessi?"

"Why would a man like that look her way at all?" Shelley sniped.

"Who wants him to just look anyway?" Maisie shot back.

Shelley Meeker gave a really annoying bray of laughter.

Sandy wrapped a towel around Jessi's rinsed hair, then gave her a light tap on the top of her head. "Your mother would kick your butt if she knew you let Shelley Meeker give you a hard time 'thout defending yourself."

"I stopped listening to Shelley a long time ago." The rest of the Windfallers, too, she thought. She'd kept her nose clean since she was sixteen, pregnant, and unmarried. But when you were the butt of town gossip, you learned fast to hold your head up and never let it show. Especially when it hurt the most. "Shelley's nothing more than a pair of fake boobs with a big mouth."

"I heard that."

"And ears. But she's harmless. Unless I let her get to me. Besides, what did she say that isn't true?"

"Pretty much everything that comes out of her mouth is crap," Sandy said philosophically.

"Which is why I ignore her. I'm happy with the way my life is going." Or she had been before temptation arrived in the form of a lanky, handsome genealogist who'd made her question. And crave.

"Sure, but you know what they say, kiddo. You can't take care of those who depend on you if you don't take care of yourself. And that includes sex. Nothing like a good roll 'tween the sheets to work the kinks out of, well, everything," Sandy said matter-of-factly. "Body, mood, mind, outlook."

"There's nothing wrong with my outlook."

"No." Sandy led the way to her station. "You were always an optimistic little thing."

Jessi shrugged. "It never made sense to me to see the dark side of things."

"Well, maybe you ought to apply that hopeful attitude toward that tasty hunk of male spending all his time out at the airport doing God knows what."

"He's not doing Jessi."

"She could have him if she wanted him," Sandy replied mildly. "Beautiful inside and out. Not that you'd understand the concept, Shelley."

"She might be able to get him in bed," Shelley said, "but she won't be able to hold onto him. Just like Lance. He had to leave the island entirely to get away from her."

The room went silent, still, dead—like all the air had been sucked out of it. And then sound and feeling and pain raced into the void. Jessi lifted a hand to her throat, trying to ease the band of sorrow and regret choking her.

Anger helped, because it didn't just sting; it pissed her off to have Shelley Meeker, of all people, throw that in her face. "Does it still burn that Lance wouldn't go out with you, even after you threw yourself at him?" she said to Shelley.

"At least Shelley didn't get herself pregnant to try to hold onto a man who didn't want her."

And now humiliation crashed over Jessi as well. She turned, as did everyone else, to see Joyce Proctor, Lance's mother, standing just inside the doorway.

"Jesus, Joyce, give it a rest," Sandy said.

"I'll give it a rest," she bit off, "the day my son can come back to his own hometown without feeling he'll be trapped into a situation not of his making."

"Um, I'm pretty sure he had a part in the *making*," Maisie Cutshaw tossed out on a hoot of laughter.

The rest of the women joined in. Jessi wanted to sink

into the chair. She would have slunk out of the place if Sandy hadn't tweaked her wet, half-cut hair again.

And sure, it was her battle—Jessi knew that—but how did she fight Benji's grandmother? He had little enough family as it was, and Joyce was good to him, even if she had no use for the mother of her grandson.

"Nobody forced that boy to leave," Sandy said.

"Sandy," Jessi began, desperate to keep the peace, even if it meant swallowing Joyce's abuse. Again.

"Hush." Sandy steamrolled over her. "She's been blaming you this whole time when it's her just as much her son—"

"My son is the kind of man—"

"Man? It seems to me the difference between a man and a boy is how he reacts to the difficult and unexpected. He turned tail and ran, and that surely doesn't make him a man."

"So he should have stayed here," Joyce shot back, "and married a girl who'd trap him with a baby he—"

"Didn't want, and abandoned?" Sandy shook her head. "He should have stayed, for Benji's sake, if nothing else."

Joyce stuck out her chin. "Men can't get pregnant. It's the girl's responsibility—"

Sandy snorted, and the rest of the room was hardly kinder. Maisie Cutshaw shouted "Bullshit!" over other comments like, "This is the twenty-first century, not the dark ages" and "Hell, let's revive the chastity belt."

"Jessi was just a girl," Sandy said when the furor died down. "Barely sixteen when she was knocked up by a kid with nothing more than a moment's pleasure on his mind. You might want to turn a blind eye so you can make it easier to swallow your own son's cowardice, Joyce, but Jessi stayed here and had Benji and held her head high when folks on this island whispered and called her names." Sandy sent Shelley Meeker a look so coldly furious Shelley hunched her shoulders and looked away.

"Jessi has raised your grandson with no help, not a dime from anyone," she continued, stepping over to Joyce and punctuating her words with the rat-tailed comb she still held. "Least of all you and your worthless offspring. Maybe you ought to stop feeling sorry for yourself and start appreciating the blessings you have, like the most amazing grandson God ever gave an undeserving witch like you."

"I love Benjamin," Joyce huffed, sounding a little taken aback. "He knows that."

"Of course he does." Sandy returned to the chair, turning Jessi's head back to the mirror with just a bit too much force, and snipping sharply with her scissors. Jessi felt the tug on her hair and closed her eyes.

"Benjamin is a very intelligent child," Joyce said.

"You bet your snooty ass he is," Sandy said. "Smart enough that it won't be long before he sees you for what you are."

Joyce pulled herself up. "You have no idea what you're talking about."

"I surely do, and so does everyone else on this island. You've made it clear how you feel about Jessi, and some of the comments you've made?" She shook her head, met Joyce's eyes in the mirror. "One of these days, some kid is going to throw that in Benji's face. Whose side do you think he'll take?"

Joyce sniffed dismissively, but she didn't look so self-righteous anymore, Jessi thought; not quite so certain.

And she was definitely speechless as she turned on her heel and slammed out the door.

"Don't you dare apologize to that woman," Sandy snapped at Jessi. But she took a deep breath, let it out slowly, and seemed the more relaxed for it.

"Remind me never to make you mad," Jessi said.

"You didn't make me mad."

"I disappointed you."

"No." Sandy tipped Jessi's head down, her scissors snicking again, sounding less homicidal now. "I just want you to stand up for yourself."

"How do I do that? It's hard enough to face her with hard feelings between us. If there are harsh words as well..." She spread her hands. "I've cost her enough."

"Cost her?" Sandy snorted rudely. "After growing up with Joyce Proctor, can you honestly say you were the one who pushed Lance away?"

"Not entirely, but I helped."

"Maybe you provided a kick in the ass, Jess, but that kid had one foot off this island from the moment he discovered the world didn't end at these shores. And what did Joyce get out of it? The sweetest grandson ever, that's what. Not that she deserves Benji. Or you, for that matter."

Jessi looked up, met Sandy's eyes, and made sure Sandy saw how much her words, her opinion—how much *she* mattered.

Sandy sniffed, fluffed at Jessi's hair. "What do you think?"

Jessi took a critical look in the mirror, then lifted her gaze to Sandy's and her lips in a smile. "I think I'm lucky to have any hair left at all."

Chapter Four

"Hey there, Jessi."

"Hi, Mr. MacDonald."

"Tomatoes on sale, just came in fresh yesterday."

Which Jessi already knew, and since Maggie had brought them in by boat, along with the rest of the market's fresh produce, Jessi already had a bowl of beautiful, ripe tomatoes in her refrigerator.

What she didn't have was milk and eggs, and the fun of spending a half hour walking the market's aisles, enjoying a simple task she usually had to rush through. Her budget meant she planned each week's meals carefully and didn't deviate from her list. She could have a little harmless fun leafing through a cookbook, though, take the time to imagine what it would be like to make some of the fancy recipes she saw the television chefs make—after a lot of cooking lessons.

For that matter, wouldn't it be fun to watch a program from start to finish, and not while she folded laundry or dusted shelves or helped Benji with his homework. But that time would come, she reminded herself, and soon enough.

Benji would be off to college before she knew it, she thought with equal parts pride and sadness. Once he graduated, he'd likely take a job on the mainland somewhere, like all the young people did. Not that she blamed them; Windfall just didn't offer enough in the way of opportunity.

Benji was smart as a whip; he'd want to do more than run a shop during tourist season or, if he stayed true to his current passion and learned to fly, squiring tourists and making mail runs. One thing she knew about her son, he would look for adventure. Windfall tended to be a lot of the same.

"What's for supper?"

Jessi kept strolling, not all that surprised to hear Hold's voice. And since it came from behind her, she found it better to keep her back turned while she absorbed the little jolt he always gave her. "It's Tuesday. AJ is probably making meatloaf down at the Horizon."

Hold stepped around her, plucked something from her cart. "I like SpaghettiOs."

Right, and he was studying the can as if it had been beamed into his hand by aliens from Vulcan. "You've never had SpaghettiOs in your life. If your heart's set on the SpaghettiOs"—she plucked the can out of his hand, dropped it back in her cart—"you can get your own in aisle three."

"Where's the famous Windfall Island hospitality?"

"It's off season."

"Good manners, as my mama likes to say, are never out of fashion."

"I wonder what she'd say about you following me around all day?"

"My mama," he said with his trademark grin, "would be hard-put to find anything objectionable about my company."

"Oh, I doubt that. Take it from a mother with a son." As much as she loved Benji, there were just times it was best to be away from him. For both their sakes.

"I hear he's a champ," Hold said, "but I could run interference, say, tonight at supper."

She shot him a look and kept moving, pushing her cart to the lone checkout, manned in the winter by Mr. MacDonald himself.

Mr. MacDonald shot Hold a look of his own. "You buying something, son, or are you just here to bother my patrons?"

"No. To both questions."

"Then supposing you make way for paying customers?"

Hold stepped aside and looked behind him, his gaze dropping to a head of white hair belonging to an elderly woman barely five feet tall. Her face was a maze of wrinkles, her smile as sweet and pure as a newborn's, and her eyes were glued to his butt.

"He's fine right where he is, Sam," Mrs. Weingarten said to MacDonald, her gaze not shifting one bit.

"No," Jessi said, "He's really not."

Mrs. Weingarten patted Jessi on the hand. "Just because you've taken yourself out of the game doesn't mean you can't admire the players."

"She's not out of the game completely," Hold said, ranging himself with Mrs. Weingarten. "She's just taking a little hiatus. I'm hoping to give her a reason to bend her rules. Or break them."

"Well, honey, if anyone can convince her to throw caution to the winds, I'm betting on you."

"It's a task Hercules himself would think twice over tackling, ma'am."

"Well, you've got the physique for it." This time, when Mrs. Weingarten patted his arm, her hand stayed there.

Jessi handed Mr. MacDonald two twenties, meeting his bland expression with a slight shake of her head and an eye roll. She pocketed the change he gave back, gathered up the handles of her canvas totes, and when Hold reached for them, shifted them away.

"Mrs. Weingarten, how are you getting home?"

"Oh, I'm walking, dear, just like always."

Jessi aimed her gaze directly at Hold. "But it's nearly a mile."

Hold popped up an eyebrow, smiled a little, then turned the full wattage of his grin on Mrs. Weingarten. "I'd count it a privilege if you let me carry your groceries home for you, ma'am."

Mrs. Weingarten dimpled up at him. "Only if you allow me to make you a cup of tea."

"He loves to hear stories about the island," Jessi put in, and this time the look she aimed at Hold was pointed. "Mrs. Weingarten has lived here all her life. She knows just about every Windfaller, present and past."

"Well, then," Hold crooked his elbow, waited until Mrs. Weingarten placed her gloved hand there, then collected her single plastic sack. "So, you know everyone on the island?"

"I do, yes," Mrs. Weingarten said, allowing Hold to squire her to the door. "But I imagine you're particularly interested in the Randal family."

"That may be." And he shot Jessi a look over his shoulder as he ushered Mrs. Weingarten out the door. A look that said, *payback is hell.*

If the general upheaval of the day had dimmed her mood, Benji brightened it right back up. How could she not be happy, Jessi thought, when he came gamboling out of the little one-room schoolhouse that served all the kids on Windfall Island? Every inch of his compact little body was in motion, and when he caught sight of her instead of Dottie Hampton, his regular babysitter, his face lit, and he raced over to throw his arms around her waist, already chattering about his day.

She let all the other stresses in her life fade away, slinging an arm around his slight shoulders as they set off to walk the short distance to their little gingerbread house on the bluff overlooking Hideaway Cove.

Not much of a breeze whistled its way along the narrow streets of Windfall Village, and the bright sunshine kept the day from being bone-deep cold. She liked to walk, and having the day off gave her the opportunity to spend a little time, just twenty peaceful minutes, with Benji before they faced the reality of homework and meal preparation, bath and bedtime.

"—and Jeff's mom—Mrs. Larimore—got really mad at him because he was cutting up in class," Benji was saying when she tuned back in to his chatter. "She said *damn* in front of the whole class, and had to give herself a time out." When his own mom did no more than squeeze his shoulder at the swear word, he peered carefully up at her. "I shouldn't've said that."

"No, but then neither should Jeff's mother." Although Jessi could understand the slip. Nobody could wind a mother up quite as effectively as her own child. While some of the parents would be giving Jane Larimore a piece of their mind, Jessi preferred to focus on the service she provided rather than a tiny little verbal slip the kids could have heard almost anywhere, including on television.

"I'll bet Jeff was disrupting the whole class."

"He was making fart noises in the back of the room. Mostly we thought he was hilarious."

"Yes, well, I'll bet Mrs. Larimore had a hard time teaching with Jeff playing class clown. And since it's her job to keep order and beat some learning into your hard heads, and as it was her son causing the trouble, she lost her temper for a second."

"You hardly ever get mad at me."

"Oh, trust me. You've found buttons I didn't even know I had."

"I'm sorry, Mom."

She ran a hand over his hat-covered head. "Don't worry about it, Benj. You wouldn't be a kid if you didn't have a knack for button-pushing."

"I could make it up to you," he said, looking up at her with wide, earnest eyes and a tentative smile. "Like, if we had pizza for dinner tonight, then you wouldn't have to cook, and you could take a bath and relax."

"I'll bet the fact that while I'm lounging in the tub you get to watch something completely inappropriate on TV has nothing to do with it."

He shook his head a little, the shock and sincerity on his face spot-on. "I'd only watch cartoons, I promise."

And although she had to fight off the urge to laugh, the certain knowledge that he was playing her gave her a pang. The charming smile, the effortless manipulation, so like his father...

And just because Benji had the knack for reading people and using it to his advantage, she reminded herself, it didn't mean he couldn't use his talent for something positive. The world needed salesmen, too.

"Well, it's been a while, and I think we've both earned pizza," she said, steering him into the warm fragrant air inside Carelli's, the island's one and only pizzeria. And to his great delight, she ordered a large, loaded, and cheesy bread, and arranged for it to be delivered before they faced the final walk home.

She unlocked the door and ushered Benji inside ahead of her, sighing as the snugness, the memories and the comfort they brought, wrapped around her like a warm blanket on the coldest day. Home, she thought as she flipped on lights to ward off the late afternoon gloom, and the people in it, made life worth living. This house had always been her home, and her mother's before, all the way back to the Duncan forebear who'd built it two centuries earlier.

Subsequent generations had added on, going up rather than out, as the house sat on a rocky shingle of land that defied the easy spread of a smooth and level foundation. The result was three stories of faded Victorian charm filled with memories, from the ground floor to the cramped and crowded attic she'd been meaning to clean out. She had the vague notion it would someday serve as

Benji's room when he hit those teenage years and needed a space of his own. At the rate she was going, she'd need all of the next six—no, closer to five—years she had left before that happened.

Her mother had been gone almost two years, and she'd yet to do more than pack her things away in an attic already filled with the castoffs of many generations. Too soon still to go through them, too painful.

She crossed the room, ran a finger along the top of a silver frame sitting on a side table by the stairs. Her parents' wedding photo always made her heart hitch and ache. Her father had died when she was too little to remember much more of him than a big, booming voice and the scent of pipe tobacco that had always clung to him. She missed what he represented more than she missed the man himself.

Her mother . . . her mother had left a hole too big for all the tears in the world to fill. And yet, she thought, wiping her hands under her eyes, there were always more.

Even when she'd gotten pregnant, her mother had stuck by her. And when Lance had left her high and dry, there'd been no question where she and the baby would live. Looking back now, Jessi couldn't imagine herself anywhere else, couldn't begin to think of a place she'd rather raise Benji than within these four walls, on this tiny speck of an island off the coast of Maine.

Some would call her provincial, small-town, but she'd learned not to care about other people's opinions. What mattered was her own. Windfall Island suited her, and if that meant she'd spend the rest of her life alone—well, every choice came with a price tag.

Chapter Five

Hold stood at the curb a minute, studying Hideaway Cottage. He'd been told this was the name the villagers used to refer to the home that had been in Jessi's family for the better part of two hundred years.

It reminded him of the gingerbread house from the story of Hansel and Gretel, or maybe the one about the old lady in the shoe. Definitely something out of a fairy tale: a narrow house on a rocky cliff, rising three stories to a steeply gabled wood shake roof over eaves decorated with fanciful scrollwork. The siding had been painted cream, the trim in shades of pale blue, tan, and brown; and the walkway was made of what he took for ballast stone, variously colored and slightly rounded from the ships that had moored—or been wrecked—off the island's shores.

There were houses to either side, set at some distance along the rocky bluff they occupied, unevenly spaced along the edge of a small cove. The rocky walls soared about fifty feet at the village, tapering down at either end to make a labyrinth of the entrance to Hideaway Cove that only a resident would know how to navigate. He'd been told this was where smugglers had secreted their caches of illegal booze during the Prohibition era.

The place suited her, he thought, suited her bright, quirky personality, her sparkling green eyes, her stubborn streak and her annoying insistence on keeping him at arm's length—which was why he'd hijacked her dinner. If he stood there any longer, however, it would be cold, and she wouldn't thank him for that. Hold took himself by the scruff of the neck—mentally since it would have been awkward to do it in reality—and walked to the front door, knocking before he could equivocate any longer.

"I'll get it, Mom," he heard a kid's voice yell from inside.

The front door flew open, and Hold couldn't help but smile. Benji Randal favored his mother. He had the same lively green eyes, same heart-shaped face, although his chin was more square. A shock of chestnut hair would have curled as wildly as his mother's if it hadn't been buzzed to a couple inches in length. His demeanor was the same, too. The boy studied him openly and solemnly, with a little wariness thrown in.

After a minute he half-turned, keeping a careful eye on Hold as he yelled out, "There's some guy at the door, Mom."

"What guy?" Jessi yelled back. "You know everyone on the island...except this one," she finished as she appeared behind her son.

Because, Hold thought with some heat, she'd kept them purposely apart. He tried not to let it irk him, knew she was only sheltering her son, but damn it, he wasn't some scoundrel come to break hearts and torture defenseless children.

"He's got our pizza."

"I see that," Jessi said, her eyes narrowed.

"Why does he got our pizza?"

Although Benji had spoken to his mother, Hold swallowed his annoyance and hunkered down so he could be eye to eye with the seven-year-old. "Had a hankering myself, son," he said. "I happened into the pizza place just as they were lamenting how busy they were, and so I volunteered to bring it out to y'all."

"Great. The whole island will know about it by now," Jessi grumbled.

"Just delivering a pizza, sugar," Hold said with a grin. "No ulterior motive."

"I'll hold you to that." And she disappeared, coming back straightaway with her purse. She opened it, looked inside, then at him again, her cheeks coloring a little when she pulled out two one-dollar bills.

"I, uh...Can I give you the rest tomorrow?" she asked faintly, looking everywhere but at him with an expression of distress that told him she thought being beholden was roughly on a par with having a colonoscopy.

Next, he supposed, she'd be offering him change from the jar on her dresser. She seemed like the type who squirreled away her nickels and dimes for a rainy day. And just the thought of it, of Jessi worrying about finding herself in a situation where she needed something she had to pay for with hoarded spare change, irritated him even more.

"It's just a pizza, Jessica."

"My pizza, that I ordered. And when Peter Carelli

showed up to deliver it, I'd have paid with my credit card."

He closed his eyes, breathed in and out, and bit back on the temper that had put a snap in his voice. "I didn't mean to put your back up. Although I seem to have a particular talent for it."

"What do you want, Hold?"

"I just want you to let me buy you a damn pizza."

"That's a bad word," Benji piped up. "Mrs. Larimore said it in school today, and now Mom says everyone is going to be mad at her."

Hold looked down into his earnest little face. "Your mom is right, son."

"My mom is always right."

Hold shifted his gaze to Jessi's, smiled a little when she rolled her eyes and sighed.

"Only where her child is concerned." She reached for the pizza.

Hold lifted it away. "I was hoping you'd share."

"Maybe if you let me out of this corner you've backed me into."

"It's just supper."

"Which I plan to have with my son, just like I told you this morning."

"You never said I couldn't come, too."

Jessi smiled a little. "You sure you're not a lawyer?"

"Now, sugar, there's no cause for insults."

"He's dressed like a lawyer," Benji observed.

"And he knows how to slide through loopholes."

"What's a loophole?"

"It's an exception lawyers use to get around rules. Don't even think it," she added as Benji looked at Hold, a considering expression his face. "Great. Now he's going to be looking for ways around every rule I set."

"Loopholes don't apply to seven-year-old boys," Hold said to Benji. "Not when it comes to the rules their mothers set. 'Course, you should never underestimate the value of a good argument, humbly delivered."

"Huh?"

"Here's your pizza, son." Hold offered the box, but Benji just stood there, watching him suspiciously.

"You can have this, too." He took the two dollar bills from Jessi and handed them over.

Benji snatched the money, shouted "woo-hoo!", and darted inside.

Jessi crossed her arms, gave him a look.

"Consider it a tip," Hold said.

"It's not the money, it's the bribery."

"Money talks," Hold said, "even to kids."

"Mom, I'm starving," Benji said.

Hold smiled hopefully, waggling the pizza box.

"You're going to behave yourself. No loopholes."

Hold crossed his heart.

Not looking entirely convinced, Jessi stepped back, pointing to a small table off to one side of the main living area. "Sorry. It's just Benji and me most of the time, and we don't need much."

"I'd call it cozy." Hold stepped close and lowered his voice. "And if there isn't another chair, you're welcome to sit on my lap."

"Get the stool, Benji," Jessi said, shooting Hold a speaking look as she followed her son into the kitchen.

Benji reappeared almost immediately with a tall kitchen stool.

Jessi's voice floated out after him. "We usually just use paper plates and napkins."

"That's fine," Hold said.

"I don't keep beer or soda pop in the house, so you get your choice of milk or water."

This time Hold followed Benji back into the kitchen. "Stop apologizing. Whatever you do is fine."

She grinned. "I'm sorry."

"You're forgiven if you tell me why you feel the need."

"I don't know. Maybe because you're all dressed up."

Hold looked down at his casual slacks, sweater and shirt, all in deep brown. And okay, the slacks were Hugo Boss, but she didn't know that. "I'm not wearing a tie."

"Alert the media." But she laughed. "Do you even own a pair of jeans?"

"Of course." But in his life, jeans were for, well, practically never.

"Mom, can I have chocolate milk?"

"Make that two," Hold said. "Does it matter? The way I dress."

"Of course. Doesn't it matter how I dress?"

And there was an invitation he couldn't have resisted, he thought, even if he hadn't already appreciated the way her snug jeans and the v-necked t-shirt she wore beneath an unzipped hoodie hugged the curves of her body.

She was a little bit of a thing, as his mama would have said, the top of her head barely reaching his shoulder. But what there was of her was well put together. And surely, the way she was dressed mattered, seeing as those jeans were tucked into heeled boots and made her legs seem a mile long. Even though the whole outfit was conservative enough to make it clear she was in Mom mode, all he wanted was to get her alone and peel her out of it—

"It's not polite to stare."

"No, son, it's not, but sometimes it can't be helped. You'll understand in a few years."

"Mom tells me that all the time," Benji said glumly. "Who are you, anyway? How come you talk funny?"

"My name is Holden Abbot," he said, absorbing another small sting that Jessi hadn't even mentioned his name to her son. "But you can call me Hold."

"Mr. Abbot," Jessi corrected from the kitchen, where she'd gone off on yet another errand.

She returned with a gallon of milk, chocolate syrup, and an expectant expression. Maybe she didn't want to ask questions herself, but she was paying close attention to the answers. He'd just have to watch his words, and be grateful he was being cross-examined by a seven-year-old.

He'd decided, after much consideration, to keep his own counsel where his origins were concerned. He'd been burned, and burned badly, by a woman who'd strung him along, accepted his engagement ring, pretended to love him, all so she could buy herself a lap full of luxury. Even the life she had to sell for it was built on a lie.

It wasn't as though he didn't trust Jessi, he told himself. Despite her clear and unapologetic yen for the ease money would buy her, he didn't believe she'd set her cap for him if she knew his net worth counted in the millions.

Still, money—that kind of money—changed everyone. He didn't know where they'd end up, but he was determined to work his way around Jessi's resistance. No, not just determined; frantic would be the better term for what churned in his stomach and whipped through his blood whenever he set eyes on her. He couldn't put a name to it—or wouldn't, yet—but he could no more turn his back on it than he could stop his own body from drawing in air, or his own heart from beating.

What sense, he reasoned, would there be in complicating an already confusing matter? There'd be time enough later, once her feelings—and his—were sorted out, to tell her about the family fortune. And if his need for her burned out as fast and hot as it had roared into flame, then what harm would have been done? It wasn't as if he was deceiving her, after all; he was just choosing what to tell and what to keep to himself.

"I talk funny," Hold answered Benji, "because I'm from Louisiana."

"Loo-Loosiana?"

"Louisiana," Jessi corrected. "It's way down south by Florida. Where Disney World is."

"Have you been there?" Benji asked, all but dancing in place. "Mom says we can go." He shot her a look. "Maybe."

"We'll talk about it, Benj."

Benji nodded, watching his mother with the supreme confidence of a child who'd never been let down.

Jessi poured milk and added chocolate syrup, looking like a mother afraid she'd have to do exactly that.

"Why are you all dressed up?" Benji asked him, and Hold had to let the pang of sympathy—edged with that snap of dislike for her predicament—go.

"What is it with the pair of you and my wardrobe?" he murmured for Jessi's benefit. To Benji, he said, "My mama isn't so laid back as yours. She frowns on jeans."

"But you're all grown up."

"You never outgrow your mama, son." He held Jessi's chair for her before taking his own.

"Yeah, that's another thing Mom tells me all the time."

"And now you have living proof." Jessi slid a piece of pizza on her son's plate.

"All the other tourists are gone," Benji said around a mouthful of pepperoni and cheese. "So what are you still doing here?"

"Just now I seem to be doing all the talking."

"Benji's got a point," Jessi said. "How is it that you can just take off from your regular life to work on a small-town gen—" She broke off, and the way she glanced at her son told Hold he wasn't the only one taking care with what he said. "Shouldn't you be manning a desk some-where?"

Hold winced. "No, ma'am, no desks for me. You might say I'm a kind of salesman."

"And what do you sell?"

"Happiness. Or at least a chance for it."

Jessi dropped her pizza and stared at him.

Hold tapped lightly on her forehead. "What's going on in there?"

"Mom, can I watch some TV?"

Jessi latched onto the diversion. "Homework?" she asked Benji.

"Did it in school."

"Okay, one hour, and keep it down."

Paper plate in hand, Benji whooped and raced all of ten feet to their little family room, snatched the remote from the top of the TV and flopped down on a beanbag chair.

"I repeat," Hold said, reaching out.

Jessi grabbed his finger before he could tap it against her head again.

He curled his hand around hers and lifted it, bringing her fingers to his lips. Those lips curved when she jolted, when he saw the pulse throb to life in her neck. She trembled, and he feared he was pushing too hard, but when her eyes lifted to his and he read the desire there, heat flared inside him and spread.

"Jessi—"

"Hold, I . . ." She eased back, but he knew if he let her think, she'd retreat entirely. So he claimed her mouth. He framed her face, nipping her bottom lip before he sank in. She stiffened, but just when he was sure she'd push him away, she sighed, softened, opened her mouth to let her tongue tangle with his. And gave. He'd known she would; she was so generous, so caring. She had a heart as big as the world, and though she tried to guard it, her heart was wide open. So he told himself as he slipped his hands into the glory of her hair. He'd just have to guard it for her, be careful not to offer more than he wanted, or let her give more than was good for her. Still, he took the kiss deeper, tasted the sweetness of her, swallowed the sexy little moan she made and felt his control begin to crumble. He wanted more, needed her like his next breath.

"Jessi," he said, nuzzling her neck, slipping his hands down the sexy outer curves of her breasts as the fire inside him burned through the leash he'd put on his desire. "Let me," he began.

But when she nudged him back, he stopped pushing.

"Benji," she said, and the fact that she had to clear her throat first, that she looked at him with dazed eyes, went a long way to making up for her presence of mind. "We have to be careful."

He covered her hand, pressed it to his chest. "Tell me you mean what I think you mean."

"Hold..." She stood and, although she'd eaten nothing, took her plate and glass into the kitchen.

Hold followed her, waited while she set her things down, and watched as her eyes filled with uncertainty and sorrow. Both ripped at him.

"My mother," she began, "my mother was my hero. I know most people would say that about their father, but I was barely three when he died."

"So even though you never knew your own daddy, you still missed him," he interpreted. He kept his distance, although he wanted to take her in his arms and comfort her.

"I missed the idea of him. And thank you for getting it." Her gaze lifted to his, skipped away again. "But my mom—I miss her every day. There wasn't anything we didn't share—except when I...with Lance. I couldn't tell her, maybe because I knew she'd be disappointed. She always told me to follow my heart, but looking back I realize it wasn't my heart I was following. I knew it, even back then, on some level."

"Do you think she'd disapprove of me?" Hold asked, and breathed a sigh of relief when she shook her head.

"I'm sorry if I gave you that idea, Hold. I think my mother would love you." She smiled. "Just like every other woman on this island."

"Gossip again?" he said, although he had to stop his hands from fisting. "I'm getting a little tired of defending myself against a bunch of exaggerations and stories turned upside down to make it seem like I was the instigator when—"

"I get it, Hold. I've lived here all my life. You don't have to tell me how stories get twisted."

"But?"

She spread her hands. "Why me?"

He laughed softly. "Why not you, Jessica? Except for that bone-deep stubborn streak."

"I don't know. You're..." She made a two-handed gesture that took him in from head to toe. "And I'm...me. Single mother, jeans and t-shirts, small-town."

"You know what I see? A beautiful, incredible woman, who works too hard managing a business, taking care of everyone else, and believing she doesn't deserve anything in return. You really need to cut yourself a break."

"People keep telling me that," she murmured.

"And let's not downplay the way you fill out those jeans." But he knew what she wanted to hear. Or at least he thought he did. "The minute I set eyes on you, Jess—"

"Don't." She whirled away from him, arms crossed, moving around the kitchen with all the energy of a small tornado.

Too bad it was such a small room—too bad for her. Hold put himself in her path, shifting when she tried to go around him, herding her back until he could box her in. And then he waited until she shifted her eyes, filled with temper and resentment, to his. "You're going to listen to me, Jessica."

"Fine, Mr. Abbot." Her eyes shifted past him, and he knew she was checking to make sure Benji was still engrossed in SpongeBob. "Have your say, and then you're going to leave."

"Fine," he bit off. But before he could even begin to order his thoughts, scattered by being so close to her, there was a knock on the door.

"I'll get it," Benji announced. Through the kitchen archway Hold caught sight of the kid popping to his feet and running to the front door, just out of sight. "Mom," he yelled a second later, "there's another strange guy here."

"I'm no stranger, kid," a male voice floated back to the kitchen, "I'm your daddy."

Chapter Six

Lance Proctor.

In the flesh. At her front door.

In a daze of pounding heart and spinning head, Jessi stared at him for what seemed like forever, felt herself transported back to the first time she'd seen him, really seen him, breathtakingly handsome and full of life. They'd grown up together, of course, known each other all their lives, and she'd always crushed on him a little. But what girl wouldn't? What teenage girl could resist a tall, dark, and handsome boy, with a killer smile and a gleam of mischief in his eyes?

The miracle, she'd remembered, was that he'd noticed her at all when he could have had any girl in school. *And had*, she reminded herself. Looking back now she wondered if that hadn't been the attraction she'd presented.

But the truth was, he'd been as eager for her as she'd been for him, and while he'd dated every girl in their age group, at least Jessi could content herself that once they'd become a couple, he'd stuck.

Until.

She bet he still set female hearts aflutter, not to mention a few male ones, wherever he went. He was still tall, still poetically handsome with his pale skin and fine bone structure, the dark hair worn just a little too long, begging to be brushed away from his brow.

He looked more... substantial now, though. He'd lost the skinny awkwardness of his teenage years, filled out to what looked to be a very healthy and well-tuned hundred and seventy pounds. He'd seen some tough times, though, she mused. His clothing showed wear at the stress points, and he carried an air of disappointment, of resignation, instead of the life-by-the-tail attitude he'd had when he left Windfall Island.

No, not the boy she'd known. But then, he couldn't be seeing the girl he'd left behind, either.

She didn't, for instance, buy into the sucker smile he gave her, the smile he'd used to finesse her into bed. The same smile he'd employed when he promised they'd be together for the rest of their lives.

That smile didn't quite make it to his eyes, she noticed now. His eyes remained cool and measuring. Calculating. Those eyes never left her face, so she could see when he figured out the smile wasn't working.

"You used to be faster on the uptake, Lance."

"I know I've been gone a while," he replied. His gaze lifted over her head, searched the stingy slice of living room he could see with her blocking the doorway.

She'd be damned if he found the new mark he was looking for.

She pulled her head back inside, closed the door behind her, and leaned against it, making herself meet Hold's eyes. He took no pains to hide what he was feeling—anger, curiosity, frustration. "Could you—"

"Of course," he said before she could finish the thought.

"Are you okay with Hold for a few minutes, Benj?" She didn't need to see him nod, not when he was already easing over to tuck his hand into Hold's.

Tears ached in the back of her throat. Nerves and stress, and the heartache of watching that little hand slip into the big one, knowing what was about to happen to her son's world and that she was powerless to stop it, made a towering anger rise up in her. It darkened her vision, deepened her breathing, trembled her hands as she reached for the knob because she knew closing the front door wouldn't stop anything. And because she wanted to confront him, to take him apart at the seams, to scream and strike and make him hurt—

Jessi stared down at her shaking hands, in shock at the violence inside her. If she'd had a weapon...But her hands were empty, thank God, and even if a part of her still wanted to watch Lance suffer, she knew that wouldn't solve anything.

She slipped back outside, coatless, and pulled the door shut behind her.

"It's cold," he said.

"I'm not a moron, Lance."

"I only meant we should go in."

"No," she said, then "no" again when he started to strip off his coat to, presumably, offer it to her.

As if a gesture of civility could erase the hurt he'd

caused in the past, or prevent the pain he was about to inflict. "You can't just show up at my door with no warning."

"He's my kid, too."

"Biology doesn't make you a father."

Lance shrugged back into his coat, shoved buttons through buttonholes, his expression going sulky. "I think the courts would disagree with you."

"Yeah? I think they'd start by asking where you've been since I was three months pregnant, and end with seven plus years of back child support."

"Aw, come on, Jess, don't be angry and bitter."

"Bitter? Are you kidding me?" She jerked away when he reached for her. "You abandoned him; you left us both. You don't just get to waltz in here like the last eight years never happened and make it out like I'm the bitch for not welcoming you with open arms."

"You're right." He shoved his hands back through his dark, artlessly tumbled hair, and although he turned away, Jessi thought she caught a glimpse of real pain in his eyes. "I was young and stupid and . . . I don't know, I panicked. Jesus, I was eighteen."

"I was sixteen, and I couldn't just walk away."

"You wouldn't have walked if you could." He exhaled heavily. "I understood that, even then. You didn't need me, Jess—"

"Now you're blaming me?"

"No. Jeez, cut me a break. I was such a screw-up, but I knew you were the best thing that ever happened to me. And when you got pregnant, I freaked, sure, but I swear I wanted to marry you and raise our kid."

"That didn't last long. But then, you always did have a short attention span."

"Not when it came to you. Remember how it was? Hell, Jess, we couldn't keep our hands off one another. Like that time we parked at the other end of the island, back when the airport was just a bunch of deserted old cannery buildings. Old man Boatwright shined his flashlight in the back windows of my dad's Buick, I jumped up, and he screamed like a girl."

"And then he hauled you home with some made-up story about you skinny dipping."

"But he let you go."

Jessi felt a smile tug at the corners of her mouth. "We were only necking."

"If he'd found us ten minutes later..." Lance reached out, let one of her corkscrew curls wind around his finger. "I always loved your hair."

Jessi tipped her head aside, then stepped back, shoving both hands back through her hair before she had to label the tingle she'd felt.

"I want to get to know him, Jess. You, too—"

"Don't."

This time Lance stepped back, and although she could see the frustration on his face, he didn't push any more.

"I'm staying at my mother's house," he said. "I'll let you set the pace, but I'm not leaving until...I want to make up for lost time."

"Do you really think you can?"

"No." He smiled, but it was wistful this time. Hopeful.

She didn't buy Lance's act for a second. But this wasn't about her—not entirely, anyway. Benji had been waiting his entire life for his father to come back to Windfall Island.

If she turned Lance away, she'd become the bad guy.

"Give me time to talk to Benji." But she already knew the time was for her, to get used to the idea of sharing her son with a man she didn't trust. If Benji had his way, Lance would be inside already, and seven fatherless years wouldn't mean a thing until...

Until.

Lance looked like he might argue over that, but she had to give him credit. He took a deep breath, let it out. "All right. Maybe when he gets to know me a little bit, we could spend some time together, just the two of us."

"Your problem isn't Benji not knowing you. It's that I do."

Lance's jaw bunched, but he nodded stiffly. "I really do want to make it up to him, Jess. I've done a lot of traveling the last eight years—"

"Oh, your mother keeps me updated. I think she's hoping you'll come back here and settle down." But not with her, Jessi acknowledged with a whole lot of relief. The last thing Joyce wanted was an outspoken, no-nonsense daughter-in-law she couldn't cow. "You shouldn't let her keep believing that."

"I wish..." Lance looked away, shook his head.

Jessi was on her guard. Still, she had to admit he looked so damned sincere.

"My mom says you don't date at all."

Okay, maybe Joyce didn't have any intentions, Jessi thought. Maybe she'd told him that out of some twisted sense of satisfaction, but she'd misjudged her audience.

"I think she takes it as a sign that you're waiting for me to come back," Lance finished.

"You should take it as a sign I don't trust anymore."

"What about the guy you're having dinner with? Do you trust him?"

Jessi stepped back, ranged herself in front of the door. "He's none of your business."

"You left him alone with my kid. They must be pretty chummy."

"Careful, Lance."

His gaze shifted to hers, and whatever she thought she'd seen in his eyes was gone. She saw only regret, sincerity, and a slight flush to his cheeks. Lance might be good, but no one could control their blush response, and the heat in his cheeks bespoke...jealousy?

Then he flashed her that smile of his, and she told herself she was an idiot for thinking, for one minute, that he wanted her back again.

"I'm sorry, Jessi."

"Give yourself a minute. It'll pass."

"I guess I deserve that."

"But?"

"I'll find a way to convince you I'm on the level."

Jessi left him standing there, barely registering when she shut the front door behind her and Hold enveloped her in the crocheted throw from the back of the sofa. She wanted to collapse, burrow in, shut out. To stay numb. The pain would crash over her soon enough—the anger, the betrayal, the welter of memories, and all the shattered hopes and dreams. Now, all she could seem to feel was fear. For Benji.

She leaned back against the door, her eyes going to her son where he sat, an assortment of superheroes and plastic army men scattered on the table in front of him. Watching her.

How did she tell him, she wondered, panicking a little at the thought? How did she tell Benji his father had returned, knowing Lance wouldn't be the fantasy Benji had built in his mind?

"I thought maybe if I could get Benji to play, do something normal..." Hold spread his hands, then shoved them in his pockets. "What did he want?"

Jessi's gaze shifted back to Benji.

"You don't believe he's sincere, do you?"

She kept her voice down, as Hold had done. "No, but—"

"You have history with him."

She rubbed at her temple, where a headache had begun to brew. "I have a son with him."

"That doesn't change who he is."

"No, but does that mean he'll treat Benji badly?"

"He left you both, Jessi."

"I remember. I was there." And when Benji jumped at her raised voice, she nearly lost her battle with the tears she'd been holding back. "Benji deserves to make his own judgment where his father is concerned."

"You're protecting him from me, but—"

"Don't finish that sentence," Jessi warned. "It's not the same, and you know it."

"No, it's not the same. He can hurt Benji more."

She went to the door, opened it and held it for Hold. "I don't need you to tell me what kind of risk I'm taking."

He stepped outside, turned back to her. "He's not giving you much of a choice."

"Lance will do whatever he can to get what he wants, no matter how long it takes."

"He'll try to wear you down, you mean."

She smiled faintly. "Remind you of anyone?"

"Mom?"

Jessi left her back against the door, just another second or two, before she found the strength to straighten and move to the table.

She picked up a plastic figure of Spiderman and slid him into a pile of army men, sending them skittering and jumping across the table.

Benji reached out reflexively, caught one of the army men before it fell over the edge. He laid it carefully on the table, watching her face just as carefully. "Was that my dad?"

Words wouldn't pass her tear-clogged throat, so Jessi nodded.

"Why didn't he come in?"

"I—" she stopped, swallowed a couple of times, and her voice cleared as she spoke. "I asked him to wait. I wanted a chance to talk to you first."

"About what?"

"About what you want."

"Oh." Benji chose a superhero, just held it.

"It's such a surprise, Benj. I just want you to have some time to get used to the idea."

"Grandma told me he was coming."

"Joyce…" Jessi clamped her mouth shut, said through her teeth, "When?"

Benji did the one-shouldered shrug he'd learned from his Auntie Maggie. "Last weekend when she took me out to lunch. She told me not to tell because it would only upset you."

And now the surge of anger distilled itself down to a cold, blue flame.

"I'm sorry, Mom. I was gonna tell you, but I forgot."

"It's okay, Benj. It was all the way last weekend." She folded her hands together so tightly they ached. The pain helped her focus, to remember who mattered most in this unbelievable situation. "There are going to be some rules."

Benji's eyes, when they met hers, were wide and filled with hope. "I can see my dad?"

"He's your dad," Jessi said simply. "You should get to know him."

"When?" Benji demanded, on his knees in his chair, bouncing. "Tomorrow? Tomorrow is Saturday—"

"And you have a birthday party."

"But—"

Jessi held up a hand. "Like I said, there are going to be rules. One of them is you won't break any commitments you've already made. But I'll get in touch with him, and as long as he agrees I'll see if he has some time on Monday."

Benji shot both fists up in the air and jumped out of his chair. He raced around the room shouting at the top of his lungs while her heart broke into small, jagged pieces.

Jessi logically understood that Benji's excitement over his father took nothing away from her. She tried not to let the hurt show, but he must have seen it because Benji came over and threw his arms around her. "Love you, Mom," he said.

She gathered him up and hugged him close, breathed in the scent of clean sweat and soap. And even as she held him, she let him go. He wasn't *her* little boy anymore.

Chapter Seven

Lance Proctor?" George Boatwright, Sheriff of Windfall, let the front two legs of the chair he'd leaned back on thump forward. "On island?"

"If he's not there yet, he will be soon," the voice on the other end of the phone said.

That took George to his feet, to pace the confines of the Windfall Island Sheriff's station. As the place was barely twenty by ten, the trip didn't take nearly long enough to settle him. "I think I'll have a talk with him, see if I can't get him to leave quietly."

"Is that really wise?"

George scrubbed a hand over his face. "Suppose you tell me why he's here?"

"Jessica Randal is working on the genealogy."

"And Lance is here to work on her."

Silence.

"Mort was bad enough," George said, referring to the young Solomon Charters handyman who'd tried to kill

Maggie. He'd been like a little brother to her, so the murder attempt had been betrayal enough without adding the pain of his suicide on top of it.

But at least Maggie was an adult; she could understand Mort's need for money to help his dying mother. Benji Randal was only seven. Lance was surely going to screw with Jessi, but what he'd put his son through would be brutal, and heartbreaking to watch.

"You know there's a kid involved, right?"

More silence, then, "If I had a choice—"

"I know," he said on a sigh, "but I'm telling you now, I'm not letting anything happen to Benji Randal."

"Proctor is only there to gather information, not to harm anyone."

"There's all kinds of harm." And sometimes, George knew, you couldn't prevent it, no matter how hard you tried. He looked at the tiny cell where Mort had taken his own life, tried not to blame himself. And failed.

George scrubbed a hand over his face. He'd gotten into this mess because he'd sworn to serve and protect the people of Windfall Island. He wasn't losing anyone else.

"I take it you've heard from Dex Keegan," he said, which was the real reason he'd called.

"Not directly. He's here in Boston, he's asking questions. It won't do him any good."

"Unless a Stanhope helps him."

"It isn't time for open warfare...yet."

"The war is here, now, on my island," George shot back. "When this all started, you convinced me—"

"No, you convinced yourself, for your own reasons."

The silence this time was on his side of the conversation. He let it spin out, not because he wanted to make a point. Because he was a slow and deliberate thinker. Because he didn't make snap decisions. And because, as had been pointed out to him, he'd gone into this insanity for what he'd thought were good reasons. If he'd let those reasons get twisted, well, that was on him.

The trouble was, he had to roll with events he couldn't predict or control. Lance Proctor, he reminded himself, was the current event. Time to concentrate on the problem he could solve in person and leave the game-playing to those whose minds were quick and agile.

He might not be the brains of the operation, but he had the brawn—and the balls—to do what needed to be done. Added to that, Windfall was his place; these were his people. He had everything to lose. That meant he'd do anything not to.

The front door opened and Josiah Meeker sauntered in. His people, George reminded himself. All of them. Even the ones who rubbed him the wrong way.

"Got company," he said and hung up the phone, settling himself back behind the desk. "Josiah," he said, and the familiarity had Meeker's jaw clenching. "What can I do for you?"

"It's about Dex Keegan, and that other man, Abbot."

"What about them?"

"Exactly."

George knew what Meeker meant, but it served his purpose to play at ignorance. Not to mention it was pure fun to screw with a man who took himself way too seriously. Someone ought to warn Meeker about the perils of underestimating others. But it wasn't up to George to set him straight.

It took Meeker a minute, during which he sighed heavily and rolled his eyes before he said, "Why are they here?"

George shrugged. "Keegan is engaged to Maggie Solomon. I'm surprised you haven't heard that. It's the talk of the island."

"Of course I've heard that. It's not why he originally came here."

"Oh? Why did he come here?"

"That's what I want to know," Meeker snapped out, not bothering this time to bite back on his impatience. "You're the sheriff on this island; shouldn't you know what they're up to?"

"I am the sheriff," George said equably, putting an extra measure of laziness into his voice. "And being as I'm up to date on the penal code, I can't think of a single law broken by either one of them."

"But Keegan claims to be a lawyer. I haven't seen him do anything…"

"Lawyerly? What do you want me to do, ask him for his time card?"

"I want to know—"

"You can want 'til hell freezes over, but you don't have any right to know Keegan's private business, or Holden Abbot's, either."

"They're visitors here, not residents."

George sat back, crossed his arms. "Last I heard we were still part of the U. S. of A., which is a free country where people don't have to account for their whereabouts or actions just because somebody gets a wild hair over it."

"We'll see what Ma Appelman has to say about it."

"She'll say the very same thing, especially seeing as Keegan is about to become a resident."

"Right," Meeker shot back, "and Maggie Solomon can do no wrong in Ma's eyes. She can lie and tell stories—"

"Careful," George said softly, all pretense at stupidity and affability gone. "We both know Maggie told the God-given truth, and you'd best be thankful she kept it between her and me. She could have cost you your family." He sat forward, locked his gaze on Meeker's. "If I hear you've been running your mouth, you'll have me to worry about."

"You won't talk about Maggie—"

"No. I won't talk about Maggie." George rose to his feet. "I won't talk at all. But we both know the truth, don't we? You tried to take advantage of a sixteen-year-old girl. If Maggie hadn't been fast, agile, and lucky, you'd have assaulted her. And you'd be dead."

Meeker swallowed hard, but George had to give him credit for sticking to his guns, even when they were out of ammo. "Your precious Maggie isn't above blackmail," he sneered.

Maggie had used the past to coerce Meeker into lending her his collection of Windfall Island journals, in order to search them for clues to Eugenia's fate. George knew all about it, but he didn't want the rest of the island finding out.

So George came around his desk, all six-plus feet of him looming over Meeker. "I warned you once, Joe. I won't do it again," he said. "I find out that kind of slander is riding the gossip train, you're going to want to watch your back. And just in case you're fuzzy on the details, that's a threat, and one I'll make good on."

Meeker held up a hand, but wisely held his tongue. He paused at the door, sending a long, speaking look over his shoulder before he saw himself out.

Gone, but not done, George decided. He'd have to keep a weather eye peeled in Meeker's direction, he told himself, wondering how many balls he could keep in the air.

As many as it took, he decided. When lives were at stake, dropping one really wasn't an option.

Chapter Eight

Without Jessi in it, the office at Windfall Airport seemed dull, boring, like an overcast day with no breeze and no break in the clouds.

Hold should have been able to get some work done on a quiet Saturday morning without the phone ringing, office machines humming, Jessi's music blaring—and her cute little backside wiggling to the beat.

Instead, he'd been restless, unfocused, unsettled. He missed her, he realized, and while it should have troubled him, he only sat back and smiled. She was so damn irresistible; why wouldn't he miss her?

It wasn't just the feel of her, the taste of her, the heat of her mouth, the way she'd kissed him back so sweetly.

She just sparkled. Despite her daily struggles, she always had a smile on her face, a kind word, an offer of assistance. Even when she'd pushed him away after they kissed she'd done it gently, without giving offense.

And he had to stop reliving that kiss. If you took your

eye off a gator, you got bit in the ass, his granddaddy used to tell him. He'd come to Windfall to create a genealogy and found himself in a life-and-death contest with an unknown enemy. Not a great time to lose focus.

Hold bent back to his research, still ruling out the off-islanders and beginning to work on some of the island families he was pretty positive would not turn out to be connected to Eugenia Stanhope. Not much more he could do at this point, he reminded himself when frustration began to eat away at his patience—not without putting Windfallers in danger. Including Jessi and Benji, and that he would not do.

But ruling out was as necessary a part of solving any mystery as zeroing in. Every avenue eliminated made the true road a little clearer.

Unless it was a road not taken. That's what Lance Proctor meant to Jessi. No matter what she said, what resentments she harbored, Jessi had to be wondering what might have happened, where she might be, if Lance had stuck around.

The idea of it pissed Hold off royally. Any man who could walk out on a pregnant girl, on his own child . . .

But if Lance had stayed, Hold reminded himself . . .

Jessi would have married him, might still be married to him. And Hold would have no chance with her.

Not that he had much of one now.

He bent back to the family Bible in front of him, determined to stop circling his mind around the what-ifs and what-thens, and do what he'd come to Windfall to do. Jessi would make the decisions that were right for her and Benji; she'd already proven that. And while she might have a forgiving heart, there wasn't an ounce of stupid in it, or in her. Whatever Lance wanted from her, he'd play hell getting it.

Still restless, and frustrated on top of it now, he got to his feet and went outside, lifted his face for a moment into the stiff, frigid wind and let it blow away some of the clouds gathered around him.

He spotted Maggie near the open hangar door, instructing a kid of about sixteen, one of several part-timers she'd taken on after Mort had died. None of them were scheduled to work too many hours, none allowed to get too close—although Hold could see the puppy-dog adoration in the kid's eyes. No big surprise he had a crush on Maggie, Hold mused. What teenage boy could resist a woman like her—tall, slender, striking, strong, and confident.

Maggie finished with the kid and started over to join him.

"The place is looking pretty good," Hold said when she was close enough to hear him over the crash of the surf.

"Yeah." She stopped beside him, turning to look around as he'd done. "Mort kind of checked out, I guess. I didn't notice."

"You overlooked," Hold corrected her. "Mort was a friend. You gave him the benefit of the doubt."

She shrugged, one-shouldered, a quintessentially Maggie gesture. "You want to know if I've heard from Dex."

"'Course you have."

"And the case?" she said with a slight smile. "He's doing background, checking financials."

"That would be a big task on a family like the Stanhopes, and Alec Barclay can't help," Hold added, referring to Dex's friend and one of the Stanhope family lawyers. It was Alec who'd hired Dex to start digging into Eugenia's fate. "Lawyer-client privilege."

"It's a stupid profession that shelters criminals."

"It's a necessary facet of the legal system, Maggie, but you know that."

"Dex is searching for motive. It would help if Alec could point him in the right direction." She shrugged. "Dex is no fool. He knows where to look."

"Resentment, greed," Hold said. "Every one of the Stanhopes probably feels some level of both. The trick is finding out if one of them felt enough to commit murder."

"Dex hasn't met with anyone in the family yet," Maggie said. "He knows Rose Stanhope hired him, but the whole family was on board with the decision, so being the one to reach out doesn't exonerate her. She may have sent Dex to find any descendants with the intention of welcoming them to the family, or taking them out."

Hold slid his hands into his pockets. "It's a dilemma, but Dex will figure a way through it."

Maggie's eyes shifted to meet his, eyebrows lifted. "Okay. So now can we talk about what you really came out here to talk about?"

Hold grinned, rocked back on his heels. "That transparent, huh?"

Transparent? The man was glass, Maggie thought. Anyone could see he was wearing his heart on his sleeve—except maybe Hold himself. And Jessi. But only because each of them chose not to see it.

"You haven't gone to much trouble to hide your interest in Jessi," she said, "and since I'm her only family, I'll ask you what your intentions are."

"I don't understand why I should have to decide where we're going to end up before we've even had our first date."

"Fair enough, but—"

"But she has a history. Everyone has a history, Maggie. It's how you choose to handle it that matters."

"Have you said that to her?"

"She'll walk."

"You've already got her on the run, Hold." Maggie crossed her arms, cocked a hip. "Men love the chase, I get that. But pursuing Jessi isn't exactly getting you what you want."

"So what do you suggest?"

"Try not to be a complication."

"I just want to be there for her. Especially now."

"I get that, too, but she doesn't know you well enough to lean on you."

"Doesn't trust me, you mean."

"Yeah, that's another way to say it."

Hold slipped his hands into his pockets, blew out a breath. Tugged the reins on his patience. "How am I supposed to earn her trust if we ignore each other?"

"I'm not saying you can't talk to her," Maggie said, "but you have to give her some room."

"Let her come to me?"

"How about the two of you meet in the middle? Wouldn't that be more satisfying, more meaningful?"

"What if she doesn't budge?"

"Then it's not meant to be, Hold. And you won't have to wonder if she gave in because you wore her down."

He mulled that in his slow southern way, then said, "It won't be easy to stay away from her."

"That's how Jessi will know it's about her, not the chase."

The stiff wind from earlier had died off, replaced by a thick, salt-tinged mist rolling in off the ocean and covering the island in what felt like a wet blanket. A freezing cold wet blanket, Jessi thought, and pulled her coat tighter around herself as she walked through the village. She hooked a right at Meeker's Antiques, and since it meant the ocean was at her back, at least the mist wasn't wafting into her face anymore. She might have breathed a sigh of relief if not for her destination.

Which she refused to think about, because thinking about it made her long to turn around. And she couldn't turn around.

So she continued down the narrow, cobbled lane lined with as wide a selection of houses as could be found anywhere. A quaint cottage squatted between a half-timbered Tudor and a single-story covered in faded redbrick. On the other side of the lane sat a pair of bungalows with little dormer windows and wide front porches.

The lane dead-ended at the driveway of a two-story, wood-sided saltbox, which had been retrofitted with an impressive—and completely misplaced—set of pseudo-Greek columns. The narrow lane picked up again on the other side of the house's brief backyard. Jessi had always thought it apt that the place created a roadblock.

Joyce Proctor certainly lived up to that reputation. She opened the door, took one look at Jessi, and closed it in her face. No surprise.

Joyce believed Jessi had gotten herself pregnant on purpose, but rather than trapping Lance into marriage as intended, the idea of being a father had driven him away. In Joyce's eyes, her son could do no wrong. Even when they'd been kids, whenever Lance got into trouble, Joyce found someone else to hold responsible, and so she'd raised a son who never took responsibility.

And this was about Benji, Jessi reminded herself as she knocked again, about raising *her* son the right way. When the door didn't open, she lifted her voice, said, "Come on, Joyce," knowing the woman was farming as much enjoyment as possible by standing on the other side or peeking through the window. Either way, she'd be in earshot. "I don't have any way to get hold of Lance. If he wants to see Benji, you're going to have to open the door."

Joyce opened the door a stingy inch. "He's got a cell phone."

But in the shock of his sudden return, she'd neglected to get his number. "Is he here?"

"Well," Joyce began.

"Mom." The door opened wider, and Lance appeared beside his mother. "I'm glad you came by, Jessi."

"That's a matter of o—"

Lance put his hand on Joyce's shoulder and she clamped her mouth shut, settling for a glare.

"Where's Benji?" Lance wanted to know.

"Bobby Cassidy's birthday party."

Joyce snorted rudely. "Holding your son over my son's head."

"Mom, you should go inside."

"No, I want her to stay." Jessi looked Joyce square in the face. The woman knew exactly where Benji was; everyone on the island knew it was Bobby Cassidy's birthday. She let it go, knowing it would gall Joyce all the more to be ignored. "I came here to set some ground rules. You should both hear them so there won't be any misunderstandings down the road."

"Rules? How dare you come to my house—"

"First," Jessi continued, talking over Joyce, "there won't be any unsupervised visits. I've told the school and Benji's sitter. He doesn't go anywhere with anyone without my permission."

"I think I'm more than capable of—"

"Manipulating him?" Jessi said to Joyce. "Like you did at lunch last weekend, telling Benji his father was coming back but that I didn't need to know."

"Well, really; you're putting it in an ugly light."

"Telling my son to keep secrets from me is ugly. I realize you don't care about betraying my trust, but you put Benji in a bad position."

"And you never asked my son to keep secrets from me?"

So, they were going to have it out. And Lance, it seemed, was going to stand back and let his mother fight his battle. No surprise there. Well, she'd be damned if she backed down again. She'd been swallowing Joyce's insults for eight long years, and she'd have gone on swallowing them.

But she wouldn't gamble with Benji's well-being.

"Lance was eighteen, not seven, and capable of making his own decisions."

"Mistakes, you mean."

"Benji is not a mistake."

"Well, for Heaven's sake," Joyce snapped out. "If you'd stop twisting my words. But you're determined to make me the villain."

"How does it feel?"

"I came back to get to know my son," Lance finally stepped in. "I thought the pair of you would be over this by now."

"Lancelot—"

"I told you before, Mother, it wasn't Jessi's fault. We were young and in love and stupid."

"You're taking her side?" Joyce asked on a gasp.

"We're all on the same side. Benji's."

Joyce worried at the strand of fake pearls she always wore, her face going sullen. "You left because of her."

"I left because I needed to leave. If you want to blame someone, blame me."

Jessi huffed out a slight, humorless laugh. "I don't care if she holds onto that grudge 'til Hell freezes over, Lance."

"Don't swear at me."

"I'll say whatever I want, however I want, whenever I want. God knows you never hold your tongue." She held up a hand when Joyce tried to interrupt. "The point is, I believe Benji should have the opportunity to get to know his father, but there are rules. Non-negotiable rules.

"Number one," she began again, "No unsupervised visits. Benji won't be having lunch with you for a while, Joyce."

"You'll keep me from my grandson?"

"You're welcome to see him, as long as I or someone I *trust* is there as well."

"Go on," Lance said, putting a quelling hand on his mother's arm.

"No discussing the past, at least not right away."

"He'll have questions."

"Evade, Lance. You're good at that."

He nodded stiffly, and Jessi could see she'd insulted him. Even if he deserved it, it made her ashamed of herself, but she put it aside. Only Benji mattered.

"What else?" he asked.

"No bribery."

"I brought him a gift."

"You can give it to him, no strings. Don't bad-mouth me," she continued.

"But you get to say whatever you want," Joyce muttered with a sniff.

"If that were the case, Benji wouldn't want anything to do with his father." Or his grandmother.

"You wouldn't stoop to that," Lance said. "I know that, Jessi."

"I appreciate that, but it would be nice if we could both—all—" she amended, shooting Joyce a look, "take the high road. Benji is not a pawn."

"There are courts."

"And I'll tell you what I told your son when he threw that at me, Joyce. No court in this world would grant custody to a father who walked out before his son was born, and has made no attempt to contact him since. And if you think I don't have enough money to hire a lawyer, here's a thought for you. Dex Keegan."

"I don't like being threatened in my own home."

"Oh, it's not a threat." They believed Dex was a lawyer, and Jessi wasn't about to disabuse the Proctors of that notion, any more than she was above using him as a club to keep them in line. "I would do anything to protect my son. Anything. And I have friends who would help me hide the bodies, no questions asked."

Joyce's hands lifted to her throat, protectively this time. *Drama queen*, Jessi thought uncharitably, and was just pissed enough to get a small kick of satisfaction that there might be a little bit of real fear thrown in.

"Is that all?" Lance asked, and if Jessi didn't know better, she'd think he was amused. Jackass, getting a kick out of seeing his mother put in her place.

"I'd tell you to use common sense, I'd tell you to put Benji's welfare above your own, but I'm not sure you can do that. Until I am sure, this is how it's going to be. Take it or leave it."

"I'll take it," Lance said immediately.

"Then I'll see you tomorrow afternoon, around four. Don't let Benji down."

"Jessi..." Lance said.

She turned back, but he just stood there, uncharacteristically hesitant.

Joyce wasn't so reluctant to speak. "It's about that Abbot person who's hanging around the airport. You've heard, of course, that he's slept in more bedrooms than George Washington."

"What does that have to do with me?"

"He's around my grandson. Don't think the courts would turn a blind eye to that kind of goings-on with a young, impressionable boy in the house."

Jessi stepped forward, not just pissed now, but coldly, quietly, enraged. "What kind of goings-on would you be referring to, Joyce? Because you want to be really careful of what kind of nasty—and untrue—accusations you're throwing around in front of my young, impressionable son."

"Stop," Lance said with a heavy sigh. "Neither of us is

going to spread the kind of gossip that would only come back around to hurt Benji. Are we, Mother?"

Jessi didn't wait for Joyce's grudging agreement. She turned, not feeling the frigid air blowing straight into her face. She made her way back to the heart of town, pausing at the corner of Meeker's store to look around. Not a single car drove by. Nobody walked the wind-scoured streets. Nobody stood—or lounged—on the next corner, watching her, waiting for her, even if she didn't want him to.

She was alone.

Just like she wanted to be.

Chapter Nine

Jesus, kid. You shoulda told me I'd be taking my life into my hands."

Paige Walker, star of stage, screen, and, currently, the Internet, looked over at Harvey Astor. He had both hands and one leg wrapped around one of the brass poles supporting the canopy over the captain's wheel, under which Paige stood to pilot the boat that was taking them to Windfall Island. "Actually, your life is in my hands."

She adjusted her balance for the roll of the old motor boat lugging along beneath her feet. She hadn't graced the deck of anything smaller than a yacht since she was sixteen, but her sea legs had been easy to find again, and her stomach barely noted the rise and fall, the side-to-side sway, of eight-foot seas in a boat barely longer.

She might be draped in silk and fur, her hair artistically highlighted and her skin pampered at a spa that charged what most people lived on for a month, but truth be told, she felt sixteen again—sixteen with all the insecurities and fears of that age, and nothing to be done about it but to put one foot in front of the other and pretend she knew what she was doing when really she didn't have a clue.

"Where are the cameras when you need them?"

Paige looked over, and when he went for his cell phone she narrowed her eyes at him until he put it away. "I've had enough publicity for a while."

"No such thing as too much publicity, darling. Haven't you learned that by now?"

"Oh, I've learned about publicity," she murmured.

She did her best to keep her exposure to a minimum and her reputation clean. She shied away from the places where photographers lurked in hopes of getting a million-dollar picture. Yet it was her quest for privacy that had proven her undoing.

"You're brooding."

Paige shook back her hair, made sure her expression was placid, if not exactly happy. "I'll be ready to work when it's required."

Harvey Astor clapped a hand to his heart, then grabbed wildly for the pole when the sea tried to take advantage of his momentary inattention. "I'm wounded," he said as he fought to keep his footing on the spray-slicked deck. "You're more than a workhorse to me." He grinned, making his gorgeous face even more irresistible. "Besides, I've made enough money on you to lounge in the lap of luxury for the rest of my life."

"Small price for the man who's given me my dreams."

"And his friendship."

Paige rested a hand on his wrist. "Priceless," she said, and meant it wholeheartedly. Harvey Astor was the only person in the world she trusted, although her so-called "friends" would have considered her insane for putting her faith in anyone in the entertainment industry. Especially an agent.

But this particular agent wasn't just the best in the trade; he was the only true friend she could count after more than a decade in a business that chewed up and spit out the unworthy.

"God, do you remember how naïve you were?"

"I was never naïve, Harve. Green maybe."

"Yes, well, lucky you skipped into my office first."

"I never skip. It isn't dignified. And yours wasn't the first office I ventured into when I hit Los Angeles. With a little foresight and imagination, someone else could have made their fortune off this workhorse."

"Oh?" Harvey's eyes lit. "Let me guess. There were strings."

"G-strings, to be exact. I passed."

"Well, aren't you just the sterling judge of character."

"Like I said, green, not naïve." At least she liked to remember it that way. Truth was, she'd still been new enough, optimistic enough, to turn down promises of stardom—at least the kind with a price tag attached. She hadn't yet discovered that she was just one of the thousand pretty, talented girls who arrived in Hollywood every year determined to conquer the fickle place.

She wondered what might have happened to her if Hollywood had had time to beat her down as it had so many others, until they took one of those offers. If not for Harve...She glanced sideways, met his eyes. "Stop looking at me like that."

"Are you sure about this?"

She watched the shoreline of Windfall Island coalesce

out of the mist, swimming into life like a quaint and ramshackle Brigadoon, rising after a century of sleep to rub its historic shoulder up against the modern day. But while the village had been kept ruthlessly historical, its people were anything but. They might be isolated, they might stay that way by preference, but they dwelt firmly in the twenty-first century, movie theaters, televisions, magazines...

Paige sighed, then put such thoughts firmly out of her mind. She hadn't been back in more than a decade, and she was coming back the way she'd sworn to, with fortune and fame tucked securely in the pockets of her mink coat.

And if—just to herself, she admitted—she hadn't so much come home as run away from scandal? What else could she have done but escape and leave the furor to die down?

"Doesn't look like the kind of place they'd take your latest cinematic offering in stride," Harve observed with just the kind of snobbery that made Paige smile again, indulgently.

"Don't let appearances fool you. A sex tape is right up their alley."

"Then I'm doubly worried."

"Relax, Harve." And when he didn't look like he would take her advice, she reached over and patted his hand. "They love to gossip."

"That's what worries me. The tabloids are salivating to find out where you are."

"Windfallers would rather cut out their tongues than talk to a reporter."

"Even one who'd offer fistfuls of money?"

"It looks like they could use fistfuls of money, doesn't it?"

"It looks like they could use spare change."

She laughed.

"There's a sound I haven't heard in a while."

"I guess it's good to be home." Even knowing what kind of reception she'd likely get.

"Paige, my love—"

She stretched up and kissed his cheek, smiling over the embarrassed blush that came to it. She'd been a bit miffed, once upon a time, that he'd never hit on her. But that had been back in the early days, before she'd realized he would have preferred her brother—if she'd had one. "Don't worry about me. I'll be safe here." *At least physically*, she thought, looking forward again, at her past.

The past had a way of hurting like nothing else ever could, and when you least expected it. Just look at the way hers was sneaking up on her, the sharp, sweet tang of wistfulness when she guided the boat alongside the weathered, rickety dock, the yearning to be welcomed with open arms, even knowing she didn't deserve it, that she'd burned bridges with the gleeful, youthful certainty that she'd never need to cross them again.

"No welcoming committee," Harvey observed as he tied the boat to the dock with pretty bows that wouldn't hold for more than a minute or two.

"I didn't let anyone know to expect me." Because she'd been worried over the tabloids' habits of picking through garbage, bribing friends and employees, even hacking phones to get the dirt they needed to sell their pitiful rags. It was a plausible excuse, one she might have believed if she hadn't always been so brutally honest with herself.

She took Harvey's hand, let him help her step off the boat and onto the dock. He didn't let go of her right away.

"You have to get back to the mainland," she reminded him. "Worry about yourself."

"If I don't make it, I'm coming back to haunt you," he said, but he squeezed her hand and added, "Give me a call sometime, kid, just so I know the cannibals haven't had you for supper."

Right. Cannibals, Paige thought as she watched Harvey leave and felt like her last hope was puttering away in that small rented boat with him. Cannibals, Windfallers, not exactly the same thing, but close enough. And she was one of them, she reminded herself. You could take the girl from Windfall, but you couldn't take the Windfall out of the girl.

Chapter Ten

Jessi let the curtain on her front window fall back in place and took a couple of deep breaths. She'd stopped looking for Hold; she hadn't seen him since Friday. Since Lance had returned. Her life was falling apart, and now Hold chose to disappear. When she needed him...

She needed him. The truth of it completely appalled her. She wasn't his responsibility. It was just that she'd gotten so used to seeing him everywhere, to feeling warm and wanted when he smiled at her, soothed by the honey-dripping sound of his voice, the center of the universe when he leaned in close and focused his melted chocolate eyes on her face.

She was an idiot, she concluded.

But she was an idiot who didn't hide from the truth. And the truth was, she'd missed Hold Friday night, when sleep deserted her in the whirl of speculation and worry over Lance's sudden reappearance. She'd missed Hold when she walked away from the Proctor house Saturday, hurt and angry and badly in need of a distraction. She missed him now, as she stepped outside because she wasn't inviting Lance Proctor in one minute sooner than she had to.

The mist that had wreathed the island the afternoon before had finally wafted away. It was still damn cold but outside she could breathe; she could feel, if only for a moment, like she hadn't been boxed in—even if it was by her own sense of justice and fair play.

After all, she had no obligation to let Lance see Benji. He'd given up any rights to his son the day he walked away. Benji, however, hadn't given up on his father; he deserved to make his own judgment.

"What's she doing here?" Lance said, his head jerking to Maggie, who'd followed Jessi out onto her front stoop.

"I'm here to support Jessi," Maggie said equably. "The question is, why are you here? And don't tell me it's because of Benji. You're working an angle."

"What angle could there possibly be? Jessi doesn't have anything."

"I have Benji," Jessi said.

But she was thinking about Maggie's observation, barely listening when Maggie said to Lance, "And I'm here to make sure you don't talk her into anything stupid."

"Like trusting me with my own kid?"

"That would be top of my list," Maggie said.

"Still jealous?"

"Still useless?"

Lance made a rude sound. "I hear you're getting married, Maggie. What's her name?"

Maggie folded her arms, her mouth shifting into a sneer. "Just because you're afraid of strong women doesn't mean the rest of the male gender is equally lacking"—her eyes dropped to his crotch before lifting back to meet his—"in courage."

"As pleasant as always, Maggie."

"Aw, Lancelot. You just bring out the best in me."

"Likewise," he snapped.

Maggie smiled broadly. "Your best was the day you left Windfall."

"I'd have thought my best would be Benji."

"There's nothing of you in that kid. Not even your name."

When Lance's face went red, Jessi stepped in. "Stop before someone gets hurt."

"Why didn't you give him my name, Jessi?"

"You left. I took that to mean you didn't want any part of him." She shrugged. "Don't tell me you're insulted after all this time."

Lance drew himself up.

"You know," Maggie said, "I never saw your resemblance to Joyce until now. She likes to look down her nose at people, just like that."

Lance spared her one last glare before he turned to Jessi, his tone heavy with better-than-thou, definitely channeling his mother. "I didn't come here to be insulted."

"It's a pretty nice side benefit, though." Maggie took a step forward. "Hurt Jessi or Benji, and you'll get more than sharp words from me."

"I can fight my own battles," Jessi said before Lance could snipe back. Or worse.

"Fine, Jess," Maggie said. "Just as long as you know I'll be happy to help you dispose of the body."

"How about you go get Benji for me, Mags," she suggested. Not that she wanted to give Lance any advantages, but the last thing she wanted was Lance having a mad on when he spent time with Benji for the first time.

"Sure, but about that angle, Lance? I'll be watching." Her eyes shifted to Jessi. "We'll be watching."

"Judging," Lance muttered after Maggie walked away.

"I'd say she has a right."

"You have a right. Maybe. But—"

"Who do you think picked up the pieces after you took off?" Jessi said quietly.

"God, Jess...I'm sorry. I just, I was suffocating even before...before. I needed to get away from here and, well, I didn't think of anything but what I wanted."

"Lance—"

"I know you don't trust me. I know you don't think I'll stick around, but you have to give me a chance."

"You're right. I don't believe you'll stay, Lance, and no, I don't trust you. But if I weren't prepared to give you a chance, for Benji's sake, you wouldn't be here right now."

Lance took one look at her face and stepped back, his earnest expression fading into uncertainty. "You've changed, Jessi. You're not the sweet girl I knew in high school."

"Sweet is easy when you're sixteen, Lance, with nothing more challenging than choosing the right earrings to wear with an outfit. I like to think I've improved with age. And experience."

"And I haven't?"

She only arched her brows, then Benji raced up, sort of plastering himself against her side. Jessi wrapped her arm around him and held on tight, just for a moment, while her stomach pitched and then finally settled. The sick feeling didn't go away, but it was only her fear for Benji, she told herself. What pitched in her stomach had nothing to do with Maggie pointing out that Lance had an angle for coming back to Windfall.

"Mom?"

She didn't want to do it, but she said, "Benji, this is your father, Lance Proctor."

He glanced at Maggie, who definitely didn't look happy about the situation. Benji arranged his pointed little features into a similarly wary expression and peered up at Lance.

Lance stuck out his hand, not hunkering down like Hold had done to put Benji at ease.

Jessi nudged him a little, and when Benji put his hand in his father's, Lance pumped it enthusiastically.

"Pleased to meet you," Benji said, curling his little hand against his stomach.

"I'm sorry, kid. I should have come back sooner. But you know how it is."

Perplexed, Benji looked up at his mother.

"He's seven, Lance. He doesn't 'know how it is.'"

Lance frowned, but she could see him tamp down his impatience. Maybe he had learned something in the years since he'd left Windfall.

"Come on," she said, and they all trooped inside.

Except Maggie. She put a hand on Jessi's arm. "Benji is going to feel awkward enough without me hovering, Jess."

"But…" Jessi sighed. "You're right." She hugged Maggie, and hurried inside just in time to hear Lance ask to see Benji's room.

"Let's all stay downstairs this first time," she said.

She'd known Lance would object, but at least he had the presence of mind to pull her aside. "You're going to watch my every move?"

Jessi very deliberately removed his hand from her arm. "Yes. And you're going to live with that because, again, Lance, it's not about you."

"I get that, Jessi."

"Do you?"

He heaved a sigh. "I just want to see his room. It's his personal space."

"Exactly. So what makes you think you can demand to see it? Why don't you wait for him to invite you?"

Now he scrubbed a hand over his face, still playing up the emotional weariness angle. And he was pretty convincing, Jessi had to give him that. Or maybe it was simply easier to understand because she was holding on to her own emotions, not to mention her patience, with a death grip.

"I'm new at this," he said.

"Well, here's a tip," she said. "Benji is seven. That doesn't mean he doesn't have rights, or that he doesn't deserve respect, or even basic courtesy."

He sighed, looked over at Benji for the first time since they'd walked into the house. "Yeah, I get it, I just don't like it. I missed the first seven years of his life, Jess. I know that was my fault, but I'm here now. And I've never been long on patience."

That made her smile. "That's the first thing you've said that gives me hope. But you can't make up for seven years in a couple of hours."

He stuffed his hands in his pockets. "I really do want

to get to know him—and you, Jess. Maybe we could start fresh?" He held up both hands, a peacemaking gesture. "I know you need time. You both need time to believe in me, but it's the truth. I just want what's best for both of you."

"Even if it means sending you away? Because I will if I think it's the right thing to do for Benji."

"For Benji or for you? So you can be with that Abbot guy who, by the way, is screwing half the women on the island?"

Jessi drew in a breath, felt her hands fist as she took a step away, then back. "My personal life is off-limits to you," she said, keeping her voice low and even, although it tried to shake as much as she was shaking inside. "You want to be angry that I don't trust you yet, be angry, Lance. But you will not—*will not*"—she bit off when he tried to interrupt—"make another comment like that. About anyone in my life. Got it?"

"Yeah, I got it."

"Use that kind of language around my son again, and you will be gone."

"Mom," Benji said impatiently.

"We're done talking, Benj," she said, but she kept her eyes on Lance, waited until he looked up, nodded. But he wasn't meeting her eyes, and if that worried her, she'd have to think about it later.

"I'll be in the kitchen if you need me," she said to Benji.

Lance answered for him. "We'll be fine."

Damn straight, Jessi replied silently, because she'd be there to make sure of it. And yeah, the idea of it made her feel utterly exhausted. *I've had it easy*, she thought to herself, wondering how single mothers everywhere put up with their jerks of ex-whatevers. Then she heard Benji's voice, tripping over his words because he was so excited about introducing Lance to his collection of super heroes, and it wasn't such a mystery anymore.

She listened another minute, smiling because Benji was already working his father over. Lance grumbled something, clearly not happy about circumstances but going along anyway because what choice did he have? But she smiled when she heard his voice lighten, when he began to respond to Benji's irrepressible good humor.

Lance Proctor might be a hell of a good con man, she thought, but in the hands of his seven-year-old son? He was toast.

Chapter Eleven

Monday morning dawned crystal clear, freezing cold, and way too early. Jessi barely noticed, sleepwalking her way through the same routine she'd performed every weekday morning for what felt like a million years. The only time she roused herself to pay attention was when she dropped Benji off at school. Then she put herself on autopilot again, pulling into her usual parking place at the airport without really knowing how she'd gotten there.

When she walked inside, though, and heard Hold humming all the way from the little office like he didn't have a care in the world, every cell in her gray matter fired up at once.

Resentment flooded her, took her to his doorway. "Where were you all weekend?"

Hold looked up, grinned. "Missed me, did you, sugar?"

Her eyes narrowed, her heart began to pound, her cheeks heated. She searched for a response, but in the wake of what she'd already given away there didn't seem to be anything to say. She turned on her heel, fuming with every step she took. One minute she couldn't step foot outside her door without running into Hold, the next he was gone completely. She'd been through Hell in the last three days, and where was Hold when she needed him?

She'd watched Benji float around the house on a cloud because his father had spent two hours with him. She still felt miserable about it, miserable that she resented her son, even for a second, being happy to finally have his father around.

And where the hell was Hold when she could have used a distraction? Maybe it wasn't fair or logical, considering how hard she'd tried to get him to leave her alone, but what was logical about emotion?

She sent one last glare toward the little office, then stood up to peel off her coat and toss it toward the coat rack. It fell on the floor but she left it there in a stupid yellow heap. What had possessed her to buy a coat that was such a happy color, anyway?

And since sitting didn't suit her mood, she decided to do the filing. There was always filing to do because who in the world enjoyed it enough to keep up?

By noon she'd finished that, cleaned every flat surface in the place, dusted, swept the floor, and finally collapsed at her desk, the long, sleepless weekend sapping her energy.

But not her temper.

Hold sat in the little office, contemplating the charts covering the walls. He'd reached a dead end on his current avenue of the search for Eugenia's possible descendants, ruled out all the families who'd moved away from the island. The time had come to move the investigation back to Windfall's shores, to the families still residing there and, even more specifically, to the other residents in Maggie Solomon's generation.

To Jessi.

Who might even now be in danger. He took a deep breath, let it out, fought off the anger and blind fear the thought always brought on. Logic, he reminded himself, made his fear unreasonable. Nothing had happened since Maggie's plane had been sabotaged a few weeks before. That wasn't to say whoever had hired Mort wasn't trying to find a new henchman.

But he and Maggie and George Boatwright, Windfall's sheriff, were all keeping a close eye on Benji and Jessi—even closer now that Lance had returned. Lance's timing was suspect, and while Hold had a difficult time believing Lance meant to harm his own son, they'd be keeping an eye on him.

And he was stalling, Hold thought, because Maggie's advice might be working a little too well. The one peek he'd taken around the door frame had shown Jessi moving around the office like a tornado, her expression just as stormy.

He felt like hell. Maybe Maggie had been right; maybe keeping his distance from Jessi had made her realize how much she missed him, but at what cost? Jessi was miserable, and so was he.

He walked out of the office, saw her spine stiffen when she heard him coming up behind her where she sat at her desk. "How about some lunch?" he suggested, smiling over the way her chin came up.

"I'm not hungry."

"Coming down with the flu that's going around?"

"No."

"Upset about Lance? It couldn't have been easy seeing him with Benji Sunday."

Jessi whipped around to glare at him. "Like you give a da—" She broke off, and he watched her clamp down on the anger until she had herself firmly under control again. It was fascinating. "I'm fine."

"You're not fine."

"Don't tell me what I am or how I feel. Go back to your little room and ignore me. You're good at it."

"But it pisses you off."

"Like I have time to think about you." She sniffed, pouted a little. "You don't even make the list."

"Maybe you could share some of the load. I have a shoulder or two that aren't doing anything right now."

Just for a moment, something flared in her eyes, something that looked like yearning. Then her gaze shuttered, and she turned her back on him again.

"C'mon, Jess, I'm not such a stranger anymore, not after that kiss the other day."

She went quiet and still, and he knew she'd gotten caught in that memory the same way he did, every time he revisited it. Which was every other minute, he admitted.

"I'm sure you can find someone who'd love to put your shoulders, and the rest of your body parts, to work," she said.

"Are we back on that again?"

"From what I hear, you've yet to get off."

He grinned.

"I mean... You know what I mean."

"You're jealous," he said, which made her spin back around and jerk to her feet.

"Of you?" she squeaked, jamming her hands on her hips. "Oh, I forgot, the whole world revolves."

"Why can't you just admit you missed me the last couple of days?"

She pasted a slight frown on her face, let it clear. "That's right; I didn't see you at all. Now I know why I had such a peaceful weekend."

"Peaceful?" Hold gave a burst of derisive laughter. "Might as well try to sell bacon to a pig, darlin'. I'd as soon believe you weren't half out of your mind with worry, seeing as Lance Proctor spent yesterday afternoon with Benji."

"It's none of your business, no matter what the rest of the people on this island think."

"Island? Hell, *you* are an island, Jessi. You think you don't need anybody else, that you can take all the weight of the world on your little shoulders forever without it burying you alive?"

"Benji and I—"

"The hell with this." Hold grabbed her by the upper arms, jerked her to her feet, and took her mouth.

He'd expected at least a token resistance, and a token resistance was all Jessi made before she melted into him. Hold let the kiss spin into a soft and lovely exchange of warmth and comfort, let that warmth wind its way slowly into his blood and haze his mind.

Jessi wrapped her arms around his waist, pressed her tight little body against him, and tangled her tongue with his. The warmth in his blood turned to heat. His brain simply emptied out—so did the rest of him—emptied then filled back up with her. Her taste, her scent, her heat.

More. It wasn't a thought, or even a word. It was a necessity, a hunger; the air he breathed mattered less than having Jessi in his arms, her mouth—

She pushed out of his arms so suddenly he let her go, then stood there bereft. Until he noticed the tears in her eyes.

"Jessica—"

"Just go away," she said.

"No." He gathered her in again, cradling her head on his shoulder. "Let go, no strings, no expectations. Just give yourself a minute to take some comfort."

It didn't take a minute. She relaxed almost immediately against him, and while he understood it was gentleness she needed, he still wanted her with every fiber of his being. Then he felt the change in her, a subtle tension in her body, a quickening of her breath.

"Jessica—"

She pulled away, taking herself across the room to retrieve her coat.

"Where are you going?" Hold wanted to know.

"To find Maggie and get a hug that's just a hug."

"What does that mean?"

"Eight years, that's what that means."

Hold caught her gaze, held it as he followed her across the room and drew her into his arms again. "That's a hell of a dry spell," he said, and crushed his mouth to hers.

She melted into him with a sexy little moan. He felt her heart pound against his, her body soften. She made him ache, yearn, crave with the kind of hunger that belonged to the dark.

He shifted, snugged her into the cradle of his hips and sipped the gasp from her lips when she strained even closer, when she dropped her mouth to his neck and he felt her hot breath and hot tongue slide over his skin.

When she slipped her hands down, though, he caught them in his, and although it took every ounce of will he possessed, he stepped back. It was either that or take her there—on the desk, on the floor, against the wall, it wouldn't matter. Until after.

He could see it already. As the heat of need left her and realization took its place, the roses in her cheeks took on the frantic color of embarrassment. She turned on her heel and fled. Hold let her go because, he reminded himself, there were times you took, and times you waited.

Chapter Twelve

Since the Horizon was pretty much the only nighttime public gathering place on the island, it was always hopping.

"How come we're going out on a school night?" Benji asked as Jessi ushered him through the door in front of her.

"Gee, you're right, Benj," she said. "I forgot it was a school night. I think we should go home."

"Aw, Mom," he said, making the word several syllables long and looking up at her with wide, pleading eyes. "I was just wondering why we're, you know, going out to dinner on a Monday?"

"Because Maggie asked us." And because Jessi wanted to hear the gossip, seeing as some of it would certainly be about her. And the Horizon's big dining room, with its wood paneling and its bar made from the side of a salvaged ship, would be drowning in gossip. The only problem left was getting there early enough. You didn't want to end up in a corner where you'd miss what happened on the opposite side of the room.

She steered Benji to a booth at the far side of the room. Not a prime location, but she had an advantage. She didn't get out all that much, which gave her virgin ears. People on the island would travel miles to be the first one to drop the biggest gossip bomb. Crossing the room was nothing.

"What are you doing here on a school night?" AJ Appelman said as he parked his bulk at the edge of their table.

AJ, owner and operator of the Horizon, was built like a linebacker, with a smile that could light the world, and the hands and heart of a culinary master.

"We're meeting Auntie Maggie," Benji said. "She's lonely because Dex is in Boston."

"That's what I hear," AJ said.

"Can I have a hamburger?" Benji asked.

"Sure, but don't you want to wait for Maggie?"

"I'm starving," he said, clutching his stomach dramatically.

"I don't think you'll starve to death in the next half hour."

Benji collapsed back on the cracked leather seat of the booth, eyes closed, mouth open, trying to impersonate a corpse.

"That's too bad," AJ said. "Can't bring snacks to a dead man, now, can I?"

Benji popped up on the bench seat, then jumped to his knees. "Can I have French— Dad! Dad's here!"

Jessi craned her head around to see Lance heading their way. He stopped, or was stopped, frequently, and while he shot her glances from time to time, he barely looked at his son.

"Hi, Jess," he said when he finally got to their table. "Hey, kiddo."

Benji clambered out of the booth and hugged Lance, his little face shining with joy.

Lance slid in next to her, sitting too close even before he slung an arm over her shoulders. "Look at us," he said as Benji climbed onto the opposite seat. "Just like a real family."

"Lance." She kept her voice even because the look she sent him said it all.

She should have known he'd choose to ignore the warning. Lance only ever saw what he wanted to see. "How about it, kiddo?" he said to Benji.

"How about what?" Benji said, his brow furrowing as he shifted his gaze to his mother.

"How about all of us having dinner together like a real—"

"Lance," she repeated, sharply enough this time to have heads turning at nearby tables. "I thought we agreed to take it slow."

Lance looked around the room. The heads that had swiveled toward their booth were now bent close together.

"You decided, Jessi," he said quietly, but with a cold undertone she wouldn't have expected from the Lance she'd known.

It only served to remind her that the man sitting next to her was a stranger.

"Mom?"

To her and her son.

"No worries, kiddo," Lance said before she could re-assure him. "I'm just anxious to make up for lost time. I guess I'm in a hurry."

"Whenever I get in a hurry, Mom says things have to happen in their own time."

"Your mom is right, Benj, but that doesn't make it any easier to wait, right?"

"Nope," Benji said with a wide smile, pleased that his father got it.

"So maybe," Lance said out of the side of his mouth, "you could cut me a break, Jess."

"You dropped me flat and disappeared for eight years, Lance. We're on my timetable now. If you keep pushing so hard, I'll just push back."

A muscle in his jaw bunched, relaxed, bunched. The expression in his eyes lightened, though, and he laid a smile on her so wide, so bright, so convincing that Jessi felt like a fool for not trusting him.

"You're right, Jess. Besides, good things are worth waiting for." He slid out of the booth.

"Are you leaving?" Benji wanted to know, his smile fading.

"I'm just going over there." He pointed to a table not far off, in the center of the room, naturally. Lance liked to see and be seen. "Maybe you could have dinner with me. If it's okay with your mom," he added, and left her little choice but to agree.

"It's okay with me," she said to Benji, adding for Lance's benefit, "as long as you stay where I can see you."

The qualification earned her a wounded look from Lance. "My mom will be here soon. She'll be joining us."

Not a recommendation, but Jessi kept the thought to herself. "What about it, Benji? Want to have dinner with your dad and your grandmother?"

He hesitated, God bless him.

"It's okay. Maggie is coming. She'll keep me company."

Not that she had time to feel lonely. No sooner had Benji trailed off after Lance than the race for gossip began. Unfortunately, Shelley Meeker led the charge. And it wasn't just information she wanted.

"Deserted by another Proctor male?" Shelley sniped.

"Really, Shelley. Could you be any more predictable?"

Her snotty grin faded a little.

"Look, you want Lance, he's right over there. Go get him. I promise I won't stand in your way."

Shelley looked over her shoulder, and when she turned back some of her snarkiness seemed to have eased off into misery. "He wants to be alone with his son."

And the anger was back, Jessi thought with a sigh.

"It's your fault," Shelley said. "If you hadn't gotten pregnant, he wouldn't have left, and now that you don't want him, it's your kid. If I had my way, all the Randals on this island would just disappear—"

"You better stop right there," Jessi said, narrowing her eyes and lowering her voice, feeling a buzz of hot satisfaction when Shelley's face paled. "You want to come at me, fine, bring it on. But don't you even think about Benji like that. Or you will be sorry."

"And when Jessi gets done with you, it'll be my turn."

Shelley spun around with a little squeak of terror and found Maggie, hands on hips and spoiling for a fight, close behind her.

With eyes wide, and for once gloriously speechless, Shelley raised a hand to her throat then fled.

"Just when it was getting fun," Maggie said, sliding into the other side of the booth.

Jessi fancied she could hear the Wicked Witch of the West's theme music as Shelley scurried away. "She's probably going to find the flying monkeys and sic them on me. Any chance you could drop a house on her?"

"Maybe not a house," Maggie said blandly, "but I could manage a piano or something."

"That would be a waste of a good piano."

"True."

"So what was that?"

"She said something about wishing all the Randals would disappear to clear her path to Lance, and I just... saw red."

"Well, you should do that more often. I won't say Shelley's gone for good, but I'll bet she leaves you alone for a while."

"She shouldn't threaten my child."

"I don't think she meant it, Jess."

"Yeah." Jessi let out her pent-up breath. "I guess I'm a little on edge."

"You're entitled," Maggie said, stopping to hug Benji when he flew up and wrapped his arms around her neck, chattering about school and his dad, so excited his words tumbled over one another and he was barely understandable before he rushed off again to light on his chair at Lance's table, like a dragonfly poised to take off at any moment. "Does that kid ever stop moving?"

Jessi shook her head. "He's thrilled to have his dad here, Maggie."

"That won't last," Maggie said, then bit off a curse that told Jessi what her expression must look like. "I'm sorry, Jessi."

"I know Lance is going to disappoint him, Maggie, and it's going to be terrible."

"You can't protect him from his own father."

"He's just so...open." Jessi let her gaze rest on the face of her son, shining with joy. He didn't seem to be holding anything back, and no, maybe she couldn't protect Benji, but she could damn well keep an eye on Lance. "When Lance leaves, Benji will be caught completely by surprise. And hurt like hell."

"I think he'll surprise you," Maggie said. "He's a tough kid. And he's a smart kid. Don't think he isn't wondering where his father has been all his life and why he came back now. And speaking of reunions," Maggie continued, "I hear Paige Walker is back on island."

"No." Mouth gaping, forgetting her own paranoia for a moment, Jessi leaned forward. "If she walked in that door right now, I'd kiss her on the mouth."

"And here I thought you were on my side."

"I'm just thrilled there will be some gossip that doesn't concern me. Tell me she really did make that sex tape, and I'll kiss *you* on the mouth."

"Dex hasn't been gone long enough for that to be an attractive proposition."

Jessi snorted. "You should be so lucky. I'm a damn good kisser."

"So I've heard." Maggie studied her fingernails, picking at a ragged spot on her thumbnail.

"Hold told you?" Jessi hissed, then swore under her breath when Maggie lifted a brow and grinned at her. She plucked a menu from the tabletop holder, pretended to study it. "I cannot believe I fell for that."

Maggie snatched the menu from her. "Give, Randal."

"Okay, fine," Jessi hissed, keeping her voice down. "There was a kiss. Or two."

"That's all? No wonder Hold has been lumbering around the office all morning, growling like a grizzly just out of hibernation. He's starving, and you're the snack he can't have." She held out her hand, waggling it back and forth like a fish swimming. "You're the salmon fighting its way upstream. Every time he gets his paws on you, you slip out of his grip."

"Very entertaining. In fact, the whole room is trying to figure out why you're making fish motions."

"I could tell them, if you like. It's not very often I get to scoop all the busybodies."

"Move and you're dead meat."

"I don't know, Jess. You and Hold in a lip-lock is pretty irresistible. And I'm almost positive I can take you."

"I'm small but scrappy, and I fight dirty when I have something to lose."

"What have you got to lose?"

Jessi thought about that for a minute, then spread her hands. "I have no idea. I just know that with everything Benji has going on right now, the last thing he needs is hearing malicious lies about his mother."

"Salacious, not malicious," Maggie corrected. "And come to think of it, they're not lies, either."

"They would be by the time people like Shelley Meeker got done repeating them."

Maggie tipped her head. "You're right about one thing.

Benji is what's important here. And he doesn't exactly look like he's suffering, Jess."

She looked over at her son, feeling heavy all over, as if lead flowed through her veins instead of blood.

"I didn't mean to upset you."

"I'm not upset. Hurt maybe, although it's not rational for me to feel hurt."

"Who ever told you feelings are rational?"

By the time AJ came to take Jessi's and Maggie's orders, the Horizon would have been in serious violation of the fire code if anyone had known how it read, and if the entire volunteer fire department hadn't been in attendance. The possibility of Paige Walker, Hollywood incarnate, making an appearance was too much for even the diehard homebodies to resist.

"It's about time, Antonio Jeremiah," Maggie said to AJ, still working her way down the alphabet in an attempt to guess his real name.

AJ just gave his big, booming laugh, and shook his head.

"I'll get your name out of you some day."

"Today is not that day. Why are you holding a menu?"

"Somebody I know was using it as a distraction," Maggie said.

AJ shook his head again, this time in exasperation. "As if," he said. "You'll have white chicken chili and my jalapeño cornbread."

"Put me down for a Maalox chaser," Jessi said.

"For you, I'll hold the jalapeños."

"Lightweight," Maggie said to her.

"You bet. I'm not good with too much heat."

"That's not what I heard," Maggie said again.

"At least you waited until he was gone to unleash the innuendo."

"You and Abbot are old news," Maggie said, just as all noise in the place died out like someone had pulled the plug.

Jessi looked over her shoulder and there was the very movie star who'd replaced her as the new grape on the island's vine. "Speak of the devil," she said.

Maggie snorted. "Paige Walker could teach Satan a trick or two."

"Still holding a grudge?"

"You call it a grudge. I call it a lesson well learned."

"Don't look now, but I think Paige wants to bury the hatchet."

"Then I'll keep my back to the wall."

Maggie watched Paige make her way across the room, stopping every now and then at one table or other, mostly so she could strike a pose and bask in the admiration. And she was downright gorgeous, damn it, every strawberry blond hair in place, her porcelain skin blush perfect, even in the Horizon where the air was always slightly smoky from a fireplace that had never vented properly.

Her mink coat gaped open enough to reveal the lush body beneath, her breasts swelling above the neckline of her designer frock with just the right balance between sexy and classy. She looked as fresh and pretty as a dewy rose.

Maggie had always felt homely, awkward, and frumpy next to her.

Nothing had changed.

"Hey, Paige," someone called out, "how about a private screening?"

Paige stopped, and for the first time since she'd broken their friendship, Maggie saw her look uncertain.

Adeline Hazelton, dressed in an eighties-era lavender polyester pantsuit and sensible pumps, looked at the loudmouth—one long, even look that had him ducking his head. Adeline ran what passed for a school system on Windfall Island. Her own kids were grown and gone, but she remained de facto principal, despite attempts to oust her. She didn't take any crap from anybody, and her motto was *once a student, always a student*.

"You're here," Adeline said to Paige. "You going to let some yahoo with a big mouth send you running?"

Paige straightened, looked around the Horizon's big dining room, then met Adeline's gaze. "I'm here."

"Question is, how?" someone else called out. "You didn't bring her, did you, Maggie?"

"And have to fumigate my plane to remove the odor of brimstone? I imagine her broom is parked outside."

The place erupted in laughter, making Maggie feel just a tiny bit guilty. For all of ten seconds, before Paige met her level stare with a pair of perfectly plucked and arched eyebrows.

"You don't have the monopoly on travel between here and the mainland, Maggie."

"I pretty much do," Maggie said. She handled the air transport herself, but even if Paige had tried to book one of her charter boats, she'd have known about it. Still, there were any number of islanders and mainlanders with small watercraft they were willing to hire out. And Paige had a way of getting what she wanted. "Tell us about the scandal," someone called out.

"Is that tape real?" another voice yelled. "Did you actually have sex with that director while his wife was right downstairs?"

"That's enough," George Boatwright said, stopping at the booth, his hands on his tool belt and a bland cop expression on his face as he panned his gaze over the crowd. "Go back to your own business. You'll all have time to visit with Ms. Walker later."

"Ms. Walker?" Maggie got to her feet, crossed her arms, made her expression just as cold and flat as George's. "Pretty formal for a man who's had his tongue down her throat."

George reddened.

Once upon a time, he and Maggie had been a couple— a teenage couple, sure, but teenagers who'd been dating almost two years. Until Paige Walker realized there was something she couldn't have, and set out to get it. She had, without considering the consequences to anyone else involved.

Paige had been a friend—hell, almost a sister—to Maggie, and there were rules about boyfriends, even exboyfriends. Maggie might not put a lot of stock in that kind of female foolishness, but loyalty, she'd always thought, ought to come before ego, greed, and ambition.

Judging by what the tabloids reported, Paige still hadn't learned to think about the people who got hurt so she could feed her selfish desires. Except this time she'd messed with the wrong man. And the wrong man's wife.

"Hollywood too hot to handle just now?"

Paige waved a hand adorned with a ruby big enough to qualify as an anchor. "I haven't taken a vacation in years," she said.

"The south of France all booked up?"

"Still haven't learned to forgive and forget?" Paige shot back, the edge in her voice the first sign Maggie was getting under her skin.

"Betrayal is one of those things that's hard to forget."

Paige huffed out a breath. "Really, I don't see why I have to take all the blame. You and George broke up—"

"We were reevaluating."

"—and you said he'd never go out with one of your friends."

Maggie took a step forward. "It wasn't a challenge; it was a compliment to George. George has morals. You might have heard of morals, maybe pretended to have them for some role or other."

Paige lifted a shoulder. But she wasn't meeting Maggie's eyes. "I just wanted you to see that no one is perfect."

"So you betrayed me in order to prove I couldn't trust George not to."

Paige sighed with very convincing regret. "I didn't reason it through very well."

"He was a teenage boy, Paige. Did you really think he could resist you when you threw yourself at him? Even before you bought those tits?"

"Ouch. And these tits are mine."

"Anything is available for a price."

"Come on, Mags. I was a kid."

"You were old enough to understand what you were doing. Better than I did as it turned out."

"I..." Paige broke off, sighed heavily. "You're right, Maggie. I'm sorry."

Two simple words. Maggie would have begged for that

apology once. Now she didn't want to hear it. "Are you going to be sorry when the paparazzi descend on us?"

"They don't know where I am. Or where I'm from."

"Oh, that's right. You're ashamed of Windfall Island."

Paige shook her head, looking truly sad. But then, she was a hell of an actress. "Are you ever going to forgive me? I was young and stupid."

"You were never stupid. Neither was I."

Chapter Thirteen

Paige flounced her way into the other side of the booth across from Jessi. Jessi ignored her to check on Benji for the thousandth time. He sat at the table with his father and grandmother, looking bored while Lance talked to Josiah Meeker, of all people. Josiah rarely lowered his standards enough to frequent an establishment like the Horizon, where the food was simple and so were the people.

Benji looked over and grinned at her before Joyce Proctor said something and turned his attention away again.

"So," Paige said, "what's going on with these beautiful men I keep hearing about?"

"Romance," Jessi said, concentrating on the chili AJ had dropped off after Maggie walked away. Stupid, she thought, to fixate on people gossiping *about* Paige and not realize they'd be gossiping *to* her as well. "At least in Maggie's case. She's getting married to Dex Keegan."

"What does he do? What's he like?"

"I think you should ask Maggie those questions."

"Well, that would be a short conversation."

"Then ask anyone else."

"Afraid of her?"

"Afraid? No. Loyal? Yes. She was here when I needed her, Paige. I'm not going to talk about her behind her back. To anyone, about anything."

Paige sat back. "You're right, Jess. I'm sorry. I'm sorry that I wasn't here when you needed support."

"I was fine. I am fine. And you were going after what you wanted. There's no need to apologize."

"Who are you?" Benji climbed up on the bench seat, slinging an arm around Jessi's neck and leaning into her. "Who is she, Mom?"

"Manners, Benj," Jessi said, but she hugged him back.

"My name is Benjamin Randal," Benji said. "Everyone calls me Benji, which is okay for now, but when I get older it's gonna have to be Ben because Benji's a kid's name."

Looking bemused, Paige took the hand he'd stuck across the table. "Paige Walker," she said. "It's a pleasure to meet you."

"I'm meeting a lot of people this week," Benji said. "I just met my dad. We're having dinner. He said I could introduce myself later, only I've never met a movie star before, and he was busy talking to adults, so..."

"I'll tell you a secret about movie stars," Paige said, "We're just like everyone else."

Benji grinned hugely. "That's what my dad said." And off he went to sit with Lance again.

"He's a great kid, Jess. And it's obvious you're the

center of his world. That won't change because Lance is back."

Jess sighed, pulled her gaze off her son. It wasn't easy, but she had to trust in the bond they shared. "Suppose you tell me something about your life," she said to Paige.

"My life is on every tabloid and magazine cover in the supermarket," Paige evaded. "I want to know what's been going on here."

"Interesting, considering you've only asked about Dex Keegan and Hold Abbot. They're not Windfallers, in case you've forgotten."

"Oh, I think I'd remember them, considering what I've heard. What's interesting is that you don't want to talk about them. It just naturally excites my imagination."

"This isn't Hollywood, Paige," Jessi said evenly, although she was more than a little irritated. "You can tell by the lack of a script and a soundtrack. Windfall is the same boring place it always was. There aren't plots around every corner." She smiled fondly. "Except the ones dreamed up by the gossips."

Paige smiled with her, just as fondly. "Then why do I smell a secret?"

"I don't know...because you're used to living in a place where everyone has an agenda?"

Paige shrugged that off—a more elegant version of Maggie's shoulder bump, but they'd gotten the gesture from each other. And they'd each have hotly denied it. "I'm just concerned, Jess. You and Maggie are my friends."

"Are we?" They'd been inseparable, she and Paige and Maggie, but high school was a long time ago now. "You left, Paige. Poof. Neither one of us has heard from you in nearly ten years. You can't just show up and expect us to invite you to a sleepover so we can braid each other's hair and share our deepest, darkest secrets."

"I wish you would. You know I could never stand to be left out."

"You left yourself out this time," Jessi said, but gently.

"Well," Paige said, "you can't get any clearer than that."

"I'm not trying to hurt your feelings."

Paige smiled a little as she slid over and stood. "I know that, Jess. You were always the kindest one of us."

"Paige—"

"And here comes a handsome man to keep you company," Paige continued, smiling brightly.

"You don't have to leave on my account," Hold said, leaning toward Paige as he did every woman, focusing on her alone and making Jessi's eyes narrow when he took Paige's hand. "Hold Abbot," he said.

"Paige Walker."

"And don't I know it."

Jessi started to slide out of the booth, but Hold dropped down beside her.

"'Scuse me, Ms. Walker," he said politely. "It was a pleasure to make your acquaintance." And he turned his attention to Jessi.

Paige stood there a moment, looking nonplussed, before someone called her name and she turned gratefully to join whoever had just spared her the embarrassment of being so completely passed off.

It was probably the first time in a decade a man had turned his back on Paige. Jessi wasn't sure how she felt about that, but as she watched Paige stop next to Lance, saw the commiseration on his face, she understood one thing. Coming home was hell.

"What's so fascinating on the other side of the room?" Hold wanted to know.

"Benji," Jessi said, relaxing as she caught sight of her son.

Benji met her eyes, at least for a second or two before his gaze shifted to Hold and his bored, sulky expression brightened. He jumped off his chair and ran over to the booth.

Lance didn't notice.

Jessi knew how she felt about that. Angry, and a little vindicated. He was talking to a movie star, in all fairness, but still.

"Hi, Hold," Benji said, barreling up to him.

"Mr. Abbot."

"Hold," Hold corrected firmly. "You and me're friends, Ben."

Ben?

"Friends," Benji said with a goofy, happy grin on his face.

As long as he was grinning like that Jessi didn't care what Hold called him.

"So what's going on?" Hold asked him.

Benji shrugged, tossed a look over his shoulder. "I was having dinner with my dad, but he said he's gotta go."

"What?" Jessi lurched forward to see around Hold. She couldn't have cared less about the black look Lance sent Hold's way. "Did he say good-bye to you?" she asked her son.

"Yep."

"And you finished your dinner, right?"

"Yeah," he said, rolling his eyes in Hold's direction.

"Moms," Hold agreed solemnly. "They can be a pain in the butt—"

"Hey!"

"But where would we be without them, Ben?"

"You got a point, son," Benji said in such a cute little mimic of Hold it was all Jessi could do not to laugh out loud. Then he laughed, and it was all she could do not to cry.

Benji's laughter was such a happy sound. Despite her own confusing welter of emotions—resentment for Lance, pride over the way Benji was handling himself, the struggle to ignore Hold's nearness—Jessi was ridiculously grateful her son was happy.

Maggie took Benji from happiness to ecstasy when she collected him to play video games with her.

The only trouble was, Jessi thought, that left her alone with Hold. Which was exactly what Maggie had intended.

The rat.

"Penny for your thoughts," Hold said, bumping Jessi's shoulder companionably with his.

She looked at him, smiled thinly. "I was thinking about Maggie."

Being a meddlesome busybody, Hold would have bet. "She cares about you."

"She definitely knows the way to Benji's heart." Jessi smiled more easily now. "He's getting pretty fond of you, too."

"He's a likeable kid. Who'd've guessed with you for a mom?"

"I'll take that as a compliment."

"It was meant as one," Hold said, tamping down on his irritation. No wonder she was guarded, he thought—what with Lance Proctor showing up out of nowhere, and now Paige Walker and whatever they'd been discussing so intensely. Hold wanted to scoop Jessi onto his lap and soothe the shadows away from her face.

He'd get an elbow in his gut for his troubles, most likely. Jessica Randal was nothing if not self-sufficient.

"You ought not to worry about Benji so much," he said anyway.

"It's my job, along with washing his clothes, feeding him, and seeing he gets an education."

"And making sure he's happy?" Hold bumped her again, stayed shoulder to shoulder this time. "Who makes you happy, Jessica?"

She nudged him back. "I do."

"Yeah," Hold said glumly, still fighting to keep his hands to himself—instead of shaking some sense into her. "Why is that, exactly? Why can't you lean a little, just once in a while?"

She exhaled heavily. "It's complicated."

"It's about your mother," Hold corrected.

"My mother was a saint."

"And that's just the problem— No, don't fire up on me," he said when he saw temper spark in her lovely green eyes. "I only meant she set a hell of an example, from what I've been told by everyone who knew her, and I know you feel you have to live up to it."

"Well, of course I do."

"Including the part where she spent the rest of her life alone after your dad died, except for you and Benji."

"She made the choice to put me—us—first."

"Exactly. It was a choice. Do you think she'd want you to be alone for the rest of your life, too?"

"Doesn't he deserve that?"

"He deserves a mom who's happy."

"Who says I'm not happy?" She reared back. "You? And you're going to fix that for me?" She crossed her arms, fuming. "Happiness starts inside you, Hold. If it's not there to begin with, looking to someone else is asking for heartbreak."

"I'm aware, Jessica, but you're so bright and giving…" He spread his hands, missing the words to capture the exact essence of everything she had to offer. "You weren't made to spend the rest of your life alone," he finished helplessly.

"You don't know the first thing about the real me."

"And you do?" Hold leaned in, kept his voice down as she had, but he let all the frustration he felt, all the disappointment, show. "When you make a decision, large or small, what do you base it on?"

"Logic, consequences…I weigh the facts and—"

"And then you ask yourself what your mother would have done. You're living your life according to the idealized version of a woman you might not have known as well as you think, Jessi."

"What's that supposed to mean?"

"Just that she was human."

"And so am I. It's all right to make mistakes, right? That's what you're going to say next."

"The only mistake I can see you've made was in choosing Lance Proctor, but you handled the consequences with a hell of a lot more maturity than most teenagers. And if Lance wasn't such an ass—"

"He was young, too, Hold."

And now she was defending him, Hold thought. He'd wanted to maneuver her into his own arms, not Lance's. "Sure, but I figure it's my luck you didn't marry him. Don't roll your eyes at me," he added when she did just that. "I'm not saying all this to get you in bed."

"Then what do you want?"

"I want a relationship, and they don't come with guarantees. People try each other on. Sometimes they fit; sometimes they don't want to make alterations to be together." He held up a hand before she could fire back. "And in your case, there are two people to get to know."

"You understand that no matter how you and I fit, Hold, if Benji is unhappy—"

"It's a deal breaker. All I want is a chance, Jessica, for all of us."

She was silent a moment. Hold could almost hear the internal battle being waged before she said, "How am I supposed to argue when you use flattery *and* logic on me?"

"You're not supposed to."

She looked up at him, and her lively green eyes sparkled teasingly into his. His mouth went dry, all the moisture burned away in a sudden burst of heat, of need. He eased forward; she stopped him with a hand on his cheek this time, rather than on his chest.

He lifted his gaze from her mouth, met her eyes, soft now with concern and something deeper, hotter. "Not here. Please, Hold."

"Where?" he rasped. "When? God, Jess, you're killing me."

"I keep trying to establish boundaries. You keep ignoring them."

"There's something about a line that just naturally

makes me want to cross it. 'Specially if you're on the other side, sugar."

"How about we take it one day at a time?"

"Does that deal include nights, too?"

"Not this one." But her lips curved, a little cat-that-ate-the-canary smile that told him it pleased her to know she had that kind of power over him.

Let her feel her oats, he thought, as long as when she got an urge to sow them she sowed them with him. And while he sat there daydreaming, she changed the subject. To him.

"My life?" he said in answer to her question.

"Gen— What you came here for is your hobby," she prompted, careful not to say too much in a room where they never knew who might be eavesdropping.

And just about the only thing he was willing to talk about. "More than a hobby," he said. "I take a lot of this kind of research. The pay isn't great, but I don't need much, and the work is fascinating. Even when I'm working for a regular, everyday person.

"Once, I traced a postal worker in my hometown back to Marie Antoinette. Not all that much of a stretch, considering the history of the state, but still, pretty good bragging rights for a man who walks the same route day after day." He'd steered the conversation carefully away from himself.

Not that Jessi noticed, busy searching the room for Benji.

"He's with Maggie," Hold said.

Jessi relaxed back into her seat. "It's getting pretty late. I should get him home."

Hold shouldn't have felt relieved, but he did. He

should have felt guilty, and he did that, too. And worried, because he'd backed himself into a corner, right and tight. And yet, having finally made progress in opening her up to the possibility they could be more than friends, the last thing he wanted was to drop his family's wealth on her.

She would cut him out of her life faster than a Louisiana cotton gin picked a field clean. Or she wouldn't, and that would be worse. He ought to trust her, he knew that. But he'd trusted before, he'd loved before.

He'd opened his heart to a woman, offered to share his life with her. For his reward, that heart had been shattered, that life turned into a thing to be bartered; the semblance of love in return for the ease and the trinkets money could buy. He knew what that had made Miriam. And he knew what it made him.

He wouldn't be a fool again, and yeah, he understood he was letting the past drive him. Twist him, if he was being completely truthful. But the past, Windfall Island's past, had also brought him to Jessica Randal, and she would take or leave the man she saw before her, the simple genealogist.

And if, a tiny little voice whispered, she learned the truth? He'd just have to find a way to stop that from happening, until he was ready to tell her himself.

Chapter Fourteen

The following Saturday found Jessi at home, settled in at her small dining table with Maggie, going over paperwork they hadn't gotten to during the week. Maggie had been in the air more often as her charter business picked up, which meant Jessi could drag her into paperwork on a Saturday without admitting that part of the delinquency belonged squarely on her own shoulders.

It wasn't so much admitting she'd fallen down on the job as facing the why of it. Or rather the whom. Ever since her conversation with Hold Abbot the previous Monday—a conversation where she'd all but given him the green light—it had been hard to focus.

In Hold's defense, he'd been nothing but a gentleman.

That had only made it worse.

She'd been on pins and needles all week, waiting for him to make some kind of move. She'd opened the door, hadn't she? So why, she wondered, hadn't he walked through it? He'd been polite, sure, but he'd kept to himself most of the week, never once parking himself at her desk like he was apt to do before, never leaning close to talk to her. And making her want him all the more.

It was annoying, confusing. And made her think about him constantly, which, she assumed, was exactly what he wanted. And why she deliberately put him out of her mind. Again.

October had passed into November, bringing snow, sleet, and sub-zero temperatures. As usual, the weather hadn't been conducive to trick-or-treating, so the Wind-fallers had gathered at the Horizon, made Halloween as much fun as possible for the youngsters without the door-to-door element. Although Hold had made an appearance, spent time admiring Benji's Spiderman costume, he'd kept his distance from her.

Lance had been there, of course, and Benji came away with enough candy to keep him on a sugar high the rest of the winter. But Jessi had missed Hold, missed his slow, smooth voice, the way he smiled and set her stomach to fluttering, and how that fluttering deepened, spread when she let her eyes wander, her body imagine how the long, strong lines of him would feel against her.

"What was that sigh for?" Maggie said, both her tone and her grin bordering on smug.

Jessi tapped on the paper she'd slid under Maggie's nose, an order for the December fuel.

"You know, I can sign my name and talk at the same time," Maggie observed. "I'm multi-talented that way."

"I can do paperwork and ignore you at the same time."

"Touché. So the question is, why don't you want to talk about Hold?"

Jessi slid the paper away from Maggie, pushed over a

stack of checks. And sighed again. "Because I'm not sure how I feel about him."

"This is me you're talking to," Maggie pointed out.

And nobody knew her better, Jessi admitted.

"I noticed he stayed away from you this week. So maybe it's not your feelings you're confused about." Maggie signed the first check, scowled over the second. "How the hell do we stay in business when so much goes out the door?"

"Because, as I tell you every month, more comes in. It's called profit, and it allows you to keep defying gravity and me to fend off starvation."

"You should get a raise," Maggie said immediately.

"C'mon, Mags, you know I'm kidding. Focus."

"Fine," she grumbled, signing the next check in the stack. "But you do deserve a raise, and since you won't take one, the least you can do for yourself is have a fling. I know a friendly, attractive man who is free tonight."

"What did you do?" Jessi demanded over the warning bells going off in her head.

"Not a thing," Maggie said. "It just seems like fate to me. Hold's not busy, and you're not busy. And before you say it, Benji can spend the night with me."

"I have all this paperwork."

"Do it on Monday."

Jessi shook her head. "I have Monday's work to do on Monday. Things have piled up, what with the time I've taken off. And," she added on a rush, "I've been a little unfocused lately. Lance coming back."

"Not to mention Hold being a few feet away all the time."

"A good friend would have overlooked that part."

"A good friend would want you to face it, Jess. A good friend would ask why you're ignoring what you feel for him."

"I'm afraid, all right?" She covered her face for a second, then shoved her hands back through her hair. The pain of her fingers snagging in the wild curls helped her bear down and face reality. "I don't want to get attached to someone who's going to leave, and I sure don't want Benji getting attached to him."

"I think it's too late for that," Maggie said, but with a note of sympathy in her voice. "The kid lights up when Hold is around."

"Yeah," Jessi said, but refused to sigh again. "Hold is so good with him."

"Hold treats him like a person, like his opinion counts. Unlike Lance."

"Maggie."

"The whole town saw how Lance ignored him in the Horizon last Saturday."

"Lance didn't ignore Benji on purpose," Jessi pointed out crankily. "And if the whole town was worried about my son, they could have left them alone instead of interrupting Lance every five minutes to score the latest gossip."

Maggie smiled indulgently. "You might as well expect the wind to stop blowing as think any Windfaller would ignore—"

They heard the tromp of feet on stairs. Maggie swallowed the rest of what she'd been about to say, which certainly would have been about Lance. Both of them bent to paperwork, looking up when Benji came over to stand by the table, favoring Maggie with a listless, "H'lo."

"What's got you looking so gloomy?" Maggie asked him.

"I'm bored."

And out of sorts, Jessi thought. How could she not see the upheaval in her son when she lived with it every day herself? The trouble was, she didn't know how to set his mind at rest. Benji had two men in his life now, a father who would surely leave again, and a man who'd befriended him, and who would surely leave. And she could do nothing to spare him those blows when they came.

What she could do, what she was determined to do, was make sure he had a soft place to land.

Benji wandered to the wide window in the living area, propped his elbows on the sill and looked out at Hideaway Cove, or what he could see of it. A lumpy rain fell straight down, splatting on the ground with half-frozen plops, and graying out the world outside. The leaden sky seemed to hang just over the roofs of the houses. Even the rocks and trees along the bluff were shades of black and gray.

Although she loved the cove and all its moods, looking out made Jessi feel as dreary as the day, and dreading the long winter coming to sock them in on the island and trap them in their houses. Then again, maybe feeling trapped had nothing to do with Mother Nature.

The search for Eugenia had come to a nearly complete standstill. Moving forward meant putting someone in danger, but if they didn't move forward, the mystery might never be solved. Lance, and his effect on Benji, was a constant worry. And then—

"Hold's here." Benji ran to the door, but he stopped with his hand on the knob, looking to his mother.

"Of course he is," Jessi muttered, even as her heart jumped.

"Sounds like just what you need," Maggie said.

"I don't know what I need."

"I do, and Hold Abbot is just the man to give it to you."

"C'mon, Mom, answer the door," Benji said, because he wasn't allowed to anymore—just one of the ways his life had changed since Lance Proctor had come back to Windfall Island.

"I'll get it," Maggie said, and was across the room before Jessi could stop her.

Not that she would have stopped Maggie; it wouldn't be polite to leave Hold on the doorstep, especially in such nasty weather. He stepped inside, wearing a buff-colored, knee-length topcoat that looked really expensive, and Italian leather shoes that were definitely expensive, both completely impractical for the weather on Windfall Island.

He shook water off himself like a dog coming out of the surf, and made Benji shriek with laughter.

Jessi stayed in her seat. She'd have liked a couple minutes to . . . *what*, she asked herself as their eyes met and her heart leapt again, beating so hard in her ears she barely heard him say "hi" to Maggie, then drop down to Benji's level to greet him.

Then his eyes lifted to hers again, held, and God help her, she couldn't look away—not until Maggie said, "Hey, Benj, how about you and I go run some errands," and she realized Maggie intended to leave her alone with Hold Abbot and her own wavering resistance.

"Maggie—"

"In fact," Maggie said, grinning unrepentantly at Jessi

while she spoke to Benji, "how about a sleepover? Dex is still gone, and I don't have anybody to keep me company out there in that big house. It'll be great to have a man around."

When Benji turned those big, pleading eyes on her and said, "Can I, Mom?" Jessi knew she was sunk.

"I don't know…" she tried anyway, her eyes straying back to Hold.

He bumped up one eyebrow, and she knew what he was thinking. And okay, maybe she was using Benji as a buffer…

"*Mom.*"

…and that wasn't fair to him. Besides, she could resist Hold Abbot, right?

"Sure," she said. "Go pack. And make sure you put pajamas and clean underwear in there. And your tooth-brush—"

"Mom," Benji said, with embarrassment instead of impatience this time, but he ran off, came back in no time flat with his Harry Potter backpack. Before she could check it, he pecked her on the cheek and Maggie whisked him out the door.

"I'd be insulted," Hold said, "if the boy didn't have the good sense to take a better offer when he got one. And if I hadn't come here to see you anyway."

He crossed the room and sat in the chair Maggie had vacated. "We kind of danced around each other all week."

"Did we?" Jessi asked. "I mean, I was right there, every day. You barely looked at me."

"Jesus, Jessica." He jerked to his feet, scrubbed a hand over his jaw. "How much do you think I can take? You were right there, every day, close enough to…and

I couldn't... If I'd so much as made eye contact with you—"

Jessi rose, one fluid motion as she laid her body against his and took his mouth. Hold went absolutely still. She could swear his heart even stopped beating. Hers definitely did, then lurched back to life almost painfully, battering against her ribcage, pumping heat and hunger through her veins, and so much desire she didn't know what to do with it all. So she stepped back. And surprised him again.

"Hold—"

"Don't, Jessica. I know it's been a long time and it feels like this is happening fast, but please, God, don't step back from me now."

"But—"

"Shhhh." He kissed her again, long and deep, tongues tangling. He tasted dark and heady; his hands on her face were strong and steady. Desire caught her by the throat again, spread through her again, twisted her in knots. And scared the hell out of her.

It hadn't been like this with Lance. That need had been softer, sweeter, not this...this deep and overwhelming sharpness that sliced through her self-control like it was so many soap bubbles.

She hadn't understood what she was getting into then. She did now. Her gaze lifted to Hold's, and she could see him holding back, giving her room as she understood now he'd given her room all week. The choice rested on her shoulders, she realized. She could let the fear guide her, or...

Really, she told herself as she stepped up to him again, there was no choice.

She laid her hands on his shoulders, lifted to her toes, and kissed him, on the neck this time. Her breath caught—the scent of him, the tang of his skin, and the roughness of it against her lips sent desire soaring. When he touched her she was lost. So she simply put herself into his hands.

His hands were gentle at first, but when she slipped hers under his sweater his touch turned a little rough, more than a little rushed, moving over her with an urgency that echoed hers. She liked it, liked his hands on her, and thrilled when she felt him tremble.

It meant he felt everything she felt. It meant she could let go, of thought, of emotion, of worrying about the after. She could concentrate on the now, on the feel of those hands rushing over her, of that mouth hot on her skin, of that long, lean body that was hers for the taking.

Take she did, fisting her hands in his hair, fusing her mouth to his and feasting on him. She nipped and nibbled, ran her hands up into his hair then let them roam down over his shoulders, over the strong muscles of his back, to cup his backside and press him, rock hard, against her.

"My God, Jessica," Hold said against her mouth.

She could feel him shudder, knew he still held back. "Let go, Hold," she whispered against his mouth. "I won't break."

"You sure, sugar?"

She stepped back, only far enough to peel out of her hoodie and hand it to him. "I want your hands on me," she said as he took it then dropped it, his eyes never leaving hers. "I don't want you to worry about hurting me." She pulled her long-sleeved t-shirt off next, not caring that she wore an old, comfortable bra beneath. "I'm not going to worry about hurting you." She slipped the straps off, slowly, smiling when his eyes dropped, finally, from hers.

He swallowed audibly—then groaned when her hands moved to the snap of her jeans instead.

"Are you trying to kill me?"

"There've been moments when I've considered it," she said with a smile, "but this definitely is not one of them." She took his hand in hers and tugged him toward the stairs. "I've waited a long time, Hold, waited and dreamed, and none of those fantasies included the couch or the floor."

He stopped her at the foot of the stairs, tipped her chin up until their gazes met. "Fantasies?"

"Years' worth. I hope you've had your Wheaties."

"Will oatmeal work?"

"I guess we'll have to find out," Jessi said, ending with a little shriek when he swept her up in his arms and raced up the stairs and into the room she barely had time to point out.

"I'm impressed," she said, taking a moment to steady herself after he dropped her feet to the floor. Who'd have known being carried away by a big, strong man would make her head spin? "Those stairs are pretty narrow and steep, and you didn't bang my head against the wall once."

"We southern gentlemen have a reputation to uphold," he said, already whisking off his cashmere sweater, and whatever he'd worn beneath it.

"That's one fantasy down, thank you."

"Sugar, you ain't seen nothing yet."

Not true, she mused. Hold Abbot was definitely

something—tall, lean, beautiful. Irresistible. And all hers, she thought, reaching out to run her fingers over the ridges of muscle along his belly.

He pulled her against him, her back to his front, all that lovely skin and those hard muscles, sliding over her when he wrapped his arms around her and dropped his mouth to her neck.

Surrounded, she thought. Hold's heat, Hold's scent, Hold's strength folding her into a world of pure sensation. She closed her eyes, let her head drop back as his hand came to her breast, making slow circles, touching her just enough to make her nipples harden to aching points and to send need arrowing down to become an even sweeter ache in her center. He bit her lightly on the shoulder, his other hand slipping down across her belly, under her jeans, into her panties. Into her.

She came apart, the climax so strong the muscles in her legs went to rubber. Hold caught her, bore her to the bed. She could feel him removing her shoes, her jeans, her panties, her bra, just the lightest touch of his hands enough to make her tremble with the aftershocks of the orgasm still rippling through her.

And then he was there, hard beside her, hard against her. Hard inside her, one strong, shocking thrust. She drew in a sharp breath, loving the feel of him, stretching her, heating her...

"Don't stop," she pleaded, barely recognizing the husky, breathless sound of her own voice. When he didn't move, she did, bucking up, shoving at his shoulders, helpless to tame the need raging through her, flexing its muscles like a caged wildcat suddenly set free.

Hold hooked a hand behind her knee, lifted it along

his thigh, and drove deep, over and over. Jessi braced her hands on his shoulders and met him thrust for thrust, the eyes she'd glued to his face going blind as she lost herself, as she flew, as she heard him groan and come with her into the sweet, sharp, ecstasy.

Hold dropped his head to her shoulder, his body still locked so tightly to hers she couldn't tell where she ended and he began, whether she felt the echo of her own orgasm or the pulsing of his.

Not that it mattered, she thought dreamily, running her hands over him, memorizing, now that she had her faculties back, the feel of his skin—a little rough sometimes, always sleeked over hard muscle.

He shifted, moved away, then got up to go into the bathroom to get rid of the condom she hadn't even known he'd used.

She missed him instantly but to her great surprise, now that she could think, she wasn't second-guessing. It had been the right decision, she realized, for her and likely for Benji. How could she give everything she could to those who depended on her if she wasn't taking everything she needed for herself? Hold had taken, too, but he'd given so much more than mere physical pleasure. Because he'd wanted her.

With the decision made she could indulge herself. And never forget, she cautioned, that whatever Hold gave her didn't include his heart.

His body and his attention would be enough, she decided. More than enough. She felt so amazing, so... well used that she started to drift off, until Hold came back and tugged at the bedclothes.

"It's a little chilly."

"Is it?" Jessi stretched, smiled up at him. "If you come back here we can keep each other warm."

"The covers would help," he rumbled, but he sat down on the edge of the bed, running a hand from her shoulder to her knee, setting off little swirls of warmth that spread through her.

He slipped under the blankets, but she didn't want anything but him against her bare skin, so she took the edge of the covers and threw them off, lifting to her knees beside him.

"You sure?" he said, more for form, she figured, as he was already reaching for her. "It's been a long time."

"Then I have a lot of catching up to do, don't I?"

She rose over him, took him in, and showed him where she wanted to begin.

Chapter Fifteen

Hold lay there, wondering how long he'd been sprawled on his back, gasping for breath like a dying man. If his stomach hadn't growled, long and loud, he could have stayed that way forever, with his hand resting on Jessi's hip while she breathed just as raggedly beside him.

If she was half as worn out and shaky as he felt, he hated to disturb her. But starvation—now that was serious business, especially if she was going to keep him burning up the calories like she had.

"Jessica," he said, patting her hip.

She mumbled something and rolled over, snuggling her tight little body against his. Any hunger he felt suddenly had nothing to do with food.

"C'mon," he said, nudging her again, "get up, sugar."

"You get up," she murmured, her breath feathering warm over his skin.

"I may, if you keep that up. And you won't be able to walk tomorrow."

"Yeah, yeah," she said crankily, rolling away from him to sit on the edge of the bed.

"We have lots more nights and days, sugar."

She twisted around to look at him. "Hold," she began.

"Don't overthink it." He scooted over and wrapped himself around her, afraid she'd put distance between them again, but knowing he had to tell her how he felt. "I won't sneak around, Jessica, I won't act like this is something to hide to spare you gossip."

"To spare Benji gossip," she said. But she covered his hands with hers. "You're right, Hold. I don't want this tarnished, either. Let's just enjoy every moment."

Hold agreed with her wholeheartedly. He wasn't going to let Miriam tarnish the brightness he'd found with Jessi. Wherever the road led, he thought, that was where they'd go. But the knowledge that Jessi wasn't in any more of a hurry to get to the end of that road helped.

"I'm taking a shower," she said at length. "There's room in there for two."

"I get in the shower with you, I'll have to carry you around piggyback for the next couple days."

"Promises, promises," she said, kissing him lightly before she eased out of his arms.

She slipped out of bed, naked and so at ease Hold would have thought she did this kind of thing all the time if he hadn't known better. As it was he just enjoyed watching her, even after he realized she'd gathered an armload of clothing to take into the bathroom.

It would only give him the pleasure of peeling her out of them later—or watching her peel herself out, he thought, remembering how it felt to see her slip those bra straps down her shoulders, one at a time. Like a punch to the gut, so seductive and so innocent at the same time, the way she'd left the bra on, left him wondering while lust caught him by the throat, the gut—the balls, he admitted, crossing his arms behind his head and just smiling over it.

He heard the water turn on, heard her groan a little, imagined those muscles she hadn't used in so long were really appreciating the heat and beat of the spray.

With her out of sight, a dozen thoughts wanted to batter at him: Benji, the search for Eugenia, the truths he hadn't told Jessi about himself and his family, concern that he seemed to be getting in over his head so quickly and so deeply.

He put the worries and concerns aside and took the advice he'd given Jessi—or, in the words of another Southerner, tomorrow was another day. Fictional or not, Scarlett O'Hara's personal mantra fit the situation like a glove.

Hold was right, Jessi decided, although she'd never admit it to his face. But she did feel a little sore, and while she intended to be well used again before tomorrow, she wanted to draw it out, savor him and what he brought her. What she brought him, she recalled with a smile. And wasn't it incredible knowing the man couldn't keep his hands off her?

All she had to do was meet his eyes and she could see that he wanted her. It sent a punch of lust rushing through her to ache in places that, well, already ached. Incredible, too, that she could want him so desperately when she'd already had him. Twice. And she'd taken him the second time. She'd slipped her body over his, taken him inside her, and pushed him over the edge.

For a woman with a nearly eight-year-old son, it shouldn't have been such a novelty, but there was so much joy singing through her that she refused to feel self-conscious over her lack of experience. Hold had made no secret of what he'd felt, and what he'd felt, even if it was only physical, was enough.

Especially since it was only physical, she reminded herself, and refused to let even that reality color her mood. She'd be foolish to fall in love with a man who'd arrived on the island with a round-trip ticket, and she'd be damned if she'd be foolish. Not a second time. She pulled on the yoga pants she'd brought into the bathroom with her, topped them with a stretchy tank, then rolled her eyes because she realized she'd dressed for Hold.

At least she wouldn't be walking back into the room naked, but when she opened the door and his eyes, filled with heat, shifted to her, she began to think naked might have been the way to go. A glance at the clock told her it was barely noon, and then she did feel . . . decadent, she decided. It would be decadent to spend the day in bed, especially when she had so much to do.

It took a lot of willpower with Hold watching her like a starving man at a smorgasbord, but she dragged herself to her closet and dug out an old, oversized sweatshirt that fell past her hips when she put it on.

Hold climbed out of bed, gloriously naked, and said, "That's not going to stop me, sugar."

A hand on the chest did. "I have to walk tomorrow, remember?" she stuttered, because skin to skin with Hold wreaked havoc on her self-control.

He wrapped his fingers around her wrist, lifted her hand and placed a kiss in her cupped palm, a soft, sweet, heavenly kiss. But the devil was still in his eyes. Tempting her.

Digging deep, Jessi stepped back and away. "I left you a towel and washcloth. As for soap and shampoo, I'm afraid I don't have anything manly in the house. You can use mine or Benji's."

"Yours'll do just fine, sugar."

His deep, smooth voice, the way he focused so intently on her, made her heart want to flutter. She simply took a long, slow breath, and let it out just as slowly when he'd gone into the bathroom.

"Food," she muttered firmly when her imagination tried to take her into the shower with him. She sat to pull on a pair of thick socks before she rose again and walked out of her bedroom. She left the bed as it was because she couldn't take much more temptation, and the twist and tumble of covers would only take her back there, with Hold.

She stepped into the hallway and stopped, her gaze drawn up the stairs to the attic. Maybe it was Hold, allowing herself to face and conquer a fear, that had her considering other challenges she'd been putting off.

By the time Hold had finished his shower she'd set the stage, and when she heard him step out into the hallway she called out, "Up here."

Hold came up into the attic at the top of the stairs and stopped, stuffing his hands in his pockets and rocking back on his heels. "Interesting place for a picnic," he said, surveying the fresh fruit, cheese and crackers, and small sandwiches laid out on a throw from the back of the couch.

She patted the floor next to her. "Come on over. I'll peel you a grape."

Hold eased onto the throw-covered floor, lounging on his side with his head resting on a crooked elbow. "Why do I feel like there's a lot of physical activity in my immediate future? And not in a good way."

"You want me to put my mother to rest, right?"

"No, Jess. I think you should live your life, not hers."

She nodded, looked around the attic, crowded with boxes and old furniture—the flotsam and jetsam of a house inhabited by several generations of a family. "This is my way of doing that, Hold. I've been meaning to clean out this place, put her things away once and for all."

"Then I'm your man, sugar," he said.

Jessi bobbled the grapes she'd picked up.

"Food first," she said, feeling like the worst kind of fool. Hold had used a figure of speech, and so much hope rose in her she all but choked on it.

She handed him the grapes and got to her feet, too wrought suddenly, too afraid he'd see it on her face, in her eyes. He'd back off. She'd have chased him off, she amended.

He wanted to take it a day at a time. Despite her recent attack of happy-ever-after-itis she agreed.

It was just the upheaval in her life, she told herself. With Lance back, Eugenia's mystery, and her own likely place in it, who wouldn't want someone to lean on? And Hold—well, he had a nice, sturdy set of shoulders. And maybe he'd offered them, but she'd spent a lot of years relying on herself. It wasn't a habit she should break now. That didn't mean she couldn't grab some happiness while she had the chance.

"Jessica?"

She glanced over, fielded Hold's beautiful, unconcerned smile, and gave him one back, relieved that he'd missed her upset. "Sorry, I guess I'm still a little anxious about this."

And a little scattered, she thought, running her fingers along the dusty top of an old dresser before pulling the top drawer open, finding only more dust and cobwebs.

"Come on over here and have something to eat. You're going to need your energy, too," he said, and she could hear the wicked humor in his voice, even if she chose not to look at him.

Hold, clearly not a man to be sidetracked, caught her hand as she wandered by, pulling her down onto his lap. He kissed her sweetly, a kiss tasting of chocolate, as if he wasn't enough of a temptation.

"You feeling awkward?" he said.

Jessi tensed, then forced herself to relax, to swallow back the instant denial. "I am, a little," she said instead.

Hold kissed her again, longer, deeper this time, pulling her back to the edge of that blurry line where she let go of thought, of control. Of caution.

She nudged him back. "You keep doing that," she said, "and I think I'll be cured."

"Glad to help, sugar."

"I hope you can still say that in a few hours." She climbed out of his lap and this time he rose as well.

"I have to admit I'm a little..."

When he trailed off, Jessi turned to look at him, and saw his eyes focused on an old bed in a far corner of the attic. No doubt it would be full of dust and god knew what else, but she had to admit it looked romantic and inviting in the soft light from the rain-washed gable window.

"Don't get any ideas," she said, as much to herself as to Hold.

"Sugar, I've had ideas since I laid eyes on you."

Really good ideas, she'd bet, as she'd already had a demonstration. She only gave him a long, steady look.

Hold sighed. "What do you want me to do?"

Hands on her hips, Jessi did a slow spin. The place had been kept pretty neat for a dumping ground; the house didn't boast a lot of square footage, despite its three stories. And the family, over the generations, had learned how to make the best of what they had.

"You know," Hold said, "There are some really beautiful things up here. Besides you."

Because she felt the heat rising to her cheeks, Jessi turned away.

Hold turned her back. "It's a pure shame a girl as pretty as you isn't used getting compliments."

"Hold," she said softly.

"Jessica," he said, leaning in.

She placed her hand on his chest, felt his heart beating hard under her palm. And with hers beating just as hard, she didn't even dare kiss him.

Hold covered her hand with his, dropped a kiss on her forehead, then stepped back and pushed up his sleeves.

"So, where do we start?"

Jessi indicated the boxes taking up most of the center of the room. "After my mom...I just boxed her things up." Because going through them would have been impossible so soon after losing her. Throwing out or giving away would still hurt, but maybe, she thought, enough time had passed so her heart wouldn't break. "Some of it I'll want to keep, but I'll need to find a place to put it."

Hold started shifting boxes. "Some of this furniture should be cleaned and used. Or you could have a hell of a garage sale."

"Meeker would love that. He's been trying to get in here for years, but my Mom would never part with anything." Jessi picked her way to an old sea chest. "Maybe I can clean this out and use it for my mother's things," she said, sinking down to sit on the floor with a sigh.

Likely every preceding generation had said and done the same, she mused, clearing out the old to make way for the new. It made her sad to think about what might be lost, but her New England forebears would frown on accumulation for sentiment's sake.

She opened the trunk and found it filled with old clothes, carefully folded and layered with what must have been cedar chips, although they'd long since lost most of their scent.

"This old dresser you were poking at earlier seems to be mostly empty already," Hold said from the other side of the attic.

"Yeah," Jessi said absently, tickled to discover a few odds and ends from her own childhood that her mother must have packed away. A little poignant, maybe, but nothing Jessi couldn't part with.

She grabbed one of the garbage bags she'd brought up with their meal and began to stuff it with clothes as she pulled them out of the trunk.

It took forever, or at least it felt like it, before she pulled out the last item, wrapped in protective paper and tied with a faded paisley ribbon. Somebody had taken some time, some care, she realized, pulling back a corner of the flowered paper to reveal a baby blanket, pink and soft when she ran her hand over it.

It made her sad, knowing Benji would probably be an only child. She'd always wanted a daughter, but she'd have taken either variety gladly, she thought wistfully, rubbing the blanket against her cheek and remembering that baby smell, powder and formula, the first smile, first word, first step. The first hug, those thin little arms clinging to her neck.

And dwelling on it only hurt her more.

She began to smooth the paper back into place, stopped when she spied a deeper pink. She eased the paper back and froze, just her eyes shooting to Hold where he was investigating boxes at the far end of the attic.

Her gaze shifted back, ran over the three embroidered letters—initials, she corrected, a large, ornate S, flanked by a smaller E on the left and an A on the right.

S, she mused, running a finger over the fine stitching that hadn't been done by any machine. The edging of the blanket had to be silk, not polyester, but the letters kept gnawing at her, especially the S. The larger size likely indicated a surname, but she could recall no surnames starting with S in the family lineage, at least not that she knew of...

And it hit her.

Stanhope.

E for Eugenia, and A must be for Eugenia's middle name. She'd have bet her life on it...

Her life.

Benji.

Stunned, terrified, she pulled the paper and ribbon back around the blanket and stuffed it into the trunk. She shoved the garbage bag full of clothes on top of it and shut the lid, jerking her hands back.

"What?"

Jessi tried to stand, made it halfway before her legs gave out. She sank down onto the chest, her mind spinning.

"Jessica?" Hold came over and took her hands, the hands she'd been wringing. "Tell me what's wrong."

She shook her head. So much had changed, and now this. She could be related to Eugenia Stanhope, and that put her—and Benji—in danger.

She flew into Hold's arms, just wrapped herself around him and held on. He slipped one arm around her waist, tipped back her chin with the other so she had no choice but to look into his face. And lie to him.

"I can't...I'm not ready for this, Hold."

"I can see that, sugar, and feel it. You're shaking."

And that was a pretty extreme reaction to sorting through her mother's possessions. If Hold wasn't questioning it yet, he would be if she didn't get a handle on it.

She kissed him as lightly as she could manage when it felt like her world was crashing in on her. Then she pulled free, bending to gather up the remains of their picnic. Hold took the tray from her. She picked up the throw and followed him out, pausing as she pulled the door shut behind her, cool relief washing over her when she heard the lock click into place.

And yeah, she felt terrible, lying to Hold, or at least keeping the truth from him, even more terrible hiding behind the memory of a woman who'd always been straightforward and honest. Still, she knew her mother would understand the imperative to protect.

And if she was being brutally honest with herself, she wanted time. With Hold. Time that didn't center around the search for Eugenia.

She was stealing that time, Jessi knew. Telling Hold about the blanket now meant shattering this little bubble of happiness and peace she'd allowed herself. It meant bringing reality back in, calling everything she'd ever believed about herself into question.

She really didn't want Hold digging into her family history until she'd had a chance to work her own mind around it all. She tended to be emotionally driven, but just now she needed to put her feelings aside and think logically about ramifications and repercussions—for herself and Benji. To take a good hard look at her life and begin to make adjustments.

She'd only keep the blanket a secret for a day, she rationalized—less than a day, really, just an afternoon.

And a night.

Soft gray light and the sound of running water dragged Hold halfway to consciousness. He pulled a pillow over his head and cursed the guest in the next room...except, he thought as the fuzz of sleep began to fade and his wits to sharpen, he wasn't at the Horizon. He was at Jessi's house, in Jessi's bed.

Alone.

He flopped over onto his back, blinked eyes that felt like they were full of sand, and figured he must be getting old when the temptation to drift off nearly outweighed the reality of a naked, wet, willing woman just feet away.

But then, he thought with a lazy grin, the naked, willing woman had spent the night in his arms, and there'd been precious little sleep. He sat up, groaning a little as sore muscles protested. A few steps took him to the door of the tiny bathroom off the barely bigger master bedroom.

He walked into the billowing steam, eased back the shower curtain printed with swimming fish and shining suns, and stepped into the tub. And just took a moment to enjoy.

Jessi stood under the spray, her petite little body slicked with water and soap, her face lifted into the spray as she rinsed her hair.

Hold ran a finger down the trail of bubbles running along the elegant length of her spine. Just as he got to some interesting territory, she shrieked and whirled around, brandishing a plastic bottle like a club.

Hold lifted his hands, palms out. "Please don't squirt me to death."

She put the conditioner beside the shampoo, on a little shelf built into the tile. "I thought you were sleeping."

"Not anymore." He grinned. "But I'm having a hard time waking up."

"Hmmmm. I can see that."

"Then I'm too far away," he said, and would've remedied the situation if Jessi hadn't set a hand on his chest.

Instead of nudging him back, she used it to steady herself while she lifted to her toes and kissed him in a cloud of warm spray and lemon that must have come from her soap or shampoo. The scent of it, of her, went straight to his head. Not so much, though, that he failed to notice her hand drifting down, over his belly, and lower—

Hold caught it before she could divert any more of the blood supply from his brain. The long night didn't seem to have sated his hunger for her. He wanted her just as desperately this morning, but the new day brought what might be the end to their affair. Benji would be back before long, and with him Jessi's sense of obligation to an idealized version of motherhood.

Now, this moment, he intended to commit to memory every glorious inch of her, to savor each sigh and moan, the way her body fit to his and how she gave so sweetly. So when she wanted to dive in to another kiss, when her hands were everywhere, when she plastered her wet, invitingly slippery body against his, he said, "What's your hurry?"

"My really small hot water heater," she murmured back.

"If you can tell how hot the water is, I'm doing something wrong again," Hold said, his voice strained when she curled her fingers around him, her other hand slipping down to cup him.

"Tell me that when you have icicles hanging off your—"

He silenced her with a kiss, his mouth brushing hers once, twice, then deepening to mate, to war as she kissed him back with a hunger that staggered him. He boosted her up; she wrapped her legs and arms around him, threw her head back when he took her breast into his mouth, when he sucked hard as he slipped inside her. He braced her against the wall, both hands under her backside. She hissed out her breath—the coldness of the tile, he decided—then drew it back in when he started to move.

When she breathed again, it was on a moan, and the moan was his name. Her lips were against his neck, and the sound of her pleasure seemed to resonate through him, to mix with the feel of her against him, around him. The scent of lemon, the heat of the water beating down on him, and the pleasure winding, tighter and tighter until it felt like every bit of him was drawn together into one single point of heat and light, burning like the sun inside him.

When Jessi gasped, when he felt her orgasm tear through her, that sun exploded, filling him with that light, that heat, and so much ecstasy he could only stand there and let it fill him. Let her fill him, he thought as the waves of pleasure ebbed, softened, and left him standing there under the cooling spray of Jessi's shower, with her draped limply over him and his legs threatening to give out any second.

"Jessica," he said, the word little more than a rusty scrape of sound rattling its way out of his burning throat.

She seemed to get the message, though—at least she stirred enough to unwind her legs from around his waist. Her arms stayed around his neck, even after her feet touched down. She held on, swaying a little and making him laugh since he was hardly steadier.

What he was, Hold decided, was freezing.

"Just in the nick of time," Jessi said, even her voice shivering. She lifted her arms from around his neck, wrapped them around herself instead until she stepped out of the shower and pulled a big, fluffy towel around her shoulders.

She tossed him a smile and hurried into the bedroom. The faint sound of dresser drawers opening and closing floated to him over the hiss of the shower head. He didn't feel the water go to ice, still dazzled by her smile, by the joy she sparked in him. Emotions tangled up inside him—

too many to sort out—but for one that ran through all
the others, a bright thread leading him to one undeniable
conclusion. No matter what else happened, they weren't
finished with one another, he and Jessi. Not by a long
shot.

Ravenous, Jessi opened her fridge and grabbed some eggs
while she listened to the water running overhead. That
shower had to be ice cold, she thought, but if Hold felt
half as amazing as she did, he'd never notice the chill.

And amazing, she decided, didn't even come close.
The word hadn't been invented that described how she
felt. Her body actually ... *hummed* was the best she could
come up with. She felt relaxed, happy.

She and Hold were ... She didn't know what they were,
but she wasn't going to waste any time or effort trying to
label it, either. No expectations. She'd promised herself
that last night. No hoping, no planning, one day at a time
because, she knew, odds were high there'd be no future
with Hold Abbot. Even so, it would hurt when he left.

But she knew how that felt.

Still, she didn't love Hold—and if the word *yet* popped
into her mind, well, she thought as she cracked eggs into
a bowl, hearts broke every day. And then they healed.

She'd been through that before, too. And she'd survived it—survived and thrived. She'd get through it again,
if she had to.

Hold slipped his arms around her waist, wrapped his
big body around hers, and whispered in her ear, "I hope
you're making omelets, sugar," which she barely heard
over the sudden lurch and pound of her pulse.

She tipped her face to his, smiling, even if she couldn't

quite meet his eyes. "I had a feeling. Any particular preference on what you want in yours?"

"Whatever you were having a couple weeks ago that smelled like Heaven. Although I have to point out it didn't smell as good as you do right now." He nuzzled her neck, and the pleasant little tune that had been humming through her body shimmied its way up to a peppy salsa.

She nudged Hold back, although it was the last thing she wanted to do. "If you want to eat any time soon, I'll need something besides eggs."

He stepped back. "Food now," he said and added a wicked grin to his raised hands, "and later—"

"Work," Jessi said firmly.

"Work?" His hands lowered, his grin notched down to devilish. "Now I'm work, huh?"

"In a sense," she teased. "I have a lot to catch up on, and since you were the distraction, you get to help."

"What makes you think I won't be a distraction today?"

"Because if you are I'll have to kick you out."

His hands went up in that warding gesture again, although this time it was meant to say, *I'm innocent.* "No distracting going on here. Though I have to point out that I didn't do it on purpose."

"I know," Jessi said on a sigh. She chose bottles from her spice rack, sprinkling in a little oregano, some parsley, just a touch of garlic into the eggs. "You can't help yourself. You're like catnip, not to cats, of course, but you can ask any adult female and I think they'll all agree you're pretty irresistible."

Hold stuffed his hands in his pockets, grinned. "Catnip, huh?"

"As if you didn't know," she muttered, sending him a look that wiped the smug expression off his face. "You're well aware you can get any woman you want into bed, and I'm including the happily married and the way-past-romance groups."

"Nobody is ever past romance," Hold said.

"In my imagination they are." Jessi set an omelet pan on the burner, sidestepped to get a hunk of parmesan out of the fridge. She dropped four slices of bread into the toaster, then handed Hold the butter dish and a knife.

"Plates are there," she said to him, indicating the cupboard. "Glasses next to the sink, juice in the fridge. Make yourself useful."

"Sugar, you don't know how useful I want to be."

"I think I have an idea," Jessi said, "but how about we have breakfast first."

The omelet tasted every bit as good as it smelled, and took about two minutes to wolf down, after which Jessi took to her feet, whisking around the kitchen to put things away and pile dishes into a sinkful of hot, soapy water.

To avoid him, Hold decided.

He caught her on one of her mad dashes, pulled her close, kissed her. Stepped back. "Again with the hand on the chest," he said, wrapping his fingers around her wrist. "Jessica."

She looked up, met his eyes for the first time that morning. "Hold. Benji is coming home... Well, I don't know exactly when."

And she didn't want him walking in on the two of them in an awkward situation. "You don't think Maggie will call and warn you?"

"It may not occur to her."

And she needed to establish some distance. He understood that—even if he didn't like it.

"So," he plucked the omelet pan out of the dish drainer, snagged a towel from the stove handle, and set to drying as she washed. "What's this paperwork you threatened me with? Or would you rather tackle the attic today?"

"Paperwork, definitely," she said, adding quickly with a fleeting glance into his face, "It has to get done." She shrugged. "The attic has waited this long."

"It can wait a bit longer," Hold finished for her, but he was puzzled.

Dealing with her mother's things had to be so much harder in reality than in theory, so he understood how she could be gung-ho one minute and shaking the next.

Seeing her still so skittish about it today surprised him. Jessi was a woman of deep feelings. She was open with her body and with her heart—sexy, warm, and loving, but not one to let sentiment drive her. She was a pragmatist. A realist. A single mother had to be both, he figured.

Still, she was a woman, and if he'd learned one thing in his life, there was no accounting for the moods of women.

Chapter Sixteen

Lance unwrapped one arm from around his middle, juggling the gift for Benji he'd hidden under his coat so he could knock.

Jessi opened the front door, her smile fading away when she saw him. Not the reaction he wanted from her, but he knew how to be patient.

"Is Benji around?" He looked past her, but instead of his son he spied Hold Abbot sitting at her little table. "What's he doing here?"

"Hello to you, too, Lance," Jessi said.

"Where's Benji?"

"He spent the night at Maggie's."

Lance opened his mouth, snapped it shut. He considered himself an expert on body language; he'd learned to read people well enough to keep his ass out of a sling during his years on the road, even to make a killing once in a while.

Add in that he'd known Jessi since they were kids, and

he didn't need to see her cross her arms and raise her brows to know he was treading on boggy ground. He had a lot to lose, he reminded himself. But he was too angry to listen.

Abbot sat at Jessi's table like he owned the place, watching them with a half-smile and narrowed eyes—amused but protective. Proprietary. They'd had sex. If Lance had been in any doubt, the flush on Jessi's cheeks would have confirmed it. She'd spread her legs for Abbot, those legs he could still feel wrapped around him, that would be wrapped around him again. No matter what he had to do to make it happen.

He took a breath, felt as if knives were stabbing into his chest. It should be him sleeping beside her, living in her house like he belonged there. Because he did.

He had to fight off the haze of fury, but fight he did, until he could focus, until he could think. He had plans, big plans. Much as he wanted to smash Hold Abbot's face in, if anything happened to the asshole Lance would be Suspect Number One. No, Hold Abbot was safe from him, but Lance would see to it Jessi made him suffer when she dumped his ass.

"You're early," Jessi said.

"Yeah," Lance shot back, then pulled himself back enough to say, "yes," on a heavy exhale. Jessi wasn't the sweet, malleable girl he'd left behind eight years ago, and he had a goal that wouldn't be accomplished by ruffling her feathers. Nor would he reach it with Hold Abbot standing in his way. "It wasn't my intention to catch you off guard, Jess, but, well, do you really think it's a good for him to be here when Benji isn't around? I mean, the talk…"

"What talk?"

"He's not here doing paperwork."

Jessi half turned, glanced back at Hold. "At the moment he is."

"Tell me he wasn't here last night." And although he'd kept his voice even and his tone non-accusatory, she fired up. "I'm not passing judgment, Jess. I'm thinking about Benji."

"And I'm not?" She shoved her hands back through her hair, barely holding onto her temper. But he could see the guilt in her eyes. "Do you really think you need to tell me—"

A muffled yip sounded from somewhere around Lance's midsection.

Jessi's eyes dropped to his coat, wriggling like he'd stuffed a dozen snakes inside.

"What the hell is that," she demanded, and Lance gave up any hope of softening her up.

He opened his coat, pulled out a small black and white, flop-eared puppy, and set it down on the floor. It squatted immediately and peed.

Jessi marched into the kitchen, coming back with a roll of paper towels and a spray bottle.

"Windex?"

"Shut up." She thrust the roll of paper towels at him. "I don't have any pet cleaner because I don't have a pet. Clean that up, then you can go. And take that," she pointed at the pup, currently gamboling over to sniff at Hold's shoes, "with you."

Lance hunkered down, swiping half-heartedly at the puddle on the wide planks of the floor. "A boy should have a dog," he grumbled resentfully.

"A boy should have a lot of things."

"Like a father?"

Jessi snatched the towels from him, mopped up the puddle in a few economical strokes, sprayed the Windex on the damp spot, then wiped again with fresh towels. "You can't win his trust in five minutes, Lance, and you can't buy his love with a puppy."

"I just want to give him a gift, Jess."

"Legos are a gift. The latest animated movie on DVD is a gift. A dog is a commitment, and not just for Benji."

"I'll help."

"For how long?"

"How long do you think Loverboy is going to stick around?"

"I don't know. He hasn't made me any promises. And just for the record? I haven't asked him for any."

"He just wanted in your bed."

"My bed, and who's in it, are none of your business."

"On this island? I think everyone would say it's their business, and I'm inclined to agree."

"Well, you can make it your business, and you can make sure the rest of the town is talking, but who do you think is really going to pay?"

Lance snorted. "You'll make sure Benji knows it's my fault everyone is talking about you, but it's not your fault for f—"

"Careful," Hold said, voice lazy, body language still relaxed right down that fucking smirk on his face.

And yet Lance had no doubt Hold was ready to back up the threat in his voice.

"This isn't about Hold and me," Jessi said. "It's about you and Benji, and me, Lance. You should have asked me first."

"It's from me, not you."

"Yeah, and it's for Benji. But who do you think is going to take it out to pee in the middle of the night? Who's going to feed it and pay the vet bills?"

"He's already had his shots," Lance said, then stopped long enough to unclench his jaw. "He's been neutered, and I have everything he needs: food, toys, bed. I didn't bring it now, but I'll drop it by later."

Jessi started to say something, ended up just shaking her head.

"Whatever it is, just say it, Jessi."

"What's the point when you won't hear me?"

Yeah, Lance decided, he'd miscalculated. Benji didn't seem to be warming up to him, at least not fast enough to suit his needs. He'd hoped the puppy would help...and maybe it still would because, unless he was a complete moron, the roar of the engine he heard was Maggie's Mustang.

Lance met Jessi's eyes, but he had no choice, really. She'd already made it clear there'd be nothing between them. Except their son. They could have been a family again; instead she was making Benji into the rope of a tug-of-war contest. Lance had been on an eight-year losing streak that had started the day he'd knocked Jessi up; he sure as hell wasn't going to let her beat him now.

As soon as Maggie turned the car off, Benji was out and rushing up to hug him—at least until he saw the puppy. The kid froze then, his eyes going to his mother, his little face, so like hers, shining with hope.

Lance could see that Jessi wanted to hold a hard line, but even as he told himself she'd never pull it off, her expression folded into lines of resignation.

Maggie, wearing a dark blue flight suit and a battered leather flight jacket, climbed out of the car. Lance fielded a long, cold stare from her before Jessi waved her off. "You've got a flight."

"Yeah, I'm already running late. I'll talk to you when I get back from Portland," Maggie said. She sent Lance one last glare before she jumped back into the Mustang and roared off.

"Mom," Benji breathed out, already hunching down and laughing as the puppy jumped on him and licked his face, then climbed on top of him when Benji collapsed onto the floor.

It was kind of cute, Lance decided.

He crouched down next to the tangle of boy and puppy. "What do you think, Benj?" He reached out a hand, only to jerk it back when the pup nipped his fingers. "You'll want to teach him not to chew on stuff." Like people, Lance thought. He kept the irritation off his face, but he reached out and gave the dog a swat that sent it ass over teakettle.

The pup scrambled back up and growled—stupid, flea-bitten mutt. He'd carried it around in his warm coat, gave it a good home, and this was the thanks he got? "You'll have to name him. If your Mom lets you keep him."

Jessi sent him a look, narrow-eyed, simmering, but this wasn't about her, any more than it was about getting dog hair inside his good coat. It was about him, Lance thought, getting what he wanted, what he deserved.

"*You* got him for me?" Benji said, finally clueing in. He climbed to his feet, watching his mom, unsure.

Jesus, she was raising the kid to be a complete pussy.

"Can I, Mom?"

"We've talked about this, Benj. Having a dog is a huge responsibility."

"I'll walk him and feed him and play with him, I swear I will." Benji spied the paper towels and Windex in his mother's hands, and his face fell. "I'll clean up after him when he has an accident, Mom, 'cuz he will until he knows—until I teach him what to do."

"I got him on the mainland," Lance said when Jessi didn't respond. "So if he has to go back—"

"If he has to go back, you'll take him," she snapped, but she pulled Benji over and gave him a hug. "You promise you'll take care of him? No whining when he has to go out, no matter what you're in the middle of?"

Benji made a huge X over his heart. "I promise."

She sighed. "Then I guess you'll have to come up with a name for him."

Benji whooped, running around in circles with his hands fisted in the air. The puppy chased him, slipping on the wood floor and tumbling head over heels before it scrambled back up.

Smiling but sure to keep it indulgent rather than smug, Lance started to peel out of his coat.

"It's not two o'clock yet," Jessi said.

"But—"

"Two o'clock," Jessi repeated, with no room for compromise.

Lance might have pushed the issue, but Hold got to his feet and stood by the table.

Lance pulled his coat back on. But, he assured himself, Jessi wouldn't always have a big, strong man around to protect her. Then the gloves would come off. It was the only option Jessi had left him.

He'd tried groveling, tried playing the game by her rules, and God knew he'd ingratiated himself—to her and the kid. Even the charm that had kept him from total failure the last eight years had failed to weasel him into her good graces.

The years had made Jessi strong. His betrayal had made her suspicious. And time had grown short.

Lance no longer had the luxury of taking the time to win her trust—even if he'd had the patience for it. He'd been brought back to Windfall for a reason, and he'd arrived armed with a goal of his own. If Jessi couldn't be convinced to help him, he'd have to find another way to accomplish that goal. And he would accomplish it, no matter what it took.

Jessi shut the door behind Lance and just leaned on it for a second before she turned around to face her new reality.

Benji still wrangled with the puppy, the pair of them rolling on the floor with the puppy nipping at Benji's ears, licking his face, and Benji laughing so hard he could barely breathe. Maybe the puppy was a good idea after all; it would give Benji something positive to focus on.

She just wished it hadn't come from Lance. Jealousy, she knew; resentment. But still, she didn't trust Lance. She'd tried to convince herself it was only the natural outcome of their history, but she just couldn't shake the feeling he was up to no good—over and above the obvious trouble he could cause.

At the very least, Lance had forced her hand. If he spread gossip about her and Hold, sooner or later it would be thrown in Benji's face—not by adults, but then adults weren't always careful about what they said in front of children.

Taking a deep breath, she looked over, met Hold's eyes. "Would you mind taking the puppy out?"

"I think we should talk first."

Jessi exhaled heavily, all her energy seeming to drain out with her breath. When Hold walked into the kitchen, she followed him, thinking, right, first she had to deal with Hold so she'd know what to say to her son.

"You're going to tell me we're through," he said the minute they were safely out of earshot of Benji.

Jessi rubbed her hands over her face, and while she understood Hold's anger, on the heels of everything else she'd been through in the last twenty-four hours, it simply exhausted her.

"The line is," Hold said, "*it's been fun.*"

"Are you a mind reader now?"

"I don't have to be when you've made your thoughts so clear."

"So we wouldn't have to do this," she said, then instantly reined in her temper.

Hold got to his feet, slipped his hands in his pockets like he did when he was amused or upset—or waging a battle within himself, just as she was.

"Don't you think you're selling Benji short?" he said after a moment, his voice calmer even if his words stung. "He's a child, but he's not fragile, Jess. People come into your life and go out of it for any number of reasons, and sometimes there's hurt. He needs to understand that, and to learn how to deal with it."

"He's already learned about people coming and going, Hold. Mostly going. Isn't that enough?"

"It's a tough break, Jessi, but it doesn't mean you have to wrap him in cotton wool. Or close yourself off."

That's exactly what it meant, Jessi thought, and that's exactly what she was doing. And so what? She'd been hurt, and badly. She wouldn't apologize for trying to protect herself, and her son. "Why is everyone trying to tell me how to raise him suddenly?"

Hold pulled his hands out of his pockets, shoved them back in. A muscle in his jaw bunched, released, bunched. "You're right," he finally said. "I'm sorry it came out that way. It's just... I know you're regretting last night—"

"I'm not." She went to him, laid her hand on his arm, tensed and hard as rock. "Last night was incredible, Hold. I wouldn't trade one minute of it. I just don't know how to explain it to my son."

"You think telling him we're not together is the answer? What will that matter if this becomes fodder for the town gossips? Will it make things better that I was barely here long enough to..." He shoved both hands back through his dark blond hair. "Hell, I don't know what, Jess, but shouldn't we figure it out before we throw it away?"

Yes, she thought immediately—although a part of her, the weak part, said *No*. It would be so much wiser to say good-bye to him now than to risk falling in love with him. She was already halfway there—

His arms came around her, and she just went into them, let herself be held.

"Remember, you asked for it," she said, taking him by the hand and pulling him out to the living room with her. "Hold and I want to talk to you about something, Benj," she said to her son.

Benji sat up, gathering the puppy into his lap. With one hand scratching the pup's head, Benji looked from her to Hold and back again. "He's your boyfriend, right? Auntie Maggie told me Hold wanted to be your boyfriend."

Jessi realized her mouth was hanging open, and closed it. She looked over at Hold. He just shrugged.

"Um...Is that okay with you?" she said to Benji.

"Sure." He sounded like it was no big deal, but he kept his gaze on the puppy, which gave a huge yawn, then tugged half-heartedly at Benji's pant leg.

Laughing, he carefully shooed the dog away, and for the second time in her life Jessi had a reason to be grateful to Lance. Whatever his ulterior motives in bringing the dog, it was just the right thing for Benji.

"Is there anything you want to ask us?"

This time he did look up, and Jessi could see that he wasn't as certain as he'd pretended to be. "Are you going to kiss and stuff?"

Hold settled on the floor next to Benji. He picked up the pup and settled it in the crook of his arm, where it promptly fell asleep. "We're going to be spending time together, Ben," Hold said, "And when I say we, I mean all three of us."

"So, you're like dating us both?"

"In a way. Your mom is a package deal, kiddo, and I'll be kissing her from time to time, if that's okay with you. And there'll be times when it's just going to be the two of us.

"You and me?" Hold continued. "I'd like us to be friends, and that means sometimes it'll just be you and me, 'cause us men, we have to stick together."

Benji's little frown faded into a smile. He took the pup

back, cradling it in his lap. "Want to help me name him?" he said to Hold.

"What about me?" Jessi said, although she had to swallow first to get the words past the lump in her throat. *How did Hold always know the right thing to say? And what had she done to deserve such a sweet kid?* "Don't I get to help?"

Benji shook his head solemnly. "He's a man, too."

"Great, already outnumbered." Jessi braced her hands on her hips, put on her best stern Mom face. "Don't get any ideas about pulling out the video games. It's lunchtime. Then there are chores to be done." And Lance to deal with in a couple of hours.

"Don't we get a vote?" Benji asked, his conniving little brain already calculating the balance of power with two men in the house.

Hold boosted Benji to his feet, then climbed upright himself. "C'mon, son," he said, "I'll explain a few things to you. First, you need to keep an eye on that puppy, because as soon as he wakes up, he'll want to piddle. Sure, laugh now," Hold added as Benji did just that, "but you won't be too happy cleaning up after him. Especially if he pees on one of your mother's rugs, and for some reason they always hit the rugs.

"Second," Hold continued, "I think it's time you learned about women. Now, when your mother said she was outnumbered, that doesn't mean this is a democracy."

"What's a democracy?"

Jessi went into the kitchen to put together some lunch, the lump that had been in her throat moving down to ache in her chest. She couldn't make out the words coming from her living room, but as she listened to the voices, one deep and filled with warmth and humor, the other young and filled with ease and trust, a little more of her heart fell at Hold Abbot's feet.

She served them canned soup and ham sandwiches, and kept her eye on the sunflower-shaped clock Benji had given her for Mother's Day.

"You didn't eat a thing," Hold said to her once Benji had finished and raced off to take the puppy out. "And the only time you spoke was to tell Ben not to feed the dog at the table."

Jessi tried a smile, and knew she'd failed when Hold didn't smile back.

"You worried about Benji?"

"No." Jessi stood, but before she could gather the remains of their lunch, Hold took her by the hand and tugged until she came close enough for him to wrap his arms around her waist and rest his head just under her chin.

When he did something like this, she thought, something so warm and loving, he made it nearly impossible for her to keep things in perspective.

"Tell me what's wrong," he said. His breath feathered across her skin, and for a moment all the stress and worry faded away.

"I wish we could stay like this..." she almost added *forever*, before she caught herself.

"But?"

"But Lance is going to be here in a little while."

"And you'd rather I not be here?" Hold squeezed her slightly, then got to his feet.

She felt instantly tense and completely alone. And absolutely justified. "It's so hard for Benji. For me, too, but before...Benji wasn't sure which way to turn."

"Yeah," Hold sighed. "I saw it, too. I don't want him in the middle either, Jessica."

She didn't have words for what swelled in her heart, that he could be so empathetic and so generous. That he thought of her son first. So she kissed him on the forehead, then stepped back before the temptation to lower her mouth to his became too much to resist.

"Jessica," he began as he got to his feet. But instead of finishing his thought, he dropped a kiss on her mouth, a kiss that lingered even if it didn't deepen. "I'll see you tomorrow?"

"I'm already looking forward to it."

"I'll just tell Ben good-bye before I go."

Afraid she'd change her mind and keep Hold there if she saw him again, Jessi finished straightening up from lunch, staying in the kitchen to start dinner.

When Lance showed up twenty minutes later, the difference between the two men was so marked Jessi nearly thanked him for deserting her eight years before.

He strode in, chest puffed out as he made a big deal over the puppy *he'd* brought. Then, as if the earlier contention had never happened, he sniffed the air, complimented her cooking, and waited expectantly. And once he realized a dinner invitation wasn't coming his way, he wrangled an invitation to Benji's room instead.

With a sigh, she turned off the stove and followed them up the stairs.

"Seriously, Jess? You're going to look over my shoulder the whole time I'm here?"

Yes. But with Benji watching so closely, she didn't say

it. Showing distrust of Lance would only make it harder for Benji to be comfortable with his father.

"Leave the door open," she said, "and keep an eye on that puppy."

Once they were in Benji's room, she headed up to the attic. If she left the door open, she could hear Lance and Benji, and she only needed a couple of minutes.

She had to see the blanket again.

She went straight to the old sea chest, flipped the lid open, and pulled out the bag filled with clothes. With Hold in the house, she hadn't been able to get a thorough look at the blanket. Now she took it out of the paper and held it up to the light.

Anyone could have seen it was hand-knit, the work done by an extremely gifted hand. There was no label, and even though the stitches on the silk edging were tiny, they weren't perfect enough to have been done on a machine. Except for the embroidered initials, there was nothing to indicate it had belonged to Eugenia Stanhope. Except for the sinking feeling in her stomach.

"Jessi."

Her heart shot into her throat; her hands shook and fumbled. The crinkle of the paper as she jerked it back around the blanket sounded like thunder. She shot a glance at the door, even as she tossed the blanket back into the chest and shoved the plastic garbage bag back on top of it. She was just shutting the chest's lid when Lance appeared in the open attic doorway.

"What are you doing?" he asked.

"Cleaning."

His gaze dropped to the chest, lifted to her face again.

"I've been sorting through some of these old trunks and chests to make room for my mother's things."

"I'm sorry, Jess. I should have told you before. Your mom was an amazing woman."

"Yes, she was." And Lance had been the only person Doris Randal had ever spoken a bad word about. "I figured maybe Benji would want to move up here when he's a teenager. His room is so small, and he'll want privacy."

"Or you will."

Jessi rubbed at her temples, which did little to soothe the headache brewing there. "Not now, Lance," she murmured.

He stiffened, but she heard no anger in his voice as he looked around at the space, crammed with furniture and boxes. "It'll take years to clean this place out," he said. "I'd be happy to help, Jess. I mean it."

And she could see it on his face; she just wished she didn't wonder what his real motivation was. "You need to understand, Lance, we're never going to be what we were to each other as teenagers. We share a son, and that's all."

Something passed over his face, something hard that she might not have glimpsed if she hadn't been watching him so closely. It disappeared so swiftly, though, that she was left questioning her own eyes.

"I'm sorry to hear that," he said with what seemed to be real regret. "I hope we can be friends."

"That's up to you, Lance. Treat Benji well, and I don't see why you and I can't get along."

"Benji and I are going to be close," he said. "I guarantee it."

"Good," she said, and although she searched his face, she saw nothing but determination.

Chapter Seventeen

I don't see how we can fit that charter in." Jessi stood in front of the big wall calendar that served as Solomon Charters' flight schedule, arms crossed, at a loss as to why Maggie couldn't see her point when it was right there staring both of them in the face.

"We have to," Maggie said, maddeningly unshakable. "I already took the job."

"You're never answering the phones again."

"You really think we're going to talk about my schedule when I haven't heard how it went with Hold?" Maggie, her butt parked on the edge of Jessi's desk, completely ignored the fact that she'd agreed to a charter she had no way of doing without a clone and a second plane. "It must have gone pretty well, seeing as you probably wore him out so much he couldn't put in an appearance this morning."

Jessi continued to study the map, because it kept her back to Maggie. "Hold had some errands he needed to do in the village—dry cleaning, that sort of thing. And it went pretty much like you'd expect," she added casually.

"Then why are you so tense?"

Because of a tiny pink blanket with Eugenia Stanhope's initials embroidered on it. She should have told Maggie. She'd been arguing with herself all morning, had started and stopped a dozen times before she accepted that she just wasn't ready to talk about it yet.

She might be a Stanhope, and through her, Benji. At the moment, that truth rested with her, and while she trusted Maggie implicitly, telling her meant telling Dex. And Hold.

The minute they learned about the blanket, everything would change. She and Benji would be in danger, and Benji mattered more than anything else in her life.

"Jessi?"

She took a couple of deep breaths, forced herself to relax before she turned around. "It was amazing, Mags. Worth the wait."

"After an eight-year dry spell, I'm surprised you didn't scream the house down around your ears."

"It's a very sturdy house."

Maggie cracked a smile, the first one Jessi had seen from her in days. "I'd ask for details, but I'm a lady."

Jessi snorted. "Since when?"

"Okay, then give me details."

"Sure." She slapped the back of her hand on the map. "Just as soon as we get your schedule nailed down."

"I'd think you'd had enough nailing."

Jessi rolled her eyes, but she laughed, too. How could she not laugh when it was the highest Maggie's spirits had been in days?

"At least tell me what that jerk was doing at your house two hours early."

Jessi made a sound that conveyed all her frustration and irritation without using any actual cuss words. "He brought Benji a puppy," she began, and proceeded to give Maggie the rundown of her interchange with Lance, how she'd wound up keeping the puppy, and Benji's absolute diligence in taking care of it. "He named it Chewie. He and Hold named it Chewie," she amended. "Chewbacca, like in *Star Wars*. Don't ask me why when there's no resemblance. Except it's a puppy and he chews. A lot," she finished, thinking of the newly mangled corner of her favorite area rug, the table legs she'd had to pad and wind with tape just in case he got a taste for oak, and one of her favorite black pumps, which Chewie had somehow liberated from her bedroom closet and demolished into tiny leather scraps.

"Of course Lance didn't come through on his 'I-bought-everything-you-need' promise, so after he left Benji and I went to the market and got the basics, including something for Chewie to chew." Which had set off her temper, even if Benji had gotten a kick out of agonizing over just the right leash and chew toys.

"Ass," was Maggie's succinct comment. "Sucking-up ass."

"I don't think Benji got that. I mean, he's grateful to Lance for bringing Chewie, but..."

"In the end it was your decision. So you're really the one who gave him a puppy."

"Is it wrong of me to get just a little satisfaction out of that?"

"If it was me, I'd be in Lance's face, going na-na-na-na-na."

"Childish," Jessi decided, "but give me a minute to at least imagine it." And smile over it. "Especially since he raked me over the coals about Hold."

"He wouldn't be an ass if he didn't. And you can expect him to be an even bigger ass now, since you've made it clear you're not interested in him that way. And by the way, you're my hero."

"I'm kind of proud of myself," Jessi said. Setting Lance straight on that score had been all too easy. Between Lance and Hold, there really was only one choice. "Let's not dwell on Lance's assitude," she decided.

"If we move the mail run here, I can take the charter," Maggie said, only too happy to change the subject—as long as she got to choose the subject.

"You have a run down to D.C. that day," Jessi reminded her, although they could both clearly see it marked on the calendar. "By the time you pick up the mail, the post office here will be closed. The mail will be a day late."

"And?"

"People will complain."

"Then *people* can find a way to get over to the mainland and pick it up themselves."

Jessi sighed, mostly because she envied Maggie that confidence. Maggie picked up the mail as a courtesy, sure, but everyone had come to expect it of her. And Windfallers weren't exactly shrinking violets when it came to voicing opinions. They weren't idiots, either. They had ample proof that anything they said to Maggie would only roll off her back. And they knew who really made Maggie's schedule.

"Moving the mail also means I don't have to move

back the marketing run, which," Maggie added pointedly, "I'm getting paid for."

"You won't have time to breathe over the next few days."

Maggie gave her one-shoulder shrug. "Suits me fine."

Jessi's heart went out to her. She'd always been a loner, always content with her life as long as she could fly. Now, well, any fool with two eyes could see Maggie was pining. And even if Jessi was the only person in the world who could have said that to her face, she wouldn't. "When's Dex coming back?"

Maggie took to her feet, pacing the office. A sure sign she was unhappy. "I don't know. He's not having much luck getting in to see the Stanhopes."

"Even with Alec helping?" Jessi asked, referring to Dex's long-time friend, Alec Barclay, who'd sent him to Windfall Island in the first place. Alec served as attorney— or at least one of them—to the Stanhope family.

"Alec has to be careful. He represents the family's business concerns, so it's a conflict of interest for him to assist Dex."

"I thought the Stanhope family sent Dex."

"They did, to investigate Windfall Island. It appears they aren't very happy to have his attention turned in their direction. Alec has a professional relationship with all of them, so he's keeping out of this right now."

"Keeping out of what?"

Jessi's gaze swung to the door, then met Maggie's when she found Paige Walker standing there, dressed to kill, from the top of her perfectly arranged blond hair to the tips of her toes, shod in something that was no doubt designer-made, probably by hand and exclusively for her. Still, her looks had helped get her on the Hollywood A-list, not to mention her talent. She employed both, pasting a bright, cheerfully snarky smile on her beautiful face, a smile that masked the hurt in her eyes when Maggie crossed her arms, took her time looking Paige over.

"I heard the outer door open, but I thought it was someone I'd actually want to see," Maggie said. She wore no smile but her tone had a bite to it that went a level beyond snark.

"You do like to sneak up on people," Jessi added.

"I've met Hold," Paige said with a casual wave of her hand. "Who's Alec?"

"Why? Haven't bagged your quota of men today?"

"Well," Paige said, her eyes narrowing over the smile she was fighting to keep in place. "Hold is off-limits."

Maggie crossed her arms. "And Dex is off island."

If Paige had been around any time in the last decade, she could have seen that Maggie was having fun. Instead, she squared her shoulders and put a haughty note in her voice. "Then I guess I'll have to wait to add him to my *quota*, at least until he returns and has time to dump you."

Grinning, Maggie started toward Paige. Jessi stepped between them. "Stop it," she said, not caring that it came out in the don't-mess-with-Mom voice she used with Benji when he got to be stubborn and contentious. They were acting like children; they deserved to be treated like children. "Stop baiting Paige, Maggie. And you," she turned to Paige, "get a clue."

"I'll stop if she stops," Paige said, not quite ready to give up her snit, or admit she'd let Maggie suck her in. "What about it, Maggie? Ready to kiss and make up?"

"Not until I get some antibiotics," Maggie said as she

walked away. But she stopped at the door, shot Jessi a warning look over her shoulder.

"I saw that," Paige said with her back still turned to Maggie.

Maggie shot up a middle finger.

"I saw that, too."

"Then I hope you can read my mind," Maggie said.

"Not through that red haze of anger and bitterness. But I know what you think of me."

"Then my work here is done."

Paige did turn around then. "Do you have so many friends you can afford to throw one away?"

Maggie studied Paige for a beat, then said simply, "Friends, true friends, aren't something you tote up on a scoreboard, Paige. They're people you can count on no matter what."

Paige smiled wistfully. "I'm finding that out."

Maggie didn't smile, but her expression softened. "Then maybe there's hope for you." And away she went, without a backward glance.

"Same old Maggie," Paige said.

"No, she's not," Jessi said. "As a matter of fact, she was never the Maggie you believed she was. If you'd spent one minute thinking about someone besides yourself ten years ago, you'd know that."

"Harsh."

"The truth often is."

"So what's Maggie's truth?"

"That's for her to say, Paige." Jessi turned her back, set to making the changes on the flight schedule.

Paige didn't take the hint. "So I'll talk to Maggie," she said.

Jessi huffed out a laugh. "The trick will be getting her to talk to you."

"Yes, well, who's Alec, and what is he keeping out of?"

"Alec is a friend of Dex's, and he's keeping out of other people's business. You should try it."

"What fun would that be?"

"None, but sticking your nose in where it doesn't belong is a great way to have it put out of joint. I'd think you would've learned that lesson."

Paige exhaled with a dainty whoosh, seeming to deflate as she did. "So you believe the gossip, too."

"It's not the sex tape; it's the release of it. The Paige Walker I used to know might make that tape, but she'd never make it public. Or maybe I should say her reputation was too precious to her."

"Well, that's something, anyway."

"Which means," Jessi continued, "either you pissed someone off and they released a tape you were stupid enough to make, or they manufactured one to make you look bad."

"Door Number Two."

"I'm sorry to hear that, but it doesn't change anything."

"Oh?"

Jessi parked herself back behind her desk. "I have a lot of work to do."

"You also have something you want to say to me."

"No, I..." Jessi braced her hands on her desk, waged a brief war with herself, and when she lost it, pushed to her feet. "Stop baiting Maggie."

"I will, just as soon as she stops baiting me."

Jessi strode around the desk, fired up now. "*You* initiate

every conversation with her, Paige. You get right in her face, maybe not physically, but your tone and your attitude are certainly confrontational."

Paige opened her mouth, shut it. "Well, damn it, Jessi, you're right. And now you're mad at me, too."

"No. Well, yes, at the moment."

"Then I owe you an apology."

"Just do me a favor and stop picking fights with Maggie."

Paige sighed. "I suppose I'm hoping at some point she'll forgive me. The two of you were—are—my only friends, Jessi. The friends I made after I left here…"

"None of them stood by you," Jessi finished.

"Like you said, I pissed someone off. Someone powerful."

"I'm sorry," Jessi said, and meant it.

"Sorry enough to tell me what's going on?"

"Nope." Jessi went back behind her desk. "Stay out of it. For your own good."

Paige smiled. "I don't think so."

"Paige—"

"I'm bored," she said with the slightest note of apology in her voice. "And I never could resist a mystery."

"No, what you are is at loose ends," Jessi said, going for firm but sympathetic. "You ran away from a problem. You should be looking for a way to fix it and get back to your life instead of meddling in ours."

It stuck with her, the advice she'd given Paige. It stuck with her, Jessi realized, because it applied to her. She'd found that damn blanket and it had paralyzed her. She hadn't been able to tell Maggie about it. She hadn't even been able to think about telling Hold.

Worse, she'd done an out-of-sight, out-of-mind. She'd run away from her problem, just like Paige. It wasn't the way she lived her life, ignoring what needed to be done. Because, she knew, the things you ignored had a way of sneaking up and biting you on the ass. So she'd face it.

First, though, she had to face Hold.

He'd come in an hour or so before and gone straight back to the little office. Before she could talk herself out of it, she got to her feet and went to his doorway. Hold was contemplating a section of the chart, half turned away from her. She stood there for a moment, just watching him.

He turned to face her, so tall and beautiful, with his dark blond hair just a little tousled, his handsome face lit with excitement.

"I received an e-mail this morning," he said, still clutching it in his hand. He turned back to the chart, excited, distracted. "It's the last off-island family I was tracking. They're all ruled out now. You know what this means?" He turned to face her again. "Jessica?"

She swallowed again. "It means if there are any descendants, they're still Windfallers."

He frowned a little.

She'd schooled her expression, but something must have leaked through. "It's great, Hold, really."

"But it means we might have to put someone in danger," he said, still watching her carefully.

"It means we should stop. Just stop until…I don't know, until we know…something."

"We won't know anything if we stop."

She walked in, joined him at the chart. She knew it almost as well Hold, could see where he'd finished the

Colby family's lineage to the point where it ended in a blunt double line after Eugenia's generation.

Not too far away, her own section of the Windfall Island genealogy sat unfinished, waiting. As far as Jessi cared, it could wait unfinished forever.

"What's troubling you?"

Being the Stanhope heir.

She'd joked about it before, only she'd refused to send in her DNA because, being the right age, there was an outside chance she could be Eugenia's granddaughter—and whoever wanted to eliminate the possible heirs had already proven they wouldn't wait for the results before taking lethal action.

She'd never really thought she was related to the Stanhopes. Since she'd found that blanket packed away in her attic like a cherished heirloom, though, she couldn't stop thinking about being Eugenia's descendant. It scared her to death. She slid her gaze away from the place where Claire Duncan, her great grandmother's name, was listed, managed to meet Hold's eyes. "I don't like the idea of anyone being put in danger."

"We can stop, but that just leaves Eugenia's descendants unprotected."

"If there are any descendants. What if we just announced that there aren't any, Hold? Then there's no reason to hurt anyone."

"How do we back it up? If it is one of the Stanhopes behind this, they'll just hire someone to finish what I started."

"They won't get any cooperation from the people here."

"They won't ask for it. It might take them longer to

trace all the island families using only public records, but they'll be able to do it."

Jessi closed her eyes. The truth trembled on the tip of her tongue, just for a second, but she knew she couldn't take the chance—with her life, maybe, but not with Benji's.

"I understand your concern, Jessica."

"No, you don't." She spun around, speared him with a look. "You can't possibly know how it feels to have a child and see him put in danger."

"I can't, no. I don't have a child, and as important as Benji is to me, there's no way I can understand how you feel." Hold took her hand in both of his, toying with her fingers. "There's also no way you'll hide from the truth, or ignore the logic of finding that truth first, when it gives us the upper hand."

No, she thought, she wouldn't ignore a conclusion she'd already come to herself.

Hold pulled her in, wrapped his arms around her. "I missed you last night."

She tipped her head up, met his gaze, couldn't speak for the war raging inside her. They were in the office, she reminded herself, where anyone could walk in and find them. But she wanted him, almost desperately.

"Jessica." Hold cradled her face and kissed her.

His hands slipped down her arms, his scent wound around her, and she laid her body on the long, lean planes of his. Heat rose in her, a sudden inferno of need growing, spreading as his hands feathered over her nipples, eased down to unsnap her jeans.

"Wait," she managed, catching his hands. "We can't. Not here."

"We can't at your place," he said, avoiding her hand to slide her zipper down.

Her heart shot into her throat.

"We can't at the Horizon. People will talk." He eased her jeans down, feathered his fingers over her.

And her breath slipped out on a slow moan.

"Here's what we have, Jessica." He slid his fingers beneath elastic and into her.

And when he dropped his mouth to her breast, hot and wet, when he drew her in even through her t-shirt and bra, when his fingers worked busily inside her, she shot to orgasm right where she stood.

She sighed, holding onto the lovely hum in her blood, the pleasant quiver deep inside. "Who'd have thought talk of logistics could be so...invigorating?"

"Speaking of logistics." Hold boosted her onto the desk.

"Hold..."

His eyes on hers, he skirted around the desk, shut the door, and shot the lock home, his eyes lighting with wicked intent.

Still watching him watch her, Jessi toed off her shoes and let her jeans and panties pool on top of them on the floor. Then she crooked her finger at him.

And made him grin. He came back, shucking his sweater and shirt, and dropping them on top of her clothes.

"You're still wearing too much," Jessi said.

"Funny. I was just about to say the same about you, sugar." Hold slipped the flannel shirt off her shoulders, lifted her t-shirt away, popped open the hooks on her bra, and stepped back, grinning. "What a picture you make, Jessica."

She wasn't one to be self-conscious, but the way he stared had her hands lifting.

Hold caught them in his, pulled them away. "I'm going to have a hard time doing paperwork without thinking of you here, like this."

She gave him an arch look. "If you don't get busy all you're going to be doing is paperwork."

He grinned, stepped in, nuzzled her neck.

Jessi eased her hands free, but her fingers, nimble as they were, fumbled with the closure on his slacks. "You really ought to try jeans," she murmured, tipping her head aside to give him better access. "I know how to undo jeans."

He brushed her hands away, unhooked and unbuttoned and slipped a condom out of his wallet, never taking his eyes from hers. She returned the favor, taking the condom and sliding it on him—slowly, with her eyes locked to his. She smiled when she felt him tremble under her hands.

"Two can play," he said.

He braced his hands on the desk and kissed her. Just his mouth on hers, his hips between her thighs, a kiss that spun in her head, burned through her body. Her hands reached for him, and a plea pushed at the back of her throat, a plea that turned to a moan when he cupped her backside, slid her forward and took her in one quick thrust that stole her breath. And her strength.

She leaned back on her elbows, everything in her focused on the feel of him filling her, moving in her. She arched, took him deeper, and felt his mouth drop to her breast, hot and insistent. Each tug of his lips, each caress of his tongue was a sharp arrow of pleasure, each stroke of his body the sweetest friction, building, tightening inside her. Reality narrowed to the two of them, bodies moving in an undeniable rhythm, the two of them, rising, hitting that peak together, the two of them, holding tight to one another while the climax ripped and shuddered through them. Fireworks exploded, bells rang—or maybe that was the phone. Jessi didn't care.

She lay on the desk—with Hold draped over her, just as destroyed as she was, just as breathless. But not—she reached underneath her and pulled out a pen—as uncomfortable. "We really need to find a better way to do this," she said.

Hold, resting on his forearms, looked into her face. "I thought we did a damn fine job of it this time."

"Funny guy. I mean a better place."

He simply grinned.

"I know, this place was damn fine," she said in a passable imitation of his drawl. "You aren't the one with paper clips imprinted on your backside."

"Your backside feels just fine to me."

Which he would know as his hands were currently checking. "There aren't any paperclips exactly there," she said dryly.

"Never hurts to be sure, sugar."

She shoved at his shoulder, but when he eased away she felt bereft, and a little embarrassed to be sprawled so wantonly on his desk. "Can you hand me my clothes?"

"If you give me a few minutes you won't need them."

"If I give you a few minutes we're going to have company, because some helpful Windfaller will have called George to find out why I haven't answered the phone."

"And he'll feel obliged to check it out."

"After what happened to Maggie? Yeah."

Hold sighed. "We're going to have to find a better place for this."

"Yeah." Jessi scooted off the desk, started dressing.

"Jessica."

When she looked up, Hold kissed her, slow and thorough and deep before he eased back, and left it sweet and gentle. "Have supper with me."

"Hold."

"This, whatever this is, it's about more than just sex."

"It's about more than sex," she agreed. And it touched her that he wanted her to know that. She just didn't know how to define that *more*. And she didn't need to. It was enough knowing Hold didn't want to sneak around. Neither did she. Hiding their...involvement made it feel wrong somehow.

But she didn't have a choice.

"How about if I come to you and Benji?" Hold said into the silence. "We can see how it goes from there."

"No. Hold...Dinner is one thing, and I know he's okay with the 'kissing and stuff,' because he hasn't really thought about what 'stuff' means." In part because he was seven, and in part, she knew, because he had so much to deal with already.

Benji was still struggling to figure out where he fit into his father's life. She could see the confusion, the uncertainty every time he and Lance were together. It broke her heart whenever Benji looked to her for reassurance now.

He'd been such a confident, happy little boy just two short weeks ago, and now it was as if he needed to know that whatever else changed in his life, she'd be the one constant. No matter what she felt for Hold, she wouldn't do anything that might seem to Benji like he wasn't getting all her love and attention.

"Right now you're his friend, Hold. Spending the night with me puts you in a different category."

Hold stopped, shirtless. "He already has a father."

Jessi stepped up to him, placed a hand on his arm, met his eyes. And prayed he'd understand. "I don't know, Hold. Neither does he, but I think we should give him the time to figure it out before anything else changes."

He nodded, surprising her. Then he gave her that bone-melting smile. "How much time?"

"Not much, I hope," she said fervently.

Hold's smile turned suggestive, sexy. "No hesitation, a lot of enthusiasm," he observed. "That's something, anyway, Jessica. You're something."

And she'd be flat on her back again if she didn't get out of there. She beat a hasty retreat, but she knew it would be a struggle to keep her mind on her work for the rest of the day. To not think about what she could have just feet away, behind a locked door...

Yeah, they definitely needed to find a better place. But then, she thought with a smug grin, she'd never look at that desk the same way again.

Chapter Eighteen

C'mon, Mom, hurry. Chewie's barking."

Jessi climbed out of her ancient Explorer, walked to the back of the car and popped it open. "That's okay," she called out. "I don't need any help."

Benji, halfway to the front door where the puppy was making a ruckus behind it, stopped, sighed, and dragged his feet all the way back to the Explorer to retrieve a couple of the canvas bags filled with their week's groceries.

She ruffled his hair. "Chewie will be okay for another minute or two."

"But he's been locked up all day."

She argued with herself briefly, then said, "I ran home at lunch and let him out," wondering why it had been a struggle to say it. Still stinging that she'd been manipulated into having a dog before she was ready, she decided. And it was time to get over it. She'd fallen for the little mutt. He was good for Benji; what did it matter that Lance had been the one to make it happen?

Benji hugged her hard, then grabbed the bags she handed him and ran headlong for the front door. He couldn't turn the knob with full hands so he stood there, fidgeting from one foot to the other while Chewie barked even more frantically, having heard their voices.

Jessi juggled the rest of the grocery bags, opened the door, flipped on the lights.

And stopped dead when she heard a bang come from the back of the house. It confused her for a second. Her mind fought to make sense of it, until she realized it was the back door slamming. And then she went cold.

"*Mom.*"

"Outside, Benji."

"But—"

"Move. Now." She followed him, dumping her bags and his in the back of the Explorer. "In the car," she said over Benji's protests, locking the doors once he'd climbed into the front passenger seat. "Don't ask, just do it. And stay in there until I say you can get out."

"Chewie," he said, his lower lip wobbling.

"I'll get him. Just stay put." Jessi could see she was scaring him, but better he be scared than hurt.

She walked back to the front door, pulling out her cell with one hand, grabbing the first weapon-like item she came across with the other.

"Boatwright," George said when he answered.

Jessi opened her front door, looked around cautiously. "I think someone was in my house."

"Jessi?"

"When I walked in I heard the back door slam, and now...I can't put my finger on it, George. Everything appears normal. But it's not. Something's off."

"I'll be there in five. Don't go in."

"I'm already in," she said. "Benji is locked in the car."

"That's where you should be."

"This is my house, George, and I promised Benji I'd get the puppy." Which had to be scared out of its little canine wits.

She eased across the family room toward the kitchen, eyes on the shadowy staircase the whole way. They'd put Chewie's crate in the mudroom off the kitchen, and Jessi could hear it rattling between the puppy's high-pitched yips.

She opened the crate door and Chewie rocketed out. He jumped on her, nipping and licking her hand when she reached down, racing off before she could actually pet him. He worked his way through the kitchen, alternating between sniffing at everything and whining at her.

"Jessi?"

Chewie, barking madly again, raced into the family room. By the time Jessi got there, the pup had squared off in front of George, growling at him although its little legs trembled.

"Game little fellow," George said. "You, too." He eyed the umbrella she'd plucked from the stand by the door.

"Are you mocking my umbrella?"

"Wouldn't dream of it." But his lips twitched suspiciously. "Might not be much use against a prowler, though. A nice sturdy bat, that's the ticket."

"I'll remember that," Jessi said, vowing to buy one at the first chance.

"You stay here," George said, heading for the kitchen. He turned back at the doorway, speared her with a look. "I mean it, Jessi. Go out and check on Benji. Poor kid has to be scared to death. And take that noisemaker with you."

Jessi scooped up the puppy and hurried out to the car. Now that George—and his gun—were there, she let Benji get out. But she kept him in the front yard until the all-clear.

"I checked upstairs," George said when they came back inside. "There's no one in here now. I'll check out back before I go, but there's no snow and the ground is frozen solid. There won't be any footprints. Tell me again what happened when you got home."

She locked the front door, turned the TV on low, and left Benji watching cartoons with the pup on his lap.

"Like I told you on the phone, when I opened the front door I heard the back door slam shut."

George glanced around. "It doesn't appear anything is missing."

Jessi circled the room. "Something..." she began, puzzled until it hit her. "The papers on the table have been moved," she said, pointing to the neat stacks of bills, contracts and invoices she'd yet to take back to the airport office.

"You're sure?"

"Positive." She kept moving, studying. She hadn't changed a thing since her mother died. Same furniture, same family photos on the walls, same knickknacks she dusted each week and placed precisely where they'd always sat. Some would call it boring, stuck in the past. Jessi found it comforting.

"What's wrong?" Benji asked, not fooled by the unexpected cartoon spree and lowered voices.

Nothing, Jessi started to say, until she realized that wouldn't be fair to him. Benji knew there was a problem; keeping him in the dark would only frighten him more.

"I think there was someone in the house while we were gone," she told him. She hated to shatter his sense of security, but he needed to take his own safety seriously.

"It was probably only kids from the mainland playing a prank," George put in.

"They're gone," she added hastily. "George already checked. There's no one in the house now besides us. But he wants me to take a look and see if anything is missing."

"Were they in my room?"

"No." George circled the sofa and hunkered down next to Benji. "And they're not coming back. I'm going to make sure of that." He reached out to scratch the pup behind his ears. "I have to say, this is quite the watchdog you have here."

"He was barking a lot when we got home."

"So I hear, and there's no better deterrent than a dog. That means just his bark is enough to make most bad guys go away."

Benji hugged the puppy to him. "Really?"

"Yep, and he growled at me, even when he was afraid. This fellow gets some size on him, and watch out."

"Why don't you come upstairs with us?" Jessi said. "We'll check your room first."

That was exactly what they did. George looked in Benji's closet, under his bed, and in his little bathroom.

"Are you okay hanging out in here for a few minutes?" Jessi asked him once George had declared his personal space prowler free.

"I'm gonna go through my stuff," Benji said.

"You do that," she said, giving his hair a quick tousle before she joined George in the hallway.

They went into her bedroom, George standing back while she took a look around. "Nothing seems to have been disturbed in here."

Still, she opened the top drawer of her dresser and sifted through the contents. The family Bible, the pitifully few pieces of jewelry she owned of any value, a gold coin that had been carried in the pocket of the first Duncan to leave Ireland, then passed down so his descendants would never want as long as they held onto it.

"Everything is here." She looked over at George, the only one who understood the implications outside of Maggie, Dex and Hold. "And I don't keep any research materials in the house."

George shoved his hat back, scratched his head. "If this is connected to the research, we have a bigger problem."

"Yeah." But George didn't know everything.

After Maggie's plane had been sabotaged, Dex had told George about the search for Eugenia's descendants, if any existed. George knew Dex was really a private investigator, not a lawyer; and he knew Hold Abbot had come to help by creating the genealogy. George knew Maggie's DNA test had come back negative.

He didn't know about the blanket. At the moment, Jessi thought with a little spurt of panic, neither did she.

She stepped out of her room, glanced in at Benji and found him still occupied with the puppy, then made her way to the attic stairs. "Just to be sure," she said when George looked dubious.

He shrugged and followed her up, making his way around the dim space like the good cop he was. As soon as he got to the other end of the room, she popped open the trunk and dug down, breathing a sigh of relief when she spied the flowered paper.

"The dust is disturbed over here."

"That was me." She closed the trunk, then went to join George. "I got a wild hair to clean this place over the weekend, which lasted just long enough for me to move some of my mother's boxes before I ran out of steam."

George grunted and kept poking around. "Just so you know, I sent Maggie a text while I had you on speaker phone."

Jessi stopped in her tracks and closed her eyes while she let that sink in. "She had a charter to New York, so it was a long day."

"That's not the reason you didn't want me to call her."

"She'll only worry."

"Maybe, but she'd have my ass for not calling."

"You're not afraid of her."

"If you say so," George said equably.

He followed her out of the attic, waiting while she turned off the lights and closed the door. George waited again while she stopped in Benji's open doorway and asked him to stay there until dinner.

For once her son didn't argue, barely taking the time to nod absently while he played tug-of-war with Chewie.

"What do you think would happen if one of us didn't call Maggie?" George said as she led the way downstairs.

"I would have told her. I just don't see any point in dragging her out on a cold, ugly night like this." The early November sky was spitting ice pellets and the wind had begun to howl around the eaves.

"Maybe she should spend the night with you."

Jessi shot George a look, then went down the rest of

the stairs. There was Hold, in her living room. Maggie stood behind him, the spare key Jessi had given her years before in her hand.

"Perfect."

"George caught me at the office, dropping off my paperwork," Maggie explained. "Hold was still there working."

"Of course he was."

"What's going on? All George's text said was *Jessi's. Now.*"

Jessi opened her mouth, closed it when she caught movement out of the corner of her eye. Benji came down the stairs, wide-eyed and big-eared, no doubt. "Chewie's hungry," he said. "So am I."

"Chewie first," Jessi said, sending Benji toward the kitchen with a pat on the seat of his jeans. "Go ahead and feed him, and make sure you give him fresh water."

Benji sent a look toward the kitchen—the big, empty kitchen.

"C'mon, Ben. It appears we're not needed here." Hold put a hand on Benji's shoulder and steered him out of the room.

But he reappeared almost immediately to lounge in the wide arched doorway, sideways, so he could see Benji but still hear the conversation in the living room.

"Someone was in here today while we were gone." Jessi kept her eyes on Hold, daring him to comment.

And he did, just not with words. She could tell by the way his eyes narrowed, the way his body tensed, that he was pissed.

"You should have called," Maggie said.

"I called George."

"From inside the house," George added helpfully.

"Whose side are you on?"

"Yours."

Jessi looked around, found three faces staring back at her with varying degrees of accusation and disappointment. "Right. So this is the part where you all gang up on me. You know, I am capable of taking care of myself."

Maggie tipped her head, smiled a little sadly. "So am I."

And look what had happened, Jessi finished silently, as they all probably were, remembering how close Maggie had come to dying at the hands of a friend. The Stanhopes had deep pockets, more than deep enough to hire betrayal.

"There's no reason to target me," Jessi pointed out.

"You're helping Hold with the research," Maggie said.

"None of which is kept here. And besides, George thinks it was kids from the mainland."

"No way an islander would be caught here when you get home," George said. "We all know your schedule."

"Except you left early," Hold said. "It was dead at the office, and you wanted to spend some extra time with Ben."

"Then it could have been an islander," Maggie concluded.

"And if it was, they're aware I don't have anything... classified here."

"Well, I'll be looking into who *they* are," George said, "even if there's no cause for anyone to bother you again, Jessi."

She breathed out carefully, almost lost it when Maggie slung an arm around her waist and squeezed.

"It's odd, though," George continued, "that someone went to the trouble to break in here and didn't take anything. Although I doubt there was much breaking involved. A five-year-old could pick the ancient lock on your front door, Jessi. You should have changed it— Hell, your mother should have changed it."

Hold jerked around to stare at her.

"This isn't the big city," Jessi said before he could put the outrage on his face into words. "Hardly anyone even locks their door."

"That's going to have to change," George said. "I'll be telling the other Windfallers—discreetly—to upgrade their locks, too."

"Great, then it's all settled."

"No, it's not settled."

"No, it's really not," Hold echoed Maggie.

"I'm not needed here anymore," George decided.

"Coward," Maggie said good-naturedly to him as he started for the door.

"I only take on hardened criminals," George said. "A woman on a rampage is way beyond my skills."

"I'm not on a rampage," Jessi said to his retreating back. "It was just a little mischief by some bored mainlander kids." It couldn't be more, she told herself. It couldn't have anything to do with Eugenia. The research wasn't the only reason for someone to break into her house, though, and as unsettled as it made her to think about finding a stranger in her home, she'd be even more unsettled if it wasn't a stranger at all. "There's a possibility we haven't discussed."

George stopped in front of the door and turned to look back at them. "I'll be talking to Lance first. The good news is, if it was Lance, I don't believe he intended any-one harm."

"I'm not sure I agree," Hold said. The lazy drawl of his words couldn't quite detract from the heat in his eyes.

"As long as you don't do anything to make me arrest you," George said. He didn't wait for an answer, disap-pearing through the front door.

"See? George isn't worried," Jessi said. "Neither am I."

"You both should be taking this more seriously," Mag-gie said.

"Maybe George knows I can protect myself."

"And Benji," Hold said.

Jessi went ice cold, then white hot, all in the space of one heartbeat.

"Hold," Maggie began.

Jessi held up her hand. Her gaze never wavered from Hold's.

"I think I'll go get a pizza." Maggie stopped, turned back. "You okay?"

"Fine," Jessi bit off.

"Your hands are shaking."

Not just her hands, Jessi realized. She was shaking in-side, too—hurt and angry, so angry it was all she could do to keep it from spewing out of her. "I can take care of my son."

"We both know that," Maggie said. "Don't we, Hold?"

He shoved his hands back through his hair, said "Yeah" on an explosion of breath.

"Good. Hey, Benj, how about you and I go to Carelli's?"

Letting out a whoop, Benji raced from the kitchen to

join Maggie. "Can I play Space Invaders while we're waiting?"

"I'm a Pac-Man girl, myself," Maggie said, referring to the vintage video games crowding one end of the pizza parlor. She draped an arm around Benji's shoulders, gave Jessi's arm a quick rub on the way by. "It's not the worst thing in the world, having people care about you."

"I don't like being maneuvered."

"Part of the package," Maggie said brusquely, shooing Benji out in front of her.

Jessi pointed, stiff-armed, to the door. "You can go, too."

"So you can ignore me again?" Hold accused.

"How did I ignore you?"

"You called George."

"Do I have to state the obvious?"

"Do I?"

Jessi shoved both hands through her hair, fisted them in hopes the pain would help her control the welter of emotions crashing through her. It didn't help much. Even knowing she'd backed herself into this corner by keeping secrets, that she was only lashing out, didn't stop her from doing it. "Someone broke in. I called the sheriff. I'm sorry I didn't stop and say, gosh, what would Hold expect me to do? There may be an intruder lurking in my house, I guess I should call all my friends and acquaintances so they don't get their feelings hurt."

"You think this is about my feelings?"

"You're not going to stand there and tell me it's not."

"Fine. I'm pissed."

"Well, I won't apologize."

"You won't trust, you mean."

She made a sound of pure frustration. "What is it going to take to convince you I can take care of myself, and my son? I've been doing it for a long time now."

"This isn't about you being strong and capable, Jessi, it's about you being too strong. Your mother chose not to get involved with another man after your father died, and that told you something about men. Then Lance came along and taught you something else. Even your father—"

"It's not like he left me on purpose."

"No, but he left all the same, just another example of how you can't trust men to be there when you need them."

"You're right, Hold." And in that moment she hated him for it, for making her realize she resented even the father she'd loved in a shadowy male figurehead sort of way. "I've never been able to count on any man," she continued. "I'm afraid to trust. What makes you different? You're here now, but will you be here in a month? A year? Will you be here when someone has to talk to Benji about sex, or hold his head when he has his first hangover, or his hand when his heart is broken for the first time?"

Silence from Hold.

"And where does it leave me when I get used to counting on you and then you leave? I do trust you, Hold, but trusting doesn't mean abdicating my responsibilities just because there's a big, strong man in the picture."

"I'm not expecting you to let me run your life, Jessi, but you could stop worrying about where I'll be tomorrow and just enjoy what we have today."

She met his gaze, knew her guard was down and didn't care. "I'm not the one asking for more."

Chapter Nineteen

You're right." Hold ran a hand back through his hair. They'd spent less than a weekend together and there he stood, angrier than he could ever remember because she'd had a crisis and hadn't called him first.

Wasn't he the one holding back? he asked himself. The one preaching to her about trust while he let the past build a wall between them? He'd been burned, and burned badly. He hadn't just let Miriam into his life, he'd been building a life *around* her, and when he'd discovered just how little he really meant to her, when he'd walked away...

It had taken him a long time to find his center again. And look how carefully he guarded it, he thought. He accused Jessi of being closed off, but wasn't he the one afraid she'd change if she knew he came from wealth? And wasn't he the one cautioning her to take their relationship one day at a time, to not make plans for the future?

Yet he'd come down on her like a swamp-rotted tree for not treating him like the solution to all her troubles.

He wouldn't risk his heart because it had been broken before, crushed by a woman who'd only wanted status and wealth. It followed that any number of women would fit into that same category.

But not Jessi.

Still, it wasn't wrong, he reminded himself, to take it slow with her. He just had to remember it worked both ways.

"Jessi—"

"Don't. Please don't say anything."

And now, where he'd seen vulnerability in her eyes, he saw fear. For Benji, he guessed. And a little, he hoped, for herself. It might be a selfish wish on his part, wanting to think she dreaded the day he might leave, selfish and more than a little telling. But there it was.

"You're right, too," she said. "I keep thinking about the future, where this is going. I can't seem to help myself."

"You have a son to worry about. It's not wrong for you to want to protect him."

"No, it's not wrong."

"Look, I don't know where this is going, either." Hold blew out a breath. "But you're right. I want more."

She sighed. "So do I."

He crossed to her and gathered her into his arms, resting his cheek on top of her head. And felt his world fall back into place. He should be worried about that, but he let it go, buried it under a kiss that was soft, gentle, and heart-wrenching in the way Jessi gave back so generously when she had every reason to put up walls.

As the kiss rolled from sweet to hot, she did put on the brakes. And he let her. To a point.

"I'm staying the night."

She rested her forehead on his chest, and as her hands clutched in his shirt, as he understood that she was afraid and she was turning to him, something rose inside him and filled places that had ached with emptiness. And when she looked up at him, when he saw the longing in her eyes, the band around his heart—a band he hadn't even noticed before—loosened.

"I want to say yes, Hold."

"That's fine, because I'm not letting you say no."

"I guess you really don't believe I can take care of myself," she said, but he could tell she was holding back a smile.

"Let's just say I want to be here in case that son of a—"

"Mom!" Benji said as he burst through the front door, pizza box in hand.

Maggie appeared behind him, one eyebrow raised. "Did we interrupt anything?"

Chewie spared them from having to answer by gamboling out of the kitchen, so happy to see his boy that his whole body wagged.

"He piddled," Benji crowed, laughing.

Jessi took the pizza, gave him a look.

"I'm going," he said, but Hold could tell he only dragged his feet for show. Cleaning up a little dog pee was nothing compared to the joy of having the dog in the first place; Hold knew that from personal experience.

"We got a large with everything except anchovies and green pepper because Maggie doesn't like green pepper," he said as he came back with pet cleaner and an old threadbare towel Jessi had earmarked for Chewie accidents. "And we got extra bread, 'cause she said I eat like a horse, and there's a note on the box."

Jessi glanced down at the box in her hands, then tipped it in Hold's direction so he could see, "Enjoy!" written on it in Maggie's bold scrawl.

He cut his eyes to the door, found it closed, with Maggie on the other side. And just in case his eyes were playing tricks on him out of hope, he heard the growl of Maggie's Mustang as it pulled away from the house. "She's sneaky."

When Jessi met his eyes, Hold shoved his hands in his pockets and rocked back on his heels. And kept his expression and voice carefully bland. "I guess she thinks I should spend the night, too."

"You're staying over?" More whooping from Benji, which set off more barking from Chewie. And more piddling.

Hold couldn't fight off the grin any longer. Nothing in the world like a happy kid, he thought, and Benji—well, there was something about him. He could say, with absolute freedom, that he was already in love with the boy.

Benji stopped in front of Hold and grinned up at him. "You can sleep in my room."

Yeah, something about the kid. "Thanks, Ben, but I'll sleep on the Davenport."

"What's a Davenport?"

"It's a kind of sofa."

Jessi handed Benji the pizza and turned him toward the little dining area. "Put this on the table and go wash your hands," she said, nudging him on his way before she turned back.

Her eyes landed on the sofa, then lifted. "No matter

what you call it, it's about a foot shorter than you are. You take my bed—"

"The Davenport," Hold repeated in a tone that brooked no argument. Much as he wanted to take the opportunity to move their relationship to a place where Benji was all right with them being together, night and day, their safety was more important to him. "It puts me down here, close to the doors."

"Really, Hold, I think George is right. There's not going to be any more trouble. Then again," she added with a slight, teasing smile, "You're in the house."

"One day at a time, remember?"

One day at a time. Yeah, she remembered.

Jessi breathed out, then in, slow, deliberate breaths. Hold's argument sounded so logical, so simple and effortless. Just take it a day at a time, enjoy what they had for the time they had it. What could be easier?

But how did she shut off her own doubts and fears? After nearly a decade of putting Benji first, how did she ignore his feelings?

She trusted Hold, but— No, no more buts, no more what ifs or tomorrows. She trusted Hold. Period. He'd never do anything to hurt either her or Benji on purpose.

"You're right, Hold. Let's just enjoy today and let tomorrow take care of itself.

He studied her for a minute. She kept her eyes on his, let him make what he would of her acceptance. He put his arms around her, pulled her in for a hug. "We'll take our time Jessica, get to know one another, and see where it takes us."

She leaned back, looked into his face. "Hold..."

He put a finger over her lips, then his mouth, one of his sweet, simple kisses. He couldn't know how that kiss, the kind one lover gave another where there was more than sex between them, got to her.

"You think you know me—"

She put her fingers over his mouth. "I do know you."

"You can never really know another person, Jessica. Not everyone is as honest—" He broke off, dropped another light kiss on her lips. "It's not important. I'm starving. Let's eat."

He stepped away, flashing her a grin before he went into the kitchen, a grin that didn't hide the shadows in his eyes.

So, he'd been hurt before, Jessi realized, and by a woman if she didn't miss her guess. It was so clear in that moment. A man as irresistible as Hold Abbot would have been involved before, and deeply, she thought. He might be naturally flirtatious, but she'd discovered that he wasn't casual about acting on those flirtations.

No, someone, some woman, had broken his heart. And his trust.

He held back, Jessi understood now, because he was waiting for her to hurt him, and in holding back, he guaranteed they'd hurt one another.

But she was already too far gone to be careful now.

With Hold bedded down on the sofa—make that "Davenport"—and Benji tucked into his own room, Jessi felt safe and secure again. Still, she couldn't sleep. Not just because of her conversation with Hold, and not because the break-in still troubled her. It was that damn pink blanket.

She flipped the covers back, hissing when her bare feet hit the cold floor as she crossed to the dresser that had once been her mother's. There, in the top drawer, lay one of the few treasures she'd made sure the intruder hadn't taken: the Duncan family Bible.

Nearly every family on Windfall had one of their own. It might seem hypocritical, the founders of Windfall being who they were and living the way they'd lived. It didn't mean they didn't value family. It didn't mean they didn't have faith. Whatever they'd done, at the foundation of it, they'd done to see to the needs of their own.

And what she did, Jessi reminded herself, she did for the safety of her son.

She propped herself up in bed, and before she could talk herself out of it, paged carefully to the birth and death records. She ran a finger over the spidery scrawls, the bold strokes of her ancestors, and her mother's careful lettering.

And jumped, her heart shooting into her throat, when Hold's voice whispered, "Jessi?" through the closed door.

She hastily placed the Bible on the nightstand and grabbed the paperback she always kept in the top drawer, but rarely had the time or energy to read.

The door eased open and there stood Hold, shirtless. "Couldn't sleep either?"

She shook her head. "Too wound up, I guess. I thought I'd do a little reading."

He came over and sat on the side of the bed, feathering his fingertips over her cheek. "You look tired."

"The words every girl longs to hear from the man she's trying to impress," she said lightly.

"Okay, you look beautiful."

"I wasn't fishing for compliments."

"Trust me, sugar, if it weren't for Benji sleeping across the hall, you wouldn't have to do any fishing. And I wouldn't be stopping at compliments."

He smiled, leaned in to give her a kiss that stayed on the warm side of sexy.

Jessi covered the hand he'd cupped over her cheek, kept her eyes on his when he leaned back. And when he smiled, slow and easy, she let a smile of her own curve her lips and warm her heart.

"So what are we reading?" He took the book she'd forgotten she held, looked at the cover, and smiled again, this one arch enough to put her back up a little. "Romance?"

She plucked the paperback out of his hands, set it on the nightstand. "And?"

"I haven't given you any romance, Jessica," he said quietly, and disarmed her.

"I haven't asked for any."

"But you deserve it." He stood, held out a hand.

She got out of bed, uncertain, and a little more than embarrassed by her flannel pants, so ancient they were all but worn through in places. Her top wasn't much better, an old t-shirt, ratty at the cuffs and hem. "I'm not exactly dressed for romance."

"Maybe not, sugar, but I can't take my eyes off you." He looked at her like she was naked and set her pulse to racing.

Instead of putting more than his eyes on her, Hold sidestepped to the nightstand, but when he reached for the clock-radio he spied the Bible, the pen she'd been writing with sitting on top. He turned to her, a question in his eyes.

While she felt compelled to fill the silence, no plausible excuse occurred to her. Since she wouldn't lie to him, she just shrugged.

Hold turned on her little clock radio and found a station playing slow, dreamy jazz. He took her hand, twirled her into his arms, and started to sway with her.

Jessi closed her eyes and let the music swirl in her head, let Hold spin through her blood—his scent, his strength, the feel of his arms around her. If this was romance, she wanted to stay here forever. Hold tucked her even closer, toying with the curls cascading over her shoulders. She sighed, rested her cheek on his chest. Right over his heart.

It felt good, swaying with Jessi while Sarah Vaughan crooned low on the radio. More, it felt right. That should have worried Hold, but he'd already made his mind up to take his own advice: enjoy each day they had together. Before one of them disappointed the other.

She sighed lightly, and the arms she'd locked around his waist loosened. Her eyes were closed, he saw when he looked down at her, and her breathing was slow and even. Asleep on her feet, he thought as he bent and lifted her. She nuzzled her face into his throat, and sent enough heat shooting through him to cause spontaneous combustion. And when he lay her on the bed, the arm she'd slung around his neck tightened enough to overbalance him. He managed not to fall on top of her, but as he dropped beside her, she wrapped herself around him and snuggled in.

Her eyes fluttered open, and her peaceful expression clouded for a moment. "Hold?" she murmured fuzzily.

"Go to sleep," he whispered. "I'm right here," and surrendering to her needs, if not his own, he slipped an arm under her head and nestled her back against him.

He was still on fire, and the feel of her tight, curvy backside snugged against him was torture. But it was a torture he was willing to suffer if his presence allowed Jessi to get some rest.

Still, as soon as her breathing evened, when he knew she slept deeply, he slipped from her bed, brushed his lips over her temple, and went back downstairs to the too-narrow, firm-in-the-middle, broken-in-at-both-ends Davenport in her lonely family room.

A different kind of torture it might be, but it was a small enough price to pay to keep the woman he cared for, and her son, safe.

Chapter Twenty

Jessi woke, smiled, rolled over. And found the bed beside her empty. She closed her eyes and flopped onto her back, bereft and grateful at the same time. As amazing as it would have been to wake up with Hold beside her, finding him gone meant he cared enough to honor her wishes.

And made her love him more.

Yeah, she thought, time to admit it. She was in love with Hold Abbot.

She'd begun to stumble the first time she'd seen him, crossing the tarmac, tall and handsome, with his gilded hair shining in the sun. And the first time she'd locked eyes with him—those dancing melted-chocolate eyes of his—she'd lost her balance even more. Looking back now, the fall had been inevitable. And nothing like she'd imagined it would be.

Falling in love should have been chirping bluebirds and circling hearts, happy, sun-drenched days and moonlit nights filled with pleasure. Falling in love should have made her heart sing, her lips smile, her world bright and fresh.

Her world had definitely changed, she allowed, but while being in love did make her heart shine, her head kept telling her to be careful, and that put a shadow of sadness over the happiness.

As for Hold—well, she didn't know how he felt about her, but he'd been so gentle, so careful with her last night. Then again, Hold was a gentle man. He'd taken care, taken his time, made sure she felt tended to because he was that kind of person. And because he cared enough to respect her feelings, in her home, with her son sleeping across the hall.

The hour was still early when she glanced at the clock, but she sat up anyway, clicked on the lamp. Picked up the Bible. She didn't open it right away.

Maggie's possible connection to Eugenia had been found first, and once they'd discovered how quickly someone was willing to strike, a conscious and calculated decision had been made to wait before anyone else was endangered. But since she'd found the blanket— God, was it just three days ago?

She took a deep breath, let it out as she opened the Bible to the births and deaths page, and faced the fact that she had to stop burying her head in the sand.

In a surprisingly short time, she had her answer. A baby had been born, a daughter, to Joseph and Claire Duncan, Jessi's great grandparents, less than two months before Eugenia Stanhope's February 1931 birth date. Jessi's grandmother would have been that baby.

She very well might have been Eugenia Stanhope.

A measles epidemic had raged on Windfall Island that

winter, taking the very old and the very young with in-
discriminate cruelty. The supposition went that Eugenia
had replaced an infant who'd succumbed to the measles.
While Jessi's grandmother had been nearly two months
older, none of the women in her family had been particularly tall, as far back as the photographic evidence
adorning her own walls attested. Not to mention her own
vertical challenge.

Her grandmother would have been small for her age,
easily replaced by a slightly younger child. Eugenia had
gone missing in October. With the winter just socking in
and with sickness to be avoided, Windfallers had kept to
their own homes. No one would have seen Elizabeth Duncan for months, certainly not recently enough to mark any
changes that couldn't be written off to those due to seven
or eight months of growth.

It wasn't proof, Jessi concluded, but the possibility existed. She'd have to tell the others. She'd have to tell them
all—

She heard a pounding, loud enough to make her jump
out of bed and run down the stairs, Benji right on her heels.
Chewie beat them both to the bottom, standing stiff-legged,
fur on end, barking so hard he bounced each time.

Jessi might have laughed if she hadn't seen Lance
standing in the open doorway, his breath frosting in the
frigid air as he squared off with Hold. Lance shifted his
gaze to her, took in her robeless, slipper-less state, then
turned back to Hold, who was shirtless, his pants zipped
but unfastened at the waistband.

"Nice," he sneered, slamming the door behind him and
moving farther into the room. "Don't worry about the kid
or anything."

Benji, a shaking, growling Chewie locked in his arms, looked up at her. Jessi drew him back against her, wrapped her arms around them both. "You can go," she said to Lance.

"Not until you tell me about this break-in."

"How did you hear about it?"

"George had a few questions for me. Thanks for the show of faith."

"I didn't tell George to talk to you."

"It makes sense, though," Hold said. "You being back on the island so suddenly. Makes a body curious as to what brought you back after eight years."

Lance stepped forward, violence clear in his eyes.

Jessi slipped around Benji, moved to block him. She agreed with Hold, but saying it would only make Lance angrier. "Not in my house."

"I don't see why not. You let all kinds of things go on in your house."

"*I* let," she shot back, refusing to give him any defense at all. Lance could think whatever he wanted to think. "This is my house, and you'll be welcome in it when you can be civil."

"I'm not going anywhere without my son."

"Oh, you really are. Get out."

Lance stepped around her, appealed directly to Benji. "It's not safe here. You should come stay with me."

Jessi put herself between them again. "Absolutely not."

"Your mother," Lance said, biting off each word, "is more concerned with her boyfriend than she is with you."

"Go home and cool off, Lance."

"So you and Loverboy can play house with my kid? Not on your life." He took a step closer to Benji, making the puppy growl even louder. "Go pack some clothes. You'll be staying at Grandma's where you're safe."

"Mom?"

"I'm your father," Lance snapped. "Do like I tell you."

"Out." Jessi pointed at the door. "If you cared— You can't put him in the position of choosing between us, Lance, even if you thought for one minute your record could stand up against mine."

Lance's hands curled into fists.

"Go ahead," Jessi dared him.

Hold stepped up behind her. "This is Jessi's business. I've been willing to stand back and let her handle it." His voice notched down to put gravel into his drawl. "But if you intend to throw a punch, Proctor, you're going to want to pick a different target."

Lance held his ground, jaw bunching.

Hold simply moved Jessi aside, and shifted his weight to the balls of his feet. He kept his gaze locked on Lance's face the entire time.

"I don't want any trouble," Lance said after a tense moment. "I was angry because of the questions."

"You didn't say where you were yesterday," Hold put in.

Lance's jaw bunched, but he answered. "I was at Meeker's, with my mother. She's looking for a new table, and well, you've seen that place. I spent most of the day shifting furniture from one part of that flea market to another."

Jessi studied his face. She couldn't see any sign he was bullshitting them. But then, he was a pretty damn good liar. Still, Meeker wouldn't vouch for Lance out of the goodness of his heart, so Lance must be telling the truth.

"You were asked to leave," she reminded him.

"Benj—"

"You want to hang around," Hold said, "we can pick up where we left off."

"I'll go. But this isn't over."

Before the door shut behind him, Jessi was already kneeling down in front of Benji, who was knuckling tears away from his eyes. "Why don't you go back to bed?"

"Okay."

"Jessi," Hold said.

"Not now—"

He drew her to her feet and a little away from the stairs. "At the moment," he whispered, "it's his mother versus his father. I'm the closest thing to Switzerland there is."

Jessi glanced back at her son, dragging his feet up the stairs, Chewie by his side. "Okay," she sighed. "Will you tell me about it later?"

Hold shook his head, shifted his gaze to Benji, and winked because he had to know they were talking about him. "It's just between us men," he said loudly enough for Benji to hear. And smile over.

Jessi could have kissed him for that alone. "It's barely five a.m.," she said instead. "See if you can't get him back to sleep for a little while. One of my men has to attend the second grade in a few hours."

"Not sure which one?"

"Oh, I know which one. That doesn't mean you couldn't use a refresher."

Shaking his head, Hold grabbed his shirt and headed for the stairs.

Jessi grinned at his back, called after him, "They teach a lot of useful stuff in the second grade."

* * *

Yeah, Benji thought when he heard the knock on his door like a half a minute after he got to his room. Usually his mom would be coming to talk to him. She was always talking to him, but it was worse when she just stared at him without saying anything. She looked so sad and worried. It made his stomach feel all squishy, and his eyes hot.

He wanted to tell her to stop acting like there was something wrong. He wanted to yell at her sometimes, he got so mad. Only he wasn't mad, exactly. He didn't know what he was, but he knew it wasn't his Mom's fault that he felt like his whole world had turned upside down.

Everything had started to change when Dex and Hold came to the island, but it wasn't them, either. The adults would glance at him and whisper when he was around, but he'd never thought they were whispering about him.

Now he knew they were, and he knew why. It made his stomach even squishier and his eyes even hotter—

"Ben?"

He sat up and said, "Come in," embarrassed when it came out kind of wobbly. It was Hold, and Hold treated him like he wasn't a kid who might haul off and cry for no reason. Hold *talked* to him, and Hold listened.

Hold opened the door and leaned against the frame, and Benji felt better just because he was there. Benji thought that might be what it was like to have a dad and that made him feel even more miserable because he didn't think that when his real dad was around.

"Hey Ben," Hold said. "Want to talk about it?"

Benji scooted his feet under the covers, smiling a little when the puppy pounced on his toes. "I guess."

"It's okay if you don't, but maybe I can help."

"What do you know about it?"

"Um…" Hold looked like somebody'd kicked him, but Benji didn't care.

"My dad said you're the reason he and my mom are fighting all the time."

"Ah. Do you believe that?"

Benji shrugged. "If you weren't around we could be a family again."

"Did you ask your mom about that?"

"I'm talking to you."

"Okay," Hold said, and then Benji could have sworn he said "shit" under his breath, and that was cool because nobody ever swore around him, not to mention Hold must be pretty nervous to slip like that.

"Do you think I'm in the way, Ben?"

"Are you going to marry my mom?"

Hold looked like he wanted to swear again, but he didn't say anything this time.

"Do you love her?" Benji demanded. "You kissed her, I saw you."

"Does it bother you?"

"Kinda. It's gross," he added, making the face that went along with the sentiment.

"You won't feel that way forever, Ben."

"My friend says you're sleeping—"

"Jesus, kid."

"You're not supposed to say that," Benji said seriously. "And you didn't answer my question. It's okay; adults don't sometimes. There's a lot of stuff they don't tell kids," he added, and waited for Hold to give him some stupid answer that wasn't really an answer.

But Hold said, "I really like your mom."

"Then you should marry her." And there it was, Benji thought in disgust when Hold looked away. Maybe he was just a kid, but he could tell when an adult was about to blow him off. "It's not hard to figure out, Hold."

Hold smiled. "Matters of the heart are never simple, kid. But I'm here to talk about you, remember? About you and your dad."

"Nothing to talk about," Benji muttered, adding a one-shouldered shrug like he'd seen Auntie Maggie do a thousand times. "It's my fault he left."

Hold straightened away from the door frame, the hard look on his face matching the hard tone of his voice. "What gives you that idea?"

"He left 'cuz my mom got knocked up. With me."

"Whoever said that needs to be knocked on their ass."

"Everybody says it."

"Okay, okay." Hold shoved his hands in his pockets then pulled them out again. "Might as well try to outblow a hurricane as get folks here to stop giving voice to stupidity."

"Huh?"

Hold came over and sat on the end of the bed, reaching over to scratch behind Chewie's ear. "Your daddy didn't leave because your mom was pregnant with you, Ben. He was just a kid, not all that much older'n you, really."

"My mom was younger than him."

"Well, some people don't grow up as fast as others."

"He didn't come back because of me." Benji said it on a rush, because it was the thing that made him want to barf sometimes, and because it made him feel better to get it off his chest.

"Did he tell you that?"

"Nah, it's just…" Benji trailed off, his fingers worrying at a frayed corner on his quilt. "He spends all his time talking to other people, or staring at Mom when he's here."

"Listen to me," Hold said. "Whatever's going on with your daddy, it's a failing on his part, not yours."

Benji looked up at him for the first time. "Are you sure?"

"Yep. He left before you were ever born, because he couldn't man up. That's before he ever met you, Ben, so how could it be your fault?"

"I guess," Benji said again.

"Sometimes life sucks—and yeah, I'm aware I'm not supposed to say that, but it's just you and me here."

"Sometimes life sucks," Benji echoed, liking the sound of it.

"It's how you react that makes the difference. You've been waiting your whole life to meet your dad, and I'll bet you spent some time imagining what he'd be like.

"Well, Ben, things may not have turned out how you expected, but that doesn't make it your fault. I'm going to be seriously disappointed in you if I think you're blaming yourself, because I know you're a smart kid."

"Yeah?"

"Yeah."

Benji looked down again, then up, sheepishly. "I guess my mom is worried about me."

"See? You're a genius. I know grown men who don't understand the women in their lives so well."

"She's my mom," Benji said, eyes rolling. "I've like lived with her my whole life."

Hold nodded solemnly, but Benji could tell he was trying not to smile. "I'll tell her you're okay, but you know what would really make her happy? You getting some sleep."

"Yeah," Benji said, sliding down in the bed. "She's always worried about me sleeping. Don't know why," he added around a yawn. "I sleep a lot."

"She's your mom. Worrying is what they do." Hold tucked the bedclothes up around him, and the squishy feeling in Benji's stomach went away almost entirely.

Must be what it felt like to have a dad, he thought again. "I wish you would marry Mom," he murmured as he drifted off, never identifying the feelings bubbling through him as hope and love, or realizing that the man lingering in the doorway to watch him sleep felt the very same way.

Chapter Twenty-One

Y ou're sure?"

"Yes, Mom," Benji said, trading a look with Hold over the back seat, a look that was pure male tolerance for the unnecessary fretting of females in general and mothers in particular.

Jessi didn't let it put her off. "There might be some talk."

"There's always talk, Mom."

"About us, I mean. Me and Hold and you. And your dad," she added as an afterthought.

Benji gathered his backpack and got out of the car, stopping by the window she rolled down. "It's okay, Mom. Me and Hold talked about it while you were in the shower."

She slanted Hold a look. "And?"

"People are dumb," Benji said with a shrug.

"Not the way I put it," Hold muttered when she glanced at him again.

"They get bored and they talk about other people so they won't have to think about what's wrong in their own lives." Frowning a little, his eyes went to Hold. "Right?"

"That's exactly right."

"And I'm supposed to feel sorry for them."

Hold nodded.

Benji nodded too, aiming for the same pious expression he saw on Hold's face. "And if they won't shut up, I just walk away because they're just trying to get me to react, and I'm not supposed to give them the satisfaction." He grinned. "And if they hit me, I can hit back." And off he ran, leaving Jessi only one target for her wrath.

"He can hit back?"

Hold hunched in his seat. "Kids are mean."

"He's a kid, too. One who's recently been told he can punch other kids."

"Only in self-defense."

"Most of the other kids are bigger than he is."

"Which means they shouldn't be picking on him in the first place. And all the more reason for him to let them know he won't be pushed around."

She looked out the window again, searching the knots of kids and adults until she found Benji. He'd dumped his backpack on the frozen ground so he could play with a couple of the other boys, including Bobby Cassidy, who considered Benji a sort of honorary little brother. That might worry her in a few years, but for now she could be grateful he had someone looking out for him.

"He'll be fine," Hold said. "He's a great kid. Who'd mess with him?"

"No one. Not physically, anyway." But that didn't make what Hold had done right.

Hold shifted around to half face her. "I was a little boy once," he said, "and small for my age. I know that's a stretch, considering the fine specimen of manhood I grew into."

"Your point would be?"

"School's a scary place when you're the little kid on the playground. I just gave him the advice I wish someone had given me when I was his age."

"Yes, well, I'm not sure I'm grateful."

"It won't be an issue, sugar. It's a small school. Every kid knows every other kid, and more importantly, their parents. It's not going to come to fistfights.

"But knowing he can stand up for himself, that's a confidence booster, and kids aren't apt to harass someone who's sure of himself."

She supposed he had her there, and since he did, she put the car in gear and pulled away from the school. "I don't imagine the break-in has gotten around just yet anyway, let alone that you spent the night at my house." That, however was about to change.

Jessi pulled up in front of the Horizon, slumping a little when she saw Maisie Cutshaw going in for breakfast. Maisie stopped with her hand on the door, peering through the Explorer's tinted windshield. A smile blossomed on her plain face, and Jessi figured she must have identified the big shadow in the passenger seat.

"Great. First you corrupt my son, now you're ruining my reputation."

Hold reached over to cup her cheek, rubbing his thumb over her lower lip. "Are you sorry?"

She covered his hand. "No." Then patted it briskly. "Go get a change of clothes. You can shower at Maggie's."

"I'll just be a minute."

A minute on Windfall could be an eternity, Jessi thought with a sigh.

Maisie followed Hold in, reappearing less than a minute later with a cigarette-puffing Helen Appelman in tow.

Maggie wouldn't have opened the window; Jessi wished she could be that rude. When Helen tapped on the glass, she rolled her window down, listened to them pepper her with questions—and save her from answering by talking over each other. They devolved into a verbal shouting match as Helen and Maisie tried to outdo each other getting the scoop on Jessi's relationship with Hold. Name-calling followed, and finger wagging. Maisie gave Helen a little shove, Helen shoved back, then AJ burst through the Horizon's door, Hold hot on his heels.

"You can thank me later," Hold said as he climbed into the passenger seat.

"I'll thank you now." Jessi backed out of the parking place and pulled away. "Considering you'll have to face Helen tonight, you probably don't want to think about later."

"You're in early," Jessi said when she and Hold walked into the office and found Maggie already there.

Maggie looked over at them from where she sat with her backside on the edge of Jessi's desk, contemplating the big wall calendar. "I'm going over my schedule for the next week or so."

Which was probably true, Jessi allowed, but a three-hundred-pound Italian tenor could have packed everything he needed for a month in the bags under her eyes.

That didn't mean she wasn't alert. "I can leave if you two want privacy," Maggie teased.

Hold grinned. "Would you be so kind?"

Jessi shooed him away. He lingered, though, ran a hand down her arm and linked his fingers with hers, lifting them to brush a kiss over their tips.

"Aw, aren't you two cute?"

Jessi shot her a look.

Still smiling hugely, Maggie picked up a pen and clinked it on the side of the little pottery vase Benji had made and which she'd put on her desk to hold pens. In case that wasn't annoying enough, she made smooching noises—loud and obnoxious ones.

Hold dropped a kiss on Jessi's lips, winked at Maggie, and headed for the little office.

"Payback is a bitch," Jessi said.

"You can be, too, at times."

"Exactly." Jessi pointed at Maggie. "Keep needling me and see what happens when Dex gets back."

Maggie turned back to the big wall calendar.

"I'm sorry," Jessi said immediately. "You must be missing him so much."

Maggie, not one to talk about her feelings, kept her eyes on the chart. "Both my birds are due for maintenance," she said, tapping a finger on the big red X in the square for that day, meaning Maggie had run up against FAA regulations for flying hours, both for her and her machinery. "As much as I love flying, I'm happy to have a day off."

"I never thought I'd hear you say that."

"Me, either, but God, Jess, I'm so tired. And not just because..." Maggie let it go, but the hand she rubbed over her chest, the hand adorned with her engagement ring, made Jessi's heart ache for her.

"This keeps up and you won't be able to wait for Benji to grow up and learn to fly," she said, going for light and cheerful.

Maggie didn't notice. "I'll have to think about replacing the Piper, too," she said, referring to the plane that had been sabotaged only weeks before in an attempt to kill her.

Maggie had ditched in the water about ten miles off the coast of Windfall Island. Dex had saved her, but the plane had been lost to the icy depths of the Atlantic Ocean.

"It's good news," Jessi said when Maggie only shook her head. Business was growing fast, but that meant they needed to keep up. Maybe, she thought, it would push Maggie past the inertia that seemed to be weighing her down since Dex had gone to Boston. "I can make a couple of calls, see what's available."

"Thanks, but that's my end of the business, Jess. You do more than your share as it is, keeping everything else running." Maggie dredged up a small smile. "We might have to think about getting you an assistant before long."

"It's the slow season, so neither of us has to worry too much at the moment."

Maggie sighed. "If this is the slow season, we're going to be in trouble come Spring."

"Spring is a long way off," Hold said. When they both turned to him standing framed in the doorway of the little office, he added, "I think we should talk about last night."

Maggie grinned slowly. "I'm all ears. Don't spare the details."

"Someone broke into Jessi's house, and we don't have any details," Hold said mildly. "That's the problem."

"And I'm taking it seriously, believe me," Maggie said. "So let's talk."

When they both stared at her, Jessi said, "Is this the part where you both gang up on me?"

"No ganging up. I'm staying at your place from now on," Hold said in the kind of tone he probably thought settled the matter.

"We'll talk about it later," Jessi said, refusing to be steamrolled.

"Hold is right," Maggie said. "And I'm sure the two of you will work that out. In the meanwhile, we ought to let Dex know what happened."

Much as she wanted to disagree, to just pretend nothing had happened, Jessi knew Maggie was right. Since the phone on her desk was ancient, Maggie dialed Dex on her cell phone so they could put him on speaker. It only took Hold a couple of minutes to fill Dex in on recent events.

Dex's first question surprised them all. "Is there anything out of place in the office?"

Hold, Maggie, and Jessi all froze, staring at one another.

"You think it was a diversion?" Hold finally said.

"It would make sense."

Jessi took a quick visual inventory of her desk, then the rest of the office. "I don't see anything out of place."

"Check the locks."

Hold took a step back and ran his fingers over the doorknob to his office. "Damn," he said, bending to get a closer look. "There are a couple of scratches here." He ducked through the doorway, doing the same kind of quick once-over with his space, Jessi figured, that she'd done with hers.

"If someone did monkey with the lock they didn't get it open," Hold concluded when he came back out. "Trust me, I know where every scrap of paper is, and nothing was out of place, on the desk or on the chart."

"My guess is someone tried," Dex said. "I would have expected both break-ins to occur on the same night."

"You think the culprit creeped my house to get Maggie away from the airport?" Jessi asked.

"That's exactly what I think."

"If it was a diversion, it worked," Maggie put in. "I was gone from here for at least an hour and a half. Should have been plenty of time to get in here and get out."

"For a pro who didn't want us to know he'd gotten in," Dex said. "You have some pretty shady characters on the island, but no one that good. Which worries me. You could have stumbled across him before he was finished, Maggie."

"There was no one here when I got back."

"I don't like it," Dex shot back. "Hold can hang out with Jessi and Benji, but you're all alone at night."

Maggie jerked to her feet. "And we're women, so we need to be taken care of?"

"You know what I mean. Any one of us is a target when there's no one to watch our backs."

Maggie calmed a little. Not enough to lean against Jessi's desk again, though. "I'm perfectly safe," she said. "And I think we're overlooking the obvious here. There's no proof anyone tried to get into the little office, and the break-in at Jessi's may not be about Eugenia at all."

"You think it could be Lance," Jessi said into the resulting silence.

"And you don't?"

"It crossed my mind," Jessi said, "especially when Lance showed up at the house this morning—early this morning. Apparently George interrogated him, and Lance was in his best dramatic always-the-victim form."

Maggie made a sympathetic face. "How is Benji?"

"At school. Taking on the world." Jessi sent Hold a look. "Probably hoping someone will make a comment so he can go Rambo on them."

"You're not going to let me off the hook on that, are you?" Hold appealed to Maggie. "I told him he could hit back, but only if someone pops him first."

"There are one or two people on this island who could use a right to the jaw," Maggie said. "If you want my opinion."

Jessi rolled her eyes. "Aside from his sudden thirst for blood, Benji seems to be taking this in stride."

"He's not too attached to Lance yet."

"He wants to be," Jessi murmured, trying not to feel relieved by Maggie's observation. No matter what she felt about Lance, Benji deserved a father; it was selfish of her not to want to share Benji with Lance.

But then, she had no problem sharing him with Hold.

"So what lame alibi did Lance toss out?" Maggie wanted to know.

"He claimed he spent the day at Meeker's with his mother. He wouldn't use that alibi if it wasn't airtight."

"No," Maggie said. "Joyce Proctor would slaughter everyone on Windfall to protect her son, but Meeker wouldn't put his ass on the line for anyone unless they were paying him. And Lance doesn't have two nickels to rub together."

"So it wasn't Lance," Hold said, although he didn't

sound completely convinced. "That leaves everyone else."

"I think it's time for me to come back," Dex said.

Maggie lit up, bouncing up to her toes a couple of times. And along with the wistfulness Jessi felt came a little hit of envy. What would it be like, she wondered, to feel so much joy your body couldn't contain it?

Although she could feel Hold watching her, she didn't so much as glance at him. Being with Hold made her happy, but it was a careful kind of happy, the kind she held inside herself like a nugget of gold she didn't dare show to the world for fear it would be stolen away.

"I can come for you this afternoon," Maggie was saying. "Just name the time."

"The sooner the better," Dex said, sounding weary and discouraged. "I'm not accomplishing anything here anyway. Although I have some thoughts on how to change that."

"Care to enlighten us?" Hold asked.

"I've got to meet with Alec first, make sure it can be pulled off. We'll talk when I get back to Windfall."

"Which will be today," Maggie said. "I'll be in Boston by noon."

"I'm not sure I can be ready that soon," Dex said. "But I'll give you my parents' address and let my father know you're going to have lunch with them."

"Um, actually, now that I think about it, my plane and 'copter are scheduled for regular maintenance today. How about I pick you up tomorrow?"

Dex laughed. "You're going to have to meet them sometime."

"I think the wedding will be the perfect time for that."

"When it's too late to talk me out of marrying you?"

"Would they try to do that?"

Dex would have laughed even harder, Jessi decided, if he'd seen the horrified look on Maggie's face. "We'll talk about it when I get back," he said.

"Not as long as I can change the subject," Maggie muttered—after he'd hung up.

Hold turned back into his office and Maggie headed for the door. Jessi scooted after her. "Maggie, do you have a minute?"

"Not really, Jess," she said without stopping. "I have to check out my plane and file a flight plan to Boston."

"It's important."

Maggie turned back, a thin veneer of expectancy sliding over her impatience. But when Maggie's gaze slid over her head, Jessi knew Hold was watching them. And listening.

"What's up?" Maggie pushed.

"It's about the, uh, thing, with the, uh, invoices."

"I don't know anything about invoices," Maggie said, not even bothering to hide her exasperation now. "Handle it like you always do, Jess." She headed for the door again, tossing over her shoulder, "Do me a favor and put the flight to Boston on the schedule."

"Okay." Jessi turned and sure enough, there was Hold, looking amused.

"'The thing with the invoices'?" he said. "You could have asked me to leave the room, Jessica."

"Not everything is about you, Holden." Jessi returned to her desk because it put her back to him, and she sat with that back poker straight. Not that it did her any good.

Hold came over and perched next to her elbow. "What's wrong?"

"Nothing." She forced herself to meet his eyes, to smile. "I'm just...worried."

"You have a lot to be worried about."

More than he knew, Jessi thought dismally.

"We'll all sit down and talk when Dex gets back, and figure everything out."

"I hope so."

"I know so." He dropped a kiss on her nose and started for his office, turning back at the doorway. "Everything will be fine, sugar."

Jessi put her head down on her desk. He wouldn't be so sure of that if she told him about that blanket. She ought to, she thought; it was just a simple conversation.

But she knew better. He'd be angry with her. On top of Lance showing up out of the blue, Benji's struggle to deal with Lance showing up out of the blue, the prowler at her house that might have *been* Lance, and her apparent connection to Eugenia, she couldn't face the prospect of destroying the one part of her life that made her happy.

When Dex got back, she told herself. Even though she knew it for the evasion it was, at least it made sense. They could all decide what to do about that blanket, she and Hold, Dex and Maggie. And it was only a measly twenty-four hours—which she intended to make the most of.

Before her world turned inside out again.

George sat at his desk in his blissfully quiet office, the only sound the click of the keys on the second-hand computer he'd been forced to learn to use as he typed— laboriously—the report on Jessi's break-in.

Eighty-some years ago some bored maid had made a very bad decision, and now he had to deal with the fallout, he thought in disgust. His peaceful little village teetered on the brink of changing in ways he couldn't bear, let alone imagine. Million-dollar inheritance, crime of the century. Fame and fortune for one Windfaller, upheaval for the rest of them.

It was bound to get out. Every time he pondered the matter of Lance Proctor's sudden return, George wondered if it already had. Sure, Lance had a kid here, but that had never seemed meaningful to him before. Why now? And was he the one who'd broken into Jessi's house? Meeker had vouched for Lance, but that didn't make the alibi airtight in George's opinion.

And then there was Paige. Again, she had a plausible reason for coming back to Windfall—

The door opened, and in Paige walked, looking like a dream and smelling like heaven.

But George had learned his lesson where she was concerned. He'd never been one to let a mystery go unsolved, though. He might be slow and thorough in how he went about it, but he got his answers.

She smiled and propped a hand on her hip to showcase the curves she'd covered with a siren red dress, beneath a coat of the same color.

George kept his eyes on her face, nearly smiled over the irritation that marred her perfect features when he said evenly, "You saved me a trip."

"Oh?"

"Jessi's house was broken into yesterday."

"What?"

And now he saw genuine surprise, real concern.

"Is she all right? Benji— Oh." She breathed out, then in again. "You think I broke into Jessi's house?"

"Not really, but I have to cover my bases. And you've always been nosy."

She laughed. "Fair enough. Suppose you tell me what I expected to find? I mean, you don't think I was there to steal her grocery money, right?"

George took in the expensive coat and dress, and even he knew those shoes with the red bottoms came dear. "No, I don't think you were after her odds and ends. I still need to know where you were yesterday between noon and five p.m."

"Lunch at the Horizon," she said with supreme indifference, "followed by a nice, long roam around the village. I caught up with Peter Carelli and his wife, and Jed and Martha. They're doing Adam and Eve," she added, referring to the owners of the island's only fuel station. Martha liked to role play, with a preference for tragic couples in history. Jed went along with her for, well, obvious reasons.

"I spent an hour in the Clipper Snip," she continued, "but I'm sure you can find a window of opportunity for me to have sneaked around in Jessi's house. You won't even have to try that hard."

"I'm just doing my job, Paige."

"Sure, and I just got back to the island, so that makes me an instant suspect. Because none of these old reprobates around here would break the law."

George sat back, grinned.

Paige smiled as she came over to rest a hip on the edge of his desk. "Your turn, Barney Fife. What's going on?"

"You know I'm not going to tell you that."

"Damn it, George." Paige straightened, both hands going to her hips. "I know a secret when I stumble across one, and nobody will tell me what it is."

George sat forward abruptly. "You're awfully curious. Maybe I should rethink your innocence."

"You have a lot of company." Paige exhaled slowly, and her gaze shifted away from his.

That made him feel guilty as hell, even if he hadn't intended to remind her of her troubles. "Paige, I... You know I don't believe you—"

"Made a sex tape with my married director, then leaked it so it's all over the Internet?" she asked when he couldn't seem to find the right words. "I know, George. I'm a little oversensitive at the moment."

He waved off her apology. "That kind of thing comes with the territory, though, doesn't it?"

"Yes. I expect people to be interested, and yes, it works to my benefit. I court the attention when there's a reason. A movie coming out, usually. It's just that..." She spread her hands, at a loss.

"There should be a line."

"There is a line. People don't always respect it."

Neither had they, back when they'd both been young and hormonally stupid. But George let it go. "If you want to know what's going on," he said, "I suggest you talk to Maggie."

Paige turned back at the doorway. "You know she won't tell me."

"She's not really angry, Paige."

"Then she's doing a hell of an acting job."

"Maybe you ought to start by talking about the past before you tackle the present."

She belted her coat and pulled open the door. "I'll think about it."

George simply stared after her for a second, then picked up the phone.

"Hello," Rose Stanhope said.

"Hi, Rose."

"George." Her voice softened the way it did when they talked to one another. The way he loved.

As always, because this long-distance contact never seemed to be enough, he built a picture of her in his mind—a cool, petite blonde, beautifully fine-boned and willowy. They were of an age; if she'd lived on Windfall, or he'd lived in Boston, they might have been in school together.

And she'd still have been miles out of his league, George admitted. If his upper lip hadn't sweat, if his pulse hadn't spiked, if he hadn't longed so deeply every time he heard her voice, he might have been able to think of her as a colleague. But even as he filled her in on the events since the last time they'd spoken, even as he kept the account concise and unemotional, he wiped his upper lip, breathed deeply to calm his racing heart, and reminded himself that even if she'd been sitting in the same room, she'd still be miles out of his league.

"You know Paige Walker didn't enter that young woman's house, George."

"No, she didn't. Trouble is, my only other suspect has an ironclad alibi."

"So, we're in the same position we were in just a few weeks ago," Rose concluded. "Someone on Windfall Island has been hired to find Eugenia's descendant, and you don't know who that someone is."

"Any more than you know which one of your relatives is out to kill that descendant."

"You're right, George, and I'm sorry. If anyone understands your predicament, it should be me."

Predicament was the right word for it, too, George thought. Rose was working to find out which one of the Stanhopes was actively trying to murder anyone even suspected of being Eugenia's descendant; George worked to protect them.

"I only have a handful of people to worry about," Rose said. "You have a whole island's worth."

"Great, I win the prize." George ran a hand back through his hair, really wishing the place was big enough for him to pace. Not that being on his feet would result in a brainstorm. He spent a lot of time upright every day, and his brain remained frustratingly blank where this mystery was concerned.

"Maybe we should talk to Keegan, let him know who he can trust."

"Sure, that would rule you out," George said, "but I don't like outing you. It could make you the next target."

She sighed. "I know someone is trying to remove any possible descendants of Eugenia's, and I understand that it could only be a member of my own family, but it's hard to face."

"I know how you feel." Windfallers were his family, George thought, all of them. And he had to face the fact that one of his kin might be thinking of murder. He glanced toward the single jail cell at the far end of the room, remembering Mort. George already knew how that kind of betrayal felt.

Chapter Twenty-Two

She brought the blanket with her.

Just as they'd arranged the day before, Maggie left first thing in the morning to pick up Dex in Boston. Jessi hadn't slept the entire night because she knew her time was up. So she'd brought the blanket with her.

Of course, she'd put it safely out of sight in her trunk while Hold was in the shower.

But there'd be no backing out this time, Jessi told herself, no finding reasons to keep the secret. She'd decided to spring it on them all at once: Maggie, Dex, and Hold. Just get it over with in one fell swoop.

They'd be angry, especially Hold, but she wouldn't let that stop her, either.

"You're awfully quiet."

"Lot on my mind," she said, her voice as quiet as Hold's had been.

She pulled the Explorer up in front of the school, and Benji jumped out almost before she stopped. It was all the proof she needed to tell her everything was all right with him, at least at school.

One worry down, she thought as she opened the window. "Don't I at least get a good-bye?"

He shot up a hand, yelled, "Bye, Mom," without losing stride. But just as she started to roll the window up, he stopped, turned back, and gave her an angelic smile. Then Maisie Cutshaw's face suddenly peered in at her.

"Hi, there," she said.

Jessi jumped about a mile and reared back until she was all but pressed against Hold. Which Maisie found extremely amusing, if her ear-to-ear grin was anything to go by.

Maisie's eyes shifted to the passenger seat and lit up. "Well, now, good morning, Hold."

"Ma'am," Hold said with a tip of a nonexistent hat.

Maisie sighed. "It's so nice to have a gentleman among us."

"Thank you, Ma'am, but we're in a bit of a rush. Ought to be on our way."

"'Course," Maisie plowed on, glancing at Jessi, "I hope he's not always a gentleman. Seeing as he's not staying at the Horizon anymore."

"Uh..." Jessi said, completely at a loss.

"I'm sure, in light of recent events," Hold drawled, "a lady like yourself would understand my concern over the safety of a woman and child living alone."

"Of course," Maisie said, instantly contrite. "I'm sorry to hear about what happened at your place, Jessi. It must be terrible, losing your sense of security."

"Yes, but I'm sure it was nothing."

"We should be going," Hold said. "Don't want to be late."

But Maisie had a death grip on the door frame, and while thoughts of stomping on the gas pedal and dragging her along beside the car held an amusing cartoonlike quality, in reality it probably wasn't a good idea.

"Well," Maisie continued, not finished confirming the latest gossip, "I hear Dex is coming home today."

"How—" Jessi shook her head, fondly, and wondered why it surprised her how quickly news traveled on Windfall. "Maggie must have told Jed Morgenstern when she arranged for the fuel delivery yesterday."

"And Martha told everyone else," Maisie said cheerfully. "But did I hear right that you're leaving us, Hold?"

"Just for a little while, Ma'am," he said matter-of-factly, before Jessi could even whip around.

And when she met his gaze, he stared calmly back. "We really have to be on our way."

Breathless, speechless, numb, Jessi rolled up the window on whatever Maisie tried to say next, put the car in gear, and pulled away.

"I was going to tell you after we dropped Benji off, but..."

But, she thought, and her aching heart wanted to give him the benefit of the doubt. But he'd had all day yesterday, all evening, to tell her. "That's why you went into town early with Maggie yesterday. To pack."

He sighed, all the confirmation she needed. "I have other commitments, Jessica. Family commitments."

"All right," she said. And left it at that.

So did Hold. That was the part that hurt. Bad enough he hadn't told her he was going away, but he so clearly didn't want to share anything about his life—his life away from Windfall.

She'd be damned if she asked a single question. She might feel like winter had settled into her bones, frozen her solid except for the tears burning behind her eyes. But it was pride that held her tongue, and self-respect that kept her on an even keel.

Hold hadn't made her any promises; in fact, he'd been careful not to. A day at a time, he'd told her, right from the start. Hell, she thought wearily, she couldn't even blame him for the pain she felt now.

He'd all but warned her not to fall in love with him.

They passed the last of the village homes, and Jessi sped up, taking the curves along the shore at her normal safe speed. The ride to the office took fifteen minutes; it felt like forever, closed in with Hold only inches away. Inches that felt like miles.

The minute she walked into the office, she heard Maggie and Dex's voices. She dumped her coat and purse at her desk and rushed back to the little office, walking straight into Dex's arms to give him a hard hug.

He hugged back, a nice, strong, comforting squeeze. The brother she'd never had, she thought, before he held her out at arm's length. His eyes searched her face, eyes that knew her too well.

"It's good to have you back," she said, putting as much lightness into her voice as she could manage with her heart feeling like a lead weight in her chest. "Now maybe Maggie will stop moping around."

"You moped?" Dex's smile spread as he turned to Maggie.

"There was a moment," she said with her trademark one-shouldered shrug. "Then I got over it." But her eyes and her smile were soft.

Dex ran a hand down her arm, then gave her fingers a quick squeeze. His tone was all business. "I'm sure you're wondering what happened in Boston," he said as he turned to include everyone in the conversation. "I'm sorry to tell you it was precious little.

"I know that Rose Stanhope instructed Alec to hire me. He wasn't breaking privilege to tell me that much. But the decision came from the family as a whole."

"So we can't rule out Rose as the Stanhope trying to kill off Eugenia's descendants," Maggie observed.

"We can't rule out any of them," Dex said, sounding weary, "and they know I'm aware that one of them is trying to take out any possible heirs." Again, he reached out, touched Maggie, as if to reassure himself.

"Not even one of them tried to convince you they're innocent?" she asked him.

Dex shook his head. "They've closed ranks. My take is they're waiting to see what happens."

"And if the heir is killed?" Jessi asked. "Even the innocent benefit."

"Doing nothing doesn't make them innocent." Dex scrubbed a hand over his face, back through his hair. "But it tied my hands pretty effectively. So, when I heard what happened at your place, Jessi, I figured it was time to stop twiddling my thumbs and get back here. There's been no change? Lance's alibi is still standing?"

"I haven't talked to George, but as far as I know Lance is still in the clear."

"It would make this whole thing easier if we could pin it on him," Dex said. "Being on the island right at this particular time, for starters."

"Yeah," Jessi murmured, "it would answer a question

or two." And maybe break Benji's heart. "But he has an airtight alibi."

"Paige doesn't," Maggie put in. "Not that we know of, anyway."

"Paige?" Jessi laughed. "Seriously, Maggie? She's dying to know what we're up to, but do you really think she'd break into my house?" Maggie sent her a withering stare.

Jessi responded with a bland expression, then smiled when Maggie rolled her eyes. "Fine. It wasn't Paige."

"Paige may be harmless, but someone on this island isn't." Hold spoke for the first time since they'd arrived, and cut straight to the heart of the matter. "There's only one direction to go from here."

A moment of humming silence passed before Jessi made Hold's point. Although it weighed on each and every one of them, she had the most at stake. "We have to continue working on the genealogy. Hold has ruled out all the families that moved away. It's time to consider the rest of us. I think I can help with that."

Jessi took a deep breath as three pairs of eyes cut to her, watching with varying levels of curiosity. None of them knew what was about to hit them. She still didn't quite believe it, and she'd had a week to come to terms with her discovery.

"My great grandparents, Joe and Claire Duncan," she began, "lived across the street from your family, Maggie, in the house I live in now."

"And my Uncle Emmett lives across from you now."

Jessi nodded. "The Duncans had a daughter named Elizabeth. My grandmother. Her birthday was December 17, 1930. Eugenia's birth date was February 10, 1931, which makes her not quite two months younger than my grandmother. Unless she was my grandmother."

Silence hummed again—ripe, this time, with shock. Not surprising as she'd shied away from any connection to Eugenia. Just the idea of it still scared her to death, knowing she was putting Benji in danger. But she couldn't keep him safe by lying to herself. The truth would come out, no matter how hard she tried to prevent it.

She slid her gaze to Hold and found his eyes on her face, his expression...unexpressive. While Dex and Maggie gazed at her with concern, in Hold's eyes she saw doubt.

"It makes sense," Dex finally said. "You and Maggie are about the same age."

Hold nodded. "So the preceding generations of your family would be contemporary to one another as well, in all likelihood. But it sounds like your evidence is anecdotal? That means—"

"I know what it means." She took another breath, a calming one this time rather than a bracing one. "The dates are recorded in my family Bible."

Silence.

"I can produce it if you want proof," she said. It didn't erase the doubt in Hold's eyes, and that hit her like a blow. "But I could have altered the dates."

Maggie took a step forward, just one before Dex put a hand on her arm.

Hold let the silence draw out.

And the fist around her heart squeezed even tighter.

Jessi wanted him to simply take her word, even when it went against all logic. Especially then. What woman wouldn't want that kind of unquestioning trust, absolute faith, from the man she loved?

What baffled her was why he held back. He'd been hurt by a woman, she'd figured that much out. She couldn't know the details; he hadn't given them to her. But it must have been a deep wound for him to close himself off so tightly, especially when she'd given him no reason not to trust her.

Until now, she reminded herself, until she stood in front of him and admitted she'd lied to him. Yes, she wanted his trust, but she'd just handed him a hell of a reason not to give it.

She rubbed a hand over her chest, tried to soothe the pain there even as she understood she'd brought it on herself.

And that was just bullshit. She'd learned a long time ago not to blame herself for events that were out of her control. Lance had taught her that. She might be perfectly willing to admit what she'd done wrong, but she'd be damned if she stood there and blamed herself for whatever was going on in Hold's mind.

"You want proof," she said to him, proud she'd gotten the words so evenly past a throat tight with unshed tears.

"If he does, he's an idiot," Maggie observed hotly.

"No, I'm not," Hold said. But he wasn't meeting her eyes anymore.

Jessi turned on her heel and stalked out, too hurt, too angry to look at him a moment longer. Or so she'd thought.

When Hold stopped her in the lobby, she rounded on him, poked a finger at him. "You think I'm after the money.

"It's a short trip from wishful thinking to reality, especially with the family Bible right there within easy reach, all the documentation in my hands." After all, hadn't she said it more than once, joked about being rich?

"No, Jess, I—" Hold ran a hand back though his hair, looked away. "Knee-jerk reaction."

"It was *all* jerk," Maggie called out from the little office, not even pretending she couldn't overhear.

Well, let them listen, Jessi thought. Then she wouldn't have anything to explain later. She wouldn't have to talk about it again. Because talking about it now was almost killing her.

"It's my job to ask those kinds of questions," Hold said.

"Maybe that's true, but it was personal, too."

Again, he didn't deny it.

"This is what you were waiting for, right?" she said, the anger draining away to leave the hurt behind. "You pushed and prodded until I told you all about my life, until I let you in completely. And yet you still don't understand me."

"I tried to give you romance—"

"That was just a dance, Hold, a wonderful dance while it lasted. But romance isn't whirling around a room in a man's arms. Romance isn't even a courtship that ends with vows given, rings exchanged. Romance is waking up with the same person, day after day, year after year. It's more than affection, even more than love. It's trust, faith, believing the best about someone even when you think the worst. Especially when you think the worst."

"You know how I feel about you, Jessica."

"How could I when you don't even know yourself?"

When he didn't answer, she stepped up and kissed him lightly on the cheek. "It's all right, I understand. And I'm sorry."

"You have nothing to be sorry about."

"Yes, I do." She went out to the car and retrieved the blanket, still wrapped in its faded paper.

When she came back, she whisked by Hold and straight into the little office, dropping it on top of his research. Then she stood back, arms wrapped around herself, stomach in knots, sick in her heart.

Maggie stepped forward and pushed the flowered paper away. They all stared dumbfounded at the blanket, with its embroidered initials, until Maggie said, "Shit, Jessi."

"I found it in my attic."

"The day we were cleaning it." Hold lifted his eyes—unapologetic eyes—to hers. But then she'd known what his reaction would be. "I thought you wanted to stop because of your mother, because it was still too early." He shoved his hands in his pockets. "Why didn't you tell me?"

"I'm telling you now."

"A week later. I get that you're afraid for Benji—"

"And I get that you're angry, but we should be talking about what it means to the search for Eugenia."

"Fine." He picked up the blanket and studied it. "It looks authentic, but it doesn't follow that the blanket came with the baby. It could have gotten into that trunk in your attic in any number of ways. And we aren't sending your DNA off to be tested."

"You didn't have any trouble putting Maggie in danger," Dex reminded Hold. "When I wanted to protect her—"

"It's not just me this time," Maggie said.

"No," Jessi put in. "If it was just my safety, I'd be happy to play bull's-eye."

"And we can't send the test to another lab," Maggie said to Dex, "unless you want to go back to Boston and get some Stanhope DNA to check against Jessi's."

"That could be problematic, seeing as they won't let me near them."

"Then we investigate Jessi's possible connection to Eugenia some other way," Hold said.

"How do you suggest we do that?" Jessi turned to look at Hold, kept her gaze cool and level although it cost her. "Don't you think it's a little curious that this blanket has been in my family's possession for so long, yet I didn't even know it existed?"

Hold scrubbed both hands over his face, shoved them back through his hair. "I don't know—the journals?" he said, referring to the Windfall Island journals Maggie had borrowed from Josiah Meeker and copied, so that she and Dex could search through them for clues to Eugenia's fate.

"We can try that," Jessi said, "but I don't think any of my people were big on writing."

"Of course not," Hold said bitterly.

Silence fell, the kind of silence that would have been filled with dramatic music if they'd been actors in a soap opera. But this was reality, Jessi thought, and in real life things needed to be said. "Can you give us a moment?" she said to Dex and Maggie.

They filed out of the little office, Maggie shooting Hold a glare as she passed him.

Jessi quietly shut the door. "I come from simple people," she began.

"I didn't mean that the way it sounded," Hold said. "It just feels like we're having nothing but bad luck."

"We both know I'm not talking about one snotty remark you made," she said, getting a kick out of the way his mouth twisted at the word "snotty." "I get that you're angry, Hold, but it's not okay for you to expect me to spill my guts every other second while you keep secrets."

"You're right. I'm not being fair, Jessica, but this," he picked up the blanket, "this is life and death."

And his secrets only felt like it, Jessi thought. "It's still my business."

"Your business." He jammed his hands in his pockets, turned away then back. "Do you think your safety, Ben's safety, doesn't matter to me? What do you expect from me?"

"Nothing, Hold. One day at a time, remember? No putting labels on what's between us."

"That's not... We weren't going to push each other for more than we were willing to give."

"I'm not the one pushing. You don't want to talk about your family, or tell me anything about yourself, for that matter. So I haven't pushed, but you can't ask me to stand there in front of my friends while you make it clear you're only in this for sex."

Now he was the one who looked like he'd taken a blow, and although it shamed her, Jessi felt that instant of satisfaction that maybe, just maybe, he understood what she was feeling. "When did I say that?"

"Never in words, but you've picked my life apart, Hold. You've questioned every interaction with Lance but you can't even tell me you're going away to spend a weekend with your family? Hell, I don't even know if your parents are alive, or their names, or if you have any sisters or brothers." She gave it a beat while her heart ached with every pounding stroke. "Okay," she said when he didn't answer, "so tell me again how this isn't just sex."

"It's just...it's not."

She shook her head, turned away.

"Jessica."

She stopped, but she kept her back to him.

"Will I see you later?"

"Do you want to?"

"Yes."

No strings, she'd told herself, and while Hold wasn't with her for the long haul, she knew he cared for her. And she—well, her heart wasn't ready to let him go. "When are you leaving?" she asked, although what she really wanted to know was when he was coming back. If he was coming back.

"Tomorrow. But I'm— The break-in. I was planning on staying at your place tonight. Unless you'd rather I don't."

"You're always welcome."

"Jessica..." He shook his head. "We'll talk later."

No, she thought, they wouldn't talk later. They never talked, not about anything Hold didn't want to discuss. She didn't expect that to change.

Chapter Twenty-Three

For the first time since Hold had laid eyes on Jessi, he hesitated. Sheer stubbornness had brought him to her front stoop; now sheer terror held him there. He wasn't sure—another first—how she would greet him. But he was damn sure he deserved to have the door shut in his face.

How the hell, he asked himself, had he gotten himself into this fix? What should have been a simple conversation had become a wall between them, a wall he'd built and now had no idea how to tear down. Not after having behaved so badly.

She'd kept the truth from him for a week, and she'd had a damn good reason for it. Maybe he hadn't told any bald-faced lies, but he'd been fully aware she wanted to know about his life, and he'd purposely left her in the dark.

Because he didn't trust her.

Jessi had that right, but she thought the problem was

with her. And that, he decided, might be the worst thing he'd done. Made her doubt herself, made her feel not good enough. Made her believe she was only temporary…

The front door opened. Benji poked his head out and said, "You gonna come inside, Hold?"

"Shut the door, Benj," he heard Jessi yell, probably from the kitchen. "We can't afford to heat the whole island. Hold will be here when he gets here."

"He's here now!" Benji yelled back. "He's just standing in front of the house."

"Thanks, Ben," he muttered as he walked through the door.

"Is Mom mad at you? Is that why you're afraid to come inside?"

"What did she tell you?"

"Nothing. She's awful quiet. Chewie ate half of a couch pillow then barfed it up on the stairs, and Mom just shook her head. And she let me have peanut butter and jelly for dinner. She usually makes me eat vegetables before a sleepover, 'cuz she knows I'm gonna have all sorts of junk food."

"Benji," Jessi said quietly from the kitchen doorway.

"See what I mean?" he whispered to Hold.

Hold grasped Benji's shoulder, but it was more to comfort himself, he decided.

Jessi just stood there, quiet like Benji had said, and it wasn't just about words. She was usually a firecracker, always moving, always smiling, crackling energy from the crown of her madly curling hair to the tips of her pink-painted toes.

Tonight she was the dead calm eye at the center of the storm raging around her.

"Go get your things together," she said to Benji.

He took off and left an awkward silence behind him.

Hold filled it by putting his foot in his mouth. "Do you think it's a good idea to let him go to a sleepover?"

For just a second her eyes fired, but the spark died almost before he saw it.

"He's just going next door," Jessi said calmly. "He'll probably be safer there than here. There's a man in the house," she added with a slight smile to take the sarcasm out of that observation, "not to mention seven kids of various ages sacked out in sleeping bags on the living room floor. They'd be like little alarm systems if someone tried to get into the house."

"I'm sorry. I didn't mean to question your decision."

"He's not in danger yet." But her gaze went to Benji, lingered as he came downstairs lugging a backpack filled to bursting.

"I'm ready."

"Okay."

"Aren't you gonna ask me if I have actual clothes in here?" Benji shared a see-I-told-you-so look with Hold. "And a toothbrush?"

"I figure you're old enough to avoid walking around naked with bad breath. Say good-bye to Hold. He's leaving in the morning."

This was clearly news to Benji. He stopped halfway to the door and swung around. "Are you coming back, Hold?"

"Yeah, I'll be back early next week."

Benji smiled and raced out the door. Jessi crossed to the window and watched him until he disappeared safely into the neighbor's house.

"I'll be back next week," Hold repeated.

"All right," she said with that maddening calm.

The fire he...okay, *loved* about her, was gone. Because of him. She stood less than three feet away from him and he didn't know how to reach her.

But he figured groveling would be involved.

"Hungry?" she asked him. "We already ate—"

"You mean Benji ate," Hold said.

"Maybe this is a bad idea." Jessi wrapped her hands around her waist, looked everywhere but at him. "You're still angry with me."

"Still? No. Again."

"Then you should go, Hold." And now she met his eyes. "I didn't invite you here so we could fight."

"You obviously don't want to talk."

"No." She walked into his arms and kissed him, and it was every bit as open, as generous, as sweet as the first time. He ought to pull back, but here was all the warmth, all the fire he'd been missing. And then he stopped thinking and simply felt.

He swept Jessi up and carried her up the stairs, loving the feel of her, slight and warm, in his arms. She hooked her hands behind his neck and he loved the feel of her head resting on his shoulder. She sighed when he laid her on the bed, sighed and reached for him, and something rushed through him, a warm gush that was only part lust. It was the other part he didn't want to think about.

Even the lust was no match for the other sensation, swelling through him like a symphony. There was no rushing this time; he wanted to give, to *show* her how much he treasured her, at least here. He drew her clothes away slowly, savoring every inch of flesh exposed, drinking in her sighs, her moans. Her skin heated under his hands and his tongue, like roses blooming. Her body moved as he joined himself to her in the slow, sensual dance.

She rose and fell with him. Her hands moved over his skin, her lips cruised over his face, his neck. Every touch, every kiss, drove the heat and need higher. She took what he offered and gave back even more, filling him with light and joy, so much joy he wondered how he could hold it inside.

He'd stayed in the finest hotels the world over—Paris, London, Rome—but here, on this rocky scrap of an island, in this tiny bedroom with its well-used furniture and somewhat saggy mattress he felt... tended. Loved. The kind of love he'd been searching for without ever realizing it. The kind of love that gave without asking for payment, that offered without demand.

Her every touch seduced, every whisper entranced; the feel of her body moving with his lifted him another impossible degree, brought him even more light, more joy.

He gave her the same caring, the same attention. He told her what he couldn't put into words, urged her slowly, gently, to peak, then fell with her.

Sated, he gathered her close, her head pillowed on his shoulder, and just drifted in a lovely haze until sleep took him away.

It started to snow during the night—soft, fat flakes that floated past Jessi's bedroom windows and made the early morning light glow like pearls. Hold slept, peaceful as a baby, with that light flowing over his face and the arm he'd flung over his head.

They'd have to get up soon, she thought, but for just a few minutes the world was quiet and soft and right. She could pretend Hold belonged there, in her bed, in her life.

For now, Hold was hers. She could slide up against him and run her fingertips over his warm skin, so she did. She could kiss his shoulder, his neck, nibble on his ear and nip at his bottom lip. She could slip her body over his, find him hard and ready, and take him in.

"Damn fine way to wake me up, sugar," he said, groaning as she began to move. His hands gripped her hips, but she kept moving slowly, even when he hissed in a breath and murmured, "You're killing me"—slow and steady until the friction, the feel of him under her, in her, became an inferno of heat and hunger raging through her.

Hold reared up and took the peak of her breast into his mouth. Reality narrowed down to his lips and tongue, drawing sharply at her nipple, his hands digging into her sides. The ache deep inside her tightened, growing with each slide of flesh over flesh until she couldn't bear it. Pleasure broke through in waves that swamped her, left her gasping for air and so weak she collapsed on top of Hold and braced herself as he came, and the waves inside her peaked, impossibly, again.

"Hell of a way to wake up," Hold said again, voice deep, breath ragged, arms tight around her.

Jessi just nodded as she slipped over to lie beside him, keeping her head turned away so he wouldn't see her tears.

"The bus is leaving in twenty," Maggie said as she walked through the office door, looking crisp and professional in her flight suit.

Jessi stayed at her desk. Business as usual, she thought when Hold came out of the little office and met her eyes expectantly. She didn't kiss and hug any of their other charter customers, and while Hold wasn't just any charter customer, Solomon Charters was still her workplace. She refused to be anything less than professional—even when he came over and settled on the edge of her desk like he always did.

Too close, she thought as his scent wrapped around her, as she could feel his warmth, as she fought the need to throw herself into his arms and ask him not to go.

"I'll be outside," Maggie said, then tapped her watch as she walked away. "Eighteen minutes."

"You're not going to see me off?"

"We said good-bye this morning," she said, managing to smile up at him. "Twice."

"That wasn't good-bye."

"No," she murmured. "You'll be back."

Hold would return, she had no doubt, to finish the genealogy. He'd made a commitment there. He hadn't made one to her. It broke her heart a little every minute she spent with him, knowing he wouldn't really let her in. But it was her heart; he'd never asked her to give it to him.

When Hold came back, they'd pick up right where they left off. She'd take every minute she could get with him, enjoy every second of those minutes, and not waste one of them thinking about endings.

"When I get back, we have to talk," Hold said.

She looked up at him again, heard something in his voice, saw something in his eyes that fed the stubborn little nugget of hope inside her, made it brighten and strain at the limits she tried to maintain. "Oh?" she said as casually as she could manage with her breath backing up and her heart pounding out of control. "Can't you tell me now?"

He took her chin, tipped her face up to his, dropped a light kiss on her lips. "When I get back."

Just the warmth of his touch was so irresistible, made her yearn so much. But she suppressed that ache, pushed away the need for reassurance, only lifted her eyes to his and smiled. "Now I'll have two reasons to look forward."

Maggie poked her head in the door. "Move it, Abbot."

He pushed off the desk, dropped another kiss, this one on her forehead, and headed out.

Maggie hung back. "You okay?"

Jessi smiled. "Fine. He'll be back, right?"

"For how long?"

"For however long he can stay."

Maggie glared after Hold.

"He's made no promises, Mags. In fact, he's been very careful not to offer more…"

"More than sex?"

"There's more than sex between us."

"But less than the relationship you want. And deserve."

"I wasn't looking for a husband, remember?"

"Sounds like the kind of denial that comes from your head, not your heart."

"What my heart feels is *my* problem, not his."

"Yeah, well, I'm sorry, Jess."

"For what?"

"For telling you to have a fling with that…that Y chromosome."

"It's the Y chromosome—among other things—that makes him interesting."

"Well, he's an ass."

"Yeah, that comes along with the Y chromosome. And he's not an ass all the time."

"Only when it counts. And why the hell are you being so reasonable about it?"

Jessi shrugged. "I can't be anything else."

"Settling for what you can have?" Maggie shook her head. "It's not you, Jess."

No, it wasn't her. "You're right, Maggie. I want it all. Home, family, husband—one who loves me so much he doesn't feel whole when we're apart."

"But Hold doesn't want that."

"I don't know what Hold wants, but it's not settling to accept that I can't force him to feel what I feel, Maggie. It's not settling to just enjoy being with him. It's not settling unless there's someone better out there for me."

"Just don't stop looking, Jess. You deserve more."

Jessi put a smile on her face, even if she knew it was a little melancholy. "Go on, or you'll be off schedule all day."

"Fine, but when I get back we're going to talk."

"Great, more talking."

Maggie frowned.

Jessi waved her off. "Have a safe flight."

"I will," Maggie said. "I'm not sure about Abbot."

Chapter Twenty-Four

Twenty-four hours had passed and she hadn't fallen apart, Jessi thought, mostly because she'd buried herself in work. Aside from the hours she'd spent with Benji for dinner and schoolwork, she'd made sure to keep herself occupied late into the night, until she'd been too exhausted to toss and turn.

She didn't have to notice how empty her bed was, to feel the ache of loneliness, to think about Hold's parting comment. They'd talk when he got back, he'd said, and she tried not to wonder what he wanted to talk about.

"When is Maggie getting back from Portland?"

She looked up, wondering how long Dex had been standing there in the office doorway watching her. Long enough to see her mooning, long enough to get that sympathetic look on his face, she decided, although she didn't feel even slightly embarrassed, since he was looking a little moony himself.

"That'll be her now," Jessi said, as the whir of the Twinstar's rotors floated in from the tarmac.

He came around Jessi's desk so they could wait for Maggie together. "I wonder how the contract talks went?"

"Maybe she should have taken you," Jessi said to him. "You know the business end of Solomon Charters better than she does. She should have taken you."

"I'm sure she did fine by herself."

Dex jerked a shoulder; Jessi wondered if he realized he'd picked that up from Maggie. Wasn't that one of the things that made them a couple, she thought, adopting each other's habits? Maggie had toned down her sometimes abrasive attitude; she tended to pause and think now before she spoke. She'd gotten that from Dex.

But she was still Maggie, confident to a fault as she strode in and dropped her clipboard on Jessi's desk. "You're looking at the newest subcontractor to the biggest charter service on the east coast," she said. "I'll be making a regular circuit for them, twice a month, year-round. And they want to make Windfall a regular stopover, four to six hours, so more business for the island. If it works out, they're already talking about expanding. We'll see after the first twelve months."

"They want a probationary period?"

"I do." Maggie paced as she talked. "Don't want to be swallowed up."

"The bump in business means you'll be able to replace the Piper right away," Dex said, "maybe take on a new pilot part-time." His phone rang and he excused himself to the little office.

"You'd never let anyone swallow you up," Jessi said.

"Us," Maggie corrected her. "You're part owner of this

outfit, and the bump in business means more work for both of us. You should think about hiring an assistant."

"I don't want an assistant. I like things the way they are."

"Things change, Jess. A smart girl changes with them."

"Is Hold is one of the things you're talking about?"

"I'm talking about the charter business. But I'd be interested to know why Hold is the first *thing* that popped into your mind."

"I don't want to talk about it."

"You want to talk about everything."

"I'm learning the art of self-editing," Jessi muttered, and was saved when Dex came out of Hold's office.

"That was Alec. There's a charity ball this weekend in Boston. The Stanhopes are patrons so they'll all be there. Alec says he can wrangle us tickets."

"Whoa." Maggie held up both hands. "Ball? As in dancing? Dancing in one of those long dresses, and those stilts some fashion sadist thinks are necessary when you wear the long dress?"

"Ball as in we can meet the Stanhopes. All of us. Imagine what will happen when they meet you, Maggie, after one of them tried to have you killed."

"Maybe it's not a good idea to stir the pot that much."

"You have to go," Jessi put in. "I can't. There's no one I feel safe leaving Benji with."

"Benji comes with us," Dex said, "especially in light of the latest revelation. He can stay with my family."

"He should be safe in a cop's house," Maggie said.

Dex laughed. "My dad may be a cop, but it's my mom they'll have to get by."

"Great," Maggie said. "You make her sound like some kind of dragon, guarding the gate."

Dex sent her a smile. "You remind me a lot of her."

"And you actually fly," Jessi added, and when she and Dex laughed, Maggie joined in reluctantly. "You know we'll have to shop for dresses, Maggie. This charity ball sounds like a pretty big deal. We can't show up in something we got down at the Emporium," she said, referring to the closest thing they had to a department store on the island. The Emporium stocked everything from work boots to lingerie, but the only current fashion to be found was between the covers of magazines. "We don't have much time, and I have no idea where to start. We're going to need an expert."

"Over my dead body."

"Well," Jessi observed, "at least then you wouldn't need a dress."

Barely fifteen minutes after Jessi called her, Paige breezed into the airport office and settled a hip on the edge of Jessi's desk. Not a perfectly dyed blond hair was out of place, and she was decked out in the kind of outfit that made Jessi sigh with envy: slim black wool pants that were likely lined with silk, fur-lined boots and a fur-trimmed coat that looked warm enough to keep out an arctic blast while still showing every line and curve of Paige's perfect figure.

"Jesus, did you fly?" Maggie wanted to know.

"You asked for my help."

"Jessi asked for your help."

Paige ignored the distinction. "I wanted to meet the man who's willing to take you on for the rest of his life."

"You could have met him at the Horizon. We eat dinner there almost every night."

"But I'm so terrible at waiting. And I gave you an hour for your reunion. That should be enough time to rediscover such limited, and rarely visited, territory."

"Some men prefer the road less traveled to the beaten path."

Paige hissed out a breath.

"If you're going to dish it out, you have to be able to take it," Maggie said.

Jessi caught the look Dex sent her way, did a palms up. "I'm not stepping between them and getting clawed."

"I only bring my claws out for special occasions." Paige crossed to Dex. "You must be the brave man I've been hearing about."

"It's a pleasure to meet you." Dex took the hand she held out, grinning when Maggie scorched him with a look.

"Don't fall at her feet or anything," Maggie said crankily. "You'll only embarrass yourself."

"I used to enjoy men falling at my feet," Paige said casually, "until I realized that the ones who do are only down there to look up your dress." When Dex laughed, Paige honed in on him again. "How's your balance, cutie?"

"Perfectly fine." His eyes shifted to Maggie and simply lit up. "I've done all the falling I'm going to do in this lifetime."

"Oh, and romantic, too. How did you manage to snag him, Maggie?"

"Be nice," Jessi said before Maggie could take the bait. "And you"—she pointed at Paige—"don't make me sorry I called you."

"I told you she'd be like this," Maggie said.

"You're right," Jessi said carefully. "I guess we'll have to buy our own dresses for the Winter Giving ball."

"What? Wait." Paige all but pounced on her. "The Winter Giving Ball? Nearly every attendee has a personal fortune in the millions, or billions. You can't go in there looking like country bumpkins."

Maggie bumped up a shoulder. "Then we'll go shopping on the mainland, Jess."

This time Paige laughed outright. "You'll buy pants, Maggie, and Jessi—"

"I'm on a budget," Jessi said defensively.

"Not while I'm around, you're not."

"You're not buying me a dress."

"No, but there are thrift shops that carry vintage gowns for reasonable prices. And if we can't find anything suitable there, I can get someone to loan you something. From one of the new designers. You can't rub elbows with the Boston elite in something from a run-of-the-mill department store."

"You're right," Jessi said. "You're coming with us."

"Sure. Why don't you invite Maisie and Helen while you're at it? It's just my plane."

"And I'm sure it's a very nice plane."

"Bet your ass, I do all the maintenance myself."

"You..." Paige gulped, the condescension draining out of her face along with every drop of blood. "Maybe this isn't such a good idea."

Maggie crossed her arms and grinned. "Afraid?"

"Yes," Paige mimicked her pose, "but I'm made of pretty stern stuff. Wait. How did you get tickets to the Winter Giving Ball?"

"A friend of Dex's."

Paige crossed her arms, gave Dex a long, dubious look. "Uh-uh. This has something to do with all the secrecy."

Jessi looked over at Dex.

"She's of an age," Dex said.

"No." Maggie tried to stare Dex down, and when that didn't work she shifted her efforts to Jessi.

But Jessi had made her decision. There'd been too many secrets already. "Dex is right, Mags. We should tell her."

"Tell me what?"

Maggie threw up her hands. "Fine, but don't blame me when she shoots her mouth off and this whole thing blows up in our faces."

"If there's one thing Hollywood has taught me," Paige said, "it's how to keep my personal business personal."

"Suppose you fill Paige in, Dex," Jessi said before Maggie could call Paige on that apparent hypocrisy. A woman who'd supposedly made the sex tape currently burning up the Internet could hardly claim to be keeping her business private. Even if Paige was ready to tell Maggie the truth, though, she wouldn't do it in front of Dex.

In any case, Jessi didn't figure she could do Eugenia's story justice, and Maggie didn't want to share, so they let Dex lay it out for Paige. Her reaction was no surprise.

"You don't really expect me to believe I'm the long, lost Stanhope heir," she said with a laugh, "although it would make quite the story. In fact, I'll bet the press would completely forget—"

"See, I told you she'd blab," Maggie said.

"My lips are sealed," Paige retorted with an edge that told Jessi she meant it.

Even Maggie seemed to relent. "Flight leaves first thing in the morning," she said to Paige, her tone firm but not cutting. "With or without you."

"I'll be here with bells on."

"Then I'll be sure to bring my earplugs."

Laughing, Dex followed Maggie out the door.

"Well," Paige murmured, "I see they're made for each other."

Jessi sighed wistfully. "They really are."

The waitress, wearing ripped jeans, a wife-beater, and a black apron crusted with something disgusting, came over to the table. "Whatcha want," she said, not even looking at them.

"Cheeseburger, loaded, and fries," Maggie said.

"Beer with that?"

"Coke. I'm flying."

That brought the waitress's eyes up, but all she said was, "Right," and sent Paige an expectant look.

Paige dropped her voice half an octave and added just a shade of southern to it as she, too, ordered a burger and fries, and a diet soda. It wasn't like she had much choice in a place where the menu was written in chalk over the bar.

Since she hadn't trusted Maggie not to leave her behind, she'd been at the airport at the crack of dawn. They'd flown out of Windfall Airport barely an hour later, and Maggie didn't run the kind of airline that served peanuts, let alone breakfast. Dex and Benji had gone to his parents' house on the South side. George Boatwright, who'd begged a ride with them, had gone off to see to his own business.

Paige had insisted the three women go straight to work, shopping. For once, Maggie hadn't argued with her.

Afraid to meet the parents, Paige had realized, although Maggie's fear hadn't amused her like it should have. She'd been too busy with envy.

"Cheer up," Maggie said. "This place has the best pub food in Boston."

Pub food, Paige thought morosely, picturing her thighs and backside dimpling instantly after the first bite.

"It's also quiet and filled with locals minding their own business, so there's less chance you'll be recognized," Maggie added, her wide grin taking the sting out of her next observation. "Maybe if you got off your high horse, you could appreciate the—what is it?—ambience. Not to mention the anonymity."

Paige looked around at the old, highly polished bar with its brass rails and fittings, the long, age-spotted mirror behind it, lined with backlit bottles. The old wooden booths along the opposite wall may have seen better days, but she'd have bet there'd been a lot of history in here, too. A man of about sixty, white-haired and ruddy, manned the taps, and when he caught her watching him, he winked and smiled, bright blue eyes shining in the dim light.

She couldn't help but smile back—before she remembered she was trying to remain incognito. *God knows*, she thought, *it wouldn't do to let Maggie figure out I actually like the place*.

"The only time I get on a horse is for a role," she said in a languid tone designed to irritate Maggie, "and I wouldn't be caught dead in a place like this in California."

Maggie snorted. "The Paige I remember would have gotten a kick out of this place."

"The Paige you remember was sixteen and green as grass."

"Emeralds more your version of green these days?"

"Oh, for Heaven's sake. Would you two stop sniping at each other?"

Paige sat back. When she turned to Jessi to apologize, she saw the unhappiness on her face. "What's wrong?"

Jessi and Maggie traded a look. Neither spoke.

"Ranks still closed?"

"No, Paige, it's just... You were gone a long time." Jessi spoke carefully, trying not to hurt her.

Jessi didn't know it was too late, Paige thought. It hurt Paige every time she realized that while Jessi and Maggie understood why she'd left, they weren't exactly forgetting that she'd turned her back on them ten years ago. Knowing it was her own fault didn't take the sting out of it.

"And Maggie's right," Jessi continued. "You're not the girl we knew anymore."

"Neither are you," Paige reminded her. "Either of you."

"That's the point, Paige. You left us behind. We— Well, *I* would have stayed in contact."

"If I'd let you know where I was." Paige sighed softly, and not for effect. "I thought I needed to shake the island off me in order to be a success. I guess I didn't realize I was burning bridges as well."

"Bridges can be rebuilt," Maggie said, "but it takes time. You were never patient."

"Neither were you." But Paige smiled, because Maggie had opened the door—maybe just a crack, but still. As much as she wanted to shove it open, she knew that would be the wrong way. But she had a lot of experience with getting her foot in, then making the most of the opportunity.

The waitress returned, carrying a tray piled with burgers and fries, with three huge sodas crammed in between. She transferred everything to the table and left them to sort it out.

"Good grief," Paige said, sitting forward languidly to survey the offerings. "Who's going to eat all that?"

"Us." Maggie crammed a couple of fries into her mouth before she began passing out drinks and the plastic, paper-lined baskets stuffed with burgers the size of bread plates.

Paige poked the burger Maggie slid in front of her, winced when Maggie took a huge bite of her own. "You know that's going straight to your ass."

"I don't store, I burn."

"Well this," Paige made a gesture that encompassed her body from shoulders to knees, "is a storage unit."

"Right. And the whole world just hates the way your storage unit works."

"Because I don't eat like this."

"For someone who wasn't actually invited, you sure complain a lot."

"I invited her," Jessi reminded Maggie.

"And I invited you, so this is my party. Why didn't I get a vote?"

"Because you would have said no." Paige hadn't wanted to hear it, hadn't been able to stomach the rejection. So she'd shoved herself in where she wasn't wanted—and maybe, just maybe, she'd made herself useful. And taken the steps that had opened that door a crack. "We had fun, didn't we?"

"I did," Maggie said, "as soon as I saw you climb out of Jessi's car in that frumpy outfit."

"I borrowed some of your clothes," Paige said sweetly. "I hope you don't mind."

Maggie grinned. "You're a little quicker on your feet than you used to be."

"Hollywood."

"So if you can disguise yourself this well, why don't you?"

"Hollywood," Paige said again, hearing the weariness in her own voice, edged with cynicism. "There's no way I'm walking around looking like this all the time." She plucked at the baggy dress and mud-brown coat she'd borrowed from Helen Appelman. A different hairstyle and a creative hand with her makeup altered her features enough, she'd figured, to withstand the kind of casual scrutiny she was likely to get. "If I was recognized and photographed in this getup it would be a disaster."

"I'm sure you could talk your way out of it," Maggie said, "seeing as you're so quick-witted now."

There were some things you couldn't talk your way out of, Paige thought. She kept that to herself, though. No point in ruining a perfectly lovely time. And no reason to starve. She licked her lips, pulled her basket closer. "Do you know how long it's been since I had one of these?"

"You had one in that movie," Jessi said.

"*December Sunshine*. I was dying. And I didn't actually eat it."

"Really? Why not?"

"It's prop food. It's meant to look a certain way and perform in a certain manner. It's almost always stone cold—can't have the actor burning the roof of her mouth on hot pizza cheese. Or say I was eating this hamburger: how would it look if it leaked all over my expensive wardrobe? Or maybe it's meant to leak on me. So it's dry as dust or loaded with enough grease and condiments to refloat the *Titanic*. Either way it's disgusting."

"That's what comes of lying for a living," Maggie put in.

"Oh, it's not that bad," Paige said, waving off Jessi's instantaneous attempt to defend her. "If the good points didn't outweigh the bad, nobody would want to be an actor. And let me tell you, there are a lot of good points."

"Money," Maggie said.

"Brad Pitt," Jessi chimed in at the same time. "You have met Brad Pitt, right? And Leo DiCaprio. You've done movies with both of them. Are they good guys? Were Angie and the kids on the set all the time?"

Paige hunched her shoulders, looking around.

Jessi clamped a hand over her mouth. "That was kind of loud, wasn't it?" she said through her fingers.

"A deaf man couldn't hear his own thoughts in here," Maggie said.

The place was a cacophony of big screens tuned to sports, the tinny sound of an old jukebox, and the bells and buzzers from a pair of old-fashioned pinball machines at the far end of the room. Just the quick glance she'd taken told Paige that no one in the place was giving them a second look—except the man ogling Maggie, and wasn't that a kick in the pants.

But then, Maggie was a hell of a looker, and in the dress she'd bought? She'd break hearts for sure.

"I think you have an admirer," Paige said to her. "It's a good thing he didn't get a look at you an hour ago."

Maggie just shrugged it off.

Jessi sighed. "That dress is so beautiful, Maggie. So is mine. I still can't believe they'd sell a vintage Valentino for so little."

"It's a used dress, sweetie," Paige said. "They can let it go for a lot less than when it was new on the runway." Especially after she'd slipped a couple of bills to the sales clerk.

Paige looked up, caught Maggie watching her, one eyebrow raised, and wondered if she'd gotten away with it as cleanly as she'd thought. Not that it mattered, as long as Jessi never found out about it—and she figured Maggie would keep the secret rather than hurt her best friend.

"Well, we're going to look gorgeous," Jessi said.

"It's a shame Hold won't be there to see you," Paige said, then immediately wished the words back when the joy slid away from Jessi's face.

"His loss," Maggie said.

Paige looked from one face to the other—Maggie's closed and angry, Jessi's closed and miserable. For once, although she was rabidly curious, she left it alone. "Well, there'll be more than enough hearts to break at the Ball, that's for sure."

But not for her, she thought, and joined her friends, angry with the press and paparazzi who only wanted to capitalize on her humiliation, and miserable that she had to hide away in a hotel room because the people who'd sought her company only weeks before would shun her now. None of them had cared to find out whether or not she deserved it.

No, she'd had to go home to find someone who cared

about her. She looked across the table at Maggie, and knew they'd turned a corner—one that wouldn't take them back to the place they'd left off a decade before, but to a new place.

A better place.

Chapter Twenty-Five

The Keegan house sat on a quiet street in South Boston, nestled between identical houses with barely enough space between them for a man to traverse without brushing his shoulders against the walls on either side.

The houses had been individualized and showed the characters of their owners. The Keegan house, Maggie thought, gave off an air of fun, of joy, of welcome. It had been painted a cheerful shade of yellow, the deep front porch accented with peach, white, and pale green.

The door was leaded glass and sported a bedraggled Christmas wreath, obviously made by the hands of children. Beyond the wreath was an interior filled with light—before the door was flung open and a woman burst through. Dex's mother, Maggie assumed. She was middle-aged and comfortably dressed in trim jeans and a sweater adorned with snowmen. One of them was flipping the bird with its twiggy finger.

"I think I'm going to like her," Jessi said.

"I think I'm going to throw up."

Peggy Keegan rushed down the steps, arms wide, to envelop Dex in a hug. She spoke to him, but Maggie's head had started to buzz, and she couldn't for the life of her make out a single word.

Then Peggy turned, their eyes met, and Maggie took an automatic step back. She didn't mean to do it, saw the flicker of surprise—and hurt—on Peggy's face, but she couldn't seem make her feet move.

Paige, bless her, stepped into the awkwardness, holding out a well-manicured hand and laughing as Dex's mother hugged her instead, and exclaimed over how she would be the talk of the neighborhood, what with a limo and a movie star appearing on the same day.

"Of course," she added, "the two do go together, after all. And you must be Jessica and Benjamin," she said, hugging Jessi next, and bending a little to shake Benji's hand.

"It's a pleasure to meet you," Jessi said, hugging back with an ease Maggie had always envied about her. "Dex has told us about you, all of you."

"And Maggie," Peggy said warmly, although her smile wavered and her hands worried at the hem of her sweater.

Her show of nerves gave Maggie the courage to step up and hug the woman who would be her mother-in-law, to murmur, "I'm sorry, Mrs. Keegan, I'm not very comfortable with new people."

Dex's mother gave her a bracing squeeze, adding a couple of soothing circles to her back that made Maggie's throat burn. "Let me take a look at you," she said as she stepped back, her hands sliding down to link with Maggie's. "Well, you're beautiful, of course, but that's not why my son fell in love with you. He's always been one to look beneath the surface."

And now the tears swam into Maggie's eyes. This, she thought, was a mother, the kind who raced out onto a snowy sidewalk in her socks because she couldn't wait to greet her son. The kind of mother who hung a lopsided wreath because it was made with love, and who cared more about the people in her house than the image it presented.

The kind who welcomed a stranger because her son was in love.

"Call me Peggy," she said as she stepped back.

"I think...Maybe at some point I could call you Mom?"

"Oh." Peggy waved a hand in front of her sparkling eyes in a move that had always baffled Maggie. "That's exactly the right thing to say, especially since I can see you mean it—look at that frown," she added, laughing delightedly.

"Maggie never says anything she doesn't mean," Dex said.

"Why would anyone?"

Maggie felt him ease up behind her and slip an arm around her waist. "Now you've done it," he said, squeezing her lightly, and although there was a teasing note in his voice, she could tell she'd pleased him.

More people ought to be honest, she thought, but she knew it was more than honesty that had prompted her.

"Come inside." Peggy took Maggie's hand, and drew her up the sidewalk and into the warmth and brightness of the old house.

"This brute lurking in the shadows is Carter, Dex's father."

"It's cold out there," Carter grumbled, taking everyone's hand in turn while his wife made the introductions.

When he got to her Maggie thought, *This is what Dex will look like in twenty-five years*. His hair might have silvered, but he was still fit, still handsome, and his eyes sparkled with strength and humor. Maggie hoped she aged half as well, but no matter what, she'd still count herself a lucky woman.

"These are my grandchildren, Katie and Kyle."

A little girl of about four had her arms wrapped around one of Peggy's legs, and Peggy's hand rested on the shoulder of a little boy only a year or so older. They were both so solemn, so serious, with their blue eyes and strawberry blond hair.

"Lou is still at work," Peggy said, her eyes going to meet Dex's. "She's turning her hand back to nursing, and I'm glad of it. I think it's helping her to be busy."

"Dex told us…We were all so sorry to hear of your loss," Maggie said.

Peggy reached over and gave her hand a squeeze.

Through it all Benji had stood back, staying close to his mother.

Thankfully Dex's niece wasn't so shy. She came over and took his hand. "You can come to my room and play," she offered.

"He don't want to play with dumb girl stuff."

Katie clouded up, her little chin trembling.

"Girl stuff's okay," Benji said. "My mom's a girl and she's never dumb, and my Auntie Maggie flies planes and helicopters."

"My Barbie has a car," Katie offered, her little voice still wobbling.

"Cars are good," Benji said, letting Katie tow him away. Kyle tagged along after them, backpedaling on his opinion of girls and their toys the whole way.

"That's some kid," Peggy said.

Jessi stared after him. "I don't know what I'd do without him," she said. "He's not really in any danger, but it will ease my mind to know he's here with you."

"Then it's settled." Peggy headed to the rear of the house. Jessi and Paige followed her while the men peeled off into what she figured was a den.

Maggie looked after them wistfully, then nearly tripped over her own feet when Peggy said, "So, I know you and Dex haven't set a date yet, but have you looked at dresses?"

"No." Maggie rubbed a hand between her breasts. It didn't do much for her wildly pounding heart. "You'll help me, right?"

Peggy's already misty eyes went damp. "If that was sucking up, you're good at it."

"That was panic. But I'd have clued in to the sucking-up factor before long."

"Your mother— Forgive me for being blunt, but she doesn't want to be involved?"

"My father doesn't want to be involved, and she'd never go against him."

"Then I'm sorry for you both, and a little bit delighted that I get you all to myself." She folded Maggie into a hug, and Maggie hugged back, if a little gingerly.

"There now," Peggy said with a laugh. "That didn't hurt so bad."

"It didn't hurt at all." But it did, in an odd way, Maggie thought. Because it showed her what she'd missed as a child.

This would be an example, she decided, of the kind of home she could make. And it was one more gift Dex had given her. The gift of family.

Chapter Twenty-Six

Maggie wore a column of black that skimmed her long, slim body. Jessi wore a gown draped Grecian style to flatter her petite curves, its deep red color teasing out the auburn highlights in her hair.

"We look pretty damn good," Jessi said, surveying their reflections in the full-length mirror in one of the suite's bathrooms.

Paige, wearing slim jeans, heeled boots and a cashmere sweater, her blond hair in a cool twist, stepped between them. "You both look gorgeous. As good as any of the idle rich you're about to rub elbows with."

"I wish you could come with us."

Paige gave Jessi's waist a little squeeze. "You know I can't. It's one of the biggest charity events of the year. There'll be reporters and photographers there, and not just any reporters. These will be society and entertainment reporters. Even if I wanted them to find me, it would take the spotlight off the charity."

"You don't have any reason to hide yourself away," Maggie grumbled.

"Well. Color me surprised."

"You've made a bad decision now and then," Maggie said, "but you wouldn't sleep your way to the top. Your ego wouldn't allow it."

"Now I'm speechless."

"Funny, your lips are moving and words are coming out."

Laughing, Paige threw her arms around Maggie, hanging on like a burr when Maggie tried to shove her off.

Jessi felt like the whole world was brighter now. "It's about time the two of you made up."

Maggie snorted. "I'm still watching you around Dex."

Paige laughed again. "You two are going to own that ballroom. Every woman is going to be jealous, because every man will be falling over themselves to meet you."

Maggie opened the ridiculously small jeweled bag Paige had insisted she needed, with the lipstick and tissues Paige had put into it. "I'm engaged, but I think you should go for it, Jess."

"Maybe I will."

"Well, then, I guess that leaves Hold free for the taking," Paige said.

Jessi shrugged. "Be my guest. He's made no commitment to me."

"Jess"—Paige met her gaze in the mirror—"you know I was only kidding."

"I wasn't. We're not in a relationship, Paige. We're just...having fun."

"You don't seem to be enjoying yourself very much."

"Of course I am. It's just a matter of curbing my expectations."

Paige exchanged a look with Maggie. "That's so . . . not like you, Jessi."

Jessi opened her tiny clutch, much as Maggie had done, but she paid no attention to the contents. "It's the new and improved me."

"New maybe," Maggie said. "I'm not sure improved is accurate. Hold has a lot to answer for."

"I'm responsible for my own feelings."

"Maybe that's true," Maggie shot back, "but how about Benji?"

"He'll be fine, too. I'll make sure of it."

Maggie started to fire back again, but Paige gave her a little nudge that shut her up. "Go break some hearts," she said, adding, "Once you've worked your way through the big shots downstairs, Jess, one lowly genealogist will be no match for you."

They made their way from the bathroom, through the bedroom, and into the public area of the hotel suite, where Dex waited for them.

"Hello," he said, giving Maggie a long, appreciative once-over before kissing her carefully.

She grabbed him by the lapels and planted a kiss on his lips, one that went deep and hot, and made Jessi just a little uncomfortable. "Now that was a hello," she said when she came up for air.

"I didn't want to muss you," Dex said, "but I am going to dance with you later."

"It's a date," Maggie said.

"Great," Paige said, herding them toward the door. "Go have it somewhere else."

"Not so fast," Dex said. "Let's go over it one more time."

"Do we have to?" Maggie said with a sigh.

"Nope, we can call this whole thing off. I'm still not convinced it's a good idea to let either one of you go into a crowded ballroom with the possibility that someone there wants you dead."

Maggie rolled her eyes, and while Jessi understood her annoyance, she wanted this to be over. If reassuring Dex that they were on their guard got her closer to ensuring Benji's safety, and her own, then she'd reassure him.

"There are two pillars of the Stanhope family," she began. "Clayton and Rose. Clayton runs the businesses; Eugenia would have been his aunt. He's divorced, has a son and daughter.

"The daughter is married to an English baron. He took her generous inheritance and built it into an egg big enough to feather every nest in Europe. They have one son, who's following in Daddy's financially astute footsteps."

"They don't come to the states often," Dex added, "and from what Alec told me, their relationship with the rest of the family is cool at best."

"So we can rule them out?" Jessi asked.

"Not entirely, but I'd put them low on the list."

"Okay. Uh, Clayton has a son," Jessi continued. "Clayton the fourth. They call him Chip. Chip is just getting into the family business, entry level. Says he wants to work his way up in the corporation. You have to give him credit for that."

"It doesn't mean he wants to give away a third of the family fortune," Dex pointed out. "He's shrewd enough to know he'll garner support and trust by paying his dues, so I'd say part of that is calculation."

"Then there's Rose," Jessi finished. "Eugenia would be her great aunt, so Rose is around our age, Maggie. Rose primarily heads up the charities."

"Rose, Clayton, Chip," Maggie said when Dex looked to her. "Got it."

Jessi nodded. "Wish us luck?"

"You don't need luck," Dex said, "not with Maggie and me watching your back." He tapped a finger to his own ear to indicate the Bluetooth Jessi had hidden beneath her hair. "Just keep the line open, and you'll be fine." He kissed Maggie, then Jessi's cheek, and left the suite.

As agreed, Jessi and Maggie lagged behind.

Jessi pressed a hand to her madly jumping stomach. "Well, here goes," she said to Paige, once they'd given Dex a head start.

"I'll be listening, too," Paige said. "Anything goes wrong and I'll have the police here in two shakes."

"We won't need the cops," Maggie said. "If Dex doesn't kick some ass, I will."

"I'll be fine," Jessi said. Even if she felt like she was going to keel over any minute. She filled her lungs, let the air out slowly, then again, until the dizziness passed. "Got any acting tips for me?" she asked Paige as she opened the door to the hallway.

"You have to believe it yourself if you're going to make other people believe it," Paige said, then gave her a hug. "Break a leg."

A uniformed security guard requested their invitations, opening the ballroom door only after he'd checked their names off his list.

It was like walking into a fairyland, Jessi decided. Potted trees strung with twinkling lights stood singly or in little groves around the ballroom. Bowers covered with flowering vines led the way to the dance floor. Tables covered with greenery held platters of food, making it seem like a picnic set in an enchanted forest.

A pair of young women in pale green dresses, tattered in the latest fashion but also vaguely reminiscent of elves, approached them. One held a basket filled with flowers that, as the other dipped in, proved to be circlets woven with trailing ribbons.

Charmed, laughing, Jessi allowed her to place one of them on her head.

Maggie politely but firmly declined. "That thing would make me look like a Maypole," she said. "You, on the other hand, look like Cinderella, Jess."

"I feel like Cinderella at the ball. I can't believe this is for charity; it must have cost a million dollars."

"Everyone here tonight can afford to give that much and more, so Dex says."

"You and I will have to settle for solving Eugenia's mystery and parting the Stanhopes of their money. Have you seen any of them?" Jessi lifted to her toes, but she couldn't see anything.

"Clayton the third is over by the bar," Dex said into the Bluetooth earpiece Jessi wore.

Since showing his face would probably send the Stanhopes running for the exits, Dex had finagled himself a place in the security room to watch the monitors. Jessi would be the one talking to Clayton, so she was wired.

"The bar," Jessi said.

Maggie started to plow her way through the press of

people. Jessi fell in behind her until the crowd thinned enough for her to walk beside Maggie. As they neared the bar, Jessi saw a tall, distinguished man, in his late sixties but still handsome and fit. His eyes, she discovered when he glanced their way, were the same bright blue as Maggie's.

Before Jessi could approach him, a taller, slimmer young man joined Clayton. The resemblance was unmistakable.

Maggie took her elbow and pulled her into a nearby arbor. "Must be Clayton," she murmured.

"And his son, Chip. My cousin."

They both spun around to find a woman around their age, smiling pleasantly. Her honey-colored hair was up in a cool twist; her crystal-embellished dress must have cost a fortune and weighed a ton. Everything about her screamed "quality." Pretty, Jessi thought, or rather she'd be termed lovely in her social circles with her flawless skin, delicate features, and...

"Jesus, Maggie, look at her eyes."

"I see them."

"Every morning when you look in the mirror."

Maggie's mouth thinned. "It's already been established. I'm not a Stanhope."

"No," Rose said to Maggie. "You're not a Stanhope, but your eyes—well, they could tell a different story. You," she said, turning to Jessi, "don't bear any resemblance whatsoever to my family."

"That doesn't really mean anything, does it?" Jessi said. "I mean, I could look like whoever Eugenia married. If she survived."

"You're an awfully cool customer, Jessi," Rose said. "Do you mind if I call you Jessi?"

"No, Rose, I don't mind."

"And you'd be Maggie Solomon." Rose held out her hand, waited until Maggie took it, then offered it to Jessi.

Jessi shook politely, but she wasn't any less wary than Maggie.

"Relax," Rose said, "I'm on your side."

"Easy to say."

"It *is* an easy thing to say, Maggie. Can I call you Maggie?"

"No."

"Don't be rude, Maggie."

Maggie whipped around, Jessi a beat behind, and found George Boatwright standing behind them. "What the hell?"

George handed one of the flutes of champagne he held to Rose, offered the other to Maggie. When she refused it and when Jessi shook her head, he downed it in one long swallow.

"Well, well," Maggie drawled, "the monkey suit looks good on you, George. But champagne? When you begged a ride to Boston, I never would have guessed *she* was the business you had to see to."

"The monkey suit," George ran a finger around his tight collar, "is for this shindig. The champagne was because of you."

Jessi stepped between them. "What are you doing here, George?"

"Shhhh." He covered the hand Jessi had set on his arm. "I'm here for the same reason you are."

"How do we know that?" Maggie demanded. "How do you know she's not lying to you?"

George rounded on Maggie, but Rose laid a hand on his arm, and he pulled himself in with a visible effort.

"It's a fair question," Rose put in. "If the three of you don't smile, it's going to look like we're up to something. And let's remember," she said pointedly to George, "my uncle and cousin don't know who you are and we don't want them wondering. As far as they know we met here, and," she dimpled, "you're just another nobody after my fortune."

"Your fortune," Maggie sniped, "is the problem."

George pinned her with a look. "If Rose wanted you dead, Maggie, you'd be dead."

"No offense, George," Jessi said, "but why would we take her word for it?"

"Because I'm the one who called George and let him know about Dex Keegan and the search for Eugenia's descendants."

Maggie crossed her arms and stared George down. "You've known this entire time?"

"You can take George apart later," Jessi said to her. "Right now we have bigger issues. If Rose is innocent, then—"

"It has to be Uncle Clay or Chip. Or both of them," Rose said with a sigh. "They won't stop until they're sure Aunt Eugenia left no one behind."

"Arrest Clay," Maggie said to George.

"For what? Having an intense conversation with his son? Even if I had jurisdiction here, there's no proof."

"We'll get proof," Jessi said.

"Great. It'll be your word against one of Boston's leading citizens. Who do you think the Boston cops will believe? And even if they did lock Clayton up, what makes you think he can't get to anyone he wants from a jail cell?"

"He's right," Dex said in Jessi's ear.

"Dex says George is right," and when Maggie swung around to glare at her, Jessi took the Bluetooth from her ear and handed it to Maggie, who, after a brief struggle, stuck it in her own ear.

She listened, and while her expression stayed mutinous, her body language didn't.

"So you're on our side," she said to Rose.

"I know it's hard to believe, but yes, I am. My great grandmother... We were very close. She died when I was a child, but she used to sit with me in the nursery, my mother said. And when I got a little older, she took a special interest in me. You see, I was the first girl born into the family after..."

"After Eugenia," Jessi finished when Rose's voice broke.

George shifted over to stand beside Rose. A blind man could have seen the care and longing his face, and the way Rose took comfort from his nearness. They might not be lovers yet, but there was a deep connection, Jessi thought.

Maggie wasn't as quick to accept this new development. "How do we know Rose isn't playing us—all of us," she qualified.

"Because we trust George," Jessi said instantly, and not just because of her automatic need to defend a friend. There were no shades of gray for George, only black and white. Even where his feelings were concerned, he'd think through every angle, every possible repercussion, before he took a step.

"Where George is concerned, nothing comes before Windfall Island," Rose said.

"We both know that, don't we, Maggie."

"But—"

Jessi elbowed her.

"Jeez, give me some credit, Jess. I was just going to tell George and Rose they make a real cute couple."

George blushed to the tips of his ears. "We aren't a couple."

Rose looked up at him, smiled, then laughed as she shared a look with Jessi. "George thinks I'm too good for him."

"George is right," Maggie teased, "but not because of the money. Because he's a hypocrite."

"Maggie," George said with a combination of guilt and rebuke that only seemed to make her angrier.

"You knew all this time what was going on, and you kept quiet about it."

"For the same reason you did, Maggie."

"You gave Dex and me a dressing down for holding out on you, as I recall."

"Don't be angry with him," Rose put in. "I made him promise not to say anything to anyone."

"You could have gone to the authorities."

"And tell them what?" George said. "Eugenia Stanhope survived, was taken to an island on the bare edges of society. Then some bootlegger, petty thief, or outright criminal, as most of them were back then, took her in and didn't ask for ransom from a family who could have bought Windfall a thousand times over? That Clayton Stanhope is looking for these nonexistent descendants in order to have them systematically wiped out so he won't have to share a fortune that would hardly notice the dent another heir would make in it? That he preyed on a troubled young man to sabotage the plane of someone he doesn't even know—a plane that is now at the bottom of the Atlantic and beyond any kind of forensic examination?"

As was Mort, Jessi thought—as they all must be thinking. "Well," she said quietly, "when you put it like that..."

"Uncle Clayton was the first to agree with me that it was time to find out what happened to Eugenia," Rose said. "He offered up his own blood as the testing sample. As head of the family, he said it was his place."

"Are you sure it was his sample?"

"Absolutely. First, we are not in any way affiliated with the lab, and while he might be able to buy a technician, why would he? He wants this business over as much as I do, and if he corrupts the comparator, how would he ever know this matter was finished once and for all without killing everyone who knew about it?" Rose shook her head. "That, I'm sure, would be more than he'd be willing to do. And with you all alive, he has numerous witnesses that the search went nowhere. He even decided to hire your Mr. Keegan when Alec suggested it."

"He miscalculated there," Maggie said smugly.

"Yes, well, so did I, it appears. I thought it only fair to alert local law enforcement. Mr. Keegan was going in with a disguise of sorts, but still, I didn't want anyone hurt. Including him. So I reached out to the sheriff, and well..."

"He reached back?" Jessi suggested.

Even as George blushed again Rose laughed. "You are,

both of you, delightful. I'd love to get to know you better, when all this is over."

"If we're still alive," Maggie said.

"You and everyone on your island will be safe," Rose assured her. "It's why we decided it would be better if George played the bumbling sheriff."

Maggie shot him an arch look. "He does it really well."

"I want the culprit to think I'm not paying attention."

"No offense, George," Jessi said, "but so far it hasn't mattered much. Nothing we've tried has mattered."

"He's smart." George stared off in Clayton's direction. "Smart enough to have worked out all the angles."

"He didn't bargain on me finding Eugenia's blanket."

"What?" Rose curled her hand around Jessi's wrist.

"Packed away in my attic," Jessi said. "Pink wool edged with pink satin, has the letters E, A, and S embroidered on it, with the S being bigger and in the middle."

"Oh, my," Rose said faintly. "I hadn't heard about this latest development."

"Because I haven't heard," George said.

"It's a fairly recent discovery, and I kept it to myself because, well…"

"Because of Benji," George said, adding for Rose's benefit, "Jessi's seven-year-old son."

"Who will be in danger," Maggie felt a need to add, "unless you can find out what Clayton is planning."

"I'm afraid that won't be possible. Uncle Clayton is very smart, and I have to say very suspicious. He knows I'm open to any legitimate additions to the family. If he's up to something, he won't tell me about it."

"Well, I won't be in danger for long," Jessi said. "My DNA is at the lab being tested even now."

"And you don't think you're a match?" Rose asked her. "Despite being in possession of the blanket?"

"There's no resemblance, and there's any number of ways that blanket could have come to my family. It could have been years after Eugenia was lost." But even Jessi could hear the worry in her own voice.

"I'm sorry," Rose's voice softened with sympathy. "I can only imagine how frightened you are for your son."

"Getting my DNA tested should take him out of danger. As long as I'm not a match."

"If you are..." Rose took a deep breath as she grasped Jessi's hand. "Is it all right if I hope you match?"

"No offense," Maggie said, "but you already said you don't know what your uncle is planning."

Jessi leaned back, peering around the shrubbery in the direction Clayton Stanhope had been, as if seeing that he was still in the ballroom could guarantee Benji's safety. Instead, she spied Hold, heart-stoppingly handsome in a tuxedo, headed in their direction. For a split second, everything else flew out of her head and she could only stare in confusion.

"Would you look at that?" Maggie said.

Rose followed their line of sight. "Oh, he's gorgeous, isn't he? Holden Abbot," she explained, adding, "Abbot Investments," when Maggie and Jessi only exchanged a look. "Commodities mostly, but they've been in banking and real estate for generations. And of course the charities, which is Hold's area of responsibility."

Jessi felt Maggie shift closer to her, appreciated the offer of support even though it didn't help much. Even she'd heard of Abbot Investments. Hold was one of the wealthiest men in the country, then. That should have some significance, but the buzzing in her head made it almost impossible to think.

"I had what you'd call a crush on him," Rose continued with a smile, "but he was engaged at the time. That was before he found out his fiancée was only marrying him to get her hands on some of the Abbot fortune. She had a shyster lawyer draw up a prenup with more holes than a wheel of Swiss cheese. Her...charms might have been enough to convince Hold not to look too closely, but his brother, James, runs Abbot Investments. James never lets emotion cloud his judgment—not even brotherly love, although you could call it love to save a brother from the grasp of a woman like that. Not that Hold thanked him, I'd imagine."

And now she understood, Jessi thought. Her mind went screaming back to shocking clarity, probably because of the pain in her chest.

"I wouldn't set my sights in that direction," Rose concluded. "He's notoriously standoffish with women now."

Shut up! The command screamed in Jessi's brain, would have shouted from her mouth if she'd been able to push words through a throat squeezed tight with agony. She wanted to shake Rose Stanhope until words stopped spilling from her mouth. But words wouldn't change the truth.

It all made perfect sense now—the fancy clothes, the manners, his ease with people. How he was able to spend those weeks doing a job that came with no paycheck. His reluctance—no, refusal—to talk about himself.

She wanted to go to him, to beat at him until he told her the truth with his own mouth. But what would that accomplish? Nothing could have spared her this broken heart, not after a betrayal of such magnitude.

Although she knew it was self-abuse of the worst kind, she glanced over again, saw Hold.

And Hold saw her.

In that instant she couldn't have cared less about what Clayton Stanhope might do, because that heady cocktail of lust and love and yearning she always felt for Hold slammed into her, made it difficult to think, hard to breathe. Impossible not to feel. But this time she only wanted to sink into the floor and keen because this time what she felt was pain. More pain than any amount of money could soothe away.

Chapter Twenty-Seven

The moment Hold saw Jessi everything faded away. She looked so damn beautiful, but it wasn't the dress that showcased her curves to perfection; it wasn't the wreath of flowers perched so becomingly atop her madly curling hair. It was her. The inner light that shone from her, the kindness, the humor, the warmth. The love.

She'd given it without hesitation and without strings, and he'd given her nothing back.

God, he was such a fool.

He had no choice now but to face the music; after all, he'd chosen the tune.

He threaded his way through the crowd, and when she turned, when she saw him and her face closed, he felt the first whisper of the desolation he would feel to live without her.

Not that living without her was an option.

She'd understand, he told himself. She'd be angry at first that he'd kept secrets. But Jessi was nothing if not open and forgiving. And he was telling her himself, right? Better late than never.

"Hold," Rose Stanhope said as he reached the edge of the bower and saw her standing there with an apologetic expression on her face. "We were just talking about you, and here you are. I had no idea you were acquainted with anyone from Windfall Island."

"Dex called him in to do the genealogy," Jessi answered for him. "Rose is on our side."

Hold couldn't have cared less about the search for Eugenia's descendants. His eyes never strayed from Jessi's face. Jessi's cold, calm face. "Jessi, may I talk to you? Privately?"

"Of course."

"Jess?"

"It's okay, Maggie. I'm fine."

But she didn't let him touch her. When he reached for her elbow to guide her out of the bower, she sidestepped so neatly he'd have believed it nothing more than happenstance if he hadn't seen the strain in the parting smile she'd sent Maggie.

He stopped under a small trellis strung with honeysuckle. The beauty of it, the fragrance, were no match for her. "I believe I owe you an apology," he began.

"Oh? Why?" she asked with a polite little smile.

"Rose didn't tell you about me?"

"Not because I asked."

"No, I don't imagine she thought it was any big secret."

"But it was," she said, still smiling slightly, as if nothing was wrong. "Clearly you didn't tell me the truth for a reason. I imagine you thought your money would change things between us." He remained silent, so Jessi pressed on. "Who was she?"

"Who?" Hold blurted out.

"The woman who was after your money. The woman you loved until you found out she only saw you as a payday."

Hold ran a hand back through his hair, swore to himself she wouldn't catch him off guard again. "Her name isn't important. Neither is she."

"Of course she is, Hold, because you still haven't gotten over her—or over what she did to you, which is the same thing. What's not important is me."

"Jessica—"

"If I mattered, you'd have told me about her. You'd have told me about your family." She stepped forward, and even in the dim light he could see she wasn't angry, just hurt. Deeply, deeply hurt. "If I mattered to you, the past wouldn't, because you'd trust me enough to realize I loved you before I knew your bank balance."

"Jessica." He reached for her.

She caught his hands, squeezed them before she let go again. "I want to thank you, Hold," she said, so gently he didn't know how she managed to keep her voice steady when his throat was tight and aching. "Next time I won't be so resistant to the people who come into my life. I'll still be careful, especially where Benji is concerned, but I will risk."

"Next time?" he said. "It's not over, Jess."

"It was over every time you chose to close me out of your life. I'll miss you," she said as if he'd never spoken, and her voice did tremble, just a little, this time, "but I've enjoyed every minute of the time we spent together. You were good for Benji, at a time in his life when he needed to be around a good man."

"I'd like to see him, Jess."

"You're his friend, Hold."

And that relationship had nothing to do with her; he got that message loud and clear. But he'd be damned if he settled for it.

"Am I interrupting?"

Hold closed his eyes for a second. Apparently, he wasn't getting his wish.

"I am interrupting."

"There's nothing to interrupt," Jessi said, turning to a woman who looked so much like Hold. She had the same burnished hair, tall, slim build, and warm brown eyes. Seeing her made Jessi's heart ache even more.

"My mother, Andrea Abbot," Hold said, stepping back to allow his mother to form a little circle with them, "Jessica Randal."

Andrea took Jessi's hand, cradled it with her other hand, and just held it for a moment. "It's a pleasure to meet you, Jessica."

"Please, call me Jessi. All my friends do."

Okay, that was a dig. It almost made him smile, because for the first time he realized she was angry. And if she was angry, then the love was still there.

"Do I understand you're involved with my son?"

"I was involved. He was just in it for the sex."

"Jessica," he strangled out.

But his mother only laughed. "I think I'm going to like you, Jessi."

"Oh, don't get too attached. Hold isn't keeping me."

"Whyever not?" she said, and although it sounded like

a question in her honeyed voice, when she turned to him, there was nothing sweet about the fire in her eyes. "Whyever not, Holden?"

"I'm not your kind of people," Jessi said before he could come up with a response. "For starters, I got pregnant when I was sixteen, so I have a seven-year-old son. And I'm from a little place off the Maine coast called Windfall Island. Windfall was settled by just about every kind of criminal and fugitive there ever was, so the only kind of blood running through my veins is red with maybe a hint of black-heartedness thrown in."

"Honey, my ancestors were pirates, swamp rats, and carpetbaggers," Andrea said. "I imagine they'd have run hand in hand with yours. Thick as thieves, you might say."

Jessi shrugged. "The current generation doesn't feel that way, so I'll just say it's been a pleasure to meet you and leave it at that." She turned to walk away.

Hold fielded a look from his mother, long and fulminating, then narrowed with disgust. But he didn't know what to do, what to say, in the face of Jessi's implacable will.

"Wait a minute," Andrea said to Jessi when words failed him. "I know my son. If he's entered into a relationship with you—"

Jessi turned back. "He hasn't. We're not in a relationship. He made that perfectly clear, and I'm sure you'll agree with him when he tells you I'm only after his money. That's no way to build a relationship, so while he's more than willing to spend time with me and my son, he's not in it for the long haul."

"I'm sure you must be mistaken, Jessi."

"Am I? In all the time we've known each other, he's never told me a thing about who he is or where he comes from, and this"—she gestured around the lavish ballroom—"is why. Here you are in a gown and jewels that would cost me a year's salary, and I'm in a bargain-basement ball gown."

"And you're feeling inadequate."

"You know, that's the funny part. I'm feeling extremely adequate. For the first time in weeks I don't feel like there's something lacking in me." She came back, gave Andrea one of her hugs that made it feel like all was right with the world, then stepped back. "And now I'll apologize for being rude and say it's a shame we couldn't get to know one another better. I think I'd have liked you."

Grinning like a fool, Hold watched her walk away. His mind was absolutely clear again, and instead of desperation he felt only confidence. Jessi had said enough, given away enough, to tell him she still loved him, and her heart was too generous to shut him out for long. "Thank you," he said to his mother.

"Go after her," Andrea hissed at him.

"I'm going."

"It's good to know I didn't raise a complete moron."

"Only a temporary one," Hold said, flashing his mother a smile before his long legs took him back to Jessi's side.

He put a hand on her arm and she looked up at him, absolutely dry-eyed. "Let me explain, Jessica."

"There's no need, Hold." She subtly shifted until his hand dropped away. "A few weeks ago I would have said you're the answer to my dreams, and that includes not having to worry about paying my bills. Now..." She looked around the room, her eyes resting on Dex and Maggie, wrapped around each other as they swayed to the music from the live band. Even seeing Dex glance up now and then to the bar where Clayton was still nursing his scotch, it was clear what they meant to one another. Her expression softened for a second or two, turned wistful before her gaze shifted back to Hold. And cooled. "I'm exactly what you're afraid of," she said.

"That's not true. You love me."

She shook her head. "Love is the most important thing in the world, Hold. But I have to love myself first, and that's impossible without self-respect. I've just rediscovered mine, so if you don't mind, I'll concentrate on me just now. Me and my son."

She walked away, and this time he let her.

"Holden," Andrea said as she joined him, "you are an idiot, especially if you don't go after that girl."

"Not now," Maggie said as she joined them.

"Great," Hold muttered, "somebody else to tell me what an ass I've been."

Maggie smiled. "I figure Jessi took care of that better than anyone else could."

"You don't know the half of it," Hold muttered as Maggie and Dex introduced themselves to his mother.

"He should go after her," Andrea said to Maggie, giving his shoulder a little shove.

"No offense, Mrs. Abbot—"

"Andrea, please."

"Andrea. You don't know Jessi."

"I'd like to, but my son is being a—a *man*."

"It is a handicap, isn't it?"

"You do know I'm right here," Hold put in.

"That's the point," Andrea said with a sniff, "you should be running after Jessi. I swear I'll be dead before Holden gives me a grandchild to spoil. And that girl, besides being lovely, gracious, and clearly intelligent, comes with a ready-made one."

"Jessi may be the kindest, most forgiving person I've ever known," Maggie said, "but if Hold goes after her now you'll never get to spoil Benji."

"But—"

Maggie rounded on him. "You lied to her, or at least kept the truth to yourself, which amounts to the same thing." She took Dex's hand. "Trust me, I know."

"I didn't do it for the reason you think," Hold said miserably.

"Then why did you do it?"

He tried to put into words the anger, the sorrow, the reluctance that had filled him, and only ended up spreading his hands.

"Until you can answer that question, do her a favor and stay away from her." And Maggie set off to offer the comfort Hold knew he couldn't.

"You just got engaged, am I right?" Andrea said to Dex.

"Yes, ma'am."

"Congratulations. Talk some sense into this one." But she smiled, her face softening as she leaned up to kiss Hold's cheek. "You love her. I can see it, sweetheart. Don't let her go."

"I'm not giving up, Mother."

"No son of mine worth his grits and cornbread would fail." Andrea sighed. "Honoria Snowdon has been hounding me all night, and she's headed this way." She shook her head, mumbling as she walked away, "Someone really ought to tell her she's too old to wear a dress cut for a N'Orleans hooker."

"Your mother is a pistol," Dex said.

"Yeah." Hold shoved his hands into his pockets. "What should I do, Dex?"

"How should I know?"

"You just went through this with Maggie."

"Maggie and Jessi are nothing alike. But I think Maggie is right; you need to give Jessi some time."

"Great."

"And in the meanwhile," Dex said, "you can help me keep an eye on the Stanhopes."

As soon as the crowd closed between her and Hold, Maggie was there, drawing her off to the side of the room where they could talk with a little more privacy.

"We have to call this off, Jessi. You're too upset—"

"No, Maggie. Absolutely not. It has to be here and now. Dex says Clayton won't risk seeing any of us in private. He won't want the personal connection. So this ball is our only chance to get to him."

"But—"

"Stop treating me like I'm going to shatter," Jessi snapped. "I'm just as strong as you are."

"Are you kidding? You're ten times stronger than me. And a whole lot nicer. At least you usually let me finish my sentences."

"I'm sorry." Jessi rubbed her temples, dug deep for some control. She could fist her hands to stop them from shaking, but what about the rest of her? "I'm sorry," she said again while she fought the tears pressing at the backs of her eyes, and the trembling that wanted to drop her to her knees.

"Let me deal with Clayton."

All it took, she realized as her spine stiffened and her chin lifted, was remembering why she'd come. "If he's seen a picture of you, which he probably has, he'll be instantly on the defensive. And he already knows you're not a match, so you're no threat to him, Maggie. And it will help me take my mind off Hold."

"Jess." Maggie shook her head. "Are you sure about this?"

"Were you sure when you took a stand?"

"Absolutely, but I didn't have to worry about anyone but myself."

"Benji is why I'm doing this," Jessi reminded her. "I'd rather face this head on than sit around waiting for someone to come after us."

Maggie blew out a breath. "I understand, and I agree with you. But I still wish you'd let me take him on."

Jessi took the Bluetooth Maggie handed her and replaced it in her ear. "It's for me to do," she said with the kind of finality even Maggie respected.

As they'd agreed, Jessi would light the fire, and the rest of them would see where the wind blew it. And now that the moment was upon her, she felt no anxiety, only a fierce determination to see their plan through.

"Here goes," she said as she turned her attention to the bar where Clayton still stood.

"Don't do anything stupid."

"It's the Stanhopes we're counting on to be stupid."

"Yeah, well, that particular commodity always seems to be in good supply."

"Says the voice of experience?"

Maggie grinned. "Bet your ass, which is how I know you won't take my advice." And with that parting shot, Maggie melted into the crowd to position herself where she could keep an eye on Clayton.

"She has a point," Dex said in Jessi's ear.

"I'll do exactly what we agreed on," Jessi muttered, smiling at a woman in a cut-to-the-navel, slit-to-the-hip dress who was giving her a sidelong look. Someone, Jessi thought, ought to tell her that a mature—and matronly—woman who wore a dress like that had more to worry about than a stranger having a conversation with herself. But it wouldn't be Jessi.

"Clayton Stanhope won't see us in private, so this is the only chance we'll have to talk to him," Dex said. "That doesn't mean I have to like putting you in the crosshairs."

"We agreed that Clayton won't try anything here, with all these people around," Jessi reminded him. "So let's get him out in the open once and for all."

"Go for it, Mata Hari."

Jessi took a minute to compose herself, with deep breaths and shoulder rolls, before she approached Clayton Stanhope. She didn't try to make it seem like a chance meeting, didn't try to charm him. With her nerves stretched to the breaking point already, it seemed best just to get on with it.

Still lounging with one elbow on the long oak bar, he took the hand she offered. "Clayton Stanhope," he said. "Have we met?"

"No."

"Well, that's a relief." His smile went from puzzled to

charming. "I'd be worried about getting old if I didn't re-member such a lovely young woman, Ms. ..."

"You won't be feeling so complimentary when I tell you where I'm from." After a beat and nothing more than a slightly bemused stare from him, she added, "I'm from Windfall Island."

He straightened, composing himself so quickly Jessi wondered if she'd only seen that split second of surprise because she wanted to.

"Never heard of Windfall Island?" she asked him.

And yeah, she definitely saw it this time—shock widening his eyes before calculation narrowed them.

"I didn't realize you were on the guest list," he said, his eyes roaming the room, even as he maneuvered them to put her back to the crowd. Anyone who noticed them would only see him conversing with a woman with no idea what she looked like. Not that it mattered.

"Oh, I know all sorts of people," Jessi said. "I'll bet I even know your latest hireling. You won't play fair and tell me his name, but I know it's a Windfaller who couldn't resist the money you waved under his nose."

"I don't know what you're talking about."

"I'm talking about you or one of your relatives hiring a young man named Mort to try to kill Maggie Solomon because you were afraid you might have to say good-bye to part of the Stanhope fortune."

"That's ridiculous. Why would this Solomon woman be worth a penny of the Stanhope legacy?"

"Eugenia."

His face cleared from mottled red to white.

"That's right. Maggie might have been your niece, Eu-genia's long lost granddaughter. She's not, and I imagine if she met you she'd be grateful. But there may be a descendant out there. What are you willing to do to make that person disappear?"

"Eugenia is dead," he hissed. "My grandmother just couldn't let her go, and she convinced Rose to continue this ridiculous search. We're all just humoring her so we can put this nonsense away once and for all."

"Oh, one of you is doing more than humoring Rose."

Clayton drew himself up, glaring down his nose at her. "I have nothing to do with any of this."

"Sure you do. If not directly, then you're willing to sit back while one of your relatives gets his or her hands dirty. That doesn't make you innocent."

He took her by the elbow. "I don't know how you gained entrance to this event, but I believe Security may be interested."

Jessi smiled thinly. "Go ahead, call Security. I wonder what those reporters over there will think about you having me escorted out after they've watched us talk very intensely."

He twisted around until he could see the gaggle of society reporters and photographers by the entrance. Most of them were watching the doors, waiting to see who arrived next, or scanning the ballroom in hopes of drama. At least one of them was watching her and Clayton with patent curiosity.

Clayton reined in his temper, but he didn't let her go, and tried to steer her into the crowd.

Jessi dug her heels in. With that Clayton let her go rather than make a scene.

"Careful," Dex said into her ear. "If he gets too angry he may just walk away."

But Dex couldn't see his face, Jessi thought. Clayton was angry all right, but he was also hooked. "I wonder," she said to him, "what would happen if I walked over to those reporters and told them all about the search for Eugenia's heirs."

"Go ahead," he said icily. "It will get press, certainly. The Stanhope name and fortune up for grabs?" He shook his head. "Every fortune hunter and lunatic in the country will come out of the woodwork. My family can retreat behind the walls of our estate, hire bodyguards, keep the press and the greedy at bay until the story blows over again. But what about that worthless little speck of land you call home?"

"I imagine the notoriety will allow it to live up to its name. Tourism is our main industry after all, and capitalizing on Eugenia's fate would certainly be a windfall for the island."

"If you're not overrun."

"We might not have walls and bodyguards, but we know how to handle crowds—and crazies."

"So it's money you're after."

"It's peace I'm after, for myself and everyone I know and love. But I don't think we'll get peace until the truth comes out. So here's my truth, Clay." She kept her eyes on Clayton's so she could gauge his reaction. "I found a blanket stored away in my attic, pink wool edged with satin and embroidered with three initials. Can you guess what they are?"

His face went white. "You're lying."

"Am I? There are no descriptions of it anywhere, and believe me, I've checked."

"*Jessi.*" This time it was Hold's voice, and that made

her pause, made her already pounding heart slam painfully into her ribs. "Jessi, what the hell are you doing? I mean, Dex told me, but what if something happens to you? Who's going to protect Benji then?"

She could hear the worry in his voice, could so easily imagine him pacing, running his hands back through his hair in exasperation. His words gave her pause, but she wouldn't let him steal her determination.

"I've thought this through very carefully," she said, and not just for Clayton's benefit. "I'll give you the blanket and sign whatever you want me to sign. I'll waive any rights to the Stanhope name and money."

"In return for?"

"Two million dollars." They'd known he would expect her to have a price. "Trust me, it's a bargain."

"Two million dollars is a bargain?"

"It is when a third of the Stanhope fortune would run in the hundreds of millions. That's what Eugenia's heir would be in line for, right? A third?"

"Jessi." Hold again, and she could hear the struggle he was waging to keep his voice calm. "He won't live up to any deal he makes, and he's too smart to say anything to incriminate himself."

Which was why she was trying to punch through his control. "I may not be able to prove that blanket belonged to Eugenia, but how do you think Rose would take it?"

A muscle in his jaw worked, and she could see his pulse beating fast.

"You want this search to be over, don't you?" she pushed. "You've gone to great lengths to make sure no heirs come forward."

Clayton's gaze jumped to meet hers, and even as she

knew she'd gone at him too hard and fast, he drew himself up. "I have no idea what you're getting at, young woman, but you should be careful."

"Why? Are you going to send someone to kill me, like you did Maggie Solomon?" Jessi kept her voice down. There was only one set of ears she was playing for.

Clayton's eyes darted around, assuring himself there was no one close enough to have overheard. He didn't deny her accusation. But he hadn't admitted anything, either.

"Does the name Mort Simpkins mean anything to you?"

His gaze shifted to hers again. "No."

She studied his face, saw only relief and superiority, and knew she'd lost him.

"He wouldn't have hired Mort directly," the voice in her ear—Dex's voice now—said. "Circle back to the money."

"So you don't do your own dirty work," she said. That didn't mean he wouldn't send someone after the blanket. And her. It was their last hope—if they could get their hands on his henchman, they might be able to get the proof they needed to stop Clayton.

"Two million dollars, Clayton. The offer is good until midnight. Not one second longer."

"And if I go to the police and tell them you're black-mailing me?"

"Go ahead, call the police. I'm sure when they hear the facts, they'll agree that I'm only selling you something that's worth a great deal more than I'm asking."

He kept his eyes level on hers, but again, she knew she had him. "How do you expect me to get my hands on that much cash at this time on a Saturday evening?"

"Really? You're going to stand there and tell me you can't pull it off? That one of the guys in this room, one of your friends, isn't in a position to open a bank for you?"

The muscle in his jaw bunched. "How will I get in touch with you?"

"I'll be right here, waiting." She started to turn away.

He stopped her with a hand on her arm. "The blanket. I'll expect you to turn it over to me before I give you the check."

She shrugged. "Of course. See you at midnight."

Chapter Twenty-Eight

Hold blew out a breath. It didn't help. Seeing Jessi safe didn't calm the fear. She'd loaded a weapon, put it into Clayton Stanhope's hands, and sent him off without the least idea who he might hand that weapon to.

He ignored Dex's attempts to talk him down, brushing people out of his way as he crossed the crowded ballroom. "Are you insane?" he asked Jessi when he got to her.

"No." She looked to Dex, who'd joined them now that their plan had been set in motion and there was no need for him to stay in hiding. "This is what we agreed to do, right?"

"Pretty much. And you did a hell of a job, Jessi." Dex turned to Hold. "Not quite so easy to justify the risk when it's someone you love on the line, is it?"

Only a few weeks before, Maggie had been on the hot seat, and Dex had refused to send her DNA off to the lab. Hold opened his mouth, then closed it without speaking. What could he say when he'd gone against Dex and helped Maggie to make herself a target?

"Fat lot of good it did us," Hold grumbled anyway.

"I didn't get him to incriminate himself." Jessi removed the Bluetooth device and slapped it into Hold's palm. "But we've got him on tape, and when he shows up to buy the blanket—"

"It still won't amount to a hill of beans as far as evidence goes."

"It will add to the case against him," Jessi insisted.

"It doesn't prove he had any involvement in the attempt on Maggie's life, and it won't stop him from coming after you," Hold said.

"It's done," Jessi said flatly.

"If I'd had a say, it never would have started."

"Well, you weren't around to object, were you?" When Hold opened his mouth to fire back, Jessi closed her eyes and held her hands up. "This isn't getting us anywhere. What happened after I walked away?" she said to Dex.

"Clayton's son joined him at the bar," Dex said. "The two of them have been tossing back scotch and talking intensely. Neither of them have left the room or made a phone call. But it's only been a few minutes."

Hold took a second to rein himself in, with the assurance he'd finish this conversation with Jess. "When I found out what you were up to, I texted my brother. James runs Abbot Investments, and he always has his ear to the ground about his competitors. It seems Stanhope Securities' finances may not be as sound in reality as they look on paper. James seems to think there might be some creative accounting going on."

"And now we have an even stronger motive." Dex

smiled suddenly, and when Hold turned around he saw why.

"Yippee." Jessi rubbed at her temple, as if she had a headache brewing. "I think I'll go to the ladies room."

"I'll go with you."

"No, Maggie, stay here with Dex. I'll be fine. I just need a couple of minutes."

Hold watched her go, and felt like scum. It couldn't have been easy for her to take on Clayton Stanhope alone. And he had to admit now that he'd calmed down, she'd done a hell of a job, just like Dex had said.

And he'd come down on her like a ton of bricks, at a moment when she was already so worn down. She'd put herself in the line of fire in an attempt to expose whoever wanted to remove any possible Stanhope heirs, and just when he needed to stay close, everything he did pushed her away.

"You don't have to say it," he said to Maggie when he caught sight of her expression.

"Have you told her you're in love with her?"

"I don't think he's told himself yet," Dex observed.

"If you don't know it by now," Maggie said to him, "there's no hope for you. I'm going to find Jessi."

Hold watched her set off in the same direction Jessi had gone. "We're not going to stand here and talk about our feelings, are we?" he said to Dex.

"My feelings aren't the issue," Dex pointed out. "As far as I'm concerned, the only person you need to discuss yours with is Jessi."

Hold exhaled heavily. "I'm not sure she'll listen to anything I have to say, let alone believe me." But he knew she had a very forgiving heart. All he needed to do was let her see he trusted her—and grovel a whole lot—and she'd let him back into her life.

Then he saw Maggie coming back. Alone.

She wasn't supposed to leave the ballroom, but Jessi needed some privacy. Paige was in their suite, but there was another bedroom, and a bath. She really wanted to soak in a steamy tub full of bubbles. What better place to nurse her pain until the first sharp edge of it passed and she could face the pity of the people who loved her?

The effort of holding in the pain, holding back the tears, made the lobby seem like a sea of marble. She'd crossed barely half of it when she heard her name from a voice that surprised her enough to make her stop, turn.

There was Lance, wearing a dark suit and a wide, easy smile. As if he belonged there.

"I've been looking all over for you," he said, taking her elbow and falling into step with her.

"What are you doing here?"

"Benji told me you were going to Boston— Don't look so irritated, you had to leave that stupid dog with the neighbors. I'd have gotten it out of them anyway."

"Not everyone knows your charm is just a veneer to hide the slime filling." She jerked her arm free.

The look that came into his eyes gave her a chill. But it was Lance, she thought. He was harmless. "So you found out where we were going and followed us. Why?"

"I thought I'd join the party."

"You have to be invited. They won't let you in otherwise."

"You are such a hick," he said with a laugh. "I didn't mean that party." He glanced back at the door to the ballroom. "They'll let me in before long. I've got my invitation right here." He wrapped his arm around her waist, snugged her close to his side.

"Ouch." Jessi looked down, but even when she saw the glint of silver it took her a minute to connect it with the prick of pain in her side. "Why do you have a knife?"

"Shut up," he whispered, coldly furious.

"What are you doing?"

"I said shut up." And he shoved the knife into her side. She cried out, stumbled.

"It's all right, darling," Lance said. Then he said more loudly, for the benefit of the desk clerks watching them, "She had a little too much to drink. We'll just get you upstairs and into bed, honey."

"Don't," he hissed when she tried to jerk away.

"You stabbed me," she said, too dazed to feel more than the wetness soaking into her dress.

"It's just a little nick. I swear to God I'll shove this knife in you, Jessi, right to the hilt next time. I know where all the exits are, and I can be gone before they finish dialing 911. Give me any trouble and you'll never see Benji again. Behave yourself and we'll have a nice little family reunion."

Her mind was reeling, but Jessi forced herself to think, to relax, to ignore the pain and the blood she felt welling from her side. To stay alive. "What is this about?"

"My ship coming in."

"I don't understand."

"Of course not," he said with a chuckle. "You just leave everything up to me, and I'll take care of it." He walked by the bank of elevators, kept going to a side door that led to a courtyard. Beyond that was a parking structure, where he let her walk in front of him. Even if she could have run, hampered by her skirts and the stupid mile-high heels she'd insisted on wearing, Lance didn't let her get far enough ahead of him to make it a possibility.

He shoved her against the passenger side of a nondescript sedan and jerked her wrists together, putting a zip tie around each wrist, then connecting them with one in the middle because they were just garbage bag ties. They did the job, though, and she had to force herself not to strain against them. She'd only end up hurting herself.

Lance shoved her in the front passenger seat. She scrambled for the lock button, not thinking clearly enough to realize it would do her no good when he had the keys.

"Christ," Lance said when he slid into the driver's seat, "if you'd just relax this will be a lot easier on both of us."

"Both of us? Did you get stabbed, too?"

Lance reached over, buried his hand in her hair, and yanked. She wrapped her bound hands around his wrist, but he only fisted his hand tighter, until her scalp felt like it was on fire and tears streamed down her face. And she realized just how close to the edge he was.

"I'm sorry," she whimpered, wanting to keep him calm.

"That's better." He let her go with a shove that bounced her head against the window.

She mopped at her cheeks, if only because the tears made her feel more panicked, more hopeless. "This isn't you, Lance."

He snorted out a laugh as he started the car.

"The boy I knew would never hurt me like this."

"Yeah, well, I had to grow up, didn't I? Thanks to you."

Grow up? He sounded like the spoiled kid he'd always been, only more bitter now.

"I couldn't stay on the island, could I?" he rambled. "Not with all those people expecting me to marry you. You and that kid—just millstones, that's all you'd've been."

"I'm sorry you feel that way. Benji is the best thing that ever happened to me, but you don't have to worry about him, or me. We won't bother you."

"Bother me? Bother me." He laughed and backed out of the parking space, still mumbling.

She heard Benji's name and a light went on in her head. Family reunion, he'd said. Everything inside her went cold, achingly cold, then hot. She'd die before she let him get his hands on her son.

"Benji is innocent in all this," she said, shaking this time with the effort of keeping her voice reasonable. "Please don't hurt him."

"Hurt him?" He laughed again. "Benji's my ticket to that ship I was telling you about. I won't lay a finger on the kid. You, on the other hand, are too stupid to see the potential."

"Why don't you explain it to me?"

He glanced over at her, shrugged. "Ever heard of Clayton Stanhope?"

The world dropped out from under her. "Did he send you after me?"

"Why would he send me after you? He doesn't do his own dirty work."

"Then who—"

"As soon as I found out about the search for Stanhope descendants, I knew I had to return to Windfall. I mean, it was like destiny, right? No one, including you, would wonder why I came back to the island."

Lance was talking with his hands, the ten-inch blade he'd apparently forgotten waving dangerously close to her face. Jessi jammed herself into the corner of the seat, as close to the door as she could get.

"What were you supposed to do?"

"Get in good with you. See where the genealogy was pointing. But he wouldn't tell me why." He was rambling now, and while Jessi wanted to ask him who "he" was, she figured it was best to let Lance talk. "I was just supposed to pass the info on to him and wait for further instructions. While we were meeting, he got called away and left me alone in his office."

"You snooped."

Lance snorted. "Who wouldn't?"

A lot of people, Jessi could have said. But then Lance had shown his true colors the day he walked away from her and their unborn child.

"He was only gone a couple minutes," Lance continued, "but it was enough. I saw Eugenia's name. I saw they were searching for her. Of course I knew about the kidnapping. Who doesn't, coming from Windfall? I got to thinking, what if she hadn't died? Eugenia, I mean? What if she wound up on the island? What if some family took her in, and she got married, had kids, grandkids? Those grands'd be about your age now. Made me wonder about you. And my son."

"Your meal ticket," she said, having no trouble putting it together now.

"And why not? What'll old Clayton be willing to pay to keep any heirs from showing up to take a bite of his pie?"

"He's willing to kill."

"I figured as much."

"You—" She had to stop, swallow the bile in the back of her throat. "You're no killer, Lance."

"Anyone can be bought for the right amount of money. But you're right, Jess. I'd rather not hurt anyone. And I don't have to. All I have to do is convince him you may be Eugenia's granddaughter. Won't even be that hard. Not when I have the blanket."

And her hopes dropped even further. But she had to try. "What blanket?"

"The one you tried so hard not to look like you were hiding that day in the attic. The one I broke into your house to see."

"Meeker covered for you?" she said. "My DNA—"

"Won't matter one bit as long as the Stanhopes don't get their hands on it."

Jessi snapped her mouth shut and sat back, realizing just how monumental a mistake she'd almost made. Telling him the DNA was at the lab already might be as good as signing her death warrant. If she didn't match, all Lance's plans would be sunk. He'd have no reason to keep her around. Or Benji.

"I'll start small," he was saying, almost to himself, "just a million or two. The Stanhopes make that much in interest every day. They can spare it without blinking an eye. We'll live high, Jess, you and me and Benji."

"And when it's gone?"

"We won't be signing away the rights to any future kids, right? It's a well I can tap forever."

Over her dead body, Jessi thought, shuddering at the thought of Lance's hands on her. But at least he wanted to keep her alive. "Fine," she said. "If you want me to be your brood mare—or maybe cash cow would be a better description—I'll cooperate. But I won't give you Benji."

"They'll kill him, Jess. That's the idea, get rid of any possible descendants. He'll only be safe with us. I don't know what you're thinking," he continued when she didn't speak, "but just forget about it. I won't let you screw this up, too."

"I won't cooperate, Lance, and you'll never get your hands on Benji."

"No. You will."

"I won't tell you where he is."

"You think I'm too stupid to figure that out?" He snorted. "It took me about five seconds to find out Keegan used to be a Boston cop. His old man still is. Where else would you leave the kid?"

"Jessi probably went up to the suite," Dex said. "Alec is keeping tabs on Clay, Sr., and there goes Chip," he finished when Clay's son eased out of the ballroom. "I have to go after him." He took off, leaving Maggie and Hold staring at one another.

"I really want to get out of these shoes," Maggie said, and headed for the door.

"I can imagine." Hold fell into step with her.

"I don't think you should come with me," Maggie said.

"You really can't stop me."

"Not in these shoes, but when we get to the room, I'm going to change them and kick your ass. That's if Jessi doesn't do it first."

"She's already made a pretty good start." Without landing a single blow or raising her voice.

"Yeah," Maggie smiled. "I don't know if it's being a mom or what, but she can make you feel about two feet tall with just a look."

Jessi had cut him off at the knees all right, Hold thought. Not because she was a mom. Because he was in love with her. Yeah, he hadn't needed Maggie or Dex to point it out to him. The minute he knew Jessi had put herself in danger he'd known, and now he was so desperate to find her and tell her that it felt like he might explode.

"You wait here," Maggie said when they got to the room.

"I'll give you five minutes, then I'm storming the gates."

Maggie came back in less than one. Paige was right behind her, and Hold felt his own face drain when he saw theirs.

"She's not here," Maggie said.

Paige added, "I haven't seen her since you all left together."

"She must be somewhere in the hotel," he said. Maggie looked at him like she'd cheerfully strangle him. Hold couldn't blame her. "Call her."

Maggie stared at the Bluetooth in his hand. "She didn't take her phone because she had that. Why didn't you give it back to her?"

"She wasn't supposed to leave the ballroom," Hold said, staring at the small, bullet-shaped device in his hand.

"Shit." Maggie kicked her shoes off—one then the

other—and the thud of them hitting the wall cut through a silence weighted with helplessness.

"I'm going back downstairs. Maybe the desk clerk saw where she went."

"I'll go with you," Maggie said. "Just give me two minutes to change."

"I'll meet you down there." Hold took off, but heard Maggie say to Paige, "Honestly, men," before she caught up with him.

"Do you really think she wants to see you right now?"

"Probably not." But he had to apologize, had to tell her he loved her. Hell, he'd settle for seeing her face, for just knowing she was all right, even if she never spoke to him again.

When the elevator opened at the lobby level, they split up. Maggie took the security guards at the ball-room door.

Hold crossed to the desk. "Did you see a woman in a red dress, petite, curly hair?"

"Drunk?" the desk clerk added to the description, with a smirk that made Hold want to reach across the counter and throttle him.

"She wasn't drunk. Careful," Hold added.

The clerk, who'd started to shrug, straightened instead. And took a step back. "The guy she was with had to hold her up," he said.

"What did he look like?"

"Shorter than you, attractive—"

"The security guards saw her with a man," Maggie said as she hurried up, "but only saw him from behind."

"I think she called him Vance," the desk clerk put in tentatively.

"Lance." Cold to his bone marrow, Hold started for the door.

Maggie dragged him back. "Where are you going?"

"I don't—" He fought to see through the red haze, to think.

"Where did they go?" Maggie demanded, rapping her hand on the counter when the desk clerk only goggled at her.

"I-I don't know."

"To get Benji," Hold said.

"Then let's go."

"You won't be any good to me barefoot, Maggie. You find Dex, let him know. I'm going after Jessi."

Maggie bit her lip, but she didn't argue with him. "I'll call the Keegans, let them know what's going on," she called after him. "They'll protect Benji."

"That'll leave Jessi in danger." Hold turned back, just for a second, saw the worry and fear in her eyes. "But not for long."

Chapter Twenty-Nine

With her hands bound and Lance driving like a maniac, Jessi had no choice but to hang on and hope. Her wrists were raw and bloody from straining against the plastic ties, her head throbbed where Lance had fisted his hand in her hair, and her side...

She knew he hadn't stabbed her very deeply, but he must have nicked something. The circle of sticky wetness on her side kept growing, and she felt a little nauseated, a little woozy.

As much as she didn't want Benji put in danger, she was relieved when Lance slammed on the brakes in front of the Keegan house. She couldn't do anything to protect her son if she passed out.

Lance tossed a cell phone in her lap. "I entered the number. Call and tell them to send Benji out."

"No."

"*Jesus.*" He shoved a hand back through his hair, a

hand that shook, Jessi was satisfied to see. "Do you want to die?"

"No, but I'll die before I see Benji end up with you."

Lance fisted both hands, even the one still holding the knife. "That's fine with me. I'll be paid for getting rid of you, then Clayton will pay me for waiving Benji's rights to the Stanhope money. Paid, and paid, and paid."

"You don't need Benji to get paid, Lance. I'll go with you, willingly. They'll pay for me, too."

"It doesn't work without both of you!" he screamed, slamming a fist into the steering wheel. "Stanhope will come after Benji, can't you see that? Do you want him ki—" He stopped, turned to stare at her from wild eyes. "You're just trying to get me away from here. There's no way you'd leave Benji unprotected."

"He won't be unprotected," she said, even though her hope of maneuvering him away from Benji was fading. "Maggie won't let anything happen to Benji. Neither will Dex and Hold—"

"*Don't*," he shrieked, "say that prick's name!"

Jessi knew she was pushing him closer and closer to the edge, but what choice did she have? She was banking on the fact that he really didn't want to hurt her. He wasn't a murderer, just a spoiled kid who'd had some hard times and was blaming her for it.

Still, he was a spoiled kid with a knife and a slippery hold on his temper. "I'm sorry, Lance."

"It's Abbot's fault as much as yours," he ground out. "If he hadn't come along, you'd have taken me back." He waved his hands, had her ducking the knife again, "All this would be unnecessary."

"I know you believe that," Jessi said gently.

"I know it," he said in a sulky voice that would have made her smile under other circumstances. It chilled her now, seeing how quickly his moods changed. Temper she'd called it, thought it, but she wondered now if he wasn't losing his grip on sanity. "I'll just grab the kid later, and you won't have gained anything by being stubborn."

"I won't put Benji in danger, Lance. Can't you see that?"

"I'm his father."

"You're holding me prisoner. You hurt me. Look, I'm bleeding."

He glanced over, shook his head. "It's your own fault," he said coldly. "I wouldn't need you if you hadn't dumped him in a cop's house." He got out of the car, came around to the passenger side, and opened her door. When she simply sat there, he grabbed her by the wrists and dragged her out.

She stumbled on legs gone to rubber, but the pain from the zip ties cutting into her wrists help her stay upright and focused.

Lance shoved her toward the house, and when she stopped she felt the prick of the knife against her back.

"That's right," he sneered when she jerked forward a step. "You talk big. Let's see if you have the guts to back it up. Now go get my son or I'll go over your dead body."

Jessi turned slowly, to face him. "No."

Lance backhanded her.

She fell to the ground, wrenching her shoulder with her hands bound and useless to break her fall. Fire shot through her side, pain grayed her vision and fogged her senses. Fury and determination pushed her to her feet.

"You can kill me with that knife, Lance, or you can beat me to death, but you won't get your hands on *my* child."

Lance raised the knife.

"You don't want to do that, son."

Jessi swung around, saw Dex's father standing on the walkway in front of his house. The rectangle of light from the open doorway behind him threw his face into shadows, but although his outspread hands were empty, she could see the gun holstered at his side.

"Mom!" Benji called out.

"Go back inside!" she yelled, but Benji ran out of the house.

Carter caught him, kept him from her. And seeing him threw Lance into a frenzy.

"I want my kid!" he screamed.

Jessi never took her eyes off Benji, took her first breath when she saw Peggy Keegan race out and bundle him up.

Benji struggled, yelled, "Don't you hurt my mom!" then sobbed as Peggy, with a last tortured look at Jessi, took him inside and shut the door.

Jessi saw the desperation come into Lance's eyes then, watched his jaw set, and knew she was going to pay for keeping Benji from him.

Lance raised the knife.

Carter Keegan stepped closer and held out his hand. "Why don't you give me the knife?"

Lance pressed it to Jessi's throat. "I just want my kid," he said, his breath sobbing out with each word.

"You hurt her, you'll never see Benji again."

"It's all her fault. First the kid, now this. I just want what I deserve!" he shrieked, dragging Jessi backward to the car.

Carter pulled his gun. "You're not going anywhere."

The front door of the Keegan house flew open again. Benji raced out of the house. Peggy Keegan followed, limping, too slow to stop Benji from racing around her husband. Benji launched himself at Lance, kicking and punching with his little fists.

Lance grabbed him, one-handed, and tossed him into the back seat, shoving Jessi away at the same time. She struggled to her feet, thanking God two steps took her to the car, and that she had enough strength to climb in with her son before Lance jumped in the front and started the car.

Everything seemed to happen at once then.

A car screamed up behind them, headlights blinding, until Hold stepped into the beams.

Lance put the car in gear and Hold started to run.

Jessi opened the rear door, held it with her foot while she scooped up Benji. "Take him!" she screamed at Hold. "Please, Hold, please," she begged when she saw denial in his eyes. He could only save one of them, and it wouldn't be her. "Please."

He reached out, his fingers just brushing hers as he wrapped his arms around Benji. She jerked to her knees in time to see, through the rear window, Hold crashing to the frozen ground. Benji was cradled safely on top of him, his little arms outstretched for her. It was the last thing she saw before Lance skidded around the corner, sideswiping a parked car and sending her off balance. With her hands still bound and no way to catch herself, she slid across the back seat to smash against the side of the car.

But Benji was safe. All that mattered was that Benji was safe.

* * *

Carter Keegan pulled up in the rental Hold had left idling in front of his house. He reached for Benji, but the kid had a death grip around Hold's neck.

"I have to go after your mom," Hold said to Benji.

"You should let the police—" the older man began.

"The hell with the police. No offense."

"None taken. If it was Peggy..." Carter shook his head. "Come on, Benji, you and I have to do the hard thing and wait. But I know you're strong like your mom."

Hold climbed into the car, looked Benji in the eye, and said, "I'll get her back, Ben."

"Promise?" Benji sniffled, his lower lip wobbling.

"I won't come back without her."

"Okay." He buried his face in Carter's shoulder.

"If he wants to get away fast there's only one place he can go," Carter said, rubbing soothing circles on Benji's back. "Take the first right, then a left, and you'll be at the highway."

Hold barely caught the last few words, already putting his foot to the floorboard. He drove faster than he ever had in his life, although it felt like he was moving through molasses. He should be a wreck, but there was a coldness inside him. He grabbed onto it tight. The alternative was to succumb to fear, debilitating fear, and he'd made a promise—to Benji and himself. He couldn't live without Jessi.

He raced onto the highway, slaloming around cars and trucks, calculating the lead Lance had on him and pushing the rental car for every ounce of speed it could give as he searched for the car Lance was driving. Just as doubt began to creep in, just as he began to fear Lance had taken a different route, just as he started to lose the iron grip on his emotions and hear the gibbering laughter of panic bubble in the back of his throat, he spotted the car.

Anger took over then—laser-focused pure rage that pushed everything else aside.

Every time Lance changed lanes, Jessi was thrown across the back seat. Luckily at some point in the swerving and shifting, the open back door had slammed closed. She barely noticed the new bruises, the ache in her side or the blood coating her wrists. She could still see Benji's face, still feel what it was like to have to hand her son off, see the terror on his little face.

Anger burned through her, the kind of anger that surged into her muscles and hazed her mind. The kind of anger that wanted blood.

She shoved her upper body over the seat, but by the time she'd located the knife Lance had already closed his hand around it. She ducked, timed his wild swings, and pressed herself into the back behind him where he couldn't reach her, at least not while he was driving.

He met her eyes in the rearview mirror, and she could see the homicidal intent there. The Lance she'd thought mostly harmless was gone.

"Kill me and you'll never get a penny from the Stanhopes."

"I think we both know that ship has sailed. You'll never cooperate."

He was too calm, Jessi thought, while anger still surged like lava in her veins, looking for a place to erupt.

Lance had already decided she was excess baggage. She knew that as long as he was alive, Benji would be too big a temptation for him.

"I told you before, you'll never get your hands on my son."

He ignored her, checking the mirrors, now driving the speed limit. He kept the knife out of sight, calm enough to think about not drawing attention to himself. There was nothing she could do but wait him out.

"You have to stop sometime, Lance."

He just hunched his shoulders, gave her no choice but to settle back to wait for an opening. But the interval worked against her: all of her adrenaline drained out of her, leaving her suddenly exhausted. She was fighting the urge to sleep when the car lurched once, then again. The movement against the car was accompanied by the sound of tearing metal.

"What the fuck!" Lance shouted.

Jessi dragged herself onto the seat, but all she saw out of the rear window was a galaxy of headlights.

A horn blared. She jerked around and saw Hold in the car next to theirs. He was shouting, words she couldn't make out, but just seeing him was all it took to put the fight back into her.

She spun around, braced herself, and put her zip-tied wrists around Lance's throat. She wanted him dead, frightened, miserable, and dead.

He clawed at her wrists, and when that didn't work, he swung out wildly between the bucket seats. She felt the knife slice her side, skitter along her ribs. But she pressed herself against the door, as far away from his knife hand as she could get, and bore down until she could hear

Lance wheezing and choking. Then reality hit her: if she killed Lance, she might be killing herself.

She forced herself to ease up, but it was too late. She felt the tires hit the warning strips on the side of the road, then heard the crunch of gravel before they went airborne for a weightless second. She saw a flash of green in the headlights and realized they'd gone off the road and onto the median just before the thud and bounce of impact shook her.

Then her hands broke free. She saw the knife and realized he'd cut the zip ties. And her. Blood ran down her wrist—too much blood. She didn't care.

"Jesus, Jessi!" Lance shoved out of the car.

She clambered out after him, giving in to all the pain and—yes, the hate—for what he'd done in the past, what he was doing to her now, what Benji would have to deal with going forward. It all twined up inside her, braiding itself into a white-hot ball of anger.

"You could have killed us," he whined.

"That's what you want, isn't it?" She stepped toward him, stumbled, and stopped to slip off her shoes. And hefted them consideringly. "You were supposed to kill me and Benji."

"Yes. No. I mean, that's what Stanhope wanted, but I never intended—"

"How much?"

"What?"

"How much is the going price to murder your own son?" She ended on a shriek, knocking the knife out of his hand as she beat at him with her shoes. When she realized she couldn't kick him with her bare feet, she used her knee, cursing because she wasn't tall enough for more than a glancing blow. But it was enough to have him staggering toward the car.

She tried to go after him, but she was suddenly lifted away and restrained.

"Let me go," she panted, watching through a red haze as Lance bolted for his car.

He jumped in and gunned it. The wheels spun in the ruts torn into the grass, not making much headway until they suddenly found purchase. Lance shot the car into traffic and there was a horrendous crash of metal and shattering glass, but the sounds seemed to come to her from a great distance as the energy drained out of her. The world grayed, which was odd, she thought numbly, considering it was nighttime.

Then Hold's face was there, filling her vision. He was talking, but she couldn't make out the words, and when she tried to lift her hand to his face, something held it back.

"Jessica," she heard faintly, smiling because she'd always liked the way he used her whole name.

She gave him three syllables back, and it took everything she had left to say them. Her last thought before darkness took her was that she wished she could stick around to see the look on his face when she told him she loved him.

Hold barely heard the crash, looking up just as Lance's car smashed into the side of a semi. Jessi had gone limp in his arms, so he laid her down. And saw the blood—on her side, her arms. So much blood. He checked frantically, lost precious time determining that the wound on her side had already stopped bleeding, but then found the gash on her wrist.

He grabbed Lance's knife and cut off the plastic tie, cursing when the blood ran faster, soaking through the strips he cut from her dress and wrapped around her wrist.

I love you, she'd said.

All he could do was hold her in his arms while her life drained away. He fought to get his cell phone out of his breast pocket, even knowing there was no chance in hell an ambulance would get through, not with the highway turned into a parking lot thanks to Lance.

He dialed anyway, then picked Jessi up and started back to his car. "Just hold on," he begged her, "stay with me, Jessica. I love you. Stay with me."

"We've got her. Sir, we've got her."

It was the operator, he thought, until he lifted his head from the sound of Jessi's slowing heartbeat, and saw the wheels of a gurney.

"You have to let us help her," a woman's voice said.

Still, it took him a minute to understand she was a paramedic, that there were two police cars and an ambulance, hazard lights strobing through the darkness, parked on the opposite side of the highway.

Hands pried Jessi out of his arms, the words coming in snatches to him as they checked her vitals and rewrapped her wrist. Her clothes were cut away so they could do a quick assessment. "Lost a lot of blood," he heard— "Touch and go," and "Get her to the hospital stat."

He tried to go with Jessi, demanded it, but a pair of Boston cops held him back. "How . . ."

"Sergeant Keegan called it in when you took off from his house," one of the cops said. "I think he figured you were going to kill that guy. Looks like you won't need to."

Hold barely heard him, and he couldn't have cared less what became of Lance. All he could do was watch the ambulance take Jessi away. He started to scrub his hands over his face, before he realized they were covered with blood. Jessi's blood.

"Sir. Sir?"

He looked up into the face of a cop about ten years older than he was.

"I'm Officer Davidson. Can you give me a statement? Sergeant Keegan filled us in on the episode at the house, but we need to know what happened after you gave chase."

"Which you shouldn't have done," a younger cop nearby, likely the older one's partner, said.

"Shut up, Mulligan."

Hold took a couple of deep breaths and reminded himself he couldn't go to Jessi until he gave his statement. He ran it through as concisely as he could for Davidson, while the younger cop wandered off to study the scene, flashlight in hand.

"Now tell me again," Davidson said.

"I need to get to the hospital."

"And I'll take you, just as soon as you run through it again. We have to get it down while it's fresh."

With no hope of ditching the police, Hold complied. "When I got here she was beating the shit out of him with those," he said as Mulligan walked up with Jessi's shoes—dirty and bloodstained—in his hand. "She was bleeding." He had to stop and swallow, and still his voice was raw. "She was bleeding to death and she fought him because she knew if he got away he'd go after her son."

"The crime techs are here," Mulligan said.

Davidson took Hold by the arm. "Come on, we'll take you to the hospital. It sounds like your Jessi was quite a woman."

"Don't talk about her in the past tense. She's too tough to let that polecat win."

The two cops exchanged a look; Hold refused to believe he could lose her now.

And yet, when they got to the hospital, he found he couldn't bring himself to go inside.

"She's tough, remember?" Mulligan said, as if to bolster him up.

Davidson just shook his head. "She's in surgery. We'll take you to the waiting room."

Maggie, Dex, Dex's parents, and remarkably, his own mother were already there. Benji threw himself into Hold's arms. Hold closed his eyes, but when he tried, he couldn't find any words of reassurance. So he just hugged Benji back—hard—and hoped he was giving as much comfort as he was getting.

Chapter Thirty

Jessi swam back from what seemed a long distance, ran into a wall of pain, and retreated again into oblivion, came back again and retreated—how many times she'd never remember. But when she heard Benji's voice, she fought to open her eyes and smile at him.

"Jessi."

Hold's voice brought a different pain, the kind no doctor could cure, and she let herself drift off because it was easier than facing that.

The next time she surfaced, it was to Maggie's voice—angry, harsh, insulting. "Stop being a wimp," she ordered. "You're scaring Benji half to death."

"Benji." Jessi wouldn't have recognized the thin rasp of sound as her own voice if it hadn't burned its way out of her throat. She fought to open eyes that felt like they were filled with ground glass. And everything hurt. Mostly her heart.

"That's it," Maggie said encouragingly. "The doctors

say you're going to be fine, but you've been sleeping for two days."

"Tired," she whispered. "Sore."

"I can only imagine. You have a stab wound in your side; it's not serious but it must hurt like hell. Your wrists look like raw hamburger, and Lance gashed the left one pretty good. Nicked an artery, so you lost a lot of blood, and you're bruised all over. You look like you were hit by a truck."

"Lance," she croaked as the memory came screaming back. She felt selfish, lamenting her broken heart when there was real suffering so close at hand. "Where is he?"

"Alive, but in a coma." Maggie shook her head. "He's not expected to come out of it, Jess."

"Benji?"

"He knows, but he hasn't said much about it."

"He'll need to talk," she forced out, each word like knives on her sore throat, "when he's ready."

"We'll all be there for him, including Hold."

Now Jessi did close her eyes.

"You can't ignore him, Jess."

She only nodded.

"Is that agreement?"

She shook her head.

"Stubbornness, then. You should know Benji barely leaves his side, even for me." Maggie sounded baffled, a little pissed off, and grateful for it. "If not for Hold...I don't know if Benji would be as okay as he is right now."

Jessi tried not to, but tears leaked out of her eyes. She let go again. She just wanted the pain to go away. Even Maggie swearing at her couldn't make her stay.

* * *

As much as she wanted to hide from everything, Jessi surfaced for longer and longer periods. By the end of the week she was almost back to her old self, awake during the day, asleep at night, and restless to get out of the hospital. She was still sore in places, still heartbroken, but ready to get back to her life.

As usual in the afternoons, her room was full of visitors: Dex, Maggie, and Paige. Benji would be along later—with Hold, Maggie had told her. She hadn't seen him since the ball, but she'd have to face him sooner or later. With everyone there as a buffer, it shouldn't be too difficult.

"Jessi?"

She looked up, tuned back into the conversation, realized they were all waiting on her. She'd given a statement, carefully edited, to the Boston police, but that had so exhausted her that the others hadn't pushed her to relive her ordeal with Lance. Until today.

And since it had to be told, no matter how much it troubled her, she repeated what Lance had told her, how he'd believed his connection to her meant he had guaranteed access to the genealogy. How Lance had hatched the scheme to blackmail Clayton instead, claiming she was a descendant, and through her, Benji.

The part about forcing her to conceive more children? That she kept to herself. As the days passed, the odds that Lance would recover grew less and less, so what point was there in making him look even more heinous than he already did?

"As far as I'm concerned, Lance belongs in the tenth circle of Hell," Maggie said cheerfully when Jessi had finished. "And he can take Clayton Stanhope with him."

"Wishing is the closest we'll get to doing anything about him at the moment," Dex said. With Mort gone, Lance incapable of talking, and no payment for the blanket, the little we have isn't enough to take to the authorities. But at least we know who we're up against now."

"Clayton won't bother us, and that's all that matters at the moment," Jessi said. The DNA test had come back negative; she and Benji were not related to the Stanhopes. Nobody would be coming after them.

She closed her eyes, just for a second, and let the relief wash through her like a cool breeze. She'd never realized just how heavy the weight of that fear had been until it was gone. Everything about her felt lighter.

Except her heart.

"The money might have been nice," Maggie said.

"You didn't want it, Mags, and neither do I. Not with that kind of price tag. No, I'm with you. We'll get there on our own." She smiled. "But I'm still playing the lottery."

"Nice to know you're open to taking risks," Hold said from the doorway.

Suddenly everyone had someplace else to be.

"I understand why you're deserting me." Jessi shot Dex a sour look. "Men are cowards about this kind of thing."

"Yes, we are," Dex said.

Jessi appealed to Maggie. "Stay."

Maggie only patted her hand. "It may not seem like it," she murmured, "but I'm on your side."

Jessi was stuck, especially when Benji peeked out from behind Hold. She greeted him with a smile and wide open arms, just holding him when he climbed into them, holding him and breathing him in. It would be a long time before either of them forgot what they'd gone through.

"Aren't you going to say hi to Hold?" Benji asked her.

She was afraid to even look at him, afraid of the hope that rose within her, but she lifted her eyes to his and smiled. He'd given her the most precious gift in the world. She'd always be grateful.

Hold had stayed by the door, uncharacteristically hesitant, although his hands were buried in his pockets, like she'd seen him do a hundred times before when he was dealing with something emotional.

"Hello," she said to him. "I'm glad to see you."

His eyes shot to hers. "Are you?"

"Of course. You saved Benji. You saved me. We owe you everything."

"I'd do anything for you." He looked at Benji. "For both of you." Hold took a step into the room. "Ask me why, Jessica."

"We're friends," she said. "At least I hope we can be."

"We're more than friends."

She smiled, though her throat ached and her eyes burned with tears she refused to shed. "So," she said to Benji, "what have you been up to today?"

"We got you a present." He held out a little blue bag. Tiffany blue. "Hold and me got it."

Jessi locked eyes with Hold, shifted them back to the bag again. She didn't take it.

"Hold wants us to marry him," Benji said, sounding a little annoyed now. "He asked me if it was okay, and I said yes, and he said we have to get you a ring or it's not official."

"Hold, I..." She had to stop and swallow because her throat kept trying to close.

"It's a present, Mom."

She had no choice but to take it, pull out the box, open it. And suck in her breath. A band of white gold held a diamond in a delicate shade of yellow, not too big and not too small, surrounded by a circle of white diamonds. "It's perfect," Jessi said. "Beautiful."

"It reminded me of you," Hold finally said. "I always feel like the sun comes out when you enter a room."

"I-I don't know what to say."

"Say yes."

She didn't hear him, couldn't hear anything over the pounding of her heart, the voice in her head telling her to take the ring out and slip it on.

She opened her mouth, then closed it, afraid she'd beg him to say the three words that would erase all the awkwardness and hurt between them. There was no question Hold loved Benji, but it would be wrong for her to trade on that.

She closed the box, even though it killed her, put it back into the bag, and held it out. "I— We can't accept this."

"Why not?" Benji demanded. He climbed off the bed and stood between them. She would have done almost anything to wipe that lost, hurt, confused look off his face, but it wouldn't be fair to any of them to live a lie.

"I was an ass, Jessica. Just tell me what you want and I'll give it to you."

Your heart. But she couldn't say that to him. If she had to ask, it meant nothing. The fact that he couldn't say those three little words, well, said everything.

"I don't know...So much has happened, and you've never...Why didn't you ever share your life with me?"

Hold came over, sat on the side of the bed, and threw her senses into such turmoil it took all her strength to focus on what he was saying.

"What held me back was never about you. I think I convinced myself if I didn't let you into my life, I could keep you out of my heart."

"Well, that's just stupid."

"I didn't say it made sense, or that I did it on purpose. It was done out of fear, Jessica, fear of giving my love to someone who only saw it as an avenue to the money. That's not you, even if, in the beginning, I was right to take it slow."

"Following me around like a puppy dog is your version of slow?"

He smiled, all the way to his melted-chocolate eyes, and it was all she could do not to throw herself into his arms.

"The longer I held back, the harder it was to tell you the truth. That was fear, too, Jessica, but then it was fear of losing you."

And now everything inside her went still, quiet. "So what are you saying, Hold?"

"I love you, Jessica."

Benji came over and leaned against Hold's side, beaming.

Hold took out the ring, held it between his thumb and forefinger. He put his other arm around Benji's shoulders. "Marry me, sugar. Make us a family. If you don't I'll just follow you around until you give in."

Her head was spinning. She couldn't seem to keep a

thought in it suddenly, but there were words coming out of her mouth. And joy filling her heart. "Are you sure, Hold? We're from such different worlds."

"I love you," he said again. "We'll make our own world, you and me and Ben. But you're the sunshine, sugar."

"There'll be plenty of clouds, Hold." But she held out her hand. Hold slipped the ring on her finger and Benji let out a whoop, dancing around the room.

"He's awfully happy," Jessi said suspiciously.

Hold shrugged. "He mentioned something about summer vacation. I told him we'd go anywhere he wanted."

"I hope you like cartoon mice and fairytale castles."

"Actually, he wants to go to Budapest."

Jessi laughed so hard it hurt.

Hold eased into the bed with her, pulled her close, kissed her softly. "One thing's for certain, sugar. Our life isn't going to be boring."

"I love you, Hold."

He sighed, rested his cheek on the top of her head. "I've been waiting to hear you say that while you weren't losing consciousness from near-fatal blood loss."

"Yeah?" She looked up at him. "I love you, Hold. Get used to hearing it."

"I will," Hold said, "but I'll never take it for granted."

She smiled. "Yes, you will, and I'll take you for granted, and our kids will drive us crazy."

"Our kids," Hold murmured in his slow, smooth voice. "When are they letting you out of here?"

Jessi's heart simply sang. She'd always wanted more children. "You have no idea what you're in a hurry for,

Hold—dirty diapers, three a.m. feedings, the terrible twos."

Hold snuggled her closer. "It sounds like a pretty good deal to me."

"No," Jessi said as she rested her head on his shoulder, "it sounds like a life. Our life. I can't wait to get started."

Caught in a sex scandal, famous actress Paige Walker returns to Windfall Island. But when she meets Alec Barclay, will their passion lead to the ultimate Hollywood ending?

Please see the next page
for a preview of

Secret Harbor.

Chapter One

Paige Walker—Oscar winner, Tony nominee, Hollywood's Darling, and America's Sweetheart—surveyed her gurgling toilet and thought about just how far she'd fallen. One minute she'd been on top of the world—hell, she'd owned the world, or at least the part of it that either made movies or saw them. And those were the people who'd mattered to her. It gave her no pleasure to admit that now. In fact, it made her feel even smaller—if that were possible—after the very people, those moviemakers and moviegoers she'd once treasured, had dropped her flat on her religiously exercised and very well-shaped ass.

Then she smiled, because instead of the inevitable rocky landing, Windfall Island had caught her. Or maybe they'd let her catch herself. It had been her idea to come home, but after ten years without a single visit, they could have shunned her. Or worse.

One call to the press would have brought reporters circling like vultures to peck at her already bruised feelings, photographers to snap up whatever scraps of her privacy remained, so they could perpetuate and feast off the scandal that had rocked her world and sent her running to the only place she'd thought she could find shelter, welcome, and acceptance.

Whether or not the Windfallers believed she'd made the sex tape currently burning up the World Wide Web, not one of them had ratted her out. Once a Windfaller, she thought fondly, always a Windfaller. There'd been a time that would have embarrassed her.

But she'd learned the value of friendship.

She'd learned the value of home, too, something else she'd discovered too late.

Her doorbell chimed the first four notes of "Somewhere My Love," and she curved up the corners of her mouth as she made her way downstairs. "Somewhere My Love" was the theme song of *December Sunshine*; Laura Galloway had been her breakout role, the one that had made her famous at the ripe old age of eighteen. Just yesterday, she recalled, and yet so long ago.

She opened the door, then managed to stop herself from shutting it again, even as her mouth flattened. Alec Barclay—tall, dark, handsome, and hostile—stood on her front stoop.

"'Somewhere My Love'?" he said, his deep voice dripping with sarcasm.

She snapped back, drew Paige Walker—the slightly raised brow, the purposely sarcastic smile, the overtly sexual body language—around her like armor. And gave him an explanation, because she wouldn't give him the satisfaction of knowing his opinion mattered to her. "I had the house renovated after my father died."

Even knowing he was gone, she'd hadn't had the heart to sell the house, although she'd had it renovated to her exact specifications. After that she'd rented it out to summer vacationers who preferred the semblance of home to the convenience of a hotel. When she'd first walked in, she'd been pleased and surprised to discover it still had the feel of a cottage, even with the modern improvements.

She'd had the back windows widened to bring the Atlantic, with all her moods, right into the house. Otherwise, she'd gone for utility, comfort and peace. The kitchen was granite, glass and stone, with appliances paneled to match the cabinets. The rest of the house boasted dark wood floors, furniture chosen for comfort, and walls in a pale cream color that seemed to glow warmly in even the tiniest amount of light.

"I'm not sure what the contractor was thinking when he chose those particular chimes for the doorbell," she continued, "but since he's a Windfaller, I'm leaning toward humor rather than flattery."

"There was nothing funny about *December Sunshine*."

"Ah, you're a moviegoer."

"I was dating a woman who liked that kind of sappy melodramatic romance."

"Oh. Well, I'm sorry she made you suffer so horribly. But you probably deserved it."

"No man deserves that kind of punishment."

Paige leaned against the edge of the door, truly amused now, instead of only acting so. "Millions of people around the world would disagree with you, including the critics. *December Sunshine* won several awards." And so had she.

He shrugged. "No accounting for taste."

"True, but it's not too late for you to cultivate some," she said, nearly laughing out loud when he only sent her a bland stare. "Why are you here?"

He hefted the toolbox she hadn't noticed he was holding. "To fix your toilet."

She felt only a split second of surprise before she retreated into her role, but Alec Barclay was nothing if not observant.

"I can fix a toilet," he said with the snap of insult in his voice.

"Who said you couldn't?"

"You did, by the way you looked at me."

"Well, Counselor," she said, "it's not every day one of the Boston Barclays shows up at my front door to play plumber."

"There's more to me than a suit and a family name."

She smiled. "Don't like it when someone makes assumptions about you?"

His brows beetled over eyes gone frosty gray. "Can we just get this over with so I can get Jessi and Maggie off my back?"

Now her smile widened, and when he stared at her she realized she'd let her guard down. But she'd grown up with Jessi Randal and Maggie Solomon, and while their paths had diverged for ten years . . . Okay, she was the one who'd neglected to maintain the connection. But now they'd come back together, and proven there was a silver lining in every cloud.

Those who'd sought to bring her down had instead reminded her of what was important in life, and therefore given her a precious gift, one she wouldn't take for granted again.

"I'll wait for Yancy," she said, referring to Walt Yancy, the one and only plumber on the island.

"Now you're just being stupid."

"Well, put another black mark in my character column, Counselor."

"This is ridiculous," Alec said, and shoved by her to stand, dripping, in her foyer. "Where's the bathroom?" He stripped off his coat and handed it to her, retrieved the toolbox from where he'd set it, then turned in a slow circle before heading off toward the kitchen.

Paige threw his coat to the floor and followed him, collecting her cell phone from the counter before she followed him into the little hallway leading to her back door, with her laundry room on one side and the downstairs powder room on the other.

Alec took one look into the little half bath, with its pale blue walls and crisp white and chrome fixtures, and turned on his heel. "That one's fine," he said abruptly, brushing by her again to retrace his steps to the staircase opposite the front door.

She whisked up the stairs behind him and into the master bedroom, and found him staring at her bed, an old iron frame she'd found online and had hired Maisie Cutshaw to paint white and dress with a quilt of her mother's.

He glanced over his shoulder, their eyes locked, and heat slammed into her, a wall of heat and hunger that arrowed straight to her belly then spread through her. When his gaze dropped, she felt it slide over her like a caress—but not a particularly gentle one, considering the set of his jaw.

"Calling the sheriff?" he said. "Going to report a breaking and plumbing?"

She looked down, remembering the cell phone in her hand. And felt foolish for thinking he'd spent even a split second admiring her body. Alec Barclay wanted nothing to do with her, lust notwithstanding.

This time when she met his eyes, she had no trouble recalling that. "I'd tell you to stop being an ass, but it's too late."

"I'd tell you a thing or two," he said with a faint smile and a quick glance at the bed, "but my mother would know somehow."

"Afraid of your mother?"

"I'd call it healthy respect."

"Nice to know you respect someone."

"I respect a lot of people."

"Just not me."

He shrugged. "That's your take."

"Right." She crossed her arms. "Nothing you've said or done would lead me to believe your opinion of me is slightly lower than subterranean."

"Gives you plenty of room for improvement."

"Maybe if I cared what you think." His grin brought a smile to her face. They both liked a little conflict, it seemed. "Now, if you don't mind, I think I'll watch one of my movies and bask in my own greatness. I'd say it's been nice, but—"

"But you don't like me. Since I'm only here to provide menial labor, you can think of me as one of the little people who are easily overlooked."

That did it. Maybe because he was right—not that she'd overlooked the "little people," but because she'd thought of them like children, whose love she never had to question. Until they'd bought into a lie—just like Alec Barclay.

She stepped in front of the bathroom door. "Get out."

He simply shifted her aside. He didn't touch her any longer than necessary, she noticed.

"I'll go," he said, "just as soon as I'm done." He walked into the bathroom and set down his toolbox. His eyes went from the still-gurgling toilet to the bathtub, a bottle of cleaner and rubber gloves on the edge of it. He looked over his shoulder, both eyebrows raised.

"I know how to clean a bathtub."

He snorted softly. "I'd take some photos, if I thought anyone would believe it."

No, but they'd believe she would prostitute herself with a director so he'd cast her, when in reality all it would take was a phone call from her agent to have them begging her to be in their little movie.

But while she didn't blame the public for being taken in, Alec Barclay should have given her the benefit of the doubt. There were two sides to every story, right? A lawyer should know that. A lawyer should at least ask her if the rumors were true. Alec Barclay—well, she didn't know why he wanted to believe the worst of her. But he did.

"Small minds always believe what's easiest," she said.

"All minds believe what they see."

"Oh, so you've watched it?"

"No." And she could see he realized how neatly he'd trapped himself. "But you haven't denied it."

"I don't owe you any explanations, Counselor. We're not in court, even if you're playing judge and jury."

"The innocent don't run away and hide."

"Get. Out." She bit off the words, let anger take her toe-to-toe with him.

He loomed over her; she glared up at him. Her heaving

chest brushed his, and with their mouths only inches apart, the heat of fury turned to a fire in her blood. Her eyes dropped to his mouth. If she lifted to her toes, or he leaned down...

She raised her eyes, saw the heat in his, the edge of temper turning to desire. But as he started to close the distance between them, she took a step back.

She had no idea what to do with the need burning through her like molten gold, but she knew if he saw it they were both lost. So she turned away. She couldn't let him see how desperately she wanted him, how it stung to know he saw her as a fame...junkie. If he knew and pushed, she'd let him think whatever he wanted, as long as he touched her. Took her.

"I'm sorry," he said, his deep voice still so close beside her, driving the ache of need even higher.

It was a need she could so easily surrender to. Alec wouldn't say no.

And she would only look cheaper in his eyes than she already did.

"Suppose we call a truce?" she suggested. "I don't like the idea of pulling our friends into"—she spread her hands, risked a glance at him—"whatever this is."

"Yeah," he said after a moment. "I'll be at the Horizon later. Why don't you let me buy you a drink?"

"No, I really don't think so."

"You're going to hold a grudge because I almost..."

"You don't matter enough for a grudge, Counselor. I've had enough experience with people like you in Hollywood—"

"People like me?" He stepped around to face her. "Care to elaborate?"

She really shouldn't have. There was enough animosity between them already. But, hell, he'd made no secret of how little he thought of her. "You're a judgmental hypocrite," she said. "The minute you met me you decided what kind of woman I was. You think I made that sex tape, that I made it and released it for publicity."

"Tell me you didn't."

"That makes me pathetic and needy in your opinion," she plowed on. Hell would freeze over before she defended herself to him. "That makes me...less," she finished for lack of a better word. "But you'd go to bed with me anyway."

"Aren't you taking a lot for granted?"

"No."

"Now there's a word you weren't saying a minute ago."

But she was the one who'd backed off first, and they both knew it. "You should go."

He held her eyes, nodded. "Just one thing. We're going to be seeing a lot of each other until this thing with the Stanhopes plays out."

"And?"

"I won't have any trouble keeping my hands to myself. Until you ask me to put them on you."

"Aren't you taking a lot for granted?" she parroted back at him.

"No."

She shook her head, smiled a little. "There's heat between us, Counselor; I won't deny that. But there's no warmth, and I find these days that I value warmth much more."

"So you're looking for love and devotion?"

"No." Not from him, at any rate. "Friendship would be nice, or at least some level of respect. You don't strike me as a man who changes his mind or his opinions."

"Not without a good reason."

She spread her hands. "I can't give you one."

"Can't, or won't?" He stepped forward, but the hand he reached toward her curled into a fist before he dropped it back to his side. "Give me a reason, Paige."

She shook her head. "As you said, we're going to be seeing a lot of each another. Best you hold on to that low opinion of me. It'll save you from doing anything you'll regret."

He stared at her for a long, humming moment, his eyes as unreadable as his expression. As he turned on his heel and stalked out, she breathed a sigh of relief. She'd lied to him, after all, Paige thought.

Alec Barclay desired her with a straight and honest lust. But she didn't feel heat unless there was warmth, too, at least on her side. Heaven only knew why she should be drawn to Alec—his strength maybe, his intelligence, his humor.

But even if he knew the truth, sooner or later she'd do something to disappoint him.

She couldn't seem to help it.

THE DISH

Where Authors Give You the Inside Scoop

♥ ♥ ♥ ♥ ♥ ♥ ♥ ♥ ♥ ♥ ♥ ♥ ♥ ♥ ♥ ♥

From the desk of Kristen Ashley

Dear Reader,

When the idea for LADY LUCK came to me, it was after watching the Dwayne Johnson film *Faster*.

I thought that movie was marvelous, and not just simply because I was watching all the beauty that is Dwayne Johnson on the screen.

What I enjoyed about it was that he played against his normal *The Game Plan/Gridiron Gang* funny guy/good guy type and shocked me by being an antihero. What made it even better was that he had very little dialogue. Now I enjoy watching Mr. Johnson do just about anything, including speak. What was so amazing about this is that his character in *Faster* should have been difficult to like, to root for, especially since he gave us very few words as to *why* we should do that. But he made me like him, root for him. Completely.

It was his face. It was his eyes. It was the way he could express himself with those—*not* his actions—that made us want him to get the vengeance he sought.

Therefore, when I was formulating Ty Walker and Alexa "Lexie" Berry from LADY LUCK in my head, I was building Ty as an antihero focused on revenge—a man who would do absolutely anything to get it. As for

Lexie, I was shoehorning her into this cold, seen-it-all/
done-it-all/had-nothing-left-to-give woman who was cold
as ice.

I was quite excited about the prospect of what would
happen with these two. A silent man with the fire of
vengeance in place of his heart. A closed-off woman with
a block of ice in place of hers.

Imagine my surprise as I wrote the first chapter of this
book and the Ty and Lexie I was creating in my head
were blown to smithereens so the real Ty and Lexie could
come out, not one thing like I'd been making them in
my head.

This happens, not often, but it happens. And it happens when I "make up" characters. Normally, my characters come to me as they are, who they are, the way they
look, and all the rest. If I try to create them from nothing,
force them into what I want them to be, they fight back.

By the time I got to writing Ty and Lexie, I learned
not to engage in a battle I never win. I just let go of who
I thought they should be and where I thought they were
going and took their ride.

And what a ride.

I'm so pleased I didn't battle them and got to know
them just as they are because their love story was a pleasure to watch unfold. There were times that were tough,
very tough, and I would say perhaps the toughest I've ever
written. But that just made their happy ending one that
tasted unbelievably sweet.

Of course, Ty did retain some of that silent angry man,
but he never became the antihero I expected him to be,
though he did do a few non-heroic things in dealing with
his intense issues. And I reckon one day I'll have my
antihero set on a course of vengeance who finds a woman

who has a heart of ice. Those concepts never go away. They just have to come to me naturally.

But I had to give Ty and Lexie their story as it came to me naturally.

And I loved every second of it.

Kristen Ashley

♥ ♥ ♥ ♥ ♥ ♥ ♥ ♥ ♥ ♥ ♥ ♥ ♥ ♥ ♥ ♥

From the desk of Anna Sullivan

Dear Reader,

There's a lot more to being a writer than sitting at a computer and turning my imagination into reality. Of course I love creating characters, deciding on their personal foibles, inventing a series of events to not only test their character but also to help them grow. And that's where everything begins: with the story.

But every writer does her share of book signings and interviews. As with every profession, there are some questions that crop up more often than others. Here are some examples—and the answers that run through my mind in my more irreverent moments:

Q: Why did you become a writer?
A: Because I like to control the people in my life and the only way I can do that is to invent them. (And

unfortunately, I still don't have much control; it's regrettable how often they don't listen to me and get into trouble anyway.)

Q: Those sex scenes, huh? (This invariably comes along with a smirk, waggling eyebrows, or a wink.)
A: I have three kids, you do the math. And please don't wink; it's almost never cute.

Q: Where do you get these ideas?
A: I used to ask my children that after they did something...unexpected. They'd usually come up blank. So do I, so I'll just say I don't know where the characters come from, but they won't leave me alone until I write them. I think there may be a clinical diagnosis and prescription meds for my affliction, but what kind of fun would that be?

But seriously, I hope you enjoy my second Windfall Island novel, HIDEAWAY COVE, as the search for Eugenia Stanhope, kidnapped almost a century before, continues.

Now Holden Abbot is joining the quest for truth, justice, and the American way... Wait, that's Superman. Well, Holden Abbot may not be the man of steel, but he's tall and handsome, and his smooth Southern accent doesn't hurt either. And even if he can't leap tall buildings in a single bound, Jessi Randal is falling head over heels in love with him. She may be Eugenia Stanhope's long-lost descendant, though, and that puts her life in danger, along with her seven year-old son, Benji. Holden may have to do the superhero thing after all. Or he may only be able to save one of them.

I had a great time finding out how this story ended. I hope you do, too.

Anna Sullivan

www.AnnaSulivanBooks.com
Twitter @ASullivanBooks
Facebook.com/AnnaSullivanBooks

♥ ♥ ♥ ♥ ♥ ♥ ♥ ♥ ♥ ♥ ♥ ♥ ♥ ♥ ♥

From the desk of Rochelle Alers

Dear Reader,

Writers hear it over and over again: Write about what you know. I believe I adhered to this rule when continuing the Cavanaugh Island series with MAGNOLIA DRIVE. This time you get to read about a young Gullah woman and her gift to discern the future. As I completed the character dossier for the heroine, I could hear my dearly departed mother whisper in my ear not to tell too much, because like her, my mother also had the gift of sight.

Growing up in New York City didn't lend itself to connecting with my Gullah roots until I was old enough to understand why my mother and other Gullah held to certain traditions that were a litany of don'ts: Don't put your hat on the bed, don't throw out what you sweep up after dark, don't put up a new calendar before the beginning of a new year, et cetera, et cetera, et cetera. The don'ts go on and on, too numerous to list here.

I'd believed the superstitions were silly until as an adult

I wanted to know why my grandfather, although born in Savannah, spoke English with a distinctive accent. However, it was the womenfolk in my family who taught me what it meant to be Gullah and the significance of the traditions passed down through generations of griots.

In MAGNOLIA DRIVE, red-haired, green-eyed Francine Tanner is Gullah and a modern-day griot and psychic. She is able to see everyone's future, though not her own. But when a handsome stranger sits in her chair at the Beauty Box asking for a haircut and a shave, the former actress turned hairstylist could never have predicted the effect he would have on her life and her future.

The first time Keaton Grace saw up-and-coming actress Francine Tanner perform in an off-Broadway show he found himself spellbound by her incredible talent. So much so that he wrote a movie script with her in mind. Then it was as if she dropped off the earth when she abruptly left the stage. The independent filmmaker didn't know their paths would cross again when he made plans to set up his movie studio, Grace Lowcountry Productions, on Cavanaugh Island. Keaton believes they were destined to meet again, while Francine fears reopening a chapter in her life she closed eight years ago.

MAGNOLIA DRIVE returns to Sanctuary Cove, where the customers at the Beauty Box will keep you laughing and wanting more, while the residents of the Cove are in rare form once they take sides in an upcoming local election. Many of the familiar characters are back to give you a glimpse into what has been going on in their lives. And for those of you who've asked if David Sullivan will ever find a love that promises forever—the answer is yes. Look for David and the woman who will tug at his heart and make him reassess his priorities in *Cherry Lane*.

Happy Reading!

Rochelle Alers

ralersbooks@aol.com
www.rochellealers.org

♥ ♥ ♥ ♥ ♥ ♥ ♥ ♥ ♥ ♥ ♥ ♥ ♥ ♥ ♥

From the desk of Jessica Scott

Dear Reader,

The first time I got the idea for my hero and heroine in BACK TO YOU, Trent and Laura, I was a brand-new lieutenant with no idea what deployment would entail. I remember sitting in my office, listening to one of the captains telling his wife he'd be home as soon as he could—and right after he hung up the phone, he promptly went back to work. He always talked about how much he loved her, and I wondered how he could tell her one thing and do something so different. And even more so, I was deeply curious about what his wife was like.

I was curious about the kind of woman who would love a man no matter how much war changed him. About the kind of woman with so much strength that she could hold their family together no matter what. But also, a woman who was *tired*. Who was starting to lose her faith in the man she'd married.

Having been the spouse left at home to hold the family together, I know intimately the struggles Laura has faced. I also know what it feels like to deploy and leave my family, and how hard it is to come home.

I absolutely love writing stories of redemption, and at the heart of it, this is a story of redemption. It takes a strong love to make it through the dark times.

I hope you enjoy reading Trent and Laura's story in BACK TO YOU as much as I enjoyed bringing their story to life.

Xoxo

Jessica Scott

www.JessicaScott.net
Twitter @JessicaScott09
Facebook.com/JessicaScottAuthor

♥ ♥ ♥ ♥ ♥ ♥ ♥ ♥ ♥ ♥ ♥ ♥ ♥ ♥

From the desk of Shannon Richard

Dear Reader,

So UNSTOPPABLE had originally been planned for the fourth book, but after certain plot developments, Bennett and Mel's story needed to be moved in the lineup to third place. When I dove into their story I knew very little about where I was going, but once I started there was no turning back.

Bennett Hart was another character who walked onto the page out of nowhere and the second I met him I knew he *needed* to have his story told. I mean, how could he not when he's named after one of my favorite heroines? Yup, Bennett is named after Elizabeth Bennett from Jane Austen's *Pride and Prejudice*. Don't scoff, she's awesome and I love her dearly. And *hello*, she ends up with a certain Mr. Fitzwilliam Darcy...he's my ultimate literary crush. I mean really, I swoon just thinking about him.

And I'm not the only one swooning over here. A certain Ms. Melanie O'Bryan is hard-core dreaming/ fantasizing/drooling (just a little bit) over Bennett. Mel was definitely an unexpected character for me. It took me a little while to see that she had a story to tell, and I always like to say it was Bennett who realized her potential before I did.

Both characters have their guards up at the beginning of UNSTOPPABLE. Bennett is still dealing with the trauma he experienced when he was in Afghanistan, and Mel is dealing with getting shot a couple of months ago. Mel is a very sweet girl and she appears to be just a little bit unassuming...to those who don't know her, that is. As it turns out, she has a wild side and she lets Bennett see it in full force. Bennett and Mel were a different writing experience for me. I was discovering them as they discovered each other, and sometimes they surprised me beyond words. They taught me a lot about myself and I will be forever grateful that they shared their story with me.

Cheers,

From the desk of Lauren Layne

Dear Reader,

I am a hopeless romantic. For as long as I can remember, I've been stalking happy endings. It started with skimming Nancy Drew and Sweet Valley Twins books for the parts about boys. From there, it was sneaking into the Young Adult section of the library way before my time to get at the Sweet Valley High books—because there was kissing in those.

By my mid-teens, I'd discovered that there was an entire genre of books devoted to giving romantics like me a guaranteed happily ever after. It was the start of a lifetime affair with romance novels.

So it shouldn't come as a surprise that as I was stock-piling my book boyfriends, I also did a fair amount of thinking about the future hero of my own love story. I had it all figured out by junior high. My future husband would have brown hair. He'd be a lawyer. Maybe a doctor, but probably a lawyer. He'd be the strong, silent type. Very stoic. He'd be a conservative dresser, and it would be strange to see him out of his classic black suit, except on weekends when he'd wear khakis and pressed polos. We'd meet when I was in my mid-to-late twenties, and he'd realize instantly that my power suits and classic pumps were his perfect match. Did I mention that in this vision I, too, was a lawyer?

Fast forward a few (okay, many) years. How'd I do?

Well...my husband has brown hair. *That's the only part I got right.* He's an extroverted charmer and wouldn't be caught dead in a standard-issue suit. He's not a lawyer, and I've never seen him wear khakis. Oh, and we started dating in high school, and were married by twenty-three.

I couldn't have been more wrong, and yet...I couldn't be more happy. Although I am a "planner" in every sense of the word, I've learned that love doesn't care one bit about the person you *think* is your perfect mate.

In my Best Mistake series, the heroines learn exactly that. They have a pretty clear idea of the type of person they're supposed to be with. And they couldn't be more wrong.

Whether it's the cocktail waitress falling for the uptight CEO, or the rigid perfectionist who wins the heart of a dedicated playboy, these women learn that being wrong has never felt so right.

I had a wonderful time wreaking havoc on the lives of Sophie and Brynn Dalton, and I hope you have as much fun reading about the best mistakes these women ever made.

Here's to the best of plans going awry—because that's when the fun starts.

Lauren Layne

www.laurenlayne.com